How to SURVIVE your SISTERS

'A rollicking read'
Carol Smith, author of *Kensington Court*

Ellie Campbell is a pseudonym for sister writing-duo Pam Burks and Lorraine Campbell. The two sisters were raised in Scotland until they were in their teens when their parents moved the family down to Sussex. Between them they have had over 140 short stories published in magazines. *How to Survive Your Sisters* is their first novel.

Pam now lives in Surrey with her husband and three children where she divides her time between writing, family, her allotment, a part-time job and chasing down her writing partner and big sister, Lorraine. After sailing the Caribbean as a charter cook and various other misadventures, Lorraine finally settled in Colorado with a husband, three horses and a dog.

7000347...

D1136045

How to Survive Your Sisters

ellie campbell

arrow books

Published by Arrow Books 2008

2 4 6 8 10 9 7 5 3 1

Copyright © Pamela Burks and Lorraine Campbell 2008

Pamela Burks and Lorraine Campbell have asserted their right under the Copyright,
Designs and Patents Act 1988 to be identified as the author of this work.

How to Survive Your Sisters is a work of fiction. Any resemblance between these fictional
characters and actual persons, living or dead, is purely coincidental.

This book is sold subject to the condition that it shall not, by way of trade or otherwise, be
lent, resold, hired out, or otherwise circulated without the publisher's prior consent in any
form of binding or cover other than that in which it is published and without a similar
condition, including this condition, being imposed on the subsequent purchaser.

First published in Great Britain in 2008 by
Arrow Books
Random House, 20 Vauxhall Bridge Road,
London SW1V 2SA

www.rbooks.co.uk

Addresses for companies within The Random House Group Limited can be found at:
www.randomhouse.co.uk/offices.htm

The Random House Group Limited Reg. No. 954009

A CIP catalogue record for this book is available from the British library

ISBN 9780099520023

The Random Ho   leading interna   Greenpeace app   (FSC), the   nted on   rement

Pri

WORCESTERSHIRE COUNTY COUNCIL	
831	
Bertrams	28/07/2008
	£6.99
MA	

For our beloved parents
Who always thought we were smashers
Whatever we achieved.

Chapter 1

Natalie MacLeod walked into the maternity ward of St Joseph's with purple daisies in her hand and profound dismay in her heart. Wincing visibly at the groans and screams audible through too-thin walls and averting her eyes from half-snatched glimpses of drip bags, plastic piping and other disgusting hospital apparatus, she pushed open the doors to the semi-private room and hesitated, examining the tableau before her.

In many ways it echoed several she'd passed along the way; the same Perspex cot beside the bed, the same medical paraphernalia and the same crowd of eager visitors, except in one important respect. This patient, with wet patches across her chest and a tired smile plastered onto her face, was her sister.

What on earth was Milly thinking? Didn't she have enough on her plate with two rambunctious boys and one insufferable teenage daughter? Hazel, their youngest sister, had said – swearing Natalie to secrecy – that Ivor's rubber had sprung a leak, but in this day and age everyone knew there was absolutely no need for mistakes. Tubes could be tied. Ivor could have the snip. Men were ridiculously squeamish about these things, of course, but if she and Jeremy were ever in that particular waterlogged barge . . .

She shuddered. Nope, it would never happen. Couldn't happen. She, Natalie, would never allow it. After all, there was such a thing as a morning-after pill.

And now here was Milly, who'd never quite lost the baby weight from Rory, sprawled out on the hospital bed like a . . . like a . . . well, Natalie sucked in her size-10 gut automatically she didn't want to be uncharitable – or, worse, clichéd – but it was hard not to get an image of scores of exhausted do-gooders trying to push a hapless orca towards a receding sea.

She ran a manicured hand quickly through her blonde bob, pasting a magnanimous smile on her face as she waited by the swinging door for her family to notice her.

'Natalie.' Milly's face was unbecomingly flushed, a lock of damp hair stuck to her forehead, but her happiness radiated the room. 'Come and meet your new nephew.' She cooed over the bundle in her arms. 'Isn't he a darling? Isn't he just perfect?'

From their chairs by the bed, Peggy and Callum rose to greet their third-born.

'Natalie.' Her mother swept upon her, all dressed up for the occasion in her best winter coat and a hideous printed dress, shapeless if it weren't for a bulging sash that tugged it too high in the front like a distorted stage curtain that exposed large bony knees. 'How lovely to see you, dear,' she said beaming cheerily. 'I was just telling your father that I don't know why I bothered to put myself through the agonies of childbirth. I swear it takes an earthquake to dislodge you or Avril from London these days. Of course I know Hazel's gallivanting all over the globe and Avril's fantastically busy with her illustrious career, but I'd think you, at least, could drag yourself away from that sexy rexy of yours to visit us once in a blue moon. Honestly, I've four daughters and, except for darling Milly, I might as well have spared myself the labour and all those nappy changes.'

Natalie's eyes narrowed, her teeth gritting, as Callum clumsily patted her shoulder. Her father smelt of peppermints and pipe tobacco but, thankfully, there were no hidden undercurrents she could distinguish and the fingers searching the pocket of his ancient tweed sports jacket were tremor-free.

'Och, don't mind your mother, she's just teasing,' he rasped. 'Come and sit by me. Tell us everything you've been up to, eh?'

'Well, as it happens, I do have an important –'

'Wow, he's gorgeous! You look fab, Milly! Well done, sweetie!' In a tumult of Opium perfume and Nicole Farhi, Avril had hijacked the limelight, rushing over to envelop Milly in her arms, praising her new nephew before she'd even given his sleeping face a glance. 'Hi, Mum, Dad, Nats.' She made the rounds of hugs and air kisses with all the insincerity and polish of someone who'd made a very prosperous vocation of working the room, coming to rest on the chair Peggy had vacated, only her circling Chloé-clad toe betraying the urgent tick-tock of precious wasted time. 'Sorry I'm so late but I got a call – Julia Roberts of all people. I brought Moët . . .' She flourished a gold-topped bottle, then caught her mother's scowl. '. . . But maybe we should save it for later. I can only stay a minute. All hell's breaking loose back at the office. I'm over the moon for you, Mills. He's a cutie! Too bad Hazel's not here.'

'Too bad?' Stung by the familiar mix of chagrin and disappointment that her family inevitably inspired, Natalie lashed back. 'If she had any consideration at all, she'd have come home for this. She knew when Milly was due. Is it too much to expect that she'd make a bit of an effort *for her family* for once?'

As always Avril was hot in Hazel's defence.

'Don't be such a witch, Nasty.' Her fingers fidgeted, clearly itching for a cigarette, her mobile or a quick clutch at her younger sister's neck. 'You know full well Hazel had planned this trip and bought her ticket months before Milly found out she was expecting. Besides, look who's talking – *you* couldn't even be bothered to show up at Hazel's leaving do. Too busy with Jeremy and his moronic City crowd, I imagine. In any case –' unable to resist she took a peek at her mobile, checking for texts, before realising hospital policy had forced her to switch it off – 'it's not as if it's Milly's first, is it?'

Into the impending war a little voice squeaked.

'Doesn't anyone want to see the baby?' Milly suggested meekly. 'He's just woken.'

There was a moment's guilty silence. Then a flurry around the bed.

Avril gently stroked the baby's left hand, visibly relaxing her usually tense, overworked gym-toned body. 'He's just precious, Mills. I can definitely see Ivor in him. And such soft skin. So have you decided on a name yet?' It had taken Milly and Ivor a week to agree on Rory's name.

'Ben.' Milly adjusted his little white hat. 'After Ivor's grandfather, Benjamin. Look, he's staring right at you, Natalie.'

Natalie peered down. 'Can they see at this age?'

'He's not a kitten, Nee Nee.' Callum laughed, what was left of his white hair apparently standing to attention.

'Hush now.' Peggy bent down and picked him up, brown eyes glistening in her wrinkled face. 'Here, Callum, you hold him and we'll call that nice nurse in to take a photo of us all.'

'No, no.' Her husband backed away, rubbing a hand over his rarely shaven chin where a small piece of toilet paper showed he'd nicked himself that morning. 'I might drop him.'

'Phooey! Four children and three grandchildren and you've never dropped one of them yet.'

'Sure you never dropped Natalie, Dad?' Milly teased. 'Might explain a few things.'

'Funny – not, dear sister.' Natalie screwed up her face. 'Where's Ivor, by the way? I thought at least at a time like this he'd be glued to your side.'

'He was.' Milly sounded instantly defensive. 'For hours and hours. All through labour. Poor man's hardly had any sleep in the last few days. He's only just left to get Erin, Fergus and Rory off to school and I told him to take a nap before he comes back. He's been a saint, really.'

Natalie looked unconvinced, as Peggy gushed forth.

'Hazel might be the most adventurous and Avril the most successful but I do think Milly's the bravest. Hours of labour with hardly a peep.' Behind her back, Milly made a face, comically suggesting otherwise, as Peggy continued in her piercing voice that could penetrate the morgue three floors below. 'Turned out little Ben here had the cord wrapped around his neck. And then there was that awful business with the placenta. I told Milly she should ask the hospital to save it for her. Lots of aboriginal cultures believe in eating it. Full of iron.'

Natalie recoiled. 'That is totally revolting.'

'Not just aborigines, Mum,' Avril chipped in, noticing Natalie looking faintly green. 'I think there's a few of the Birkenstock Brigade partial to a little nosh. Or you could always bury it in your garden, have a little ceremony. That's quite a trend too.'

'Anyway' – Natalie's voice cut through the unpleasant conversation – 'now we're all here, I have some news too.' She waited till all eyes were on her and then dropped the bomb. 'Jeremy and I have picked a date for the wedding.'

'Oh, but that's wonderful, wonderful!' Peggy's eyes flooded with tears as she rushed to hug her daughter.

'About bloody time.' Callum grinned, rubbing his unlit pipe between smoke-stained fingers.

'Gosh, Nats, that's brill. When is it?' Milly smiled happily.

'Early July. We've booked the church in Little Hooking. Isn't it superb?' Basking in her family's excitement, Natalie's face looked as pink and pretty as any bride's.

Avril rose to her feet, towering over everyone in the room, even without her four-inch heels. 'Superb.' It was sardonic, her face shuttered, eyes cold. 'Well done, Natalie,' she whispered in her sister's ear. 'You couldn't wait to steal Milly's thunder for your own little portion of glory, could you?' She swivelled to face the others. 'Well, sorry to walk out on all the excitement but I really do have to go.'

And out she swooshed, sucking with her all Natalie's joy.

Caught off balance, Natalie wavered between guilt and anger.

'I'm sorry, Milly. I never meant . . . I just thought with us all being together. Anyway' – she took refuge in leaning over Ben, trying to conceal the hurt of Avril's words sparkling in her eyes – 'Avril's right, he is a beautiful baby.' She could feel her throat slightly choked. Why was it no one could wound you like a sister? 'Utterly perfect, thank God – even if he was a mistake.' The words slipped out before she realised her mouth had formed them.

'A mistake?!' Milly clutched her child to her breast, outrage widening the blue eyes that were so similar to Natalie's and the infant in her arms. 'Why on earth would you say that! Ivor and I wanted this child more than anything else in the world. We were trying for an absolute age.'

This time there was no ambivalence about Natalie's feelings. Rage rushed through her as she realised that, once again, she'd been had.

Damn! With every ounce of her heart, and for the thousandth time in her life, she wanted, longed, yearned to kill that bloody Hazel.

Chapter 2

Avril MacLeod <Avril@avrilmacleodagency.
co.uk> wrote:

Hazel, where are you? I emailed you twice
in November and haven't heard a peep. In
case you missed the big news, sweetie,
Natalie's getting married. July wedding,
Little Hooking church, all the frills.
Sorry to break the ghastly news to you but
she wants us all as bridesmaids. Aren't
you due back sometime soon?
  Mum sends love. Stopped by at Christmas
for a quick visit but too much going on at
office to stay long. Got to run, we miss
you.
Happy Xmas, Av.
PS And what on earth did you tell Nats
about the baby? Milly went into huge huff
and Natalie was ranting about you for
weeks.

From: Hazel MacLeod [mailto:backpacker666@
hotmail.co.uk]

Sent: 16/01/2008 17:12
To: Avril MacLeod
Subject: Re: EXTREMELY URGENT - didn't you read my last email?

Yeah, sorry about that. Been hanging on the beach at Parque Tairona in Colombia, drinking rum and Coke (no, Av, the kind you squeeze lime into), Christmas and New Year are a total blur.

Re Nat wedding, I don't really have to go, do I? I'm sure Nats won't notice if I'm not there . . . or she might prefer it. I'd probably just trip over her train or say something rude to JJ, you know me.

Think it'd be OK if I skip it? Anyway someone swiped my credit cards and plane ticket from my hammock, only have $40 left. Off to Ecuador with cool Canadian hippy couple in VW camper bus.

Send kisses to Mum.

Haze

Avril MacLeod <Avril@avrilmacleodagency. co.uk> wrote:

Sweetie, you are the giddy limit, why do I have to wait months for your replies? I'm sending $2,000 to you c/o American Express, Quito. Assume it'll cover travel expenses and air ticket. Re your last email, no, you absolutely cannot 'skip' the wedding, and yes, your absence will most definitely be noticed. If you don't

come, then I'm warning you, Hazel, neither
will I, and nor will Milly. We MacLeods
have got to stick together. Nats has
ordered the dress material, says she needs
us all by mid-April at latest for dress
fittings. Wants to know your dress size –
are you 10 or 8? Email her, will you,
she's driving me nuts.

From: Hazel MacLeod [mailto:
backpacker666@hotmail.co.uk]
Sent: 11/02/2008 15:23
To: Avril MacLeod
Subject: Re: EXTREMELY URGENT – didn't you
read my last email?

Thanks for dosh. Spent a week in the
Galapagos and now heading to Iquitos,
Amazonia, met guy with jeep, said he'd
take me there, want to see giant
anacondas.
  Tell Natalie not to get her mohair granny
knickers in a twist.
  Canadian couple turned out to be total
freaks – scary! Internet café packed,
there's a huge line for this computer so
catch ya later.
  Haze

Avril MacLeod <Avril@avrilmacleodagency.
co.uk> wrote:

Hazel, you little creep. If you don't book
that air ticket right now, I swear no one

in this family will ever speak to you
again. Natalie is up to calling me five
times a day and you've already missed
first two dress fittings. You were
supposed to be home months ago. Bridezilla
needs your measurements, ASAP!!!!!
  Av

From: Hazel MacLeod [mailto:backpacker666@
hotmail.co.uk]
Sent: 23/05/2008 13:04
To: Avril MacLeod
Subject: RE: EXTREMELY URGENT - didn't you
read my last email?

10, I think.
Waist 26, Bust 32, Hips, 32.
Amazon super interesting. Hoping to bring
surprise gift but v. bulky, might have
trouble dragging it back.
  Haze

*

Bobbing like a float on the high seas, Hazel's sleeping head
beat a tempo with the rackety bus as it slowly lurched and
wheezed its way up the dizzying mountain pass.

It had been a hellish couple of days. Travelling by foot,
dugout canoe, riverboat and a variety of decrepit vehicles
from the mosquito-ridden swamps of Amazonia to the thin
clear air of the snow-covered Andes. For the last innumerable
hours, she'd been crushed like a currant in a Garibaldi
biscuit, stuck between a pair of contorted legs that were too

long to fit into the two-person midget-sized seating and the sprawling hips of an indigenous rooster-clutching woman who'd planted herself on the corner and began a relentless invasion of Hazel's space.

But of all this Hazel was temporarily, blissfully, unaware; oblivious to the rooster's evil glares, the burnt-out wrecks of less fortunate buses that had plummeted over the precipitous cliff, or the anchor of drool trickling from her open mouth onto the man's shoulder on which her sleeping head was resting.

She was a kid again on one of those long lazy summer days that had filled her childhood. Four or five years old, like a naked painted savage, squatting in the wigwam her mum had made her, fishing the small stream at the bottom of their gloriously overgrown garden, plundering the brambles for snacks. The air was thick with the scent of flowers and fresh mown grass, the bushes humming with the bees, like one of those perfect Sunday afternoons when the whole world is tranquil and sleepy.

And now her dream state took her over to their old wrought-iron garden table laden with a sumptuous afternoon tea that bore no resemblance to the rock-hard scones and fairy cakes Mum baked for company and hid from the family until they were stale and tasted like sawdust. The sleeping Hazel salivated, her lips making little smacking sounds to her neighbour's amusement.

Around the table were Hazel's three older sisters: Nasty Nats, always trying to be all grown-up and show-offy; Milly, Hazel's protector, never out of horse-smelling jeans; and the eldest, Avril, who lived in America with the real Red Indians.

The grass tickled her bare skin as she wriggled on hands and knees to lie unnoticed beside Mum's chair. Her mother's canvas hat was jammed over a fresh perm of tight curls, her jaw clicking as she chewed. She seldom wore make-up like other mothers. Her sole lipstick – a nub of coral pink – was mostly used as Hazel's warpaint, though today Avril had contributed a very dark red.

'My face I don't mind it for I am behind it,' Mum always joked, ''tis the people in front take the blow.' But really she had lovely eyes like a deer and strong bones worthy of a tribal chieftain. Hazel thought she was beautiful even in her gardening trousers and the loose blouses she wore to cover her 'battle of the bulge'.

Stealthy as a snake, Hazel's mud-streaked hand sneaked up and was painfully seized. Just as quickly, she retaliated.

'Ow!' Natalie leapt up, chair clattering backwards. 'Look, Mum, blood!' There were teeth marks in her flesh. 'That's it, Honkhead. You're dead.'

'Have to catch me first.' Hazel streaked across the garden but when she dropped her Lady Muck pretensions, twelve-year-old Natalie was a whippet. Swerving and spinning to evade her pursuer, Hazel realised it was time to call for reinforcements. 'Mummy! Milly! Help! Help!'

As Natalie's arm wrapped round her throat, Hazel clutched a chunk of Natalie's blonde hair and yanked with all her might. Natalie screamed. Hazel twisted under her and turned, kicking, hitting and scratching until Mum caught up to grab Natalie and Milly pulled Hazel away.

'Good heavens, girls! Aren't you ashamed of yourselves, squabbling in front of Avril when she's come all this way to visit? And you, Natalie, don't be such a bully. You're so much bigger than she is.'

'But she *bit* me!' Natalie's wail reverberated through the garden. 'Don't say you're on her side.'

'I'm not on anyone's side,' Mum said patiently, her hand an ungiving band round Hazel's wrist as she dragged her firmly back to a chair. 'Hazel, you microscopical speck of animosity,' (her scolding was spoilt by her half-jesting turn of phrase – a favourite in Peggy's repertoire – and the unmerciful tickling that made Hazel squeal and laugh and kick her legs wildly), 'have you no instinct for self-preservation? Do you want Avril to think you don't know how to behave?'

'Well, she doesn't!' Natalie burst out. 'She's a spoilt little baby.' She began to chant in a sing-song voice, 'Baby of the family, baby of the family . . .' only stopping as Matt walked out of the kitchen, a huge grin on his mischievous sun-freckled face.

Though he was really Milly and Natalie's friend, Hazel had known Matt all her life. He'd been hanging out with the MacLeods since the day they'd arrived from Edinburgh when Hazel was just a tiny baby. He was like a brother to her except that at night he slept in his own bedroom two houses down the road.

'You are a love.' Mum took the lemonade jug from him. 'You know, if one of my girls were to marry you, they wouldn't go far wrong.'

'Sorry, Auntie Peggy.' Matt's smile revealed a chipped tooth from when Natalie had shoved him out of a tree. 'One's too old, two are too young and the other's far too scruffy.' Laughing, he ducked Milly's attempted thump.

'Well, Hazel's too scruffy too.' Natalie was straight on her youngest sister's case. 'Your hands are filthy,' she scolded. 'How are any of us supposed to eat after your disgusting mitts have mauled everything?'

'Oh, just leave her alone, why don't you?' Milly sprawled with one leg over the arm of her chair, her tumble of golden hair tamed by two elastic bands. 'You're a nag, Natalie.'

Ignoring this, Natalie turned on her mother. 'And how come you don't make Hazel wear clothes? I'd absolutely

14

die if any of my friends saw her like that, I tell you, I'd just die.'

'Come off it,' Matt said. 'You were always the first to run around in your birthday suit on a hot day. Wasn't she, Mills?'

'That's a vulgar lie.' Natalie threw an instant huff, storming back to the house with Matt ambling after to bring her back.

Avril sent a curl of blue smoke into the air, the top of her shirt unbuttoned to expose her suntanned skin. 'Are they always like this?'

'Little monsters,' Mum sighed. 'Oh, we miss you so much, Avril. Aren't you ever coming home? Lec Refrigeration are always looking for staff. They give you a nice pension scheme and luncheon vouchers to boot.'

Avril's face screwed with horror and Mum hastily swerved course. 'So how do you like California? Have you found yourself a nice chap yet?'

Hazel felt the usual shyness that swamped her before her oldest sister, so different from anyone else in her life, with her chain-smoking, ripped denims, studded belt and tough American-sounding voice. She was always sweet to Hazel on her rare visits, ruffling her hair, commenting on how much she'd grown, but since Avril had left home shortly after the move to Sussex, she still felt like a slightly scary stranger.

Avril tipped her sunglasses down, hiding contemptuous eyes. 'You're forgetting – I don't like nice chaps.'

'Oh, Avril.' Mum's voice quivered. 'All your father and I want is for you to be happy.'

A chill seemed to enter the sunny garden. Avril chewed on her lip, glaring into the distance. Her mother's hand shook as she put down the teapot.

Hazel saw their father approach before anyone else. He had a goofy grin on his face and he was walking strangely. He stumbled on a paving stone and fell into a rose bush, cursing as he thrashed around. Mum leapt from her chair and ran towards him. Her efforts to help him to his feet proved futile, so instead she ushered her youngest daughters inside leaving Avril to try and placate Callum.

Loudly he started to sing in his deep Scottish brogue, his voice ringing in Hazel's ears.

As the bus lurched into the pothole to swallow all potholes, Hazel woke. Everything was tilted to one side, chickens squawking, bundles falling from the luggage racks above.

'*Madre de Dios!*' the woman beside her exclaimed.

Hazel jerked her head up, only to discover a sticky line of spittle was still connecting her to the shirt of the man she was using as an unofficial mattress.

'Oh, Jesus, I'm sorry. I've been dribbling on you.' She mopped at it with the bottom of her skimpy vest.

'So that's what it was?' His eyes gleamed with amusement. 'I thought the roof had sprung a leak.'

Hazel stretched as she took in the scene with amazement. The bus was angled at an alarming degree, a mob of passengers fighting to get to the doorway, which was a whole foot from the dirt. Inches from the back wheel the road dropped off in a sheer cliff with a tiny ribbon of river visible far far below.

'What happened?'

'Seems our driver here decided to take a snooze and aimed us straight for a hole. Come on.' He nudged her towards the crowded aisle. 'Maybe with everyone pushing, there's a chance we can get this thing upright.'

'If we don't all go over the edge . . .'

He shrugged. 'Better than sitting like zombies, cooking in this oven on wheels.' Unlike Hazel, he had to stoop, head bent, to walk between the row of seats. 'Unless you've another suggestion?'

Hazel looked out the window at the searing drop. 'Parachute? I could call a taxi. Ask them to wait at the bottom.'

He laughed. 'You reckon your mobile can get a signal?'

She patted the pockets of her favourite travel trousers, baggy cotton pyjamas she'd bought years ago in India. 'Darn it, Tarzan, I must have dropped it when we were swinging through those jungle vines. Christ' – she turned serious again as she followed him down the narrow aisle, squeezing past a man struggling with a huge wicker basket big enough to contain a boa constrictor and its accompanying snake charmer – 'I can't believe there's another delay. At this rate I'll miss the bloody plane *and* the wedding. Avril will have my guts for Nat's bridal garters. I knew this was a terrible idea. Why the hell did I let you talk me into it?'

'You said you wanted to see your niece and nephews, remember?' Swinging lightly down, he headed for the driver's side where an animated crowd was gathering.

She hopped to the ground, slinging her daypack over her shoulder, as her companion set about organising the bus salvage.

Of course, mentally Hazel hugged herself with secret glee; even if she did make Natalie's wedding on time, there was a good chance at least one of her sisters would be out for her blood.

Jesus, she couldn't wait to see everyone's faces, when she turned up with you-know-who.

Five words sprang to mind.

Fox

And

Sleepy Unsuspecting Henhouse.

Chapter 3

Natalie had tried on and taken off almost every garment in her entire wall-to-wall wardrobe. She'd narrowed it down to her gold Miu Miu miniskirt and her creamy apricot stripy two-piece with the ruffled hem that just skimmed the top of her calves. But then again there was her long sapphire silk jersey dress. Elegant and it looked great with her eyes. No one could fault the classics.

Or maybe – an awful doubt ran through her – she was on the wrong track altogether. Looking at her selection again, did they all smack of the ultimate sin, *trying too hard*? She dug desperately through the heap of discarded clothes and pulled out an oyster sleeveless linen shift and a daffodil-yellow wraparound summer frock.

Slipping into the latter, she admired the V that hinted at her cleavage and the fitted waist that showed off her enviably flat stomach before flaring out into a sexy but not too short skirt. *I am playful, sassy and confident*, the dress said to her through the full-length mirror. *This is a fun occasion and we're all here to have a super fantabulous time.* At least that's what she thought it said. But what if she'd misheard. What if it was really saying *I'm a cheap slut, Mrs Potterton-Smythe, and your son is making the biggest mistake of his life?*

'So how about this then?' She gave a twirl that sent her

helmet of honey-blonde hair swirling along with the skirt. 'Yes? No?'

'Yes. Definitely yes.' Stretched out over three-quarters of the mattress, Jeremy omitted to raise his straw-coloured head, which had been buried in the *Financial Times* for the last fourteen outfits.

'Not too tarty? Or too girlish for a thirty-five-year-old?' She bent down to put on the matching daffodil T-bar shoes.

'So what happened to those last two birthdays?' Of course Jeremy had to point out the discrepancy in her age, so annoyingly literal about the tiniest inaccuracy. He momentarily flicked pale eyes a fraction in her direction. 'No. It looks nice.'

'Nice?' Natalie felt a scream rise up her throat and pushed it back down. 'What do you mean, nice? Nice all right? Or nice nice?'

'Nice nice.' Jeremy turned a page.

'I'm not supposed to look nice nice, am I? I'm supposed to look good good.'

'Well, you do look good good, then.' He sighed. 'It's only Sunday lunch. Does it matter?'

'Of course it matters,' Natalie said sniffily as she stripped back to bra and pants. 'Of course it bloody matters,' she repeated for emphasis. 'It's your parents meeting my parents for the first time. It has to be just right.'

He tossed the newspaper onto the bedroom floor and gave a wide yawn. 'Look, if it's all such a mammoth deal why not throw the whole dashed pile in the car. The boot's large enough.'

'That's not the point.' Irritably she kicked off the shoes. 'I don't want to be making final choices at Mum and Dad's. It will be chaos as it is.'

'Well, you still have a whole twenty-four . . . or rather –' he checked his watch, 7.25 a.m. – 'twenty-six hours before we have to leave. Why do we have to go down so early anyway? I'm going to miss the cricket.'

'Because, dear Jeremy' – her voice was muffled from the inside of the linen shift – 'I want to make sure your parents are served something that's actually edible. And in case you've forgotten, the wedding's only a month away. Can't just leave it all to the last minute, you know.'

'Hell, if you're going to go all crotchety this weekend' – Jeremy drew aside the covers and jumped to his feet – 'maybe it's better if I just skip the Saturday and meet you there Sunday. You take the Fiesta and I'll pop down in the MG.'

'No. You can't!' It was a wail. 'Listen, I'm sorry.' Natalie ran forward and put her arms round his neck. 'You have to come with me, babypie. Please. Pleease.' She snuffled into his neck, covering it with conciliatory kisses. 'I'm just a teeny bit nervous, that's all. You know what my parents can be like. Avril and Milly are coming down too. I need to make sure everyone's aware of what they have to do on the big day. You don't want things to go wrong, do you?'

She might have succeeded in halting his progress but his face was still stiff. He unfastened her arms and replaced them by her side looking as dignified as any man – even a hefty commanding presence who regularly played prop forward on his amateur rugby team – could be dressed only in his tighty-whiteys.

'You know, Natalie, sometimes I wish I'd never agreed to have it all at *your* house, *your* church. Mother's still very disappointed we're not marrying in Oxford. The way she handled my sister's wedding – people are still marvelling over it.'

'I know, but getting married in Little Hooking church, it's been my dream since I was a teenager.' She walked back to her dressing table, sitting down to apply her eyeshadow. 'You have to admit it's picturesque. That quaint little archway leading to the original Saxon church door. Your Baltimore cousins will love it. You can even boast about all those films it's been featured in. And whatever you think of Mum's housekeeping, her garden's gorgeous, way bigger than your parents'. We just won't let the guests inside, that's all.'

In the mirror she caught Jeremy's reflection as he zipped up his tennis shorts. His face couldn't have been sourer if he'd got his underwear and more caught in the zip's nylon teeth.

'Oh, I'm teasing,' Natalie chided. 'Don't look like that. They're getting the whole place cleaned from ceiling to floor. And Mum's promised me Dad will be on his best behaviour.'

Jeremy sat heavily on the bed to put on his socks. 'We've heard those promises before. Remember our engagement party?'

Natalie shuddered. How could she forget? Flashbacks of her father turning up uninvited to the swanky west London pub they'd hired for the occasion two years ago, wanting to buy his 'sweet Nee Nee' a good-luck 'dram o'whisky'. How he'd ever found out its top-secret location she still didn't know to this day. It was too terrible to think about . . . staggering drunkenly around the pub, throwing his big clumsy arm over Jeremy's shoulder, insisting on buying him a drink. Or thwacking her girlfriends on their skimpily clad backs, wittering on about how his little baby was finally getting married. Eventually he fell asleep in a chair, his snoring only punctuated by loud yells of 'Angus! Angus!' whoever the hell Angus was.

Natalie was relieved to find he'd disappeared as the guests were leaving, only to discover him lying face down outside in everyone's path of exit. 'Who's he?' some people had asked. 'Haven't a clue,' Natalie replied as she stepped over him and

21

hurried off to the car. The memory still made her blush with shame, but really, what else could she have done?

'This time it'll be different. After all he's been on the wagon almost two years. And Mum'll keep him under control.'

'Yes, but who'll do the same for her?' Jeremy asked, too many incidents of Peggy's eccentricities etched deeply in his mind. He swung his arms in a limbering motion then stretched up to whack an imaginary ball into the perfect serve. 'I'm sorry to say it, Natalie, you're the only one of your whole family that's halfway normal.'

'Oh, Jeremy.' Natalie's laugh was a little anxious. 'You don't mean that. They're fine once you get to know them properly. Anyway, it's only a couple of days, we hardly ever all get together.'

'Thank God. I suppose Milly's bringing those hideously spoilt kids with her?'

Natalie nodded, not thinking to defend Milly's energetic but mostly quite well-behaved brood. 'Ivor the Invisible's got to work the weekend again. Don't worry, I'll make sure they don't bother you. And I'll do all your packing,' Natalie coaxed, sensing a weakening. 'And you can watch the match in Dad's study and . . . and we'll leave immediately after your parents. We can stop at that pub you like on the way back.'

'Oh OK, if I must,' Jeremy groaned. 'But don't forget to stick in my jogging gear, at least then I can get away from everyone when the fur starts flying.'

'Who said the fur's going to start flying?'

'What, you three sisters under one roof for two whole days? Let's just say I'll lay down pretty good odds. Got to dash – meeting Ratters for a quick game before work. I'll shower at the club.'

He closed the door to the bedroom.

Natalie waited to hear the front door shut firmly behind

22

him before she turned back to her wardrobe and, standing on tiptoe, pulled a shoebox from the top shelf. She checked the outside. Blank and unrevealing except for an almost transparent strand of honey-blonde hair.

Yes. Good.

It was still there.

Milly was having a crisis. It reminded her of that old Fred Astaire joke. The one where Fred's left the steam pudding to explode on the hob and Ginger calls down the stairs, 'What's happened, Fred?' and he replies, 'I've got pudding on my white tie, pudding on my black suit, pudding on my tails.' Only in Milly's case it was poo. Poo on the dazzling white towel, poo on the dazzling matching bathmat, poo on the loo seat. Even poo on the pristine stripy wallpaper. She wouldn't have minded so much if it had been her own pristine stripy wallpaper. Not that anything in her house was, or ever could be, pristine.

Of course she could have changed Ben down in Lorena's lounge like all the other mothers had done this afternoon, but his eight-month-old bottom was twice as big as their newborns and with Ben being on solids . . . Well, she didn't want to put them all off their choccy biscuits. Plus – she pulled a wet wipe from its box and began dabbing at the bathmat – they all had those new environmentally friendly Velcro terrycloth things and here she was losing the battle of containment with – heaven forbid – a disposable. Tree killer. Forest wrecker. Ecological heathen. She could almost hear the other mothers clucking and tutting in disdain, elbows folded and positioned high in the air like bad Les Dawson impressions. See, Mrs Simpson. Told you so, Mrs Simpson.

A knock on the door made Milly pull herself into action. She poppered up Ben's trousers, put the shamefully non-biodegradable nappy into an equally non-biodegradable nappy bag and hauled herself and Ben up from the floor.

'Are you all right in there?' came an anxious whisper from the other side of the door. Rachel, her ally, her friend, the only one of the bunch downstairs who, like Milly, had more than one child, her son, Tristan, being Rory's best mate and little baby Jessie a few months younger than Ben. Rachel had begged Milly to come along today. Safety in numbers, she'd said. Bloody NCT and their teas, Milly had muttered.

'You've been ages. Everyone's beginning to worry.'

'Oh, Christ.' Milly opened the door a crack. 'Look, can you take Ben for me, just for a moment?' She squeezed his chubby body through the door into Rachel's arms followed by a pair of dinosaur-adorned dungarees.

'What is it?' Rachel slung Ben expertly onto her right hip. 'Is something wrong? Can I come in?'

'Believe me, you don't want to come in.'

A look of understanding came over Rachel's face. 'An up-your-backer?'

'An up-your-backer. Down-your-legger. All-around-the-bathroomer. I just need to clean up a bit.'

Rachel shot Milly a look of sympathy and headed back to the pack with Ben tugging her hair. Milly lowered her bulk onto the toilet seat, sweat pooling in her armpits, and counted slowly to ten. Of all the gin joints in all the towns, Ben had to conduct his dirty protest in Lorena Lovett's house. Ironic really. The most anal-retentive woman in the neighbourhood . . . and Ben chose her house to crawl around with a dangerously leaky nappy. He'd thought it a great game as, chuckling away, she'd tried desperately to pin him down.

Taking a deep breath, Milly began searching under the sink. Everything was in alarmingly perfect order. Even the cloths and dusters were neatly folded. She should introduce

Lorena to Natalie. They were two of a kind.

The nappy bag began to ring. Fumbling around, she eventually traced the sound to her much neglected mobile and gazed in dismay at the display. Natalie. Telepathic or what?

'Hi, Nat. Coincidence. I was just thinking about you.'

'Good.' Natalie sounded pleased. 'I was worried you might forget.'

'Forget?'

'This weekend . . . meeting my future in-laws . . . dress-fitting tomorrow afternoon.'

Oh, bottom, Milly groaned inwardly, was it this weekend? The thought of trying to fit her size 16 and rising body into a shimmery satin bridesmaid dress filled her with dread. Diets? She'd tried them all. Fought the flab, struggled with her cellulite, made war with her wobbly bits. She'd done Scarsdale, Atkins, Slimnastics, gymnastics, high carb, low carb – all to no avail. There was no getting away from it. Milly's lardy lumps were here to stay.

'So what are you doing?' Natalie said ultra casually. 'Getting ready? Deciding what the children might be wearing?'

'Something like that.' Milly put the stained towel in the sink, squirted some liquid soap onto it and began scrubbing at the poo marks. 'Not sure whether Ben should wear his manure-brown shorts or his piss-yellow leggings.'

'Pardon?'

'And Rory and Fergus, now do you think they should be matching or polar opposites? Like white shirt black trousers Rory and white trousers black shirt Fergus. Total contrast.'

'Oh, I don't think you need to go to that much bother,' Natalie reassured her without a flicker of irony. 'I mean, obviously smart but –'

'OK, fine by me. We'll go casual. Got to fly, Nats.'

Milly pressed the end-call key and slipped the mobile back into the rear pocket of her military-grey elasticised-waist maternity trousers (the only decent item of clothing she'd been fitting into lately) – who said breastfeeding made you thin? Bollocks.

She rinsed out a J Cloth and set to work.

Note to diary: Don't whatever you do, Milly Winifred Simpson, give Ben that canned beef-and-bean mixture again.

Ever.

Chapter 4

Avril reclined in her ergonomically designed mocha leather chair, mobile to her ear, feet propped on the burled oak desk, admiring her slim legs all the way down to her Christian Louboutin leopard stiletto shoes.

'Really, darling, if it wasn't for the dropping jaws as we walked into Langan's, one would hardly guess he's such mega box office. Hysterically funny too − not like most actors, completely up their own arses. We had a two-bottle lunch and the people next to us almost fell out their chairs, they were so agog, eavesdropping, of course.'

Outside her window the rush-hour traffic was building up. She loved her new offices, perched above the South Bank, with stunning views of the river and conveniently close to the National Film Theatre and Royal Festival Hall.

The voice in her ear buzzed excitedly.

'No. Well, he *is* married to you-know-who. I know, normally that wouldn't slow me down, but they're very happy, alas. Anyway, he's at least five years younger than me.' She laughed again. 'All right, ten, you bitch. And his head barely reached my chin in three-inch-heeled cowboy boots. The point is, he loves Baxter's work. He's desperate for him to direct his next project . . . Yeah, seen everything, even the early commercials. Well, darling, obviously CAA would love to nab him but Baxter hates LA. He's still more Oor Wullie than William Morris, thank God.'

She rubbed her ear, hot from overuse and glanced at the clock.

'Got to go, sweetie. Big shindig at the family pile this weekend, Natalie's got some frightful ordeal planned for us all, even the sun's had to change orbits to accommodate her . . . No. I am not taking him. Fucking hell. One glimpse of my family and he'd be clinging to his wife's neck, begging to renew their vows. Oops, got a couple of calls on hold, I'll catch you later.'

For the next hour and a half, much as her head throbbed, and her eyes ached from the strain of scanning through endless small print, the phone kept her tethered. First New York, then Los Angeles.

Strange to think she owed her current career to a fluke, as much as anything. She'd been sitting in an economy seat on Continental Airlines, on her first visit to the States, when a Beverly Hills literary agent had passed her his card, intrigued as much by her teenage cynicism as her auburn tresses and lilting Scottish accent. Though more than one producer would suggest that her tall slender body, sultry mouth and fuck-'em-all swagger might have made her a movie star, she'd become his assistant, to the delight of his screenwriter and film-director clients.

But after eight years, she'd found herself sick of the LA frenzy. She longed for home where people understood your sense of humour and didn't pretend every stranger was their best friend and where waiters refrained from sitting uninvited at your table to harass you with their screenplays or head shots.

And besides, her boss's wife was becoming suspicious. Soon after he'd let her start her own client list, they'd begun an affair. But only a few flickering embers remained of all that white-hot passion, and though he had lots of good qualities, she had no intention of getting caught in a nasty divorce and getting stuck with the sap.

Rejecting countless job offers, she'd flown back to England and started her own agency. True, the British film industry couldn't hold a votive candle to Hollywood, and what the BBC paid their writers would barely cover lunch on Melrose, but there was a new buzz of optimism in the eighties since *Chariots of Fire* had won its four Oscars. For a while at least all things UK were hot and Avril had the transatlantic contacts and youthful energy to make it work. Although the fabled Second Coming fizzled out like a fireworks party in a Californian deluge, by then Avril had another lucky break.

It came in the form of one Baxter Donaldson, fresh from film school, shy as Bambi and eager to join the fledgling client list of a fellow Scot. By the time she'd manipulated his raw talent into an A-list career, her reputation for hard-hitting negotiation had all kinds of doors jerking open, mostly for fear she'd kick them in, and the trade press were having a field day with her high cheekbones and almond-shaped jade eyes.

Looking at her now, few people would realise how often she'd had to hide from the landlord or listen to her stomach growling, complaining that it had been too long since the previous meal.

Damn Natalie, she thought now. The last thing she wanted to do was drive down to Little Hooking tonight but her sister would get her way, always had.

There was a tap and Brenda stuck her head round the door.

'I read that script you gave me. *Ode to Mr P.*'

'What do you think?'

'Crap. You're right, it's Toby's worst effort yet and by the way, he's on Line 2. Are you going to tell him?'

Avril sighed. 'Is there any point? He'll never believe me and besides the jerks involved in this production make Dumb and Dumber look like Einstein and Baby Einstein. Hell, they'll probably love it if they ever learn to read. Oh well.' She drummed her long fingernails on the desk, debating her best course of action. 'Put him through, will you?'

She girded herself, pasting on a smile.

'Darling, it's in front of me now! Absolutely fascinating! That thing with the gorilla and the pogo stick – outrageous! Brad Pitt?' She cast her eyes up for Brenda's benefit. 'Well, yes, that's a novel idea . . . Yes, certainly I'll mention it to the suits. Although quite honestly, sweetie, I'm not quite sure his fans would stand for him playing in an ape costume. Let alone Angelina . . .'

Patiently she listened to the babble on the other end, then broke in: 'Look, let me courier it over. I'll call you as soon as I have any news.' She put the phone down and looked pleadingly at Brenda. 'Get me a G and T, will you? Light on the tonic, lots of ice. Oh, and Richard might stop by. If he does, show him in, will you?'

'I think he might know the way himself by now.' Brenda winked.

That was the trouble with assistants, Avril thought as the door quietly closed, they thought they knew everything. She certainly had.

Collapsing on the matching mocha leather couch, she pulled her compact from her handbag. Another fine line between her eyebrows, unfortunately not too fine to be noticeable. A telltale trace of grey among the auburn suggesting it was time for another hairdresser touch-up. Giving a heavy sigh, she began applying a smidgeon of foundation. Forty-five years and three days old. Depressing or what?

*

30

Half an hour later. Another tap on the door. Brenda stuck her head round.

'Natalie called three times. I told her you were in a meeting. And Richard's arrived.' She had a big suggestive smile on her face. Avril realised the reason why as Richard walked in, carrying the hugest bunch of lilies she'd ever seen.

'Rob the florists?' She stood up to greet him, once again struck by the notion that his thin hawk-like face would be perfect for a tragic-hero role – though she could also see him cast as a sneering lordly villain. Take away that sharp suit and he'd look great with a sword and tights.

'Who's Rob?' he joked. 'Not another rival?' He kissed her cheek and shoved the flowers at her. 'Belated birthday present. A little bird told me.'

'More like a large singing canary.' Avril screwed her eyes at Brenda. 'Take a pew, Richard. Drink?'

'Scotch would be good.'

'Brenda, sweetie, fetch Richard a Scotch and put these in water, will you? Thanks. You know I'm leaving for Sussex tonight.' She turned to him reprovingly, as the door closed. 'Might as well give them to blabberchops out there. They'll be dead before I return.'

He kissed her full on the mouth. 'Well, at least you can enjoy them now,' he whispered into her lips. 'And you do always say you live for the moment.'

'That I do.' Avril snuggled into his arms, enjoying his warm familiar scent. She liked the way he made her feel small and fragile instead of a towering giantess. His hand slid into her shirt, cupping her breast as their lips met in another bruising kiss. Ice rattled behind the door and they both sprang apart as Brenda brought Richard's drink in.

'So how's Diane?' she asked, mainly for her assistant's benefit but also to remind herself how impossible this whole thing was. Hadn't she learned her lesson with married men? As her friends often remarked, Avril had a knack for picking them. Beautiful drug addicts, tormented artists, would-be priests and, of course, the married. If they were good-looking, unattainable and hopelessly screwed up, they made a beeline for Avril. Or was it she for them?

But now, as she told Brenda she could leave for the night, anticipating a quickie on their favourite couch, she realised Richard was glaring at her.

'Why do you always do that?' he asked after Brenda slipped back out.

'What?' Avril's mouth fastened on his, her hands reaching for his fly, but he pushed her irritably away.

'Mention Diane.' He stood up, the mood definitely broken. 'I told you when we met that our marriage is long dead.'

'Really?' she said sardonically. How many times had she heard that before? She pulled out her compact again, repairing her smudged lipstick. 'I thought you took a trip together last Saturday?'

'We drove Kath to look at universities, that's all.'

'None of my business.'

'Isn't it?' He eyed her shrewdly. 'Well, maybe we should change that. Let's go away together. I could come to Sussex with you this weekend? Meet your folks.'

'God, no!' She snapped the compact shut.

'Why not? Are you ashamed of me?'

Ashamed of him? That was a laugh. When she had so much to be ashamed of herself.

Things she hoped nobody would ever find out.

And every time she went home it became harder not to scream them aloud.

Chapter 5

A flat tyre. How could she have a flat tyre? And as clichéd as it was, there wasn't a hope she'd be able to find the spare, let alone change it. Milly glanced at the dashboard clock. She'd so wanted to prove Natalie wrong – that she wasn't *always* late. And this morning things had been going so well. Ivor had supervised the washing and dressing of Rory and Fergus in their best clothes, only fair as he was working all day, missing all the fun (fun!?) while she'd fed Ben an early but light helping of Ready Brek considering yesterday's bowel explosion. Even teenage tyrant Erin had actually managed to drag herself from her bed before eleven thirty. Unheard of for a Saturday morning.

'When are the repairmen coming?' Fergus asked for the hundredth time.

'Any minute now.'

'You told us that half an hour ago.' Erin gave a petulant sigh as her MP3 player chose that moment to run out of battery power.

'And you'll probably tell us it again in another half an hour,' moaned Fergus, who at twelve was the double of his elder sister.

'They said they'd text when they were five minutes away.' Milly turned on the radio. 'I'm sure it'll be very soon.'

'I'm not sitting here while some weirdo man changes our tyre. It'll be *so-o* embarrassing.' Erin twisted her long blonde hair round and round and began breaking off the split ends. 'What if one of my friends sees me?'

'Even if they did happen to speed past, they're hardly likely to recognise you.'

'Yeah, right. Everyone knows my parents have the crappiest car in the whole of Sussex.'

'Well, when you're earning bags of money, you can buy us a better one, can't you?' Milly found herself snapping. 'And that won't be long, because you sure as billy-o aren't going to get into college with your grades.'

'Take a chill pill, *Maman*.' Erin put her feet up against the windscreen and released a chewing gum from its packet. A pretty girl with a wide round face and clear complexion, she could drive Milly round the bend with her world-weary, aren't-adults-so-o-o-dumb routine. 'It's only coursework. It doesn't matter.'

'What do you mean, it doesn't matter? Some of that coursework will go a quarter towards your GCSEs.'

'Whatever.' Erin rolled her eyes.

'Do you want to end up stacking shelves in a supermarket?' Milly wasn't prepared to let it drop. 'Or –'

'Don't say it, pouring petrol from a pump, or what's that other one you use? . . . sitting on a factory line with stumpy fingers . . . Jeez, if you're going to keep moaning on at me, I'm going home.' Erin unclipped her seat belt.

'No you're not. Everyone's expecting you.'

'Yeah, expecting me to waste my whole day listening to Auntie Natalie drone on about her boring wedding and Jockstrap Jeremy witter away about the stupid stockmarket. It's so unfair.'

'Life's unfair, Erin. Sooner you realise it the better and

don't call Jeremy that. You know how Rory repeats things.'

'You know how Rory repeats things,' echoed five-year-old Rory.

'Freak!' Erin snarled at her brother seated directly behind her.

'Chav!' Rory retaliated.

'You don't even know what a chav is, dog's breath.'

'No, but I do,' Fergus cut in. 'Girls who wear horrible tracksuits and go out with chav guys like Peter Mickleforth.'

'Who's Peter Mickleforth?' Erin narrowed her eyes.

'The one whose face you were snogging off round by the ICT block.'

'I was *not* snogging anyone!' Erin retorted crossly. She hated that Fergus was now in her secondary school, albeit three years below. A right little spy in the camp. 'Butt out of it, loser.'

'Stop it, all of you, you'll wake the baby.' Milly attempted to intervene but was powerless to halt the insults that ricocheted from back to front and side to side.

'Gaylord!'

'Dumbhead!'

'Shut up!'

'No, you shut up!'

'Will all of you shut up, please!' Milly ordered.

'I will if she will,' said Fergus.

'I will if she will,' repeated Rory.

'Moron!' Erin turned and slapped his head.

'Don't you dare hit your little brother!' Milly's voice was at full pitch now as Rory gave a puppy-like yelp.

'At least I never *bit* him,' Erin said pointedly. 'I can't believe he went and attacked Sophie Mason's cousin. I mean, he's worse than an animal. Should be stuck in a zoo with the apes.'

'*You* should be stuck in a zoo!' Rory yelled back through tears.

'Now leave it!' Milly tried vainly to regain control. 'We went through all that yesterday afternoon.'

And what an afternoon it had been, pulled aside by Rory's form teacher in front of all the other reception parents.

'Ah, Mrs Simpson.' Miss Ledbetter cleared her throat. 'Could I have a word please?'

Obediently Milly followed her into the classroom, Ben strapped to her chest in a ring-sling baby carrier, as the other children began fanning their way outside. Rory was nowhere in sight. Miss Ledbetter closed the glass door and motioned Milly to sit on the other side of her desk. 'I'm afraid there's been a bit of an incident.'

Milly's stomach went into free fall. A million scenarios flashed before her eyes. Choking on a stick of chalk, falling off that new scary-looking playground apparatus, being tripped over by some bully boys and banging his head. She was winded once herself at school when one of the kids in the playground bellowed 'Bundle!' and she was caught in the scrum. The memory could still produce palpitations of excruciating terror. 'Where is he?' She tried to suppress the rising panic in her voice. 'Is he OK?'

'Yes, *Rory's* OK,' the teacher said witheringly, sitting bolt upright on her leather chair. 'But Darren Hammond isn't. I'm afraid Rory bit him.'

'But . . . Where? How? Why?'

'The where is on the arm, how we can guess, but the why we've still to discover. The Head and I have both talked to him, independently, but he's not given either of us a satisfactory response.'

'He's not?' Milly said weakly, wondering vaguely what a satisfactory response might be. A high Benny Hill-type salute and a 'Sir, yes, sir. Sorry, sir' followed by a click of the heels.

36

'As far as we can ascertain, it was entirely unprovoked. He's in Mr Mitchell's office at the moment. I told him I was going to speak to you or Mr Simpson. There is still a Mr Simpson, is there?'

'Yes, Miss Ledbetter.' It was all Milly could do to stop her voice from going all slow and sing-song.

'Just I hadn't seen him around since Fergus was in Year 5. I thought perhaps . . .' She cocked her head to one side like a tabloid hack scenting a juicy scandal.

'He's been busy, that's all,' Milly found herself explaining. 'He can't always make parents evenings.' Nor sports days, cake sales, nativity plays, school concerts . . . OK, admittedly, she'd turn up to those school concerts in a state of high excitement only to find everyone else's little darlings doing the star turns and all that was visible of her child was a corner of their ear; still Ivor would have loved to have been there. But he was working every hour he could to get his new company off the ground and had been since he'd got off the corporate ladder that had also kept him slaving like a dog, nights and weekends too. It had been the same old story from the moment he and Milly left university.

'Look, Mrs Simpson.' Miss Ledbetter's eyes expressed sympathy. 'I don't want to worry you unnecessarily but you know we take biting extremely seriously in this school.'

'I'm sure you do, and so do I . . . in the home, I mean.' Milly became flustered. 'Er . . . not that it happens in my home. But if it ever were to . . . I'd stamp it down . . . Not that it would . . .' She trailed off.

'Good. That's fine.' Miss Ledbetter stood up and brushed down her skirt. 'Helps tremendously if parents can reinforce school rules. Anyway, Darren's mother's implied she's happy enough to let it drop this time and we've had strong words with Rory, so hopefully there'll be no more to be said on the subject. Now if you wait here I'll go and fetch him. In the meantime, have a look at our vegetable jigsaw display. It's really rather impressive, especially cauliflower corner.'

'I'm sure it is,' Milly said as she felt herself morphing into Alice in Wonderland, just after she'd drunk the shrinking juice. By the time Rory was brought back into the room she was three centimetres tall and about to dissolve into the floor. Minutes later she slinked back across the still crowded playground, followed by a glowering Rory. She could almost feel the thud of stones on her back, followed by shouts of 'Bad mother! Useless mother! Shun her. Shun the inadequate bitch!'

'When are they coming?' Rory whined, bringing Milly's thoughts back to their current predicament.

'Won't be long, I'm sure.' She turned to release Ben from his baby seat and snuggled him under her blouse.

'Shouldn't he be taking the bottle by now?' Erin looked on in disgust as Ben suckled away.

'He could.' Milly gently stroked his small head. 'But this is far better for him. Anyway, formula's expensive.'

Erin visibly cringed, then her eyes lit up as her mobile gave a bleep. 'I gotta go,' she said seconds later.

'You can't.' Milly watched helplessly as Erin yanked open the car door. 'You have to stay here. Erin . . . Erin!' Milly felt her third migraine of the week beginning to surface.

'I'm telling you, Erin Simpson,' Milly shouted as she watched her daughter clomp down the road in her wedge-heel shoes, 'if you leave here now, you're grounded . . .'

'. . . for a month . . .' was the last thing Erin heard as she turned the corner.

Chapter 6

'No sign of Millipede yet?' Callum raised his head from the *Telegraph* crossword.

'Not since that last text,' said Avril who was sprawled in an armchair in her parents' living room watching Jeremy who in turn was watching the cricket with a kind of orgasmic relish. Every now and then he'd jerk his right elbow back and mutter 'Yes! Yes!' under his breath.

'What did it say again?'

'"In a jam wagg feed."'

'"In a jam wagg feed"? What the heck does that mean?' Her father peered over his spectacles.

'Probably got her cell stuck on predictive again.' She'd bought the phone for Milly's birthday but she could count the times she'd used it on one hand. Either there was no credit, or she'd forgotten to charge it – the excuses were endless.

'Maybe feed yourself I'm in a jam.' Callum's fountain pen was busy scribbling on the top of his newspaper, trying to arrange the letters into an anagram, clearly not grasping how predictive texting worked. 'But what's the wagg for?'

'Search me. I tried ringing back but all I got was screams, shouts and obscenities. I think the kids were murdering each other.'

'Saves their mother the job at any rate,' Callum chuckled,

as he rose to his feet and flicked a switch. 'Let's put a bit of light on the subject . . . Oh . . .' A shriek from outside. 'I think that was you, Jeremy, being summoned.'

'What? What's that?' Jeremy's eyes shifted away from the screen for a millionth of a second. 'Well done, Worcester! Good show. Good show!'

'Jeremy, don't you think Natalie might need a hand?' Avril urged.

But it was no use – Jeremy only had eyes for the cricket.

'No answer was the loud reply,' Callum muttered under his breath as he rose to his feet.

'Right, now, start walking.' Natalie pushed aside the honey-suckle and placed the tip of the tape measure against the wooden trellis.

Her mother took the other end and trotted obediently down the path.

'And stop there, by the statue,' Natalie instructed. 'No, not that one, Mummy. The one with the broken birdbath. Next to the willow.' She must make a note to have that birdbath removed before the big day; it was a real eyesore with its whopping great crack down the middle and chipped claw foot. In fact, the whole garden could do with a makeover. Could she stretch the budget any further? 'That's perfect. Stay right where you are.' She hurried across, took the tape measure from her mother and began making notes in a small spiral-bound book.

'Are you finished with me?' Peggy was itching to fit in a little weeding before she had to serve lunch.

'I suppose,' Natalie said, distracted. 'Bloody Jeremy, what's happened to him? I'm sure he must have heard me call.' She consulted her previous measurements and frowned. The figures just didn't add up. 'It doesn't make sense.'

40

'Oh it does all right.' Peggy stooped down and plucked some chickweed and two dandelions from the rose bed. 'Minute a chap's got you, they turn a deaf ear, although they usually have the courtesy to wait till the honeymoon's over.'

'No, not Jeremy, Mum.' Natalie took a sudden gasp of breath staring at her pad, and dropped her head in her hands. 'Oh Christ! Oh Christ! Help! Somebody! Help!'

'Sounds like a cat's caught its claws in something,' Jeremy muttered as Natalie let out another wail. 'What on earth's going on?'

'Pre-wedding nerves, I guess.' Avril perched herself on the edge of his chair and studied her future brother-in-law at close range. As much as she disliked the turgid Jeremy, he had stuck by Natalie for the last six years; he deserved a bundle of credit for that. He never blew their shared deposit account on wild nights out, never drunk himself stupid, brought in a decent wage. In fact, on paper, he would make a perfectly respectable husband. And yet . . .

'Looking forward to the big day, huh?' she enquired gently. Maybe it was partly her fault that he seemed so, well . . . blank. Perhaps she hadn't spent enough time getting to know him properly. She'd never delved deeper than the surface niceties. Of course his appearance was slightly against him, his robust Saxon fairness spoilt by a rather vacant face with those pop eyes and pronounced forehead so that in her humble opinion he was far from the Greek god that Natalie touted. But then again, he couldn't help that and she was often criticised for being too judgemental with people.

'Looking forward to it being over, that's for sure.'

Romantic not! Avril sighed. Well, that was something they had in common. Last thing she'd ever contemplate was getting married. 'Ciggy?' She offered him her pack.

'Only smoke cigars. And only on special occasions.'

'Yeah, me too,' Avril said, taking one herself. 'Except I seem to be having more and more special occasions these days.'

'In what way?' For a second he appeared almost interested. She opened her mouth to respond but his head jerked back to the television as another batsman came up to play.

'Skip it.' Avril stood up, seeing his eyes glued to the screen, his mouth half open, as he leaned forward again as if preparing to launch himself into the action. Or lack of it. It was all white noise to her, the sporting equivalent of watching clothes spin round the dryer.

Too bad, she thought, dismissing her future brother-in-law as she slipped out of the room unnoticed and headed upstairs, missing the sound of Milly's tyres arriving on the gravel. Try as she might to like him, she found him duller than a lump of soggy clay.

Probably why he appealed to Natalie.

She could have so much fun moulding him into shape.

Milly was two hours late by the time she finally drove into her parents' driveway. She parked her old Astra estate between Avril's classy Sprite and Jeremy's gleaming MG. 'Now listen carefully.' She turned to face the boys in the back. 'I need you to be on your best behaviour these next couple of days. No fighting, biting, shouting, hiding and definitely no terrorising Jeremy. Do you understand?'

'Ya, Ma,' muttered Fergus.

'Ya, Ma,' mimicked Rory.

'Good. I'm depending on you guys.' She gave them a loving grin and then checked her face in the mirror. Sweat was beading on her brow and above her lips and her fringe was pasted to her head. Ugh. If Milly could remove one season from the calendar, it would be summer.

'Take this.' She handed Rory a box of breadsticks and a bag of soft toys. 'And, Fergus, if you can bring in the pushchair, I'll carry the car seat. Quiet now. Don't disturb Ben whatever you do.'

Loaded down, all three crunched across the gravel path to the kitchen door.

Milly loved coming here. Natalie had scarpered off to London as soon as she turned eighteen, sharing a flat in Earls Court with a couple of other girls, and Milly had often stayed with her during her breaks from university. But while Natalie had lapped up city life, the clubs and party atmosphere, Milly had never really felt at ease and when she dropped out of uni and married Ivor at the age of twenty, they'd almost immediately settled back in Sussex. They'd found the perfect starter home in Codmoreton. Three miles from Little Hooking and her beloved parents.

Once, when they were kids, Matt had asked why they didn't just call Codmoreton Big Fat Hooking. Its handy commuter location on the direct train line between London and the coast had mushroomed a once appealing market town with a smattering of half-timbered historic houses into a fairly characterless urban sprawl that extended almost all the way to Little Hooking, only the presence of the dual carriageway ring road preventing the two from merging into one. But while the straggling curve of Little Hooking had only one pub (the Dog and Donkey), Pheasant Farm Riding Stables and a small arcade of shops, Codmoreton possessed the schools, a monthly farmers' market, a regular old high street with all the usual suspects, plus a couple of dingy bars-cum-nightclubs and a rather depressing caravan park, catering to the hikers who came in droves to tackle the Downs.

Really, there were much prettier places in the area – not a duckpond or village green in sight – and tourists usually forgot to linger on their headlong rush to the sea. But even if the other MacLeod sisters found it all dull beyond belief, to Milly it was fresh air, safe playgrounds and the familiarity of home.

She pushed aside the bedraggled wisteria that straddled the door frame and righted the battered old sign that read 'The Briars'. Years ago, homesick for her Edinburgh friends, hating the new school and the way they made fun of her accent, Milly had found a tiny compensation in this garden and, of course, the riding stables, just a mile away.

She loved the flower beds with their riot of hollyhocks, foxgloves, geraniums; the patio where the oregano jostled with the weeds for space; the little winding path that led to the tumbledown shed where her dad kept his carpentry tools. Most of all she loved the herb garden, the out-of-control mint, the marjoram, sweet basil and the purple sage which had trebled in size this year and was now crawling with bumble bees on its lilac flowers. She wanted to lie down in their heady scents, close her eyes and breathe them all in.

Thank God her parents hadn't paid any heed to Natalie's insistence that they should swap the 'draughty, crumbling edifice' for a modern energy-efficient bungalow which in her 'humble opinion' would be 'far more appropriate for their age'. Callum had bought the Victorian four-bed family home as a fixer-upper, from an ancient couple almost as dilapidated as the house, but somehow the much-vaunted renovations had failed to come about. No matter Natalie's dreams of sky-rocketing house prices and developer's potential, Milly was quite certain that any self-respecting builder would probably throw up his hands and suggest bulldozing the lot.

But where was everyone? Hearing raised voices coming from the back garden, she rounded up the boys and went to investigate.

*

'What do you mean, the lawn's too small?' Peggy peered over Natalie's shoulder at her scribblings.

'Because it is.' Natalie was wringing her hands. 'By at least ten metres.'

'Oh dear. Will it make much difference?'

'Much difference! Much difference!' Natalie's voice rose with each repetition. 'It will only mess up the whole wedding, that's all.' She checked her sheet again. 'What am I going to do? Jeremy!' she suddenly blasted out. 'Jeremy, come here urgently!'

'Cheer up, Natalie. Worst things happen at sea.'

Natalie swallowed an insane urge to pummel her mother for her relentless cheerfulness, and tried with ever-increasing dread to imagine how Peggy would be perceived by her future in-laws.

At seventy-six her iron grey locks were brutally hacked into a short back-and-sides style that only emphasised the sunken hollows between her prominent cheekbones, the strong jaw that clicked when she ate and the sharp chin worthy of the Wicked Witch of the West. Even her purple bri-nylon trousers with the foot stirrups were hopelessly unflattering and decades old.

'Mummy, I don't think you quite understand. The marquee's going to be too big and just say by the micro-chance I do manage to find another, smaller one at such short notice, I'm not going to be able to fit everyone in. I'll have to do the seating plan from scratch.' She closed her eyes in frustration. 'Do you realise how long I've worked on that seating plan? Going through it again and again, so that Jeremy's Uncle Ralph isn't placed anywhere near his ex-wife who he once wrapped in a rug and threatened to set on fire, and his feuding cousins won't be sitting next to the one who got all their great-grandfather's money, and –' She suddenly took a breath and her face lit up. 'Do you think Dad can cut the fence down? Use some of the land that's behind the garden?'

Her mother shook her head. 'Sorry, dear, but I'm afraid we've had our own feud of sorts with the owners. Remember Joyful Beasley?'

'Hateful Beastly, yes. Not still alive is she?'

'More than alive and twice as hateful as ever. Silly nincompoop. She's been on the warpath for the past five years, ever since your father paraded up and down the lawn in his string vest when Mr Beasley was showing round some potential buyers.'

'String vest? Well, that's not that bad, is it?'

'No, dear, it was *only* his string vest. He was a bit tiddly, I'm afraid. Anyway the next day she cut down our clematis. Pure spite. I could murder Callum sometimes. Uh-oh, speak of the devil.'

Callum ambled over to the two women, leaning heavily on his wooden stick. Since his retirement, he'd let his whiskers grow, his face was as weather-beaten as any farmer's and the nest-shaped ring of hair around his bald pate was covered with a canvas hat to prevent sunburn. In his old frayed corduroy trousers with his shirt hanging out, he looked more like a tramp than a retired doctor.

'Are my ears burning?'

'We were discussing Mrs Beasley, darling.' Peggy plucked at a piece of goosegrass that had attached itself to his arm.

'Ah, rotten to the core that one. I'll bless the day she manages to sell up and ship out.' He caught Natalie's pained expression. 'What's the matter, Nee Nee?'

'The lawn's too small for the marquee,' Natalie informed him.

Callum scratched his brow. 'But you measured it, three times on your last visit. We both did.'

'Well, it must have shrunk or something.'

'What, you mean with all the dry weather we've been having?' he chortled. 'Away with you, girl.'

'It's not funny, Daddy! It's going to ruin everything. Everything.' Natalie could feel her chest tighten.

'Look, there's your sister,' Peggy said with relief. 'Milly will help. She always has bright ideas.'

Milly could tell something was up. Peggy rushed to greet her, while Natalie stood wailing in the middle of the lawn with Callum helplessly lingering by her side.

Her mother gave her a brief hug. 'Oh, Avril –' She stopped, flustered, getting the name wrong as she often did. 'I mean, Hazel, Milly, whoever you are, thank the earth you've arrived. Natalie's driving us all –' She stopped again, the word 'nuts' freezing on her lips as Milly's nose starting twitching a warning like a rabid rabbit. Natalie and Callum had wandered over too, closing in behind her just in time to hear her last words. '– to the shops later,' Peggy improvised.

'No I'm not,' Natalie sniffed. 'I never said that.'

'Suit yourself,' Peggy said cheerily. She ruffled Rory's and Fergus's hair, then squared off her fists for a spot of impromptu sparring, landing gentle taps on their noses and chests. 'Here, let me take Ben.' She reached for the car seat, peering at the sleeping child within. 'Doesn't he look darling? Where's Erin?'

'Uh, Erin . . . er . . . couldn't come at the last minute,' Milly fudged. 'She had an appointment we'd forgotten. I'll take her to Gayle's later in the week, Nats, I promise. And I already picked up the boys' suits.' It had been decided for economy's sake that Milly should rent her husband's and sons' outfits. And Jeremy still had his morning suit from his sister's recent wedding.

'Hello, my little cherubs.' Natalie stooped, her attempt to kiss Rory and Fergus foiled as they expertly ducked away and rushed headlong for the stream.

Milly shrugged at her younger sister. 'That's children for you. You might think you're a glamour model but to them you're just the warty old aunt.'

'Oh ha.' Natalie failed to smile, inwardly seething. One day, when she and Jeremy had a child, he or she would be a hell of a lot more polite than Milly's grotty offspring. And it wasn't like her sister hadn't all the time in the world to clean them up or discipline them. After all, she wasn't working.

Callum patted Natalie clumsily on the back. 'Sit down with your mother. Milly and I'll have a wee look.' He took the notes from her limp, unresisting hand, while Peggy put her arm around Natalie's shoulder.

'I'm sure it'll be OK,' she soothed, leading her to the patio and placing Ben on the ground by the table as Callum set to work with the tape measure.

'It won't.' Natalie pulled out a chair and sat down. 'It's started already.'

'Not your asthma again? I thought you'd grown out of it.'

'No, my nightmare. Where it all goes terribly wrong. I've been having it almost every night lately.' Tears welled into her eyes. 'Oh, Mum.' She shook her head sadly. 'Why does everything bad happen to me?'

'Look, dear, the main thing is you and Jeremy love each other. Everyone gets the heebie-jeebies when they're under stress. Even the Queen. Here, have a blow.' Peggy pulled out the ragged square of cotton, torn off her husband's old shirt, that she was using as a handkerchief.

'Did I ever tell you the story about Frazer? A lovely man. Six foot two, eyes of blue. Frazer Alexander Stewart, he was called. You know I've always had a soft spot for Scottish men.' Peggy was English herself, her family from Yorkshire originally, a shameful fact that her daughters had tried to hush up in the Edinburgh years when every history book and playground patriot painted her nation as black-hearted villains.

'I met him when I was nursing at the Royal West Sussex in Chichester,' she continued, patting Natalie on the back. 'He was building a boat, the *Black Swan*, and I'd help him with it when I was off duty. He used to promise me that one day we'd sail it round the world, he'd show me the pyramids and Niagara Falls and the Taj Mahal and then we'd settle in the South Seas, living free on bananas and coconuts.'

'What's this to do with the wedding?' Natalie sniffed.

'Actually, it's to do with *my* wedding, dear. Frazer wanted to marry me when he'd got his boat-building business established – the *Black Swan* was just the prototype – but I was almost thirty and I just couldn't bear to wait. I wanted to have children, you see, and Callum was there on the sidelines, already wooing me.' She bent to release one of her broad ugly feet from its leather sandal, rubbing a large raw-looking bunion on a big toe that looked to Natalie's eyes deformed. It was hard to picture her as the slim pretty girl, with the wavy hair and twenty-four-inch waist, that smiled out of her black-and-white photos; harder still to think she'd driven these two men crazy with lust. 'I'd met your father in the hospital before he transferred back to Scotland and he'd send me postcards every week and come to visit one a month. So persistent.' She laughed uproariously at her own unflattering description of the romantic contender for her hand.

'Anyway, Frazer – such a lovely man – was completely crushed when I chose Callum. When he heard we'd got married, he sent me a letter, giving us the *Black Swan* as a wedding present. He said he could never look at her again without seeing me.' Peggy sighed. 'But Callum wouldn't let me collect her. We'd moved to Portree by then and Frazer had sailed the boat to Devon and settled there, starting his boat-building yard. Callum said it was too far away. He didn't want Frazer to sail it up either. Broke my heart.'

Natalie wiped her eyes and stared at her mother, incredulously.

'Ah well.' Peggy laughed, shrugging. 'It's just a story.'

'Jesus, Mummy, if someone were offering *me* a boat, I'd have Jeremy shunting off to get it, even if it were frozen in the South Pole and he had to run behind a dog sleigh with only a shovel to dig it out. Why didn't you *insist*?'

'The men ruled the household in those days.' Peggy brushed off the notion with an airy wave of her hand. 'Besides, your father was just starting his practice and we had no money for gadding about.'

'Typical man, just thinking of himself.' She had little patience for her father.

'Well, not all men are like that.' Her mother furrowed her brow. 'You don't feel that way about Jeremy, surely? Because if you're not absolutely certain, Natalie . . .'

'Oh, Jeremy's different. At least he's responsible. He'd never put me through all the crap you took from Daddy.'

Peggy blinked and then bent down awkwardly to fuss over Ben's sun bonnet and Natalie immediately regretted opening her big mouth.

Across the lawn, Callum and Milly headed towards them, arm in arm, chuckling.

'Natalie, you're a right div,' Milly teased as she drew close, not noticing the silence she broke.

'I always told you to pay more attention to your studies.' Callum handed her the notebook.

Natalie stared at them and then the notebook crossly.

'Sorry?'

'You might think I'm a useless lump, should have been put down years ago.' He nudged Milly, sharing the joke. 'But one thing your father knows is the difference between feet and metres.'

Feet and metres. Feet and metres. Natalie felt the bile rise in her throat.

Why was it that by the rest of the world, she was considered extremely together, respected not only for her looks, her style, but also her brains and business skill? But five minutes at home and it was Natalie the dolt, Natalie the thicko, Natalie who everyone made fun of for not being able to catch a ball, for not knowing her eight times table or for once mispronouncing mystery as micetery.

Well, she fumed silently, when she finally walked up the aisle to become Mrs Jeremy Potterton-Smythe, all that would be gone. There'd be no one sneering that she couldn't spell Constantinople; no one remembering that as a teenager she was the lazybones who'd sleep in till 2 p.m., no one deriding her for being the fussy conventional one. No, for once everyone would be admiring her, the glowing bride. It would be her day to shine and her family would just have to lump it.

Chapter 7

'Avril? It's Richard.'

Son of a bitch. The sound of her lover's voice in her parents' kitchen, where she'd just descended to make herself a coffee, jolted Avril into feeling like a guilty teenager again.

'Why are you calling?' she said curtly, stirring sugar into her mug. She'd specifically asked him not to phone her over the weekend.

'Now there's a greeting.' He laughed, unfazed where a lesser man might quake or take offence. 'I take it you didn't get my message then? On your home answerphone?'

'I drove straight from the office. So what did you want?'

Her gaze swept through the window into the garden, noticing most of her family gathered round the wrought-iron table, seeming highly amused at something, except Natalie who, typically, looked ticked off. At some point while she was upstairs, reading a few pages of the scripts she took with her everywhere, Milly and the kids had arrived. Well, she could say hello later.

'Hmm.' Richard pretended to ponder. 'What *did* I want? Do you know for the life of me I can't quite remember. I think your passionate response has swept it away.'

'I'm hanging up,' she growled.

'Frankly, my darling, I'm the teensiest bit terrified of telling you now. I hope you won't take this the wrong way but . . .'

But . . . How often had she encountered that word? 'But . . . I've been thinking . . . time to call a halt . . . wife beginning to ask questions . . . been to counselling, etc., etc.' She was almost relieved. Richard was gorgeous: distinguished, powerful and maybe the sexiest man she'd ever dated, a heady combination. Too many nights recently she'd found herself glancing at the phone, itching to dial his number, just to chat for a few minutes before she fell asleep.

That was definitely a no-no. There might be room for the occasional guest appearance in her life but she'd been burnt early and the wounds sometimes still hurt. Freedom had come at too great a cost ever to give it away. And if she wanted confirmation that she wasn't missing out on the whole commitment/kids thing, five minutes with Milly and her brood usually did it.

She realised Richard was still rambling on about his plans on the other end of the line. She picked up the brimming coffee mug and headed upstairs where she could talk – and even yell if necessary – without Jeremy intruding in search of beer or the whole family suddenly bursting in.

'. . . I've actually found myself in your neck of the woods. I'm in Arundel. Charlie's throwing a huge bash here this weekend.'

'Arundel?' She felt the hairs on her neck stand on end. The celebrated castle and adjunct town were less than sixteen miles away.

'No. You can't,' she cut in. She put the mug on the fake oak nightstand and flopped down on the bed beside her laptop and a sheaf of manuscript papers.

'Can't what?' Richard queried playfully. 'Stay up after midnight? Have a sleepover? Do I detect a tinge of jealousy?'

'Don't talk crap,' Avril shot back, sharper than she

intended. 'I meant come round. You can't come round. I'm extremely busy. I haven't the time to entertain you.'

'How *extremely* fortunate then,' he drawled, 'that I'm quite entertained where I am. I called merely to say hello, *bonjour, laissez les bon temps roulez*, and all that . . .' Now she could hear the sounds behind him, glasses clinking, music playing, shrieks of laughter. 'I think I know rather better than to suggest you actually accompany me on a social occasion. Forgive me, I'm clearly intruding. I do apologise.'

Avril could hear his irritation – and maybe something else? Could his feelings be hurt? Surely not. Richard was tougher than that.

In the background there was a girl's voice, coaxing yet insistent. 'Ricky, darling, get off the phone. You promised me a martini. Don't be such a bore.'

'Who's that?' Avril hated herself for asking.

'Saskia. Charlie's sister. She drove down with me. Very entertaining, I must say, the darling girl hardly took a single breath the whole way. Oh well, apparently I'm being summoned. Don't worry, I won't impose on you again.'

The phone went dead.

Shit. So he *was* angry at her. Maybe she had rather jumped down his throat. Well, too bad. And who the fuck was this Saskia girl? But she couldn't dwell on any of this now as her nose was being assaulted by an alarming burning smell wafting up from below. Leaping down the stairs two at a time, she hurried to investigate just as a shrill whistling threatened to rupture her eardrums.

'Oh blow it! Not again!' Peggy raced down the hallway, tea towel in hand, flapping it in the air like a manic Robinson Crusoe signalling a passing steamer. Too late. The smoke alarm screamed its piercing message throughout the house.

'What burnt?' Avril shouted through the din.

'Everything, sausage rolls, pizzas, nuggets,' Peggy answered, prodding at the alarm with a broom.

'Is there a problem?' Callum appeared at the back door just as the alarm stopped.

'Keep the ruddy door closed,' Peggy hollered, 'or it'll go off again. Give me gas any day. I'll never get used to that blooming electric.'

Avril opened the oven, leaping back as a black puff of smoke billowed out. She peered in at the charcoaled remains. 'It looks like you've two shrivelled potatoes in there.'

'So that's where they went! Didn't I tell you, Callum, when I baked that halibut for dinner last week that something was missing?'

'Is there anything else in the fridge we could cook?' Avril asked.

'Might be some old pork chops.'

Avril sighed. With her mother old really meant old. She had this habit of keeping food long past its sell-by date, which she insisted was the scam of all scams. 'Anything else?'

'There's mould on the cream cheese, but I can wipe that off. It's penicillin anyway, you know. It's good for you. Oh, and there was some gammon I was going to use, but apparently your father finished it off.' She gave him an accusing look over the top of her glasses.

'You did?' Avril turned to her father.

'Aye, but I didn't know it was for today. It was in the fridge winking at me. Your mother never feeds me.'

'My heart bleeds.' Peggy sighed. 'Dr Proudfoot says if he doesn't lose weight, his blood pressure's going to hit the roof.'

'Och, don't listen to that daft gowk. The cleaning lady in my practice knew more about doctoring than that windbag.'

Callum settled himself into a chair by the kitchen table and began feeding his pipe with tobacco.

Peggy scrubbed at a non-stick pan with a Brillo pad. 'Poor Jeremy. That's his lunch spoilt. What shall I tell him?'

'Jeremy this, Jeremy that,' Avril tutted. 'God, you treat the guy like royalty. Who gives a toss if he thinks your cooking's a disaster zone?'

'*Disaster zone*? I'll have you know my tattie scones were the talk of Skye.'

'Yeah, didn't Nana lose a tooth once biting into one of them?'

Avril had been absorbed in the self-imposed and rather scary task of going through the refrigerator, pulling out wilted lettuce and pots of mouldy yogurt, when she realised her parents had gone ominously silent. She looked up to catch them exchanging anxious glances.

'What? What is it?'

'Now don't take this the wrong way, dear,' her mother began hesitantly, 'but your father and I wanted to have a word with you alone. We think it's time –'

'Gone time,' Callum interrupted. 'It's no fair on the poor wee thing.'

'Well, anyway.' Peggy blinked, nervously. 'You know what we're going to say. One of these days you're going to have to –'

'No,' Avril said sharply. 'You're wrong. I don't *have* to do anything.'

'You cannae avoid it forever.' Callum sucked on his pipe stem, embers glowing as the match flame dipped down.

'Why can't I? It's better the way it is, don't you see? Besides' – she felt her temper rise – 'I can't imagine why you'd want to bring this up now, right before Natalie's wedding.'

'You know, the truth has a funny way of coming out.' Callum shook his head.

Avril fixed him with an icy glare. '*You're* talking to *me* about truth? Too bad you didn't think about it earlier.'

Trembling, she walked into the garden, leaving her parents staring at each other in dismay.

An hour later, Peggy, Avril, Milly and all three children were seated glazy-eyed in front of the TV on a worn-out old sofa and both armchairs, empty pizza boxes on the floor. Sensibly Jeremy and Callum had vanished the moment they saw what was in store. On-screen an elaborately coiffed bride was suspended mid-march up the aisle, groom and best man waiting patiently at the end.

'Now watch carefully,' Natalie commanded as she unpaused the video and pointed to a tuxedo-clad boy of about seven. 'This is where the pageboy drops the train. See . . . right there.' She pressed pause again and tapped her cue on the little boy's fingers. 'Everyone took their eye off the bride at her big moment and it spoilt the whole atmosphere. Now remember, Fergus, as chief page the train is your job...'

Milly couldn't help her mind from wandering as Natalie played the third video of the session. She wished Erin hadn't stormed off like that. She was impossible these days. So stubborn. And wilful. And Erin hadn't even thought to phone to say she'd made it home safely. Let alone apologise.

And then there was Rory. Milly picked idly at a loose thread on her blouse. He still refused to talk about the biting incident. She had made him promise never to bite again, but should she have been more forceful, asked Ivor to have words? Fergus had never done anything like this and she'd always thought Rory the milder mannered of the two.

'. . . using real petals, not paper confetti. The church doesn't like it. Did you get that, Milly? Milly?'

'Pardon?' Milly snapped out of her daydream.

'About the ushers scattering rose petals at my feet as I walk through the churchyard and you're to distribute the hand-made cones of freeze-dried petals to the guests.'

'Oh yes . . .' Milly nodded. 'I can do that.' She glanced at the list on the floor in front of her and tried her very darnedest not to feel resentful. What Natalie was spending on the caterers was enough to feed her family for a year.

'Anyway, I have handouts here, just in case you forget what you're all meant to be doing.' Natalie opened her well-worn folder, bulging with brochures, handwritten lists, neatly cut-out magazine articles and – was that, Milly wondered, a spreadsheet? 'And there will be a final chance to iron out any last-minute hiccups at the rehearsal. Oh, and one last thing.' Natalie gave a big wide smile. 'Colour coordination. It's all arranged with the florists, the caterers, everyone. Dusky-pink bows at the ends of the pews and all over the marquee. Dusky-pink calla lily twinned with a blue thistle for the men's buttonholes, dusky-pink sash for flower girl Erin of course, and dusky-pink satin gowns for the bridesmaids.'

'Which will set off the dusky-pink salmon on the dusky-pink tablecloths,' said Avril. 'While we drink our dusky-pink champagne. And groove to the sound of dusky Pink Floyd.'

'And Ben will have a dusky-pink nappy.' Milly began to giggle, tickling Ben who'd been contentedly playing on Peggy's lap.

'And we'll all have dusky-pink nail varnish on our dusky-pink toes.' Avril tried to keep a straight face.

'And Fergus can wear dusky-pink shoes,' Milly snorted.

'No way I'm wearing pink shoes!' Fergus's expression of horror made Avril and Milly laugh uncontrollably.

'Sorry, buddy.' Avril dug him in the ribs. 'No choice. Hey, relax, you can take them off the minute Natalie rides away in her dusky-pink limo.'

'With her dusky-pink husband.' Milly rolled around the sofa, clutching her sides, her hot rosy cheeks flushing with each movement. 'Oh crumbs,' she howled, 'I think I'm going to wee myself. And they can have a pink dog and call it –'

'Dusky!' Fergus and Rory said together.

That was it, the whole family was gone, hollering and hooping.

Natalie's eyes flashed with fury. 'Well, all I can say is, you two had better not be like this at Gayle Cutting's this afternoon. She's the finest seamstress in the South-East and she's not going to welcome grown women acting like a pair of hysterical hyenas!'

Chapter 8

Surveying her figure in the narrow changing-room mirror, there were two occasions that sprung to Milly's mind.

One was when she was sitting in the university sports hall changing rooms, at the age of nineteen. She and her friend Alison had just played a game of squash. Milly glanced over at Alison who was struggling out of her gym clothes and couldn't take her eyes off the width of her friend's legs. Her thighs had chafed from rubbing together and her poor friend was complaining about the size of her rear end, despite her efforts to get fit. Milly clucked sympathetically and made all the correct noises, while secretly thinking, 'My God, if I ever get like that, shoot me quick and bury me deep.'

The other occasion – Milly turned to her left, yuck, the side view was even worse with that dimpled skin around her thighs – was when Erin was about two and some mother at playgroup mentioned cellulite. Milly replied, in all innocence, 'What's that?' And the woman chuckled knowingly and said, 'Don't fret, love, you'll find out soon enough.'

Well, she certainly knew all about it now. Oh, how smug she'd been in her youth. How certain of everlasting beauty. What had happened? Those loose folds of skin where there used to be a waist, where did they come from? And the bingo wings under her arms, when did they appear? She didn't dare step on the scales these days, let alone undress naked in front of Ivor. Even her baby-blue eyes, so admired in the past, seemed to have shrunk into the podge of her face. Her smile overshadowed by her double chin.

Of course, the approaching forty thing might have something to do with it, and the fact she'd had four children couldn't have helped.

Reluctantly she stepped into the dress and pulled it upwards only to discover that somehow the inner petticoat seemed to have got all caught up with the sleeves. She twisted the garment round, tugging at the slip which was protruding like a bustle.

This is ridiculous, she thought, hot with shame, drenched with sweat and mortified that her armpits would stain the material if she ever hoisted it that far up. When had it all got so out of control? Was it because Ivor was working all hours up in his Pimlico office that Milly, starved of adult conversation, was reduced to raiding the biscuit tin every fifteen minutes, storing up cookies to get her through the famine like a camel about to cross a hundred-mile desert?

Desperately she yanked at the silk and heard an ominous whisper, the sound of overstrained seams and ripping fabric. Forcing herself to slow down, she shimmied the skirt millimetre by millimetre up her thighs and over her hips but that was the best she could manage. The zipper rose two inches and stuck fast.

Perhaps there was another reason for the weight gain? A colossal cyst like that lady on LBC she was listening to a while back: two stone, or was it three? And then when they removed it, she was back to normal, albeit with a scar from breast to bikini line.

'Are you ever coming out?' Natalie called through the curtain.

'In a moment.'

Milly sighed as she surveyed her overhanging tummy. Two years older than Natalie and almost a third as large. Now was that fair? Good job it wasn't her getting married. Here comes the bride all fat and wide . . .

Leaving the room, sucking in her pot belly, back gaping to the breeze, she finally emerged.

'Milly . . .' Natalie's eyes were on stalks. 'That's . . . that's . . .'

'Too small, I know.' She could hardly bear to look at Natalie, trim in her slim white sheath. What a comparison to Milly's dusky-pink satin fiasco. The pull-you-in pants Rachel had recommended were only serving to push the folds of fat higher up, so that it looked like she had two sets of boobs. Under no circumstances could this be regarded as a flattering look.

'It doesn't even shut at the back!' Natalie shrieked as Milly attempted to retreat back into the changing room. 'Oh Christ . . . You've put on weight, you promised me you wouldn't. Gayle, come over here, we need you!' She grabbed Milly's arm and pulled her in front of the mirror to stand on Gayle's pedestal.

'Maybe you should just forget me as bridesmaid.' Milly scowled at her reflection.

'No. I can't. It's all settled. Couldn't you . . . I don't know . . . Go on a . . .'

'Diet?' Milly glared at her. 'Don't even go there, Natalie.'

'I wasn't suggesting you *need* to, you're not . . . *overweight*,' Natalie said quickly as she pulled at the fabric. 'It's just I don't know what Gayle can do here. Gayle?' She called out again. 'Crisis!'

'Just been with chief bridesmaid.' Gayle glided across the thick pile carpet. 'Says she hates strapless and the length makes her resemble a beanpole.'

'Oh, Avril's always complaining, don't listen to her. What about this catastrophe? Can you fix it?'

Standing on the pedestal, looking down at the immaculate, manicured Gayle and the glowering bride beside her, Milly felt her heart skewered like a piece of butcher's meat, prickles of heat staining her exposed chest and flabby arms with big red blotches. Being stared at like this, labelled a catastrophe as if she were deaf or lobotomised, could not have been worse if she were Typhoid Mary, surrounded by doctors and students in gloves and masks, discussing her repulsive yet fascinating case.

'Looks like we'll have to move the seams, *again*,' Gayle said through a mouthful of pins as she spun Milly round. 'Might work. Another couple of pounds and there'll be no hope. What about bridesmaid number three?'

'I could murder her,' said Natalie. 'She promised she'd be here and –'

'And here I am!' In the flap of exclamations surrounding Milly's dress disaster they hadn't noticed the bell clang as the shop door opened. 'Ta-da,' squealed Hazel as she threw her arms up to embrace her sisters.

'Hazel!' Milly leapt from the pedestal she was standing on and rushed to hug her, with Gayle dragging behind as she tried to keep the dress pins in place. 'However did you find us here?'

'Talk about leaving it to the last moment.' Natalie pouted. 'I've been frantic with worry.'

Hazel laughed. 'Didn't I say I'd be on time for the final fitting? Oh ye of little faith.'

'Actually, no, you didn't. And it would have been helpful if you'd been here weeks before. Poor Gayle's had to manage with the vague measurements you sent in that one poxy email. And then never a word from you.'

'It was a little difficult getting connected in the middle of the bloody rainforest.' Hazel yawned. 'Jesus, I am *so* fucking jet-lagged. So you're going through with it, Nat?' She gave her sister a quick kiss. 'Jockstrap Jeremy, still the man you want to grow old and wrinkly with, then?'

'Of course I'm going through with it.' Natalie grabbed the headdress, adjusting the veil. 'And I wish everyone wouldn't keep calling him that. Are you –' She swivelled away from the mirror to stare more closely. 'Christ, Hazel, you're a bag of bones! What on earth have you been doing?'

'No size ten.' Gayle assessed her expertly. 'Lucky if she's an eight.'

'Touch of dysentery,' Hazel said with a smile. 'Fortunately I had expert care.' The olive skin she shared with Avril and Peggy was tanned to a healthy-looking deep brown, but her ribs stuck out below the unhemmed edge of her cut-off T-shirt so that she looked on the verge of painfully thin.

Hard to believe Hazel was already thirty. She was the smallest of the MacLeod women, a petite five foot three, with – Gayle Cutting lamented inwardly – the body of an undeveloped twelve-year-old. No breasts or hips to speak of – why, she might as well stick to the children's department for her rather wacky wardrobe – actually, she probably did looking at the rather immature design on her top.

'This is like some ghastly nursery rhyme nightmare.' Natalie sank to the ground. 'One's too fat and the other's too thin.'

'You forgot the one that's too tall. I'm definitely wearing flats.' Avril stepped through the curtain. 'Hazel, hallelujah! We thought the crocs had got you. Were the Galapagos fabulous? Did you see the giant tortoises?'

'Out of this world!' Hazel's eyes sparkled. 'I swam with sea lions. Did you know they come right up and look in your mask? And there are these birds – the boobies –'

'Oh my God, your hair!' Avril fingered the locks. 'The colour of it.'

'Au naturel, yes. I know, I haven't seen it in years myself.'

'It looks lovely,' Milly said.

'Rot.' Hazel scrutinised her reddish-brown locks in the mirror. 'I'm going out first thing tomorrow and picking the first packet of scorching red or strawberry blonde or whatever they have on the shelves. Or maybe I can dye it purple again, that might look good with pink. Oh, that reminds me, I brought something back.'

'Not bedbugs again, I hope.' Milly took the veil from Natalie and passed it to Gayle who placed it carefully down on a nearby table like it was the Crown jewels. 'Poor Mum was in despair after that Bombay thing. Had to throw away all the bedding and I still itch every time I stay there.'

'Like the old days, eh?' Hazel snorted. 'Remember, Natalie, when you and Milly got scabies? And had to be doused daily with that stuff that stunk like skunk's piss.'

'I've absolutely no idea what you're talking about,' Natalie said, shooting furious looks at Hazel. 'Excuse my sister, Gayle. She has the oddest sense of humour.' Gayle smiled politely and decided to busy herself in the back room, not wishing to join in with the family reunion.

'So what did you bring us?' Milly tried to keep the peace as always.

'I left him outside. Hang on a sec.' She dashed out of the door, the bell jangling behind her.

'Him? What is he? Monkey? Stray dog? Amazonian headhunter?' Avril guessed.

'Or a pygmy.' Natalie sighed. 'I wouldn't put anything past Hazel.'

The bell rang again, Hazel towing an unshaved, scruffy-looking man behind her. No pygmy, he was at least six foot and he had to stoop to enter Gayle's admittedly low threshold. In a threadbare denim shirt, he looked like a suntanned gypsy, with an open friendly face and tawny sun-bleached hair that he had to push back from his eyes.

His gaze moved from sister to sister with a teasing familiarity, flashing an ear-to-ear grin made wolfish by a slightly chipped tooth.

Milly gasped. 'Matt! I don't blinking believe it!'

Spontaneously she ran forward to hug him and then, just as if someone had stepped a foot on her hem, awkwardly jerked to a halt, hands clutching frantically at the dress which was threatening to leave her, stricken by the sudden realisation of exactly how much more of her there was to expose than the last time they'd met.

'I didn't believe it either, when Hazel walked into the clinic.' He took two steps forward and wrapped his long arms around Milly and squeezed her tight. 'It took a while to recognise her all grown up and gorgeous.'

The instant Matt let go, Milly bolted to the changing room to escape from her half-on half-off bridesmaid's dress as Matt exchanged a quick hug and kiss with Avril. 'Matt.' Her lips brushed his cheek. 'How amazing. When Hazel said a package, I was sure she meant an anaconda or something equally ghastly.'

Matt looked over at Natalie, who was intently examining a line of stitching on her waist, and quirked an eyebrow. 'Hi, Nats. You . . . you look stunning in that. He's a lucky man. Congratulations.'

There was a fractional silence. As Matt rubbed at his sunburnt neck, motes of dust seemed to billow from his travel clothes, making him look like an unwashed hobo next to Natalie's gleaming white gown.

'Thanks.' Natalie's reflection stared at him coldly through

the mirror. 'So what brings you back to sunny Sussex?'

'Hazel. I'd planned to stay in London but she insisted I visit you all.'

'Once I told him about the wedding and how everyone was getting together for it' – Hazel put her arm around his waist – 'there was no stopping him.'

Chapter 9

'. . . there I was travelling in the rainforest around El Oriente with this guy I'd met who had the most boneshaking wreck of a jeep imaginable. And out of nowhere we both get attacked by this ferocious dog, practically foaming at the mouth, a sure bet for rabies.' Hazel grinned appreciatively at her sisters' looks of horror and perched her non-existent bottom beside Matt on the pedestal Gayle used for pinning clothes.

'So . . .' She drew it out with relish. 'The locals told us there was a doctor downriver, two days' journey by boat. And when they managed to contact him, he only had one rabies vaccination left. So we had to kill the dog and bring its head with us to get it tested, and all the way down, paddling away in this dugout canoe, the two of us were looking at each other secretly checking for signs of hydrophobia. Because if one of us had it the other would have to push them overboard for the piranhas. So when we finally reached the clinic, who do you think was the noble doctor . . . ?' She pointed to Matt who stood up and took a bow.

'In the middle of the rainforest!' Avril exclaimed. 'What are the odds of that?'

'You killed a dog?' Natalie was appalled. 'That's so cruel.'

'She had to.' Milly defended her youngest sister. 'Rabies is deadly.'

'Sorry to tell you,' Matt said with a laugh as he placed a hand over Hazel's mouth, 'but it wasn't quite that dramatic. A dog in the next village nipped her hand. Her friend insisted she came in for a tetanus booster. And the only one foaming at the mouth was lover boy Lance when she ditched him.'

'I didn't ditch him and he wasn't my lover boy. Honestly, you spend more than two days on the road with someone and they think it's a lifelong commitment.'

'I should have known,' Natalie said in disgust. 'You are such a liar, Hazel.'

'I prefer to think of it as creative storytelling. Anyway, it did happen to someone I met. And they did chop off the dog's head, so there!' She poked out her tongue.

'So, Avril . . .' Matt grinned, diverting the tension. 'It's been – how many years? Congratulations on the agency. Hazel's been filling me in on your superstardom. And wow, look at you. Who would have believed it? I always think of you in black leather, black lipstick and studs. You had us shaking in our boots as kids.'

'Did I heck,' Avril snorted.

On the first day of their move to Little Hooking, Hazel still a tiny babe, Avril a sulky teenager, full of rage and fury against her parents, nine-year-old Matt, already an independent spirit, had wandered over to show them all his new boxer puppy. He stayed all day, watching them unload the removal lorry, full of curiosity, knock-knock jokes and cheeky comments, until his mother had finally come searching and found him sitting on an upturned packing case having dinner with them all.

Of course he'd been far too young to be anything but a nuisance to Avril and she'd moved to London a scarce year later. But whenever she visited home, Matt was always there, by then inseparable from the younger MacLeod girls, leading them into adventures and childhood scrapes and although Matt and Avril's paths crossed infrequently, he'd still managed to make his presence felt. Wrestling with Milly during the kissing scenes of Avril's TV programmes, jumping up and down in front of the screen doing wicked imitations of all Avril's favourite musicians during *Top of the Pops*. Avril had been torn between finding him funny and wondering why his mother hadn't drowned him at birth. Now he was all grown up, his freckles replaced by a tan and laugh lines, his round boyish face morphed into manly cheekbones and a narrow chin dominated by a temptingly mischievous mouth that spoke of experience. Only the long eyelashes fringing wicked slate-grey eyes remained the same. Dusty and travel-stained, he looked perfect for a casting call as the next Indiana Jones, and as out of place among Gayle's pristine silk and lace as a musket-toting backwoodsman.

Matt watched her shake her head in wonder, his grey eyes crinkling. 'What about that day we threw a bucket of water over you from Milly's bedroom window?'

'God, did I want to kill you then!' Avril grimaced. 'One minute I was all dressed up, sneaking out to meet Billy Mitchell at the Blue Grotto, the next I'm drenched and howling blue murder. And all I could hear was you three giggling away above me.'

'Did you know I have four children now?' Milly had emerged again, feeling marginally better in her normal clothes, though there was nothing like a tussle with zips and formal wear to make you freshly self-conscious of your excess rolls of lard.

Matt nodded. 'Hazel showed me the photos you emailed her. Very proud auntie she is, you know.'

'Anyway,' Hazel interrupted, 'did I mention the cow-tossing incident. We were just leaving . . .'

How different she and Hazel were, Milly thought. While Hazel had travelled the world, trekked through the Andes, discovered hidden ruins, dodged Colombian drug lords and found herself lost in jungle paradises with handsome lovers, Milly's dreams of travel rarely extended past Majorca and now they couldn't afford that, even if Ivor could be prised away from work.

At age thirty, Hazel had never met a job, a flat or a man that she could stick with for more than a year. Her ease at finding all three and even greater ease at dropping them to jump on an aeroplane for somewhere remote and tropical made Milly's head swirl.

'Does Mum know Matt's here?' Avril enquired.

'Not yet,' Hazel bubbled. 'But I can't *wait* to tell her. She's going to be *so* excited to see him again. And there I was thinking that I didn't have a date for the wedding.'

'For the wedding!' Avril caught Natalie's shocked face as Hazel stroked Matt's arm.

'Because after all he will be staying at The Briars with me.'

'He will?' Natalie said, surprised. 'Does Mum know about that?'

'Can you imagine her letting him stay anywhere else?' Hazel said in a sing-song tone.

'I told Hazel I'm happy to book a hotel in Codmoreton,' Matt said, shifting uncomfortably beside an indignant-looking Hazel. 'Really, I don't want to be a problem.'

'Course you're not,' Milly insisted, her heart wrenching at the idea he might feel unwanted. 'You're practically family. And, well, if Mum can't fit you in, Ivor probably wouldn't care if you kipped with us for a while,' she added somewhat doubtfully. 'That is if you don't mind a put-you-up in the lounge. Our house is rather poky.'

'By poky,' Hazel teased, 'she means that at the crack of

dawn you'll be woken by the kids jabbing you with toy light sabres, demanding their sofa to watch TV.'

'Beats spider monkeys peeing on you in your hammock just for the hell of it or tarantulas visiting your tent.' Matt seemed to relax again. He absent-mindedly stretched out his broad shoulders as if to loosen out some travel kinks, as Natalie shuddered at the thought of tents and creepy-crawlies. 'You forget I've been living in the jungle. What's a little poke here and there, compared to that!'

'As the actress said to the bishop,' Hazel said, taking the low road as usual, nudging Matt with a raucous dirty laugh. Matt shook his head, giving Avril and Milly one of those 'what can you do with her' looks. Only Natalie was deeply unamused, acutely aware of Gayle patiently waiting in the other room.

'Not that now is the appropriate time to discuss this, but if Matt would feel more comfortable in a hotel . . .' Natalie stood her ground as she was met with Hazel's glare and Milly's doleful eyes. 'He'd probably prefer the privacy. And I happen to have a list . . .' She pulled her voluminous skirts behind her with a swish of satin and threw them all a haughty stare worthy of Queen Victoria.

Hazel sniggered. 'Don't you always.'

Watching Natalie with amused interest, Matt put his arm around the shoulders of Gayle's dressmaker's dummy, pretending to lean against it as he waited for the dust to settle.

'You know full well Mum'll raise the roof if Matt doesn't stay with her and Dad,' Avril said. 'What's rattled your cage, Natalie?'

'Nothing. I'm not rattled,' Natalie protested as Gayle came across, looking purposefully at her watch.

'Right, so who's next?'

Matt quickly released the dummy and seized his chance to escape.

'Look,' he said with a smile, shrugging good-naturedly, 'you lot sort it out. I'm fine with the Coach and Horses, the poky sofa, or even a sleeping bag on the lawn – it'll be a step-up if I'm not sharing with scorpions. And don't forget I still have friends I can call on in Codmoreton. They didn't all flee to far-flung ports as soon as school was over. Hey, when you've finished here, meet me at the corner pub. I've had this desperate craving for a ploughman's and a pint of Old Peculiar ever since our plane touched tarmac.'

As the door closed behind him, they all stared at each other.

'Nice work, Nasty,' said Hazel. 'You managed to make him really uncomfortable. He kept saying he didn't want to intrude but I told him everyone would be thrilled to see him.'

'We are,' said Avril, 'only, it's a bit awkward, isn't it?'

All eyes turned to the sofa, where Milly had sunk beneath a pile of silk-edged throw cushions.

'It was a long time ago.' Milly's face was a violent shade of red. 'Don't mind me.'

'Certainly she should mind you,' protested Natalie. 'Matt was *your* boyfriend. I think it's incredibly tactless to bring him back here and as her date of all things.'

'Yes, but under the circumstances . . .' Avril reasoned. 'Especially meeting up like –'

'You are *so* making this into a bigger deal than it is,' Hazel interrupted, staring incredulously at Natalie. 'Christ, we grew up with him after all. I can't believe you didn't invite him or Aunt Dorothy. And all that other stuff was twenty years ago.'

As if they'd only been parted minutes, Natalie and Hazel had already reverted to their usual bickering mode.

'What the hell difference does that make?!' Natalie exploded, forgetting Gayle's presence. 'He ditched her. Even if I had a clue where in hell he was or felt in the least bit inclined to find out, he'd already lost all right to any kind of consideration in my eyes. You'll notice Milly didn't have him at *her* wedding.'

'Well, actually –' Milly's faint protest was squashed by Hazel's louder one.

'God, you're hard.' She glared at Natalie. 'You never forgive anything, do you? All those years he was like our *brother*.'

'Oh yeah,' Natalie shot back, 'and I'm sure it's just a *sister* thing you've got going now. Coming in here, hanging on his arm. In most cultures they'd call that incest.'

'Oh, think what you want to think.' Hazel crossed her arms. 'You will anyway.'

'OK, let's everyone calm down.' Avril put up a commanding hand. She turned to Hazel. 'This thing with Matt. Is it serious?'

'Course not,' Natalie scoffed. 'When has she ever been serious about anyone?!' Her eyes bored into Hazel. 'Have you slept with him?'

'Jesus H Christ! Stop with all the questions. You lot are unbelievable! Anyone would think I'd brought home Adolf Hitler not sweet darling Matt. Why don't you all keep your nose out of my frigging business? That way we'll be a lot happier.'

'But it's not just your business, is it?' Natalie shook her head, reminding Hazel of a pit bull with unrelenting jaws. 'It's Milly's business too. She went out with him first.'

'Well, it was more a logical progression with her than anything, wasn't it?' Hazel flopped on the sofa next to Milly and scratched the freshest insect bites on her scarred brown legs. 'Boy next door, best friend, go out for a while, split up. Anyway, you told me you and Milly were both virgins till you were twenty. So if she didn't shag him, what does it matter?'

'I can't remember saying anything of the sort.' Natalie stormed into her changing room and began undressing. 'And

74

even if I did,' her voice echoed over the top of the door, 'it was more than likely to stop you jumping into bed with the first available guy you met. Not that it did any good. But I'll tell you one thing.' She emerged barefoot, doing up buttons, eyes flashing sparks. 'I don't want him staying with Mum and Dad, the house is going to be crowded enough as it is, and I definitely don't want him at my wedding. And neither does Milly.'

'That's a bit harsh, Nats.' Avril stared at her. 'He's here now. Mum will have a fit. And I'm sure Milly –'

'The guest list is full.' Natalie folded her arms firmly and set her chin. 'We don't have room.'

'Oh, don't be so stupid,' Hazel burst out. 'Milly's cool with it, aren't you, Mills? And if he can't go to the bloody thing, then neither will I.'

There was a huge sob from the sofa. 'Why don't you all stop talking for me! If you want to know how I feel, I'm right here beside you. I do exist, you know.' Milly burst into tears and ran out of the shop.

They all stared after her in astonishment.

'Now see what you've done,' Natalie hissed at Hazel, suddenly aware that Gayle was still in earshot.

'You mean what *you've* done,' Hazel spat back. 'So are you going to get her, or must I?'

'I will.'

'No, I will,' Avril snapped, as she grabbed her purse and stormed out the shop, leaving her dumbfounded younger sisters finally speechless.

When the doorbell rang, Peggy was deeply engrossed in the Harry Potter book she'd been reading to Ben to cajole him off to sleep. Not that her youngest grandson would have the slightest knowledge of what the book was about, but it was an excuse as ever to indulge in her favourite pastime. And Callum and Jeremy had disappeared right after lunch, giving her a few precious moments.

At first she'd thought they'd gone off together – unusual as this was – but Jeremy had returned a while ago, clambering up the stairs to the guest bedroom, muttering about a nap, and Callum was still missing in action, out for one of his walks perhaps, or pottering through the village, engaging in political discussions with one of his cronies.

Hastily she shoved the book under a cushion, a habit acquired in the early days of her marriage, when she'd always have a cloth and polish close by to quickly feign busyness, and hustled to the door before the sleeping baby woke.

No doubt her husband had forgotten his keys again. She could see a silhouette through the frosted-glass pane. Something about it made her innards sink.

It was Callum. He stood half propped against the porch, his eyes bloodshot and bleary, humming snatches of his favourite song, 'The Road to the Isles'. With him were two old ladies at least fifteen years his senior, so small and frail it looked as if a strong breeze would blow them both to Bognor. They were breathing hard, with anxious expressions on their powdered, wrinkled faces. One's hat was askew on her pure white hair, a hand on Callum's arm. The other, in lacy gloves with a blue rinse attempting to disguise her thinning scalp, had her arm around his waist. The smell of whisky that assaulted Peggy's nose caused her to take a sharp intake of breath.

'So sorry to bother you,' White Hair stammered. 'We found your husband – well, he was flat out on the side of the road.'

Callum slid into singing again.

'The poor man couldn't get up,' Blue Rinse chimed in. 'He could have been run over.'

'We helped him to his feet . . .'

'But he kept falling down . . . So upsetting.'

Poor man, my nelly, thought Peggy as she noticed a dirt stain in the knee area of Blue Rinse's woollen skirt and a rip in White Hair's left stocking. She could only imagine. Callum was a big man. If he'd stumbled – and in that condition she was amazed he could take three steps without toppling – he must have taken these two down with him like skittles.

She shuddered, imagining hip replacements, wheelchairs and dry brittle bones.

'I'm afraid' – White Hair straightened her hat and leaned forward, quivering – 'he might have been *partaking* . . .'

One year, three hundred and forty days into sobriety, Callum MacLeod had once again tumbled off the wagon. And the first thought of his long-suffering wife was: Lord, let me hide this from Natalie.

Chapter 10

Milly brushed away tears as she raced through the narrow cobbled streets. It wasn't only everyone talking like she was invisible that had caused her to flee like a petulant toddler, it was seeing herself reflected through Matt's eyes that had made her feel so desperate.

In family lore, Natalie might have been labelled 'the pretty one' and Milly lauded for her academic brilliance, but even so, in the old days, men in pubs often pulled Milly aside to tell her she was beautiful, the most attractive of all the sisters. Well, they couldn't say that now, could they?

There was Hazel, youthful and cute, with her gamine looks and boundless energy; the willowy Avril, so elegant and full of confidence with a fantastically fit figure, thanks to all that time spent with her personal trainer. Even Natalie was looking better than ever, her hair stylishly streaked for the wedding, not a spare ounce of weight anywhere. And then there was Milly . . . reduced to a fat old mama.

She glimpsed her reflection in a shop window and shuddered. But it wasn't just losing her looks that was so depressing Milly, it was the person inside she'd grown to loathe. She used to have a real life, real ambitions, but who was she now? That clever brain which her father had been so proud of, those hours she'd spent with him discussing Greek and Roman mythology, and the finer points of philosophy, what had she done with it?

And now Matt had turned up as some kind of Albert Schweitzer, out there in the trenches with Médecins Sans Frontiéres, making a difference the way she'd once dreamed of making a difference. No wonder she couldn't bear to have him look at her, imagine what he must think.

She came to a halt as she reached the railings overlooking the sea. She leaned over them and peered into the swirling water below. 'Catastrophe' Natalie had called her. And yes, she wasn't wrong, she was too fat; no self-control, no discipline, her children didn't respect her, her husband didn't have time for her and who could blame him, she cooked the same boring meals every night, the house was always a mess. She was a bad mother and a bad wife.

Of course she could never abandon the children but, honestly, who would be the worse off if she weren't there? How long was it since anyone at all had seen her as anything more than a not very capable domestic drudge? Or even noticed her existence except when she was needed to find a missing item or pick them up from school or be moaned at because she hadn't done something they'd asked her to three times already.

Natalie was right. She was a catastrophe. A bloody fat useless catastrophe.

The tide was in, the waves churning up as the sky darkened. Thunder cracked overhead. Seagulls swooped yelling their protest into the wind. Milly's mouth tasted of salt and her head swirled as she pushed her way along the pier.

Avril trotted down the road, looking right and left down each and every side street, but Milly was nowhere to be seen in the maze of the Brighton lanes.

Why had she run off like that? She wasn't even wearing a jacket and that black thundercloud looked like it was about to burst any second. Crack. Lightning streaked across the sky, the first drops of rain spotting her new Nanette Lepore summer coat.

God, how Avril hated the female psyche sometimes. Theatrics, dramatics, screaming and sulking. No wonder most of her closest friends were male. Why couldn't Milly express her opinions from time to time rather than just holding back, trying to please everyone until she finally flipped?

That was the problem with Milly. Didn't she realise passivity was just plain irritating? Take a simple thing like offering her tea or coffee. It was always 'whatever's easiest' or 'whatever you're having' and you were left trying to second-guess and choose for her. Or like when Avril took her to see *Reservoir Dogs* and only after it was all over did Milly murmur, green-faced and apologetic, that she hated films with violence.

Probably a whole heap healthier to be self-centred like Hazel or explosive like Natalie, rather than bottle things up all the time.

In fact, she considered, as she found herself at the promenade, she was the only one of the four of them who wasn't overemotional. Milly used to teasingly call her the Tin Woman from *The Wizard of Oz* endlessly searching for her soft spongy heart. Little did Milly know Avril wouldn't want a soft spongy heart if it came free with a company car and a pension plan. Underneath that hard shell was an even harder one and she liked it that way.

Passing a row of small shops, Avril glimpsed into a wine bar and suddenly stopped short with shock. There inside, at a table in the back, was Richard. He was sipping a long glass with a miniature paper umbrella in it and he was laughing. Opposite him, also laughing, was a woman. Sky-high cheekbones, full pink-painted lips. Mid to late thirties. Vibrant red hair and the most voluptuous figure.

Avril stood rooted like a rabbit caught in headlights as she tried to make sense of it. Why was Richard with her? Who was she? Saskia? And why was he in Brighton? He was meant to be in Arundel . . . But then again . . . they weren't that far apart, and Brighton was *the* place to go these days. For a second she considered going in and surprising him, but then she thought of their earlier conversation . . . She'd all but bitten his ear off for even ringing her and there was she muscling in on . . . what appeared to be . . . a rather intimate . . .

. . . tête-à-tête.

She carried on walking.

Across the road, the bright interior lighting of the Arena Fitness Centre displayed taut, slim female bodies, leaping about in a way that any other day would have Milly bolting to the nearest doughnut shop. But today was no normal day. She stared for a few seconds, even debating venturing in. But everyone knew gym memberships were ludicrously expensive and she and Ivor weren't exactly rolling in money.

She shivered and pushed a wet strand of hair from her eyes as she made her way to a bus shelter.

The rain began to fall in earnest. It swept into the open sides, hammered against the glass and ran in rivulets down the graffiti-sprayed, poster-clad building behind her. Hugging herself against the cold, she stared unseeingly at ads for jumble sales come and gone, posters for bands she'd never heard of, flyers for bizarre miracle products. Somehow seeing Matt again had triggered something she'd been shoving aside, made her take a good look at herself and realise there was no way she could go on like this. She had to change or hate herself forever.

Then suddenly she saw it, partially obscured by scrawled numbers for Busty Babs, Nellie the Naughty Nurse and Heidi Ho's Escort Service, the words 'Special Offer! This month only!' jumped out at her.

A big smile filled her face.

She knew she had the answer.

Peggy hauled on her husband's unresisting arm but she might as well have been hauling a dead elephant by the trunk. It was no use, his eyes were half open, showing the whites, but he wasn't helping at all. 'Come on, Callum. Please . . . they'll be back soon.'

Callum lay half on the foot of the stairs, looking barely conscious. She shook him until he roused enough to flap a hand. 'Ach, away with you, woman. Let me sleep.'

'No, you mustn't.' She shook him again. Callum was at least thirteen stone; even at the height of her nursing days, she couldn't handle that dead weight. Her mind was filling in the blanks like one of Callum's crosswords. His disappearance at the same time as Jeremy. Jeremy's return alone, the worse for wear – he was sleeping it off himself in the bedroom. She'd wring her future son-in-law's neck with her bare hands when she laid eyes on him.

No doubt he'd wanted company, she fumed, as she struggled to move Callum before everyone got home. But didn't he realise what he might have started? Just one month before the wedding . . . That was the trouble with some people, they didn't understand alcoholics. Think one little snifter won't hurt.

'Jeremy!' she bellowed. 'Jeremy! Come down here and give me a hand. Damn you,' she added under her breath. But there was no response.

She turned her attention to Callum who was now starting

to snore. Shaking him again, she whispered conspiratorially in his ear: 'Natalie's upstairs. She wants to ask you something. She has a problem.' One of her oldest tricks, but it usually worked a charm.

'Nee Nee?' Sure enough Callum began to rise.

'Yes, yes. Nee Nee. She's upstairs. He's just coming, dear,' she called loudly into empty space. 'He'll be up in a jiffy.'

'Oh my little baby. My little princess . . .' Then he stopped. 'But she's off to try on her bridal gown . . . Och, Peggy, Peggy, you're no trying to make a cuddy out of me, are you, hen?'

His accent, usually the soft Highland burr of a native Gaelic speaker, grew thick and loud as any drunk Glaswegian at the docks.

'Course not.' Fiddlesticks. Some part of his brain was still compos mentis. 'But . . .' Peggy's mind worked fast. 'Did I say Natalie? I meant, Hazel. You know me, always getting names wrong. She's back from South America.' Well, she was supposed to be, soon, she reasoned. 'She wants to show you what she's bought. A whole suitcase full of Peruvian treasures,' she improvised, 'blowpipes and panpipes and Inca carvings.'

'Hazel?' His eyes opened, he made a shaky effort to get back on his feet. He started to rise again.

'Yes, come on . . .' She put one of his hands on the banister and tugged at his arm. 'There's a statue that looks like a man with a jaguar head, really interesting.'

He was like a lead weight. How those old ladies had managed, she'd never know.

But like a walrus dragging itself across the sand, slowly he began to move, wobbling on each step as if they might both topple backwards to the start again. If he fell, she wouldn't be able to hold him, she knew.

Fergus appeared from the kitchen. 'Nanny, can you –'

'Just check Ben's still asleep, please, will you? And bring

Rory in from the garden, I don't like the look of those clouds.'

She saw the alarm in Fergus's eyes. How she wished he didn't have to witness this, but it would be even worse if Nat found out. With all the added stress of the wedding, she'd been so dreading this might happen.

At last they were outside the bathroom.

'Shower, now!' She pushed Callum, fully dressed, into the cubicle, turned the water on cold and slid the door shut, sitting on the cold tiles in a state of exhaustion, back against the glass.

As the water hit his head, running down his shirt and trousers, Callum lifted up his face like a turkey in the rain and began to sing . . .

'. . . ye've never known the tangle o' the isles . . .'

Avril spotted a heavy figure on the opposite side of the street, trudging along, head lowered to the wind.

'Milly!' Avril ran across the road. 'Milly! What were you doing running off like that?'

Her hair was dripping and her clothes were sticking to her. 'I didn't mean to cause any fuss.' She shrugged. 'I just wanted time to think.'

'Are you OK?'

Milly gave an odd smile. 'I am now.'

'Was it Matt?' Avril was curious. 'Was that what upset you?'

'In a way.'

'You still have feelings for the guy? Really?'

'If you don't mind, I'd rather not talk about it.' Milly wiped some rain from her forehead and tucked her arm through Avril's. 'Let's just say I got a bit claustrophobic in there for a second. But I'm OK now, honestly. Let's go back to Gayle's. See what she can do about my ever increasing dress.'

As they walked back through the passageways, Avril's mind kept returning to the wine bar.

She sighed as they opened the door, and the bell clanged again.

Milly wasn't the only one feeling mixed up.

Callum safely settled, comatose and snoring in bed, Peggy went to find the children. She was shaking visibly, her legs trembling with exhaustion and frayed nerves. 'I'm an old lady,' she told herself. 'I just can't handle things the way I used to.' And then, 'Poor Natalie. This'll break her heart.'

Was there to be no end to it then? she wondered. Was this the way it was always destined to be? She'd been so hopeful with each passing month of sobriety that Callum had finally conquered his demon.

Fergus and Rory were in the kitchen playing with Rory's train set when Peggy walked in.

Peggy noticed Fergus look away as she came in, ducking his head to avoid her gaze. He knew, obviously. Her heart twisted for him. Should she say something, talk about it? Or had Milly already discussed Grandad's drinking with him? Perhaps she should leave it to his mother. It was a sensitive issue that needed careful handling and Peggy would probably shove her big clumsy foot in her mouth and make the situation worse.

'Grandad's having a nap,' she announced brightly, pasting a cheery smile on her face. 'I'm afraid his tummy was bothering him, must have too much sun on his walk or maybe he ate something bad.' She grabbed both boys by the hand, pulling them to their feet. 'I know – why don't we all surprise Mummy, make her some *dee-li-cious* fairy cakes!'

Chapter 11

Sunday was another blistering morning, yesterday's storms already just a distant memory. Milly drew open the blinds and peered out. Humid and sticky again. And what would she wear to this gathering of the clans? She had no decent dresses that fitted and shorts would be too obscene.

Military grey maternity trousers it was again.

But not for much longer, she vowed. Not for much longer. She crumpled the piece of paper that represented salvation and threw it in the wastebasket. Yesterday had been a turning point. For once she'd acted on her inspiration instead of squashing it back down. Still, the memory made her feel slightly sick. Last night she'd hovered with her credit card for ages before going ahead, fingers shaking as she filled out the form. All that money. It was sinful, daylight robbery. But if it really worked . . . Ivor never checked the accounts and after all she owed it to herself. Didn't she?

How soon would she see results? she wondered. A couple of weeks? A month?

Quickly she shoved the wastebasket under her dressing table as Ivor came into the room, wearing mismatched socks hidden by the hanging hem of his trousers. She really should sew that up one day.

Whatever he ate and despite the hours spent in front of the

computer, Ivor stayed eternally skinny so that sometimes Milly felt people must look at them and see Jack Sprat and his plate-licking wife. His wiry dark hair was greying but still appeared as if he'd stuck his finger in a light socket; the rimless glasses over intense, black, Russian Jewish eyes gave him the look of a slightly worried intellectual and his mobile was almost permanently attached to his ear – so much a feature, in fact, that once he'd turned the house upside down looking for it, all the time chatting to a client through the mouthpiece.

He was brilliant, of course, and intensely driven. It hurt her that now he was almost forty-two, the newbies in his profession were so ready to write him off as a dinosaur. Since the bankruptcy of his last software company – Ivor's partner having basically stolen and mismanaged it into an early grave – he'd been putting all his energies into some truly innovative ideas but unless he could raise the funding that was all they would remain.

'One of my clients cancelled Wednesday's meeting, and well, I know it's short notice but why don't we go out instead?' He gestured at his dangling tie, soliciting her help. 'Maybe we could ask your mum to babysit.'

'But it's a school night. The children need to be at home, in their own beds,' Milly said, flustered.

'Well, then let's get a babysitter. Or ask Erin to help out for a change. She's old enough.' Ivor wasn't giving up easily.

'She'll be going out herself.'

'She doesn't have to. I'm sure even she can sacrifice one night for her decrepit parents.'

'Besides, where would we go?'

'Leicester Square, maybe see a show, grab a bite to eat? I'll ask Erin now.'

Once Ivor left the room, Milly began to try to dampen down her worries. Ivor was right, they hadn't been out alone together for ages . . . Not since she was heavily pregnant with Ben. A restaurant might be rather lovely, a candlelit meal to put a bit of spark back. Maybe she'd even go shopping Monday, buy something for the occasion. The more she thought about it, the more her spirits rose.

Ten minutes later, Erin walked in, towel wrapped Carmen Miranda-like round her head. 'Dad says I'm babysitting Wednesday.'

'If that's OK?'

'Sure . . . yeah . . .' She held out her flattened hand, palm upwards. 'How much?'

As she chivvied the boys into their clothes, dimly in the background of Milly was aware of Ivor's mobile ringing. A muttered conversation and suddenly he reappeared. He didn't have to say anything. His whole body was an apology.

'Sorry.' He made a face. 'Really, I'm sorry. It won't be like this forever.'

'No, of course not.' Milly sighed. 'Of course it won't be.'

At least she hadn't wasted money on a dress.

Later that morning, Matt wandered into Peggy's kitchen, yawning, his stretch ending in an abrupt collapse of arms as a chill blast hit him, coming, he realised, not from the open refrigerator door, but from Natalie's icy glare. Goosebumps freckled his legs under the boxing shorts and T-shirt, both of which had seemed perfectly respectable when he'd left the bedroom.

Natalie's hair was pushed up off her forehead – a sure sign of stress – with a big smear of flour on her brow. She'd covered her church clothes with one of Peggy's wacky aprons, this one flaunting a well-filled bikini, with teeny cartoon waist and gigantic boobs. Surrounded by vegetables, pots, pans, chopping board and a colossal chunk of meat dripping blood, there was a crazed look in her eye, and Matt really didn't care for the way she was waving that cleaver.

Braving it out, he crossed the flagstone floor, heading for the half-full coffee percolator.

'Hi, Nasty.' Perhaps, thinking about it, their old childhood nickname wasn't the most tactful choice but it automatically slipped out. 'Where is everyone?'

'If you're looking for *Hazel*' – she whacked an innocent carrot – 'I've no idea. Everyone else had breakfast hours ago. It is twelve o'clock, you know.'

'That's jet lag for you. I didn't get to sleep till three.'

'Not too cramped in that single bed?' It sounded accusing, rather than concerned.

'Oh, it wasn't bad. I made Hazel sleep on the floor.'

If anything the chopping got more manic. Matt half expected to see a digit join the vegetables in the pan.

'Need any help?'

'No. No. As I've said at least five times this morning. No, I do not need any bloody help!' Natalie seethed. 'Least of all from *you*.' She pulled at a drawer, which moved a few inches before sticking. He watched in amusement as she tugged wrathfully until it finally exploded open. Broken pens, half-eaten pencils, toenail clippers, yogurt-pot lids, loose keys, napkin rings, a single gardening glove and a grinning, pink, shorn-headed troll all crashed to the tiles.

Matt rushed forward to help her pick them up. Bending down, he was uncomfortably aware of her face and apple-scented hair only inches from his and even more self-conscious about his half-dressed state.

'Damn Mummy. Who in God's name would save all this rubbish?'

'Everyone has a junk drawer.'

'*A* junk drawer?' Natalie straightened. 'They're *all* full of sodding junk. Look.' She yanked at the drawer underneath. 'Bits of string. Brown paper. More string.' She pulled a piece out so he could see.

'Very eco.'

'Fine.' Natalie jerked furiously at the next. 'And I suppose it's also eco to save . . . ancient half-empty seed packets, half a toy soldier, candle stubs, a zillion pens that don't work, empty matchboxes, loose toothpicks, dirty old Sweet'N Low packets and – what's this?' She grabbed something wrapped in a red paper napkin and opened a corner. 'Yee-uck!'

In disgust, she flung it from her hands. Deftly Matt caught whatever it was, still sticking to the napkin, and peeked.

'Ah.' His deep voice pontificated in the manner of an expert at the *Antiques Roadshow*. 'A hunk of prime English Cheddar, well aged. Quite a rarity these days.'

'How can she live like this?' Natalie's response was vinegar. 'It's revolting. I should call in the social services. And how can I possibly cook when I can't even find a simple piece of silver foil?'

'Up there.'

'Sorry?'

'Up there.' He pointed his finger at the top of the cabinets. 'Hang on, I'll get it for you.' With his long legs, he hopped easily on to the counter and handed it down.

Natalie snatched it from his grasp. 'I mean, who the hell keeps tinfoil where it's totally out of reach?'

'Well, obviously, there's no room in the drawers.' Matt landed on the floor with a bounce. 'All this is for the in-laws, eh?' He peered in the roasting pan. 'What are they like?'

'What are who like?' Natalie reached up to the cupboard to pull out some spices.

'Jeremy's parents. Don't they say if you want to know what

your husband'll be like in twenty years' time, check out the father? Or is it the wife and mother?'

'I certainly hope not. Because I can promise you, I won't be *anything* like Mummy.'

'Too bad.' He reached for a carrot and flinched as Natalie banged the cleaver inches from his hand.

'Just tell me, Matt, what are you doing?' Natalie fought to suppress her anger.

'You know, the secret of a good Yorkshire pudding is double the egg quantity. Little tip for you.' He tapped the side of his nose.

'You're not funny and you're not clever.' She faced him, arms folded, the smudge of flour still on her brow. 'And you are not welcome here. Milly doesn't want you around, I don't want you around and you can bet your life that Hazel will lose interest the minute she's got over the novelty of showing you off. And what's more' – she picked up the knife again and bayoneted the beef – 'I'm not inviting you to join us for lunch. I will *not* go through the embarrassment of explaining to Jeremy's parents which of my sisters you're going out with now and have Mum telling her endless stories about who was caught playing doctor with whoever.'

'Aha – so you remember that, do you?' His grin looked like the wolf discovering Grandma in bed. Of course, of everything she'd said he would pick up on that. Natalie was annoyed to find herself blushing.

'It's a figure of speech,' she said, flustered. 'And it wasn't –'

'Keep your knick-knacks on, Nasty. I'll stay out of sight. Wasn't really all that keen on dining with the Poshy-Washies anyway.'

'The who?' For a second she looked ready to throw the roasting pan at his head. 'Get out! They're going to be here in three hours. Just get the hell out of my way!'

Obediently Matt ambled to the back door.

'On the other hand' – his face was innocent, but his eyes spoke mischief as he kept well out of firing range – 'while I've caught you in this obsessive domestic mood, if you suddenly feel the urge to whip up some brekkie, I like a three-minute egg, soft-boiled.'

To his astonishment, Natalie, already overwrought, completely lost it. 'You've a bloody nerve, Matthew Harkness! Showing up back here after all you've put us through. How do you think it felt listening to Milly cry herself to sleep, night after night, because you were messing her around. You fucked up her life, you know that, don't you? I mean, look at her. Have you ever seen anyone more unhappy?'

To her satisfaction, she noticed Matt flinch, seeing in his eyes that she'd got to him at last.

'Come on, Nat.' He took a few paces forward. 'You're blaming me for something that isn't the twisted drama you've created in that overheated head of yours. I'm not saying I didn't make mistakes. I'm not proud of everything that happened. But my break-up with Milly is our business, hers and mine, not yours. And if you want to know the truth, I actually don't think she was all that upset.'

'No. You wouldn't.' She faced him squarely. 'I suppose it was merely a coincidence that Milly dropped out of university right after it all happened.'

'Because she fell in love with Ivor,' Matt said deliberately. 'She wrote to me about him.'

'Don't be so dense. She married him on the rebound. Anyone could see that. The man totally neglects her, wholly obsessed with his crappy, worthless projects while she scrimps by, practically penniless. And now you come traipsing back, with her much younger sister, boasting that you're in love. I think you're incredibly selfish, you and Hazel.'

'For Christ's sake!' Matt said in frustration. He moved towards Natalie again but she turned her back, feigning intent concentration on preparing the lunch. His arm stretched out to grab hers, then he dropped it and irritably shoved his hands into his pockets. 'If you'd just, for once in your life, just listen . . .'

'I can't hear you.' She started to hum loudly, an infuriating tactic he remembered from their childhood. 'Go away. I don't want to know.'

'Natalie . . .'

She hummed even louder.

'Oh, what's the use!' The wisteria above the back door shook with the impact as he slammed the door behind him.

Chapter 12

In the garden, Matt found Peggy stretched out in a faded canvas deckchair, fanning herself with a paper plate.

'Been kicked out of my own kitchen, by my own daughter, can you merit it? We don't see her for months on end and then she takes over the place.'

'Well, you know what they say about too many cooks,' Matt said as he sat down next to her in the deckchair's mate, angrily pounding heart slowly returning to normal.

'Blooming gall of the girl! One thing I can do well is a Sunday roast. She gets herself in such a state. A worrier like her father. I never had to fret about the children, he'd do it all for me. Staying up past midnight pacing the floor when they were out at some party, convinced they'd been murdered.' She leaned over and grabbed his hand. 'Oh, Matt, it *is* good to have you here. Just like old times. You know your mum was the best friend I ever had. It broke my heart when she decided to emigrate. I miss her so much.'

'Mum misses you too. I mean, she loves it in Adelaide, living close to her brother and all that sunshine, but she talks about you all the time. All the stuff you got up to. Just the other day she mentioned on the phone that time she stopped by and caught you digging up some rocky patch in the front that was full of weeds and she was giving you a hard time saying nothing would ever grow there. And half an hour later, when she got back from the shops, every inch was full of plastic tulips and roses that had come free with some washing powder. She says she never laughed so hard in all her life. And then what about that bloody castle the two of you wanted to buy?!'

'It would have been wonderful, wouldn't it? Callum and I saw it on our way up to Skye one summer. I still have the brochure. Eighteen bedrooms, four towers, with just a touch of dry rot, no plumbing and a few wiring problems! Dorothy was going to have the west wing and we'd have the east. Unsurprisingly Callum refused outright when he heard it needed more than a little love and attention, it needed a whole new roof!'

Milly strolled over, Ben propped on a hip, just in time to overhear Peggy's mournful sighs at having missed out on the castle. 'Nothing a few million pounds wouldn't fix, eh, Mum? No, don't move, Matt. If I sit in that thing, I'll never get out of it.' She lowered herself onto the grass, rolling her eyes. 'Old Nasty's having a hissy fit but she won't let me do anything. God, she's in a foul mood.'

'Yes, I had a taste of that too,' Matt said, searching her face for clues of the emotional torment Natalie had implied. But today she seemed cheerful, happy even.

He had no way of knowing that Milly had stood at the kitchen door for ages, steeling herself to face him again, terrified that Hazel might have spilled the beans about her humiliating outburst the day before.

'And that dreadful woman you called Cross-Eyed Ginger.' Peggy was still happily reminiscing. 'What a temper she had. That day she found out about her nickname and stormed over to complain. I could hardly keep from laughing, it was so apt.'

Milly remembered her well. A stout middle-aged woman

with bright orange hair, a tongue that could lacerate from fifty paces and an unfortunate squint. Just one of the many they'd tormented with that age-old game of ringing the doorbell and running away. God, they'd been demons but what freedom they'd had. No one worrying if they didn't show up from breakfast to bedtime. Riding their bikes to the windswept hillsides of the South Downs. Running unsupervised through Little Hooking Woods, playing *Robin Hood*. Poor Natalie, always typecast as the dastardly Sheriff of Nottingham.

'Why am I always the baddy?' Milly could still visualise the stubborn set of little Natalie's chin on the infamous day she'd rebelled. 'I want to be Lady Gwendolyn and Will Scarlett rescues me. OK, Matt?'

'OK,' Matt had agreed, obliging as ever, home-made bow strung as always in those days over his shoulder. Though he was definitely co-leader with Milly, at times he had this annoying (to Milly) tendency to let Natalie get her way.

'There's no such person as Lady Gwendolyn in *Robin Hood*,' Milly said, exasperated. She was a stickler for details in those days, and besides, who could they fight and jump out at if there wasn't a villain?

'Maid Marian then. And I'm tied to this tree,' Natalie insisted, clinging dramatically to the nearest tree trunk.

'Oh, let her be whoever she wants, dear.' Peggy raised her floppy canvas crown and spoke up. It must have been one of those rare occasions the weak Prince John (Peggy) and baby squire (Hazel) were allowed to come along (though not really part of the game), their castle an ancient tartan picnic blanket, because here she was butting in again, showing the faulty favouritism that could drive her subjects up the wall.

'All right,' Milly seethed, 'you're the stupid Maid Marian. And Robin rushes to your rescue to attack King John's men.' She brandished her wooden sword against a bunch of nettles, managing, in her fury, to get stung on the hand. 'But, alas, his blade slips and poor Maid Marian dies.' She poked at Natalie's armpit menacingly. 'Go on, Nasty. Die!'

'I don't want to.'

'But you do it so well,' Milly urged. 'You're far the best at dying.'

Unable to resist the flattery, Maid Marian crumpled gracefully into a pile of dead leaves.

'Then along comes the Sheriff of Nottingham.' Milly jumped on her imaginary horse and cantered off with Matt in tow, leaving Natalie in a bewildered heap on the ground.

How terribly she'd treated Natalie, Milly thought, but at least she'd felt brave and bold back then. When had it all changed?

Was it when things had got so bad at home? When Mum and Dad seemed to never stop fighting over Dad's drinking? When none of the neighbours except 'Auntie' Dorothy, Matt's mum, would talk to them any more? Or when everyone at school started to tease and ignore her after that one disastrous birthday party where Dad had lurched into the living room, stumbled among her friends as they played blind man's buff and fallen on her Black Beauty birthday cake? Milly could still hear the screams and see poor Carol Cox sobbing hysterically in her party dress, trying, panic-stricken, to pull off the blindfold, clueless as to what terrible chaos had swept up all her friends.

Of course Carol Cox had turned into a little bitch, tormenting Milly every time she found her alone in the corridor, but still it had to have been a nightmare experience for the poor kid. Last Milly had heard, she'd become a therapist, specialising in abused children.

'Oh my, would you look at that!' Peggy pointed at the drooping willow tree that overhung the stream. Hazel was underneath its dangling branches, crawling on her stomach, dressed in a feather headdress, while Erin frogmarched Fergus, hands tied, towards the plank bridge that crossed the stream's one-foot span.

They all laughed.

'Can't believe she's got Erin involved too.' Matt laughed. 'I thought she'd be much too cool for those kind of goings-on.'

'You'd better believe it,' Milly said. 'Hazel's going to make a great mother some day. Much better than me.' She felt grateful for the diversion and for the normal way Matt was acting, just as if all that other stuff between them was the furthest thing from his mind. He'd always been someone in whom she could confide anything; he'd had that easy-going acceptance that made her chest tighten when she thought about how estranged they'd become.

'I don't think that girl will ever grow up,' Peggy said, raising her eyebrows. 'Or get a proper job. I wish Avril would take her under her wing a bit, but then again . . .' Her mind seemed to drift. 'Where is Avril by the way?'

'Gone to the pub with Jeremy,' Milly informed her. 'Said she'd get him out of Natalie's hair. Very noble of her, I'd say.'

'Your father's not gone too, has he?' Peggy looked suddenly anxious. Last thing she needed was a repeat of yesterday.

'Don't worry, Mum, he's fast asleep snoring under his newspaper. Looks a bit rough this morning though.' Milly tentatively tried to broach the questionability of her father's ongoing sobriety but she knew better than to push her mum on the subject. It was something they'd all learned to live with, either way.

'As well he might,' Peggy muttered under her breath.

There was a crash from the kitchen and a startled yelp.

'Sound familiar?' Milly said with a grin.

'Should we go in and lend a hand?' Matt suggested.

'You first then. I don't want my head bitten off.'

Another crash. Natalie opened the kitchen door and stared accusingly in their direction.

'Why can't any of you *help*?'

'They're here! they're here!' Rory squealed as a shiny meteor-blue Bentley rolled up the gravel path.

'Don't stare!' Natalie dragged the children away from the window. 'Now remember, kids, no burping, squabbling or making poo-poo jokes. And if you have to use the loo, do flush the chain. How do I look?' She smoothed her hair, pulling off her apron. 'And please, Avril and Hazel, mind your language. The Potterton-Smythes detest women swearing.'

'No shit!' Hazel grinned.

Natalie gave her a disdainful look. She could have at least made an effort, brushed that tangle of hair or changed out of her FCUK T-shirt. Hardly fitting for a lunch party with the Potterton-Smythes. Mind you, Milly wasn't much better in those faded grey baggy trousers she always wore.

'And, Mum' – she fluffed up the cushions and pulled at the washable cover of the sofa so the calico back wasn't exposed at the base – 'no talking with your mouth full. And above all, no family stories – especially about me.'

'You'd better get out there.' Avril gave her a little shove. 'Go and curtsy to the in-laws.'

'Mummy, Mummy, come down quick! The Poshy-Washies are here!' Rory shouted excitedly up the stairs, just as Natalie opened the door.

Chapter 13

'I have to say,' Mrs Potterton-Smythe ('call me Beryl') commented over a spoonful of carrot-and-coriander soup, 'Natalie was right about the village. Absolutely charming. And the church is darling. Your Sunday services must be magnificent.'

'Afraid I wouldn't know,' Callum contributed in his polite soft-spoken way. An exceedingly shy man, he found all social occasions an ordeal.

'My husband was raised Free Presbyterian.' Peggy scooped more soup into Godfrey's bowl. 'Very strict Protestants, I'm afraid they'd find Little Hooking's church organ the height of sin. And I don't go because much as I'm a believer, churches have a dreadful effect on me. Though of course when we were in Edinburgh, Callum's mother insisted we sent the girls.'

'Nana wouldn't even let us watch TV on a Sunday,' said Milly. 'Or play.'

'We had to sit in our bedroom studying the Bible,' Natalie told her future parents-in-law, sounding as virtuous as if she'd actually done it. 'But she wasn't all bad. She bought Milly and me rocking horses once, for our birthdays. Mine had a white mane, Milly's black.'

'That was a one-off,' said Milly. 'Mostly she was really strict. Natalie and I ran away once, that time she had to look after us just before Hazel was born when Mum's mum was really sick and poor old Mum went off to Harrogate to help her out. Only one of the neighbours saw us and took us home.'

'Avril was lucky,' Natalie cut in. 'She was in boarding school, she missed it all.'

'Oh yes,' Avril said bitterly, 'I was *so* lucky.'

Milly glanced at her, remembering the fights and shouting that had preceded Avril's departure. Avril yelling at their father that a nine o'clock curfew was so unfair when no decent club got going till after ten, hysterically throwing herself on her bed when he refused to give in. She had long hair then, almost to her waist, which Mum was always threatening to cut while Avril was asleep – never dreaming that not much later it would be replaced by orange and black spikes.

A vision came to her of sitting beside Natalie on Avril's bed, watching her conceal a love bite on her neck with a slathering of make-up. She'd have been the same age as Erin, Milly realised with a start.

Funny how, in the past, it was Avril she'd felt sorry for. Now, being a mother herself, she had nothing but sympathy for her parents. Perhaps that was what Erin needed – a good old-fashioned boarding school?

Avril had hated it though. Much as Milly had loved watching *St Trinian's* and Natalie had begged to go too, the oldest MacLeod girl had plainly resented the whole experience. Mum had enrolled her in Codmoreton High after they'd all moved to Sussex but she hadn't liked that any better. Before the year was over, she'd dropped out, decamped to Camden and become a punk.

'My mother was a fine God-fearing woman, that she was,' Callum said, interrupting Milly's thoughts.

'We're churchgoers ourselves, aren't we, Godfrey?'

announced Beryl, trying to regain some of the attention. 'Anglicans.'

'Dad's lot loathe Anglicans,' Hazel said cheerfully. 'Think they're one step away from Catholics. Pass the salt please.'

Natalie gave her a fierce look. 'That's not true, is it, Dad?'

'Not at all. Not at all. Butter, anyone?' Callum pushed the saucer to the centre of the table.

'But I remember, dear Daddy, that once I wore a cross and you told me it was papist rubbish.' Hazel dunked her bread into her soup.

'It was such a super service this morning,' Natalie said hastily, throwing Hazel the filthiest look she could muster without being spotted by her future in-laws. 'Jeremy and I went for the reading of the banns, didn't we, babypie?'

'What hymns did you decide on?' asked Godfrey.

'Well, "Amazing Grace", obviously. And I quite like that one that goes, "Sing Aloud Loud Loud", oh and –'

'And my favourite, "Jerusalem".' Peggy wandered back in with a large serving dish.

'Wine anyone?' Natalie said quickly in case Peggy decided to sing.

'Make mine a large one.' Avril held her glass out.

'No thank you,' Beryl said briskly. 'We don't drink.'

'Very wise,' Callum reflected as he poured them iced water from a jug. 'As it says in Proverbs: "Wine's a mocker and beer a brawler, whoever is led astray by them is not wise."'

'Exactly how we feel.' Godfrey nodded.

'Ruination of many a fine man.' The old hypocrite did a great imitation of a pious head of the household, Avril thought, taking a huge swig. But now he was standing up pushing against Godfrey's chair. 'Excuse me, Godfrey, will you? Nature calls.'

Godfrey squashed himself against the table as Callum

squeezed between him and the wall, making a break for the staircase under Peggy's suspicious gaze.

Beryl glanced out the window at Fergus chasing Rory.

'Your children, are they?' She turned politely to Avril.

'Heck, no.' She shuddered. 'They're Milly's.'

Milly automatically followed Beryl's gaze. Matt was on his knees, fending off Fergus's stranglehold around his neck, while holding Rory at bay with one hand. They were all laughing hysterically. When did Ivor last play with them like that?

'And who is that young man out there?'

Natalie didn't miss a beat. 'Oh, that's Matt.' She glared at Avril and Milly. '*Our gardener.*'

Too late, she saw Jeremy's look. Damn – not only had he witnessed Peggy's ecstatic reunion with Matt but they'd all had dinner together. 'Mum just took him on yesterday,' she mumbled. 'He used to live down the road.'

'Really? And does he always act like that when he's at work? Extraordinary outfit. He seems to have forgotten his trousers. Oh my.' She stared through the window, looking slightly boggle-eyed. 'He's sunning himself now, on one of your deckchairs. They do take advantage sometimes, don't they?'

Avril and Milly battled the sudden urge to snigger. Milly stared determinedly out of the window, shoulders shaking, and Avril put her head between her hands and feigned an intense interest in her empty bowl.

Fortunately, Callum's return provided a diversion, as once again Godfrey shuffled in to let him pass.

To Peggy's experienced eye, her husband's face looked a little flushed. More worrying, his hands that had been trembling at the start of lunch, were a little steadier suddenly. To her it could only mean one thing.

The hair of the dog.

Twenty minutes later and they were all tucking into the roast beef, astonishingly still pink and tender. Natalie had outdone herself. The roast potatoes were fluffy, the parsnips sweet, and she'd even thrown in a gigantic portobello mushroom for Milly, remembering, for once, that she was vegetarian.

The only fly in the ointment, Peggy thought, had been Callum, who'd had more 'bladder calls' than an incontinent terrier determined to mark every tree in the forest. Each time he'd returned a little unsteadier, eyes a little redder. Even Mrs Potterton-Smythe had noticed his excursions and mentioned something in a confidential whisper about Godfrey's prostate.

'So your husband couldn't make it?' Mrs Potterton-Smythe enquired of Milly.

'Too busy, I'm afraid. He's launching a new company to market his software programs. It's at a very delicate stage.'

'Software?' There was a pause as Beryl chewed delicately at a smidgeon of beef, keeping her lips primly closed. 'I'm afraid I know nothing about computers. What do these programs hope to achieve?'

'Hard to explain really. Something to do with CTI – you know, computer telephony integration, only of course light years ahead of what's out there now.'

'Immigration, you say?' Godfrey cupped his hand to his left ear. 'Criminal, isn't it? All those Romanian Gypsies coming over here, living off our welfare. When's it going to stop, that's what I say?'

'Hear, hear,' said Jeremy.

Hazel stared as if she'd encountered a pod of Martians.

'You can't be serious!'

She yelped as Avril kicked her under the table.

'Well, stands to reason, we don't have limitless resources,' Jeremy lectured. 'This is a small island, there simply isn't room, even if we wanted to take them in. Let them go somewhere else. France or Spain. Or stay where they are and get their act together.'

'And be killed or starve? "Them" being political refugees, victims of war, for example,' Hazel said heatedly. 'It's all right to sit here, like big, privileged fat cats, saying people should be able to take care of themselves, but have you ever been to any of those countries, Jeremy? Seen how these people live?'

'I have to say you're right, son,' Godfrey said, purposefully ignoring Hazel. 'Don't approve of all these handouts myself. Oh, I'm not saying we can't help in some small way – send over some books maybe, or show them how to plant their corn. You know the saying, give a man a fish and you give him a meal. Teach him to fish and he eats for a lifetime. Only they need to remember they owe us for that fishing line. I'll have some more roast beef, Peggy, yes please.' He held his plate high in the air for a generous serving.

'But what if the rivers have dried up, the crops have withered in the drought and the grain is being robbed from you by the warlords who are killing and torturing people at random?' Hazel carried on indignantly. 'What use do you think his fishing line is then?'

'I don't think we really want to discuss politics, do we?' Natalie glared at Hazel.

'Other countries manage.' Godfrey reached for the horse-radish. 'They need to get their act together. Choose responsible leaders. Fight for them, if necessary.'

'Right. And you expect people too weak to stand, let alone pick up a stick, to defend themselves against Kalashnikovs. Interesting perspective.' Hazel flung down her napkin. 'Excuse me, everyone. I think I'll go outside. Chivvy that *idle gardener* along.'

'Good idea.' Callum stood up again, lurching noticeably. 'I might join you. I'll just fetch my pipe.'

'Callum. Sit down!' Peggy's tone was sharp, commanding. 'You don't need to get a thing!'

Milly and Avril froze. To their surprised relief, Callum dropped back in his chair as everyone stopped eating.

'Actually, I think I hear Ben waking. I'd better go check on him.' Milly's cheeks were as pallid as Callum's were red.

'Isn't it wonderful?' Peggy smiled sweetly at Beryl as Milly scuttled out. 'These two lovebirds getting married. I can hardly believe it. My little girl.' Her eyes grew wet and then started to gush. She lifted up her glasses and futilely pressed her napkin against them to stop the flow.

'Oh, for fuck's sake, Mum!' The words were out of Natalie's mouth before she caught Mrs Potterton-Smythe's disapproving look. Shit.

Deftly, Natalie turned the conversation to Jeremy's upcoming promotion, but in her deepest core, she could feel the damage was already done. Her humiliation grew when Avril somehow missed her mouth with her glass, causing red liquid to trickle down her chin and breasts, spreading across her new high-collared Karen Walker blouse.

Avril dabbed at her breast with a generous splash of Chablis but only succeeded in looking like the last man standing at the OK Corral.

'Oops!' She laughed gaily. 'Maybe this would be a good time to fetch dessert.'

'Grand idea,' Callum said, jovially. 'How about a nice sherry while we're at it? Godfrey? Meryl?'

'Beryl. And no thank you.' Her voice was frigid.

'Oh, come on. A small one never hurt anyone, don't you think?' Callum patted Beryl's knee.

Peggy came to the rescue. 'I've a better idea. Why don't we take dessert and coffee on the patio. The rhododendrons are heavenly at the moment.'

'Yes, I noticed them as we arrived. Very beautiful.' Beryl relented slightly, as the Potterton-Smythes allowed Peggy to lead them out the French windows, dessert plates in hand. 'I wasn't entirely convinced when Natalie suggested holding the reception in your back garden,' (she made it sound as if Natalie had suggested a party in a septic tank) 'but really it's quite a spectacular setting.'

'Mummy knows everything about plants,' Natalie said, in a rare moment of daughterly appreciation, grateful for this safer ground.

Over by the willow trees, she saw Hazel boxing with Matt, feinting and jabbing as he easily parried her blows. Laughing, he grabbed Hazel by the waist and dropped her in the stream. She yearned to kill them both.

'Anything that gets me out of housework,' Peggy added cheerfully, easing into a patio chair. 'Always hated it. I used to pray to be a boy because I had to help my mother with cleaning while my two brothers never lifted a finger. Just because they had penises and I didn't. Oh yes,' she carried on, oblivious to Beryl's open-mouthed expression, 'everyone thought they were all so wonderful just because they had something to wag underneath their trousers.'

Gratitude withering now, Natalie wished ardently for a meteor to drop into the street outside or a telephone pole to come crashing to the ground, anything to provide a diversion and change of topic. As a retired nurse, her mother often forgot that not everyone shared her lack of inhibitions in discussing genitalia.

'Missed that, I'm afraid.' Godfrey followed behind. 'My bad ear. What didn't she have?'

107

'Nothing, Father.' Jeremy grabbed his arm. 'Let me show you around while we wait for pudding. I need some advice on the marquee.'

'It was terrible when this rabble were small.' Crossing her varicose-veined legs in front of her, Peggy was on a roll. She had Natalie's gift for pushing unpleasantness aside to think about later and so for the moment her annoyance and frustration with Callum were forgotten in the pleasure of a brand-new audience. 'So much laundry and all I had was a battered old machine and wringer. I'd throw the dirty sheets in the corner of the basement staircase for Mary the maid to do later.'

'You had staff?' Beryl, who'd been hovering beside the weathered, green-tinged patio chairs finally relented, brushed off the seat and cautiously sat down.

Natalie silently cursed herself for not having checked the chairs were clean, but in all honesty even her wish to please the Potterton-Smythes was wearing thin.

'Did I cocoa! No, later I'd be Mary and do them myself! So anyway, one day Callum slipped on the dirty washing and fell all the way down the stone stairs . . .' She chuckled at the memory.

'Mummy, I don't think Mrs Potterton-Smythe – Beryl – is interested,' Natalie hissed, noticing Beryl's faintly appalled expression. 'Oh, look, here's Avril with the coffee,' she chirruped, hoping to distract the attention from her mother who was writhing in hysterics at her own unfinished story, croaking like a seal on heat and showing off rows of ugly amalgam fillings. There was no stopping her, Natalie realised. More than any time even in her turbulent childhood, Natalie wished she'd been adopted.

Beryl took a chipped mug from the tray Avril offered, her eyes still fastened on Peggy in horror. Unable to contain her anger, Natalie made some excuse about putting on some more water to boil and fled to the kitchen.

'Thought I'd killed the bally man.' Peggy chortled on, fighting to get the words out through snorts of hilarity. 'He turned every colour under the rainbow afterwards. Rory, dear' – she grabbed her passing grandson – 'come and say hello. Want some lemon meringue?'

'Not hungry,' he mumbled, head thrust shyly into her lap.

'Well, delicious as it is' – Beryl put her plate down firmly – 'I really think we need to go. Thank you so much for lunch – it's been . . . lovely. What a darling little boy. He'll look so smart in his pageboy suit.' She patted him on the head. 'Goodbye, young man.'

At the kitchen window, Natalie stood alone, taking deep breaths as she attempted to remain calm. 'Almost all over,' she said to herself, grateful that everything had gone relatively smoothly – given the relatives she had to deal with.

Milly came into the kitchen carrying a still sleepy Ben. She was about to pour Natalie another glass of wine, thinking she needed to relax a bit more, when they were both startled by a blood-curdling, high-pitched scream from outside. They looked through the window in horror. Rory had just sunk his teeth into Mrs Potterton-Smythe's plump stockinged calf.

Chapter 14

Milly woke the next morning to a tangle of legs she quickly identified as Ben and Rory. Patting her hand further along the mattress, she realised Ivor had deserted her again. Musical beds for the third night in a row. Rory started off in his own room all right, but in the night she'd wake to a shaft of light in the door frame, a creak on the floorboards, followed by a duvet being lifted and a tiny icy foot against her calf. And then Ben would start to cry and she'd bring him in to soothe him and next Ivor would be leaving the now crowded mattress for the haven of Rory's top bunk.

Her husband sauntered into the bedroom, naked apart from a navy towel fastened round his skinny hips. 'You were out like a light when I got home.' He smiled down at her, dripping water from his hair.

'How did your meeting go?' She stretched her arms and sleepily pulled herself up to a sitting position. 'What time did you get in?'

'About midnight. And you know what these people are like. Promise you the sun and the moon but I won't believe a word until I have that contract in my hot and clammy hand. Good time with the family?'

'So-so. Rory bit Mrs Poshy-Washy. Dad got drunk. When I left, Hazel was fuming about how Natalie was joining a family akin to the Ku Klux Klan and even suggested she should stitch her a sheet and pointy hat as a wedding present. Oh, and Avril drove home in a mammoth huff because Nat got shirty about her drinking. The usual.'

'Sounds a laugh a minute.' Ivor towelled his hair vigorously.

'Yes, but it's dreadful, really,' Milly fretted. 'Poor Dad. You know the doctor warned him last time he fell off the wagon that another binge could kill him. His liver's shot, he said. The funny thing is, Natalie was so obsessed with sucking up to the Poshy-Washies, I don't think she even noticed. God, why can't we be a normal family?'

'Because "normal" families are a myth.' Ivor kissed her forehead. 'Propagated by American TV. I'll go put the kettle on.'

'Come on, Rory.' She shook the lump to the left of her. 'Rise and shine. Don't lie there dreaming while the sun scorches your eyes out.'

'You're always saying that,' grizzled Rory. 'Just like Nanny.'

'And my granny used to say it to her. Now get up, lazy sloth. Action stations! School's in less than an hour.'

'It's for you, Mum,' Erin sang out fifteen minutes later as Milly strapped Ben in his high chair. 'Auntie Nat.'

'Oh dear,' Milly said, flustered. 'Rory, pour yourself some Shreddies, and Fergus, can you feed Ben for me?'

'Milly.' Natalie sounded stern.

'I'm sorry, Nats,' Milly said into the mouthpiece. 'Like I told you yesterday. I'm sorry, I'm sorry, I'm sorry. I'm dealing with it, I'm just –'

'Oh, Rory savaging Mrs Potterton-Smythe, you mean? Well, yes, that was monstrous, but I think we got away with it.'

'We did? How?'

'I told her he had special needs.'

'You did what?' Unable to believe her ears, Milly choked back a stream of unsaid words.

'That he was deprived of oxygen at birth and that the cord was wrapped around his neck and that he took Ritalin three times a day to help control his ADHD. Well, I had to say something. I couldn't let her think he was an undisciplined tearaway, could I?'

'I suppose not.' Milly bristled, deciding it was too early in the day to get into a row about this.

'And it was partly true, at least it was Ben that had the cord around his neck, wasn't it?' Natalie continued, oblivious to the crucifying hurt she'd just inflicted on her sister. 'And Avril was way out of control . . . I mean, getting smashed at functions may be a blast in your twenties, but she's practically fifty . . . so unbecoming . . .'

'I don't actually think she was –'

'And then all that militant drivel Hazel was spouting. Practically calling Jeremy's parents fascists. Doesn't she even care that they're my future in-laws?'

'What did Jeremy say?'

'Nothing. Literally. The only words he spoke on the way back were, "Can you plug in the satnav?" He hardly uttered a thing this morning either.' She sighed. 'And I so wanted the day to be perfect.'

'Well, I thought it went pretty well considering.' Milly just wanted to stop the post-mortem and forget the whole debacle. There was a bleeping on the line. 'Hold on a tick, there's another call coming in. Erin! Erin!' she shouted. 'Tell Rory and Fergus to finish up now and brush their teeth!' She switched lines before Natalie could protest.

It was Hazel.

'Hi, Hazel. I'm just on the phone to –'

'Can you believe those people?' Hazel burst in. 'Jesus, Addams family or what! I actually feel sorry for JJ now having those two weirdos bring him up.'

'Oh, they're probably OK, we just didn't get a chance to know them. Listen, I can't talk, I've got Nat –'

'Would you even want to get to know them? They're practically Nazis. Stuck-up snobs. I bet if you look closely you'll find snot marks on the ceiling. And Natalie was practically licking their boots. Yes, Mrs P-S. No, Mrs P-S. I'm surprised she didn't jump up and give the *Sieg Heil* salute. Pretending Matt was the fucking *gardener* for Christ's sake! How awful is that?'

'I'm sure Matt thought it was hilarious, he knows what Natalie's like. Oops, hang on.' She switched back to the other line. 'Sorry, Nats. It's chaos here.'

Unfortunately it was true. Erin, Fergus and Rory had emerged, all clamouring for attention. She held out the phone so Natalie could hear.

'Mum, Fergus has taken all the Chunky KitKats.' Rory.

'Mum, Rory's taken all the crisps.' Fergus.

'Why do we never have any milk in this house?' Erin. And on it went, 'Has anyone seen my trainers?' 'I can't find my history book.'

Ignoring the fighting and taunts that were routine for every weekday morning, Milly focused back on the handset again. One of these days she'd get a walkaround one that she could lock herself in the bathroom with. 'Sorry about that. You know, bottom line is they're Natalie's Nazis and it's really none of our business if she chooses to join them goose-stepping around Codmoreton bypass.'

'What do you mean, *my* Nazis?'

Oh plop! It was Natalie.

'I meant . . . What I was saying' – Milly got flustered – 'was

113

Hazel was probably jet-lagged or something yesterday.'

'That's her on the other line, isn't it? Well, you can just tell her from me that I'll never forgive her. Never.'

'Oh, Natalie, don't be like that. She's your sister after all. Listen, I think we all need to talk. You, me, Hazel and Avril. You don't want to be still fighting at the wedding. Let's all meet up. How about Wednesday night?'

'Personally I'd just as soon not bother,' Natalie said brusquely.

'You'd better.' Milly forced her voice to sound assertive. 'Or you'll be having a wedding without bridesmaids.'

There was a long silence. Natalie was obviously weighing it up, trying to calculate how it would affect her seating plan.

'All right then,' she said reluctantly. 'Where?'

Chapter 15

'So how did the big weekend go?' Vera arrived into Natalie's office Monday morning clutching a cappuccino, caffè mocha and two iced buns.

'Oh, all right.' Natalie kept her eyes on the computer screen, punching details of their latest listing into the company website. 'Listen to this. "Georgian town house . . . remote-control gadgetry . . . acoustic glazing . . . plasma screens . . ."' It sounded fabulous. If Jeremy's parents did give them that loan, then who knew . . .

'Only all right?' Vera's pug nose twitched as if scenting a juicy piece of gossip.

Well, Natalie wouldn't give her the satisfaction.

'No, no, I mean brilliant.' She carried on typing. 'You know, I'd give anything for remote-control gadgetry.'

'Oooh, you could switch your oven on before you came home.'

'Have muted lighting and soft music playing as you walked back through the door.'

'Swish back your curtains to save you getting out of bed in the morning.'

They both sighed a moment.

'Still, it's three point five big buckaroonies.' Natalie shrugged. 'Slightly out of budget.'

'Even with the Potterton-Smythes' inheritance?'

'Will you stop it!' Natalie giggled as she rechecked the measurements from the notepad beside her. 'They're not even in their seventies yet.'

'Oh well, one day. By the way did you use those table decorations I lent you?'

'Yes. Mrs Potterton-Smythe asked where they came from.'

'Tell her Harrods, third floor.' Vera plucked a brochure from the filing cabinet and began leafing through. 'Oh, this is mine . . . "Historic country house, wealth of period features, paddocks . . ."'

Natalie wasn't listening, her mind engaged in an imaginary tongue-lashing with Hazel. 'I'll have you know, you cocky madam,' she blasted her mentally, 'the Potterton-Smythes have more class in their little finger than you have in . . .'

With a click of the mouse, she closed the site down and turned to her colleague. 'Vera, can I ask you a question?'

'Mmm?'

'How do you get on with your sister?'

'I loathe her. We've always been like oil and water. I stabbed her hand with a fork once, impaled it when she stretched across me to grab some butter. Another time I whacked her in the head with a metal swing, nearly knocked her unconscious. And at least twice I pushed her down the stairs, hoping she'd die.'

'Wow.' Natalie stared at her with a mixture of horror and admiration. Vera always seemed to be such a happy, uncomplicated soul. She hadn't known she was sharing an office with devil child Damian.

'Oh yeah. She still gets up my nose. Why do you ask?'

'No reason really.' Natalie turned back to her keyboard.

For some strange reason she felt quite cheered up.

*

'So what's the timeline?' Avril clicked her mouse onto her computer diary and began counting forward. 'Right, today's June fourth, three months would be say early September. Mmm. Pushing it a bit, isn't it? OK, sweetie. I'll see what I can do.'

She snatched a sip of her coffee. Her desk, immaculate at the start of every day, was already littered with contracts and scripts and she had two new clients coming in this afternoon before she bolted to a meeting at the BBC. It was always this way, like juggling a dozen eggs over a cement floor. Too bad she had no audience to appreciate her skill.

Staring at the email that had just come in, a wry smile unconsciously creased her lips. Wally Walton was at it again, trying to coax her to come work for him, run his Beverly Hills office. She could be back living in the Hollywood Hills, earning three times what she did today with half the headaches. On the proviso, of course, that she brought with her certain clients, Baxter being one of them.

Tempting. She'd known Wally for years. He was a native New Yorker, sharp as tacks and, if not exactly laid-back, astute enough to trust her and give her free rein to run things the way she wanted. But still, only in her deepest, darkest moments would she ever faintly consider it.

In business, as in her personal life, Avril's was strictly a one-woman show. No partners. No help. Not a single penny from her parents. Peggy's cheques, when she was just a sixteen-year-old, making her own way in London, had all been returned. And she was proud of it.

Brenda buzzed through. 'Milly on line four.'

'Milly? What's up, sweetie? You never ring me at work.'

'I don't usually like to disturb you,' (Milly sounded tired) 'knowing how busy you are but this is urgent. I have to be quick because I'm just about to get called in to the doctor.'

'Are you OK?'

'It's not me, silly. It's Ben, just a snuffle probably. Look, I need to ask you something.'

'So shoot.' She began flipping through the papers on her desk.

'Well, I think we should have a kind of powwow. Hazel and Natalie are at each other's throats.'

'What's new?' Avril shrugged. 'Anyway, Natalie's impossible. Did you hear the way she talked to me?'

'I know, I know. But the wedding's less than a month away, and it's her big day, we don't want there to be an atmosphere through the whole thing. So I've kind of arranged for us all to get together Wednesday evening.'

Same old Milly, Avril thought. Even as a child she was the peacemaker, trying to patch things up, hoping to jolly everyone into forgetting their grudges.

'Who's all?'

'Just the girls, I thought. I mean, I would invite the guys except Ivor's busy, Jeremy's hardly speaking to Natalie, Natalie's cross at Matt, Hazel hates Jeremy and . . .'

'. . . and besides, Avril, the green old gooseberry, doesn't have anyone.'

'Oh look, Avril, I never meant that. Naturally if it was guys too and you were seeing someone –'

'Actually, darling, I am. Seeing someone.' She didn't know why she said it. She was just thoroughly pissed off with this image everyone had of her as the loveless workaholic. Well, of course it was partly her fault. She liked to keep her affairs secret. Especially from her family.

'You are?' Even through the phone, Milly's surprised enthusiasm made her flinch. 'Who, what, tell?'

'His name's Richard.' Funny, Avril felt almost shy. 'Richard Burdock. He's in publishing.'

'And this has been going on how long?'

Too late to backtrack now; she'd opened the bag and the cat was out and halfway down the alley. 'Three months.'

'Three months! And you haven't let on. You sly old dog, you.'

'Less of the old if you don't mind.' Avril laughed. Maybe Richard was right. Perhaps it was time for her finely drawn line to get a bit smudged around the edges.

'But that's brill. Look, I'm going to call Natalie and Hazel right back, tell them to bring the blokes. With any luck, they'll forget their squabbles in the excitement of meeting your new fella.' Milly's voice turned anxious suddenly. 'You will invite him, won't you?'

'I might. Was that all?' Without noticing it, her gaze had returned to her laptop, clicking on three new messages, only listening with half an ear as she read the first one.

'There is another thing. I'm really worried about Dad. I mean, obviously he was drunk yesterday and you know what Dr Proudfoot said –'

'Oh, Milly, leave the man alone. It was one tiny slip-up, don't make a huge issue out of it. He's probably fine today. I mean, he might have been a little tipsy but that's his whole culture, think of all those old shepherds in Scotland who drink like fishes, and they all seem to live to ninety-nine. Heck, did you hear the way Natalie went on at me! All I had was a couple glasses of wine and you'd have thought I was an incontinent lush. Whatever you do, don't say a word about Dad to her, she blows everything out of proportion.'

Brenda stuck her head through the door, splaying out finger and thumb, and doing a weird kind of sword dance. Baxter was on the phone.

'Gotta go, sweetie. Call me back when you know where and when.'

'Oh, but I want to hear about the new man – all the gory details. Where did you meet him? How did you get together? What's he like?'

'How big's his dick?' Avril laughed, in a good imitation of Hazel. 'All in good time. You'll just have to wait and see.'

Natalie had barely stepped into the office when her mobile rang.

'Avril's got what?' Natalie dropped her briefcase and headed for the coffee area. Half the morning had been taken up with some complete time wasters, a married couple who'd spent hours lovingly examining a Holland Park mansion they clearly couldn't afford.

'A new man. One she's been seeing three months!'

'Three months!' Astonished, Natalie splashed her caffè latte over the edge of the styrofoam cup on to her skin. She mopped at it with a napkin, phone pinned between shoulder and ear.

'His name's Richard and she's bringing him along to meet us.'

'My, aren't we honoured?' Avril's secrecy about her love life irritated Natalie no end. More than once she'd walked into some Soho hot spot to see her clearly on a date. There were spies in MI5 with looser lips. 'Is it serious?'

'Could be. She sounded, well, different. Less brittle. God, you don't think she's falling for him, do you?'

'Avril? Don't be ridiculous. He'll do something unfor-givable – pull her chair out in a restaurant or hold her hand in public and that'll be it, the old heave-ho. She's as fickle as Hazel in her own way.'

They both laughed.

'Well, about time she did.' Milly rocked Ben's pushchair back and forth. 'Fall for someone, I mean.' Faintly from the nearest clinic room, she heard the abrupt beginnings of a baby's outraged scream then silence.

As the nurse ushered out the latest inoculation victim, she recognised the familiar guilt-ridden, tear-stained, lip-quivering look on the stricken face of the new mother, emerging with her pushchair. The baby had already forgotten the insult of the jab, chortling as he waved his chubby arm in the air, but the shock and agony of betraying her little darling would ruin that woman's entire day, Milly knew. She'd been there.

'Did she give any details?' She switched her attention back to Natalie.

'Only that he works in publishing.'

'And what's his name?'

'Richard Burdock. You don't know him, do you?'

'No, but his name sounds familiar. I might throw out some feelers.'

'Richard? It's Avril.'

'Avril. *Quelle surprise*. And what might you want?' Well, she deserved that, she supposed. As she hesitated, momentarily wrong-footed, his voice relented, becoming a little less cool. 'Fun weekend?'

'If your idea of fun is razor-sharp splinters driven under your fingernails. You?'

'Terrific.'

He didn't have to sound so cheerful about it.

'Enjoy Brighton? Sizzling Saskia enjoy her cocktail? Have a good time staring down that ample cleavage?' is what she wanted to say, but instead she just said, 'Enjoy Arundel? How was the house party?' Because no way would she let him know she'd seen him. She despised people trying to pull the wool over her eyes. He says he's in Arundel; she sees him in Brighton. He's supposed to be visiting Charlie; she catches him at lunch with some younger version of wifey. Oh, it could all have some perfectly innocent explanation but she wasn't going to demean herself to find out. It wasn't like they had any hold over each other.

'Absolute blast. I've known Charlie since we were in knickerbockers. Great crowd. You'd like them.'

'I'm sure I would.' Avril wondered if one solitary female constituted a crowd and doubted very much that she'd care for her at all. 'Look, I was thinking, say no if you're busy, but you talked about meeting my folks . . .' To her annoyance she suddenly found herself sounding like a shy teenager. 'And, well, my sisters and partners are hooking up in a pub Wednesday evening and I wondered –'

'Oh, Avril, I would have loved to, but Wednesday . . .' She thought she could hear his pen tap against his teeth, imagining him raising what-can-I-do-the-girl-won't-leave-me-alone eye-brows at the voluptuous Saskia opposite. '. . . I'm away in Birmingham, won't be back till Friday morning. We could do Friday night maybe?'

Yeah, right. First she'd heard of this Birmingham trip. How ludicrous – she actually felt humiliated.

'Friday?' She pretended to check her diary. 'Actually, sorry, I'm off to New York. The Cameron Baxter movie – he's been after me to visit the set for ages.' Why not after all – she could squeeze in the shoot and a meeting with Wally at the same time. If nothing else it would be a morale boost.

'Oh. You didn't mention it.'

'Just booked the ticket. Hey, look, I'm pretty busy . . .' It was no good, she felt all wrong talking to him now. She quickly picked up a sheaf of paper and shuffled it in front of the speakerphone. 'Got a heap of things to complete before I go and Brenda's asked for the rest of the day off, toothache, but I'll catch you when I get back.'

'How about lunch or a drink before I go?'

Well, naturally he'd be too busy for dinner. That figured.

'No, I've too much on, but thanks anyway.'

She put the phone down, plucked the handful of flowers from the vase and chucked them in the bin. Then she flung open her office door.

'Brenda, I need you to book me a ticket for New York, JFK.'

'You do? When?' Brenda paused in her typing.

'Wednesday. No, why not make it tomorrow? Coming back in about a week. Oh, and can you get rid of these?' She held out her waste-paper basket. 'They're beginning to whiff.'

'OK.' Brenda took them, looking bemused.

'And, Brenda, one more thing . . .'

'Yes?' Her assistant glanced at her warily.

'You can take the rest of the day off.'

The package was there Tuesday afternoon when Milly and Rory arrived back from school. Sitting on the doorstep, covered in urgent express stickers. Her hands shook as she picked it up. So small and light. What had she done? she wondered. What would Ivor say if he ever found out? Was she a complete sap, throwing away his hard-earned money on what might be no more than a hoax, a scam for the gullible and desperate? But even as she thought it, she was tearing open the packing tape, using her teeth to force her way through the layers of plastic to get to the cardboard below. Then more plastic and a leaflet full of printed warnings that she gave barely a glance. Americans – so paranoid, so petrified of getting sued.

After all, great wars weren't won by the faint of heart . . .

Chapter 16

The next evening, as planned, Peggy's purple Mini came to a screeching halt under an ancient oak in the car park of the Flying Ferret.

'Nice.' Matt nodded his approval as he peeled himself off the windscreen and unfastened his seat belt with the relief of a repentant survivor. 'Who recommended it?'

'Milly thought it'd be a good halfway meeting point.' Hazel switched off the ignition and hopped out. 'Apparently she and Ivor used to come here a lot when they were first together.'

'Did they? I can see why.' Matt stared out at rolling hills and winding footpaths, thinking how rural and peaceful it all was. Since he'd arrived back, everyone had been complaining in true English fashion about the heat and clamminess. If only they knew. Give them one of those thirty degrees Celsius days that had almost become normal for him, throw in a few thousand mozzies and a hundred inches of rain in the 'dry' season and then let them talk about humidity! One instant you'd be sweating so hard it seemed the patients would find a melted puddle instead of a doctor, the next you'd be hastily moving boxes in a thunderous downpour away from a gushing flood and a frantic retreat of ants. (Didn't they say there were more ant species on a single Amazon tree than in England, Scotland and Wales put together?) No wonder he was gawping like a tourist at these ivy-covered stone walls, rustic picnic tables and mullioned glass windows. How 'frightfully charming' it looked. A lot of people apparently shared the same opinion because the picnic tables and garden area were buzzing with activity.

'Very olde worlde England-ee, isn't it?' he said, appreciatively. 'You sort of expect to see Dick Turpin galloping up on old Bess. Hard to believe we're in good old suburban Surrey, don'tcha think?' Grinning, he started to sing: '*Dick Turpin was a highwayman . . . who sailed the Spanish Main . . . la, la, la . . .*' Lacking words or tune, his voice trailed and stopped.

'I wouldn't give up the day job quite yet.' Hazel laughed as she locked the car. 'You might want to work on that before you audition for the *X Factor.*'

Together they walked across the gravel, Hazel holding on to his elbow, so she could keep up with his long legs and study him at the same time.

Not classically handsome, she assessed, and not for the first time since they'd met again. His nose was a bit too broad, his mouth too wide, on the whole more ordinary and way more cheerful than the sulky male models that graced the pages of *Vogue.* But then again, hadn't she read somewhere that a heart-shaped face denoted sensitivity? And he looked naturally athletic – though not bodybuilder, ugh – with that tight bum in faded black cords and a great set of abs too, not that you could see them under his shirt. She skipped a few steps to avoid the sensation of being towed.

By the time they reached the flowering half-barrels and coach lanterns that adorned the entrance, Hazel had almost definitely decided once again that the secret to his charm lay in his eyes – frank, clear, wrinkling sexily at the corners – and his daredevil grin that promised nothing but trouble. One look and you just knew this was a madman who'd think nothing of snowboarding off cliffs or bungee-jumping Angel Falls – and yet he could be just as happy having tea with an old lady like her mum. Best of all, from Hazel's point of view, he was someone you could be silly with, have a real laugh. They had so much shared history.

Had it been tactless to mention Milly and Ivor's whirlwind romance, which had followed so soon after Milly's break-up with Matt? Surely not, it had all happened so long ago. And yet she couldn't help remembering Milly's disappointment when Matt didn't come to her wedding. Typical Milly; if she had her way, the whole world would be holding hands, with Milly herself teaching them how to sing.

Still, she wondered, as he pushed at the heavy oak studded door, how *did* Matt feel about seeing her sister again? Hazel was good at getting men to bare their souls, whether it involved three bottles of wine in an intimate restaurant, a six-pack of beer and tequila shooters, or a balmy night under the stars with a blazing campfire; but in all those conversations since they'd hooked up in Ecuador, Matt hadn't once mentioned his teenage romance with Milly and had answered – or rather failed to answer – all questions of his love life with a sequence of jokey responses or hilarious anecdotes, the bastard.

'Holy sardine cans, Batman, it's packed.' Matt reeled back in momentary shock at the standing-room-only crowd. 'How are we supposed to find anyone in this mess – sonar?'

'Sissy,' Hazel teased him. 'You haven't been gone *that* long.' Bouncing up and down, she stuck her arm in the air, trying to see over a sea of shoulders. 'Milly! Milly!'

From a corner, Milly stood up, beckoning them across, her mouth forming their names, though you could barely hear her in the laughter and chatter. Hazel watched Matt grin and raise his hand. Quickly she grabbed hold of his belt as he started to forge a path.

'OK.' He squared his shoulders. 'Hang on. We're going in.'

Well, the fact that he wasn't spilling any secrets only added to her curiosity, she mused as she tripped along in his wake. Maybe he was one of those men who, once their heart had been bruised, built themselves an impenetrable shield. But Hazel had worn through those defences before. There was nothing she loved more than intrigue – unless it was a challenge.

In this case – she grimaced as a heavyset man lurched back and almost sent her flying – her inquisitiveness was more like a sisterly concern whatever Natalie's low-minded suspicions. After all, you wanted the people close to you to be happy, didn't you?

At last after a lot of squeezing and elbowing (by Hazel) and complaints (by other people), they arrived triumphantly at the table and Hazel's spotlight turned to her sister.

Jesus, that's a first – her sharp green eyes glinted speculatively, as Matt bent down to kiss Milly's cheek – *she's wearing make-up.* And a long, pleated skirt and fancy cheesecloth top with nary a food stain in sight. Milly's hair was adorned with a butterfly clip, her eyes glittering and happy as she launched into a breathless account of her drive over.

'And then I turned left at the crossing, when it should have been right, so I've only just got here. And I didn't dare leave the table to get a drink in case someone nabbed it. Isn't it a shame Avril couldn't come?' she shouted happily in their ears. 'Going off to New York like that. After we invited the menfolk just for her. Oh, sorry, Matt, I was thinking of Jeremy, not you.'

'Would you rather the menfolk sat at another table?' Matt suggested, smiling down at her. 'We could have manly drinking matches and compare the size of our, er, Filofaxes while you sisters get down and dirty.'

'Filofaxes?' Hazel laughed, hovering beside him in flip-flops, a sleeveless white cotton shirt and a pair of mid-length shorts that would reveal every one of Milly's varicose veins. 'You're in the twenty-first century, you dodo. No one has Filofaxes any more. Ouch!' She yelped as Matt stepped not-so-accidentally on her bare toe.

'Oops.' He ruffled her hair, smiling dangerously. 'Sorry! Were you saying something?'

'I have a Filofax,' Milly lied sweetly, 'and we all have to sit together. Natalie won't go apeshit in front of outsiders. Not that you're an outsider. Oh Christ, I keep putting my foot in it, don't I? Help me out, Hazel. Say something.'

'Shepherd's pie looks scrummy,' Hazel said, studying a nearby table. 'I'm so starving I could eat the whole shepherd. What are you drinking, Milly? Lager and lime?'

'Oh, gosh, I don't know. Glass of wine, I think. No, wait, pub wine's disgusting. I'll have a screwdriver. If they do them,' Milly dithered. 'Or maybe a gin and tonic. Sorry, sorry, it's just I'm so nervous.' She made a face at Matt. 'Did Hazel tell you about my Nazi phone cock-up?' A shadow fell over them. 'Oh, hi, Nats, Jeremy. Grab a seat.'

'Is this place always so packed?' Natalie grumbled as her gaze moved around the pub from its aged dartboard in the corner to the rusty farming implements hanging from the overhead beams. 'I can't hear myself think.' For the last thirty minutes, she'd been ignoring Matt, swivelling her chair away from him in the ostrich view that if she didn't look at him, he couldn't really be there.

'Ladies' night,' Matt answered, pointing to a notice in the corner. 'Two-for-one special for the ladies. But I see they let you in anyway.'

What the hell. He'd already alienated Jeremy. The big goof

had stared down his nose at Matt the minute he'd reached the table.

'Ah, the putative gardener,' he'd sneered, not offering to shake hands. 'Natalie tells me you're actually some kind of a doctor.' He might as well have said backstreet abortionist, the way he managed to make it sound both shady and a veiled insult at the same time.

''Fraid so. And how is your mother's leg?' Matt gave Jeremy a huge smile in response. (Mrs P-S had been quite strident in fighting off his attempt at first aid.) 'So, your fiancée's been chatting about me, have you, Nasty?' he continued, with a wink at Nats. His eyes met Jeremy's, showing nothing but bonhomie. 'And she tells me you're quite the wa–banker.'

His tone was a wicked mimic of Jeremy's and Natalie practically choked on her slice of lemon. Had he almost insulted Jeremy by calling him a wanker? She just knew that's what he meant and she had the awful feeling Jeremy knew too.

Hazel bounced back with a trayful of drinks.

'Sorry about that. One of the bartenders saw my bag and asked if I got it in Nepal. Turns out we were both in Kathmandu at about the same time, isn't that wacky?'

'Yes, well, far be it from us to get between you and your raging hormones.' Natalie glared at her icily. 'And I wanted a Perrier, not Evian. Fetch it for me, will you, Jeremy?' She waited until her fiancé departed. 'Now, if Hazel can pull her mind from her groin for a second, I have some news. I googled Richard Burdock.'

'Ooh, and you practically married.' Milly giggled, nudging Matt. 'Don't tell Jeremy.'

Natalie gave her a scathing glance.

'Sorry.' Milly buried her nose in her drink.

'As I was saying, I've got news. Good and bad,' said Natalie mysteriously.

'What's the good news?' Milly asked eagerly, popping her head up again.

Natalie absent-mindedly took a sip of the unwanted Evian, stirring her slice of lemon to prolong the suspense. 'He's loaded. Stinking rich. Just sold his publishing company to a big American corporation for millions.'

'Millions, eh?' Hazel's eyes lit up.

'What's the bad news?' Matt tipped some of Milly's peanuts into his hand. 'Don't tell me, he's a hundred years old, on life support and too weak to say "I do".'

'He's already said it.' Natalie pulled a printed sheet of paper out of her handbag and threw it on the table. 'To someone else!'

They all studied a picture of a tall gaunt man, early fifties, arm in arm with a sophisticated, immaculately made-up redhead. 'I came across an article in one of the Sunday mags – "A Day in the Life of Married Moguls". His wife set up the business with him, they work together, equal partners.'

'Married! Oh no!' Milly subsided back on the blue-striped velvet chair. 'Do you think Avril knows?'

'Obviously,' Natalie said. 'They're not exactly low-profile. It's his wife I feel sorry for. Our sister, the home-wrecker. She has the morals of a rutting rabbit. No wonder she didn't let on.'

'It can't be that happy a marriage,' Hazel countered, 'or he wouldn't be cheating, would he?'

'Well, naturally, with your warped values, that'd be *your* attitude.' Natalie was still bitter about the Nazi slur. 'Anyway, Milly, it gets worse. This time there's a daughter involved. Katherine.'

'That's rough.' Matt's clear-sighted gaze met Natalie's angry eyes. 'But maybe you don't know all the circumstances? And people *have* been known to make mistakes.'

'No, I agree with Natalie.' Milly surprised them with her vehemence. 'This is typical Avril. What she's doing, it's, well, it's just plain wrong. Imagine that poor little girl's life if her parents end up divorced. You should never hurt the children, never ever.' She took a big gulp of water, looking embarrassed at her outburst.

Natalie stared at Milly's flushed face and then at Matt, who now pored over a newspaper, trying to look absorbed by an article on the price of organic meat. Natalie was putting one and one together and coming up with three! She hardly heard Hazel's rebuttal that children might be better off divorced than with two warring parents. Something was going on here. It wasn't often Milly got so worked up. Interesting or what?

'Someone should talk to her,' Milly continued, 'before it becomes messy.'

'And suppose the press got hold of it?' Natalie focused back on the conversation. 'I'm actually very glad Avril didn't bring him here tonight. I mean, if some floozy went after Jeremy . . .'

Matt swapped a sly glance with Hazel as they both looked at Jeremy standing in the queue, his lack of chin even more apparent in profile. He knew immediately what she was thinking. Unlikely. He shoved his face in his pint glass to conceal a smile.

By the time the food arrived and was set upon like a baby deer strolling into a den of starving wolves, the earlier tension had dissipated. Even if Hazel hadn't apologised for her Nazi remark, she offered a verbal peace pipe by asking Natalie questions about the wedding preparations and even managed not to yawn at Natalie's long-winded descriptions of menus and place cards and other bridal concerns. And Milly was in an amazingly bright mood, making everyone laugh with stories about the children and, of course, her mother.

'What about that time, Hazel, when you brought home that black actor and you overhead Mum ask him, "Can I rub your little woolly head? I've always wanted to rub a little woolly head."'

'What a riot!' Hazel giggled. 'There she was rubbing away at this ultra-PC, super-racially-sensitive American and he actually didn't mind. They loved each other. It was a hoot.'

'I like the story about Matilda,' Natalie joined in.

'Oh yeah.' Milly started laughing again.

'Who's Matilda?' Matt asked.

'Mum's bicycle,' Milly explained. 'She was working in the cancer ward of this hospital and apparently she was always talking to her patients about Matilda. Matilda this, Matilda that. So one day this man who was dying told her he wanted to see Matilda as his last wish. So she decorated her bike all over with flowers and ribbons and wheeled it in to show him.'

'She took a bicycle into a hospital? I hope she sterilised it first,' Jeremy said sniffily. 'Sounds like a breeding ground for germs.'

Everyone ignored him.

Heading to the bar, Matt was surprised to discover Natalie had followed him.

'Must be my new aftershave,' he joked, as she brushed against his chest trying to squeeze in beside him. 'Girls have been mobbing me all night. It's called L'eau de Honking Great Cuckoo.'

'Don't flatter yourself,' Natalie said witheringly, as a huge backside, its owner struggling to carry four beers, pushed her into Matt's arms. In danger of tipping off her heels, she teetered for a second before feeling him steady her and then abruptly pulled away. 'I'm just concerned that if you're anything like Hazel, it could be closing time before we get a

132

drink.' Flipping back her blonde hair, she searched his eyes and summoned her sweetest smile. 'Milly's on good form tonight, don't you think?'

'I guess.' Matt glanced around warily, feeling unexpectedly like the Lone Ranger riding into a dangerous canyon and suddenly realising Tonto has disappeared and the row of rocks above his head each has a little feather tip.

'No, I mean she's acting completely different. She's all dressed up and did you notice? She's actually wearing eye pencil.' Even though she'd put the eye pencil on in a rather odd way, Natalie mused; angled at an alarming degree at the corners, it resembled Samantha's mother in *Bewitched*. 'And lipstick. Usually it's a red-letter day if Milly just manages to brush her hair. And look at her laughing and joking – it's like the old Milly back again.'

'Natalie.' He rubbed his nose, his eyes creasing with concern as he said gently, 'You forget, I only know the old Milly.'

'Well, take my word for it. She's been miserable as sin recently. For years really. Until all of a sudden *you* turn up.' She stressed the 'you' in a way that sent a shiver down Matt's spine. 'And look at the way she keeps patting your leg, touching your hand.'

He felt very tired all of a sudden. He settled his old man's body on a recently vacated bar stool.

'Spit it out, Natalie. Not that I could stop you.'

'Well, it's obvious, isn't it? The big effort to look good, the way she's jabbering on, too excited to eat. And her eyes are positively shining, especially when she looks at you. I can't think when I ever saw her look that way at Ivor. Any fool could see it. Except a guy. Milly's head over heels in love.' She spun his bar stool round so that he faced Milly's table and added, her breath warming his ear, 'With you!'

*

'Need to splash my boots,' Jeremy said gruffly. 'Back in a mo.'

Hazel shuddered. 'How can Natalie stand it?' she said as soon as Jeremy was out of earshot.

'He's probably an OK bloke really,' Milly said doubtfully. 'I mean, he must be if Nat wants to marry him. You never know what people are like when it's just them, on their own.'

'Yeah, maybe he turns into an intellectual genius when they're alone. Starts doing his Mensa quizzes between giving Nat back rubs. Or maybe he's a maestro in bed, plays her like a violin.'

'Better than a banjo, I guess.' Milly glanced over at the bar in time to see Natalie spin Matt round, her lips a scant intimate inch from his ear. Hazel followed her gaze, catching the attention of the stocky man pulling a beer, who grinned at her and winked. With his shaven head, squashed nose and tribal tattoos, he looked like a good-natured thug.

'There! I caught you,' Milly said triumphantly as Hazel grinned back. 'Flirting again.'

'Oh, give me a break. That's the guy I told you about. The traveller. He's a laugh, that's all. He's been halfway round the world on his motorbike. Drove it all the way from Australia. Anyway his buddy there behind the bar, the good-looking camp one, says he's totally gay. The way they were larking around I'm pretty sure they're an item. And in case you haven't noticed, he's spud-ugly.' She popped a peanut in her mouth. 'Though he does have melt-your-heart eyes.'

'Honestly, Hazel, you are a one.' Milly watched Matt and Natalie gather up drinks, not sure in the swirl of confusing emotions how she felt about any of this. 'One minute you're all over Matt. The next you're going on about melt-your-heart eyes.'

'What on earth has one to do with the other?' Hazel looked baffled. 'Why would Matt care if the barman has cute eyes?

His are just as yummy. So unfair, don't you think, when men get those great eyelashes. Anyway, Matt and I are completely cool. In fact, if you can keep a secret . . .' She leaned forward, head close to Milly's, her eyes sparkling with mischief.

'What? Tell, tell.' Automatically, Milly mirrored her conspiratorial pose. But despite her curiosity, she was aware how dry her mouth had suddenly become and the loud pounding of her heart. There was a feeling close to dread in the depths of her chest.

'No, it's nothing.' Hazel straightened up as the clink of glasses announced Matt and Natalie's approach at the same time as Jeremy converged from the bathroom. '*Non importanto*. Forget I said a thing.'

But that was the problem. Milly moved over on the bench seat to make room for Matt.

She hadn't said anything at all.

Milly stepped quietly through the piles of clothes littered around Erin's bedroom floor, treading carefully so as not to wake her snoring daughter. Not one iota of floor space was to be seen. Erin was always complaining that she needed a new carpet, but what was the point? She began tidying up. She'd read that teenagers should be left to sort out their own mess. Sounded sensible enough, but probably the authors of that great revelation were childless psychologists who weren't faced with a bundle of washing hidden at the back of Erin's wardrobe that would take Milly a full day to get through.

Not to mention if Erin couldn't find her textbooks in this mess, she couldn't study. The school suggested letting them have a quiet space and this room was the only quietish place in their overcrowded house. Milly wasn't materialistic but still, three bedrooms for six of them was quite a squash. If only Ivor was earning again, more than just the odd freelance

135

project to keep the creditors from the door. If only this new company would take off and 'almost in the bag' meant 'finally in the bag'. Milly quickly banished the disloyal thought. Her head was spinning again; she needed physical activity to calm her jangling mind. All day her brain had been racing and the alcohol this evening had left her buzzing with an unaccustomed high. She kept going over it all in her mind. The sudden reappearance of Matt. The evening in the pub. The revelation about Avril's boyfriend. Now it was twelve thirty and Ivor still hadn't returned from his meeting. What if *she'd* wanted to stay out late, clubbing and things? She sniggered at the very idea. Even in her short-lived heyday, she'd loathed all those strobe lights and loud music. She hadn't been in a nightclub since before Erin was born.

But thinking of Erin made her remember Fergus's comment about Erin's snogging.

Should she be concerned? Most fifteen-year-old girls kissed boys, herself included; it was just that, well, Erin was so secretive. Not like her neighbour's eldest daughter, a year older than Erin, who seemed to tell her mother everything, guys she fancied, petty arguments at school. Erin was confiding less and less in Milly. Was there always going to be this distance between them? Would she leave home early like so many other teenagers she'd heard about, only dropping by with a load of washing? Or end up like Avril and Natalie, who hardly visited Mum at all?

She stuffed old sandwiches in the bin, torn magazines, bent hair clips. Suddenly she heard a beep. She found Erin's phone underneath a mound of skirts (if you could call them that – they were so miniscule). Hastily she picked it up, muffling it in a pile of clothes with a nervous glance at the bed. It beeped again. Surely no one would be texting at this hour? In her sleep Erin muttered something and rolled over. Stepping quietly into the corridor, Milly stabbed a button at random and managed to open up a message.

Soz I 4gt. MM's goin 2 kil me. Bet meet me b4 9
C u l8r

Now who was going to be killed? Why? Who was MM? And what on earth was eighteen R? Restricted videos? Internet porn? So many hazards these days to contend with, but ten to one if she asked Erin, there'd be the most almighty tantrum and it would turn out to be something trivial, like not doing her maths homework. But what if it wasn't? Yet another reason she wouldn't get any sleep tonight.

It was the early hours of the morning when the red-haired woman was woken by the shrilling phone on her bedside table. Yawning and rubbing her eyes, she glanced disbelievingly at the clock and picked up the receiver.

The line was bad, the voice muffled.

'Mrs Burdock? I think you should know. Your husband's having an affair.'

'Pardon me?'

'This is Mrs Burdock, isn't it? Wife of Richard Burdock?'

'Yes.'

'Your husband's unfaithful, Mrs Burdock. He's cheating on you.'

'Who is this?'

'Let's just say, I'm a friend.'

Click.

The line went dead. Rolling over, Olivia Burdock threw a black look at the ceiling. Damn, now it would be hours before she could go back to sleep.

Chapter 17

'Can you believe this mob?' Hazel whispered to Avril.

'I'd no idea so many people could be involved in one small wedding.'

Saturday morning, one week before the 'big day' and they were perched in the front right-hand pew of the famous Little Hooking church. Reverend Chatham was chatting to Natalie and Jeremy, clasping Natalie's hand in both of his while the Potterton-Smythes were examining the famous Little Hooking stained-glass window, a bandage prominently featured on Beryl's lower leg. They'd exchanged only the barest of civilities with the MacLeods, giving the merest icecap nod in response to Peggy's exuberant greeting.

'And this is only the fucking rehearsal, darling.' Avril yawned as she ran her fingers through her hair. 'I wish they'd hurry up with it. I've been back from New York for over a week but I swear my body still thinks we're on East Coast time. Plus I was up till three in the morning; Baxter needing babying again. All I can do to keep my sodding eyes open.'

There was a scuffle of activity and Milly plonked herself in the seat beside them, a big milk stain down the front of her blouse. She was wearing one of her usual shapeless outfits but something about her looked different, Avril thought.

'Everything OK, Mills?' Avril asked, as she and Hazel moved up. 'You seem a little feverish.'

'Touch of Delhi belly,' Milly hissed back, her eyes glowing as she grinned triumphantly at them.

'Hope it's not catching. Natalie'll marmalise you if she has to cancel the big day for a lousy stomach bug.' Hazel brought her bejewelled flip-flops up to rest on the back of the pew. With her poppy-print halter-neck top and the tiniest of denim shorts, she looked hardly older than her niece sitting two rows behind, fiddling with the earpiece of her MP3 player.

'And if she doesn't, I will.' Avril had a quick check of her mobile to see if any messages had been left. 'There's no way in hell I'm going through this again.'

'I see Mum's bawling her eyes out.' Hazel giggled before screwing her eyes at Natalie who was being attended to by the fluttering, fawning Reverend Chatham. 'I thought the bride was only supposed to be the centre of attention for a day. Nat seems to be turning it into a vocation.'

Reverend Chatham had let go of Natalie's hand, though not before putting it to his lips. She hurried over to her sisters, discreetly wiping his spittle off her lilac chiffon dress as she went.

'We're starting. Milly, do keep the kids under control, will you? They're running all over the gravestones outside. And whatever you do, steer Rory away from Beryl. Put him on a leash if you have to.'

Milly put her thumb to her nose and waggled her fingers at Natalie, the moment her head was turned. 'Well, look at the daft ha'p'orth with her bandage.' She leaned over, whispering to Avril behind her hand and pointing her chin at Natalie's future mother-in-law. 'Are we supposed to think her leg's about to fall off? It's been weeks and he barely broke the skin.'

They chuckled like naughty choirgirls in their pew as

Natalie spun on her heel to deliver more orders to the rest of the family.

'All right then, everybody. Attention now.' Reverend Chatham cleared his throat and clapped for order. 'Bride, father of the bride, bridesmaids, flower girl, ring bearer, why don't all of you go by the door, and wait for your cue? Ushers, we'll deal with you later. Let's take it from the arrival of Jeremy and his best man. Cedric, can you start the music please. Snip snap.'

There was a scurried reorganisation. The four sisters found themselves squashed in the small church vestibule with Erin, Rory and Callum who was looking red-eyed and deathly hung-over, body juddering like a clapped-out diesel tractor.

'Everything OK, Dad?' Milly leaned across to whisper in his ear.

'Your mother's cross with me. Says I disgraced myself with Jeremy's parents. You were there, Millipede, I didn't do anything that bad, did I?'

'Well, you were a tiny bit merry,' Milly admitted reluctantly.

Natalie's eyes narrowed in appalled realisation as her head snapped round.

'Och, Millipede.' Callum shook his head, reproach shining from his watery eyes. 'Millipede, I'm so disappointed. So you're against me too?' His head kept up the motion, like a plastic Alsatian in a car rear window.

This was an old routine. She thought of all those times she'd seen him slumped comatose in his favourite armchair, with its threadbare, typically English horse-and-hound fabric, a tray on his lap, his shirt stained with the food that was falling from his mouth, and the only word he could rouse himself to say was 'Millipede'.

'Millipede.' His bleary eyes would open. 'Are you there?

Millipede?' And when she finally gave in and answered, 'Yes, Dad,' he'd shake his head and repeat again sorrowfully, 'Och, Millipede.' As conversations went, it was more than a little tedious.

What a waste. She loved her dad but really he was too much sometimes. She'd really thought his sobriety was going to last this time but she should have known it was too good to be true. If only he'd go to AA the way Mum had asked him a thousand times. But you couldn't even mention it without causing a huge fight so why even bother? And poor Mum having to try and cover up for Dad yet again. She looked haggard under her make-up. Dad's drinking was wrecking both their healths.

'So disappointed,' Callum muttered.

'Be quiet, will you?' Natalie dug viciously at him with her elbow.

'Now when you hear the bridal march, Jeremy,' Reverend Chatham was saying, 'that's your cue. Some people think the groom shouldn't turn to watch the bride. Personally, I think you're missing something very wonderful if you don't, especially with such a delectable creature as your future wife.'

Hazel nudged Milly. 'Does that mean if she was a right minger, he shouldn't bother?' She dodged another glare from Natalie.

'Natalie, dear,' Reverend Chatham beckoned, 'if you can just start your walk up the aisle with your father? Keep it slow.'

Natalie felt Callum's arm shaking as they started forth. The funeral pace of their progress allowed her to hold on to him for all her worth, but she couldn't lose the uneasy sensation that if she were to slacken her vice-like grip, he would land straight on the worn stone floor.

Oh fuck, what had she been thinking? It finally dawned on her. He was on the booze again. The stupid, stupid bastard.

How could she have missed it and how would she ever tell Jeremy?

She should have got married on a beach, in another country (on another planet ideally), kept her family as far away from the whole thing as humanly possible.

'Now,' Reverend Chatham continued, 'I do my dearly beloved bit. And when I say "Who giveth this woman …" the bride's father – that's you, Callum, old chap – should snap out of his daydream and say "I do". Place the bride's hand in the groom's hand.' The vicar directed Callum like a puppet, moving his arm over to Natalie's hand. 'That's it. Fine. Now you can sit next to your lovely wife at the front.'

No one could miss Callum's tremors. As soon as he found his place, the whole rail started to rattle as he clung on to it for support. Next to him, Peggy snuffled into her handkerchief, futilely trying to mop back the floods of tears.

And well she might cry, Natalie thought viciously, married to a man like Dad. Longing to shrivel up and vanish into the flagstone slab below her feet, it was suddenly blatantly clear that her decision to marry in Little Hooking had been the worst one of her life.

Dad's pissed as a newt. Drunk as a skunk. Bladdered, slaughtered, rat-faced. The words buzzed like angry hornets in her brain. This was the epitome of every nightmare that had ever woken her, sweating and terrified, in the dead of night. And why now, of all times? One measly week before the wedding. Even if Mum could keep him under house arrest, the reception was at their bloody house.

She must have been out of her mind, setting herself up like this. Hadn't she learned a damn thing over the years? You couldn't trust Dad – ever. Getting married in Little Hooking – suddenly she couldn't imagine anything that looked more like a recipe for a shockingly public humiliation. Jeremy would never talk to her again. Hell, he'd probably leave her jilted at the aisle, and who would blame him.

Unless . . .

Through the buzzing of the hornets a seed of a plan began to form. It was heartless, possibly even wicked . . . but it might just work. But could she do that to her own father?

You bet she could. The selfish inconsiderate prick didn't seem to care a jot about *her* feelings.

When Rory stepped forward in his role as the ring bearer, Milly saw Beryl shudder and whisper something to her husband. Milly felt like slapping the older woman. Rory might be naughty at times, but he'd been so proud to have a part in his auntie's wedding and now everyone was treating him like he was a leper and the Potterton-Smythes like they'd just discovered the colony was slated to move in next door.

Rehearsal mercifully over, everyone made a quick exit, welcoming the fresh air outside. Peggy took a moment to pull herself together, deciding to overlook the rehearsal's atmosphere. She sauntered over to Beryl, her arm around the waist of Matt who she'd found waiting by the church gate for Hazel, dressed in paint-spattered jeans. Anxious as he'd been not to overstay his welcome and with several other friends he was keen to visit, Peggy had absolutely refused to let him go. Cunningly, she ensured his continued presence by persuading him the whole outside of the house needed painting, every window and door and, when he'd finished that, half the inside too. Natalie had thrown a fit when she'd found out but she couldn't deny the peeling paintwork could use a facelift.

'You and Godfrey will be joining us for lunch, I hope,' she said to Beryl cheerfully. 'There's quite a good restaurant just ten minutes drive from here on the Midhurst road. We've booked a table. Our treat.'

But Beryl and Peggy's attention was suddenly distracted by a familiar raised voice coming from beyond the yew trees at the edge of the graveyard. Callum was standing toe to toe with Godfrey, swaying and prodding aggressively at Godfrey's overstuffed chest. Despite his younger years Mr Potterton-Smythe looked terrified. He took a step backwards, only to find himself pressed against a tall headstone.

The two wives hurried over but Matt was there first, putting a restraining arm on Callum's tweed sports coat.

'What is it? What is it, Callum?' Peggy panted.

'Och, nothing.' Callum rubbed his white hair, making it stand on end even more than usual and gave an abashed smile. 'We were just having a wee word, weren't we, Godfrey?'

'Oh . . . ah, yes. Yes.'

Godfrey had sidled round and hidden behind Beryl, clumsily straightening his tie, just as Natalie appeared.

'What's happening? Godfrey? Beryl? Is everything OK?'

'Time to go, I think.' Godfrey grabbed Beryl by the sleeve. They began a quick march to the churchyard gate, heads bowed in a conspiratorial whisper.

'Jeremy!' Beryl suddenly screeched, causing several rooks to scatter. 'Jeremy, we're leaving! Now!'

Natalie whirled accusingly to face her parents.

'Dad was threatening him, wasn't he?' She looked from one to the other and settled on her mother. 'That's it, isn't it? He's got himself pissed and so he decides to pick a fight with my fiancé's father. Well, I wish he were dead.' Her eyes filled with tears as she stared at Callum. 'I mean it, Dad. I never want to speak to you again. Beryl, Godfrey, please wait! Wait for me!'

She tottered across the grass in her lilac high-heeled sandals while Peggy gave a heavy sigh and took Callum's arm. He rubbed his whiskers, looking old and confused. Gently, Matt led him to a bench where he sat staring into space, a battered old man with red watery eyes and the picture of abject misery.

Natalie caught up with the Potterton-Smythes just as they were stepping into their Bentley. 'Wait,' she said. 'I'm so, *so* sorry.' Her eyes widened as she noticed Jeremy, on the other side of the car, opening the rear door. 'Jeremy, I thought you were driving back with me? We were going to go flat-hunting this afternoon, remember?'

Jeremy shuffled his feet, looking awkward.

'Sorry, Natalie. I thought I told you. Mother and Father want a bit of a chat. About . . . eh, mortgages and stuff. Don't worry, you can take the car. They'll drop me off.'

'But . . . but . . .' Natalie stammered as Jeremy dipped hastily into the car, 'shouldn't I be there? If you're talking mortgages?' she persisted, louder now that Jeremy had shut his door.

Beryl, swinging her bandaged leg into the front seat, gave her a glare that could have cracked a coconut.

'Why?' she snapped. 'I doubt you'll be paying much of it.'

'Of course I will. We'll be sharing all the bills, won't we, Jeremy?' Natalie blinked in bewilderment as Beryl took off her jewelled beret and placed it in clenched fingers in her lap. 'Besides, we estate agents know about mortgages. And don't I have a right –'

'Yes, well, I'm sure we'll be hearing plenty about your rights if and when you marry my son,' Beryl said stiffly, through the half-open window. 'And probably a whole lot less about your job, I don't doubt. Permit us a few hours alone with Jeremy. You'll have him all to yourself soon enough. And we have the pre-nuptial to discuss. Godfrey – drive!'

*

There was an awkward silence. The three MacLeod sisters surrounded Natalie and watched the car slide away like a grey submarine with its nuclear cargo.

'At least you're not marrying the parents,' Milly observed.

'Yep, and it looks like Jeremy's been trained to come to heel,' Hazel added. 'Now you just have to make sure it's your heel in future.'

'She detests me.' Tears sprouted at the corner of Natalie's eyes and she curled a finger to wipe them away. 'She absolutely detests me.'

'Course she doesn't, darling.' Avril gave her a hasty hug. 'And even if she did, anyone can see she's an out-and-out bitch. Natalie, sweetie, no one wants to burst your bubble but I have to ask – are you sure you know what you're letting yourself in for? Jeremy utterly failed to stand up for you, slinking off like a spineless worm, while his mother treats you like trailer trash. I mean, she obviously dominates both those men. If you ask me –'

'Ask you!' Natalie spat with fury. 'Well, I'm not asking you. You bet I want to marry Jeremy. You don't get it. I'm thirty-seven, Avril. Thirty-seven! I should have been married at least seven years ago. Almost every newspaper, radio station, TV programme is about the ever-ticking biological clock. It might suit you all right but I've no intention of ending up a childless old maid . . .' She stopped as Avril jerked back, her face stricken with hurt. There was a sudden uncomfortable silence in which the rooks' harsh cawing seemed unnaturally loud.

'Oh, Avril, I'm sorry.' The steam went out of Natalie's anger and was replaced by horrified shame. 'I didn't mean . . . I wasn't talking about you.'

'Why not?' Avril said through a forced show of teeth that miserably failed to resemble a smile. 'It's true, isn't it? What

146

would I know? I'm just a childless old maid. Sorry I tried to interfere. Well' – she stared round at the ring of horrified faces – 'I guess I'll see you at the hen night.'

And then she was gone.

Chapter 18

Hazel and Milly gawked at Natalie. She flushed, looking defensive.

'What?!' she snapped.

'Honestly, Nats.' Milly's big blue eyes were full of reproach. 'How could you!'

'Talk about going for the jugular,' Hazel chimed in.

'Oh, go boil your heads, the pair of you,' Natalie fought back, her insides twisting wretchedly with guilt and self-pity. 'Leave me alone. This is possibly the most miserable day of my entire life. The last thing I need is you two making me feel worse.'

'Fine with us.' Hazel shrugged and turned away. 'We know when we're not wanted. Come on, Mills.'

Milly hesitated. 'But aren't you coming to the restaurant?'

'After what Dad did? You must be joking,' exclaimed Natalie.

'So what are you going to do? Your car's back at The Briars. I'd drive you but I've got the car seats in the back, and the children are squashed as it is. Maybe I can get Fergus or Erin to go with Mum and Dad?'

'I said leave me alone.' Natalie turned her back. 'Go to your stupid restaurant. Don't bother about me.'

Milly relented, wordlessly rounding up the children, who'd been happily playing, oblivious to all the commotion.

Out of the corner of her eye, Natalie watched her two sisters walk across the car park where her mum was trying to persuade her dad to drink some coffee from the flask she'd brought. There was a hasty conference, then her mother handed the flask to Hazel and strode over.

'Natalie,' she soothed, 'please, darling, don't cut off your nose to spite your face. Come and have lunch with us.'

'I will not eat with that man. I don't want to speak to him ever again.'

'Then how are you getting home? Maybe we can –'

'I'll walk,' Natalie interrupted.

'In those shoes?' Peggy eyed her strappy sandals. 'It's at least two miles.' Unfortunately, The Briars and Little Hooking church were at opposite ends of the strung-out village.

'I've got transport,' piped up a cheerful voice. They'd forgotten Matt. 'I can take her back.'

'Oh, will you?' Peggy gave him a relieved smile. 'Well, good, that's sorted. If you change your mind, dears, join us at the restaurant.'

'Over my dead body,' muttered Natalie as she watched them drive off.

She turned to Matt, irritated that he'd sabotaged her martyr role but relieved to escape the ordeal of stumbling home in new shoes with an ankle strap that was already making its presence painfully felt. 'I suppose I'm meant to be grateful,' she challenged, ungraciously.

'Let's not expect miracles.' He pushed a strand of hair from his eyes. 'Considering you've already crucified Avril and your dad. All I ask is I'm spared any lectures.'

'Why waste my breath? You wouldn't listen anyway.' She stalked towards the car park. 'So where's the car?'

Matt was squatting beside some railings. 'Here.' He unfastened a padlock and wheeled forward a tatty old bicycle, paint peeling from its rusty mudguard, broken basket hanging by one leather strap from the front. 'Borrowed from Mr Dodds across the road.'

Natalie recoiled, pushing down her skirt as a breeze lifted the flimsy material. 'Are you nuts?'

'Possibly.' Matt's eyes glinted dangerously. 'Watching your whole family bend over backwards to avoid one of your tantrums has that effect on me.'

A blistering remark sprang to Natalie's lips, but with unusual discretion she held it back.

'I haven't been on a bike in years,' she said instead, witheringly.

'You know what they say' – he rode in a circle, showing off with his arms outstretched like a tightrope walker – 'you never forget. Come on, hop on the saddle, and I'll do all the work.'

'I have a dress on, you know.'

'So?' He popped a wheelie over the kerb. 'Hitch it up and stuff your skirt in your knickers. I'll give you a bunk-up.'

'This is preposterous.' Her head swivelled wildly, looking for rescue. 'Why did they all go and leave me?'

'You told them to clear off, remember? You could still walk.' He skidded to a halt beside her, spraying up gravel. Natalie's palms itched to shove him over. His face looked ridiculously boyish, evoking that mischievous eleven-year-old whose relentless cheek was always getting them into fights with the local bullies. 'Or wait for the Codmoreton bus.'

Natalie remembered seeing one depart as they came out of the church. 'It's three-quarters of an hour till the next one,' she groaned.

'Well then, doesn't seem like you have much choice. Come on, giddy-up. Daylight's a-burning.' He raised the front wheel, imitating a whinny.

Seeing no option, Natalie gathered her skirt and, grabbing

150

Matt's arm for balance, hopped on one leg and swung the other over the saddle. She felt ridiculous and helpless, her feet dangling with no place to put them, the bike wobbling when she wobbled and her face in line with Matt's rear end as he bobbed up and down in front of her. A bunk-up – how long was it since she'd heard – or done – that?! The summer Milly had fallen off a horse and broken her arm, she and Natalie had travelled all over the place like that, Milly perched on the back with her arm in a sling, Natalie straining to turn the pedals.

At least she had no friends left in Little Hooking. No one to recognise her doing a 'bunk-up' with her skirt tucked in her knickers.

Matt began peddling briskly up the main street, through an alleyway, then took an unexpected sharp right down a narrow sludgy path.

'What are you doing!?' Natalie shrieked as they gained speed. Mud spattered from under the tyres and she clutched Matt's waist tighter as branches whipped at them, trees flying past.

'Thought it'd be more fun to cut through the woods. Which way is it?' He pressed hard on the brakes as they rapidly approached a fork. 'Left or right?'

'How would I know? I haven't come this way for years.'

'This way then.' He swerved left as the path flattened out for a short distance. 'Hate to tell you this, my sweet Nasty, but I think you've put on weight.'

Ahead, Natalie saw their route crossed a brook and then rose up a steep bank, studded with tree roots. Maybe one of those lunatic dirt bikers with souped-up engines could handle it but Matt on Mr Dodds's decrepit old three-gear with Natalie risking life and limb on the two-inch-wide saddle? No way.

'Let me off, you bonehead.' She whacked his back harder than strictly necessary. 'You're stark staring bonkers, you know that?' Matt skidded to a stop before the water's edge and Natalie slid down. 'Oh bloody hell!' she wailed as her descending heel sunk into the soggy ground beneath them. 'These sandals cost almost two hundred pounds. Jimmy Choo!'

They were ruined. There was nothing to do but to take them off, wincing as her bare feet met first mud then the ankle-grabbing coldness of the river and the sharp stones that littered its bed. Matt stretched out a hand to help her but she swatted it away.

As kids they'd been barefoot as often as they'd worn shoes, clambering over rocks in swollen rivers, scrambling through the woods, racing along pebbly Brighton beach, soles of their feet hard enough to take thistles, branches and gravel in their stride. So what if it had been forever since her size 5s had dealt with anything tougher than carpet. After all those years of fighting to keep up with Milly and Matt, she wasn't about to prove herself a sissy now.

'Two hundred quid for those things? Estate agency work must be lucrative,' Matt observed, pushing the bike up the bank in front of him. 'That's more money than most of my patients see in a year.'

'Yes, well, we're not in the bloody jungle now, thank God.' Natalie swore as her arm brushed against a stinging nettle. 'And I need shoes, not a sermon. I thought we said no lectures?'

'No, the deal was you couldn't lecture me.' He pulled back a tree branch to let her duck under, resisting the childish temptation to let it swing back in her face.

'I could murder Jeremy,' she said, straightening up. It wasn't just her shoes that had suffered. Her layered chiffon dress was also looking like a sheet of tissue wrapping on Christmas Day after Rory had ripped it to shreds. 'Abandoning me like that. And then Avril, taking offence at nothing. Honestly, she acts like a complete child sometimes.'

Matt gave her a slant-eyed look but wisely held his tongue.

At the top of the hill they surveyed the territory. There were paths in all directions but somehow with the sun hidden by the trees, they'd got all turned around.

'That way, I think,' she pointed at random. They set off down the hill.

Avril was haring along the M25 watching the needle hover around the ninety-eight miles per hour mark as vehicle after vehicle grew closer and disappeared into a tiny blip in her rear-view mirror. If only it were as easy to shake off her family. After an hour of driving Natalie's hurtful remark still reverberated in her head.

'Childless old maid. Childless old maid.' Yes, that'd be how they saw her. Never mind that she'd just received yet another notice from *Who's Who* asking if she wanted to be included in next year's edition. Never mind that her personal address book looked like the invitation list for the Academy Awards or that in her last *Guardian* interview they'd called her 'a phenomenal success, with movie-star looks and a razor-sharp brain'. Never fucking mind that she only had to snap her fingers and at least three of *People* magazine's 100 Most Eligible Bachelors would ditch their bimbos and fall slavishly to heel.

No, just because she wasn't running after some lazy slob, fetching his pipe and slippers, sweating over home-cooked meals and wantonly adding to the world's overpopulation, they saw her as half a woman. A workaholic freak. How dare they! How dare Natalie, with her stuffy self-important fiancé and his pompous parents, or Milly with her useless unhelpful

153

lump of a husband and her brood of squalling brats. They hadn't a clue. And even her mother. How often had she complained that 'all her fun stopped when she got married'? And no wonder when you saw what Dad had put her through.

She allowed herself a delightful vision of strangling Natalie, seeing her cornflower-blue eyes pop out of her thoughtless little head, before the memory returned of Brenda's call to her in New York.

'. . . oh yeah and Handsome Harry phoned again. That makes four times in the last five days. Wants you to call him back. He didn't sound like his usual sparky self. And he asked me about some toothache? You two haven't had a row, have you?'

'No. I told you to tell him I'm tied up in meetings.'

'And I did. So what *are* you doing? Truthfully?'

'Walking down Fifth Avenue. Bit of window-shopping. Lunch with Wally at some hot new place near Central Park. Supposed to be fabulous. Says they're booked up three weeks in advance but he has influence. And then he wants to take me on the Ellis Island tour of all things. I told him I don't do "tourist" but he's persistent.'

'Sounds like you're *very* tied up.'

'Brenda.' Avril opened the door to Saks. 'I love you but – butt out.'

That had been two weeks ago and although he'd called once or twice, she still hadn't got round to calling him back.

She pressed her foot on the accelerator as she zipped past a lorry with a tank plastered with Esso on the side, then swerved round a Lamborghini convertible with a yuppie-looking couple, his arm over her shoulders, her platinum-bleached hair blowing in the wind. Their fleeting astonished looks were worth any amount of speeding tickets. In her breast pocket, next to her heart, she could feel her mobile vibrating. With one hand, she pulled it out and looked at the display.

Another message . . . She pressed read.

ND 2 C U TONIGHT. URGENT. RIC.

Tonight, eh? And why so urgent? Well, she couldn't call from the car. He'd just have to wait.

Chapter 19

'Ow! Ow! Ow!' Natalie screeched. 'Damn it.' Coming to a halt, she pulled furiously at the twig that had caught in her hair. Stubbornly it refused to yield, little spiked branches entangling it further.

'Wait, you'll make it worse. Let me.'

Taking his sweet time, Natalie thought as Matt dropped the bike and strolled back, reaching for her trapped tresses. Head down, staring at the few dark curly hairs peeping over the neck of his T-shirt, she could feel the warmth of his flesh, inches from her own, smell the sweat of his body, dangerously close, as his fingers worked dexterously to release her. Every second seemed an eternity. He'd almost finished when she jerked her head, pulling the last bit free at the expense of what felt like an inch of scalp.

Eyes watering, she glared at him. She looked like a wild woman, a couple of tiny sticks still caught in her messy, tangled hair. Matt reached to fish them out but she got there first.

'I can get it.' She tugged ruthlessly, ignoring the pain. 'This is all your fault, you know. If you'd taken the road, we'd have been home ages ago.'

'And miss this whole adventure?' His smoky eyes sparked with amusement. 'You were a lot more fun when we were kids,

Nee Nee. Don't you do anything spontaneous any more?'

'Don't call me Nee Nee.' She flopped down on the ground, needing a rest. 'And why you think traipsing in circles like a pair of blithering idiots is some great accomplishment, I'll never know.'

'Oh, being an idiot has its moments,' Matt said as he sat beside her, selecting a slender strand of grass to chew. 'So . . .' He lay back and stared at the almost cloudless sky. 'Do you think you and Jeremy will have children?'

'Definitely.' Natalie rubbed her aching feet. 'I want a boy and a girl.'

'And Jeremy?'

'Well, obviously, Jeremy wants them too . . . I mean, he wouldn't be marrying me if he didn't want children.' She felt a momentary flicker of doubt. Had they ever really discussed it?

'And whatever Nat wants, Nat gets.' He tickled her chin with the grass blade.

'Oh shut up.' Irritated, she pushed it away then remembered she was supposed to get him on her side. 'You know we've always been friends . . .'

Matt propped himself on one elbow. 'I know it,' he said, looking down at her. 'I was beginning to wonder if you did.'

For an aching moment her eyes stayed glued to his then she mentally shook herself and tore her gaze away, unsure how to phrase the next bit. 'Look, I need you to do me a massive favour.' She took a deep breath. 'I need you to kidnap Daddy.'

Matt laughed and sat up, grass blade falling from his mouth.

'Good one, Nats. I thought you were going to ask something serious.'

'Oh, not really kidnap. Only, you know . . . just keep him away from the wedding somehow. You can imagine what a disaster it will be if he's drunk. Jeremy's parents will never speak to me again and Jeremy'll probably sulk for at least six months and . . .' Her voice faded.

'Shouldn't you have thought of that a teensy bit earlier? Before you invited ninety-five people to your parents' home?' He stretched out his hand to pull her to her feet.

'He was supposed to be on the wagon,' Natalie said, exasperated. 'And I mean, wherever we got married, they'd be there, wouldn't they?'

'Not if you have your way, apparently. So what exactly is the dastardly plan?' Matt still wasn't taking her seriously.

'I don't know. You're inventive. You could think of something. Take him out in the car and get a flat tyre or run out of petrol, whatever. Or engine trouble. Shove a potato in the exhaust. I saw that in a film once. If you found a nice pub to leave him in while you went to get help, he'd be in no hurry for you to come back.'

'Hmm . . .' His eyes held a tinge of sympathy. 'Not to throw obstacles in your wicked scheme but isn't he giving you away? Are you planning to go up the aisle without him?'

'*You* could give me away. A last-minute replacement.'

Matt flinched, dropping her hand, his eyes suddenly stormy. 'Yeah, *right*. Marching up in my monkey suit after sabotaging your dad,' he scoffed. 'Thanks but no thanks. You know, I never figured you for such a bitch.'

Natalie bit her lip, flushing.

'I didn't mean . . .' She went on the defensive. 'Look, don't you get it? I'm just trying to save my wedding. And the rest of my life. It's all right for you. We can't all be saints.'

'Oh, so I'm a saint now?' Matt's half-laugh was devoid of mirth. 'That's refreshing. Ever since I got here, you've been treating me like Lucifer on a quest for souls. Make up your mind, darling.'

He noticed that the chain had fallen off the bike when he dropped it. He squatted over it, turning his back to her. She reached out to his shoulder.

'Look, all I'm saying –' she started.

He flinched from her touch and stood up, snatching a clump of grass to wipe his hands. 'And where am I supposed to leave Callum? Lost in the woods like Hansel and Gretel? Get real!'

'Wouldn't be the first time he couldn't find his way home,' Natalie muttered. 'All right, fine. If you won't do this one simple thing for me, I'll just get Hazel to slip him a couple of sleeping pills.' She kicked barefoot at a tree stump, ruined sandals dangling from her hand. 'I should have listened to Avril, opted for a registry office.'

'You know you don't mean that,' Matt said, his tone softening. Natalie's slumped shoulders and dejected face were having an effect. He picked up the bike again and started moving so that Natalie was obliged to follow. 'Honestly, I think you're underestimating your father.'

'Easy for you to say.' Tears sparked on her lashes, always her best weapon. 'Do you know how many times he's promised . . . and promised . . . that is, when he'd even admit he knew what you were talking about? Remember how we all used to hate Christmas? And Easter? And birthdays? And weddings and funerals. Any excuse to go out and "celebrate". And May Day . . . and Armistice Day . . . and bank holidays and all the saints' days . . .'

'OK, OK.' Matt surrendered with his free hand. 'If it makes you feel better, I'll swear to keep him from the bottle. I'll shadow him all day, stick to him like a tick to a tapir. Will that help?'

'What about the reception? There'll be champagne, an open bar . . .'

The woods had thinned out so that they were walking side by side approaching a split rail fence. With a jolt Natalie realised she knew where she was. They'd be home in minutes.

'I said I'll take care of it.' Matt threw the bike over the fence and vaulted it easily. 'Besides which, I think you're misjudging him. He won't want to embarrass you.'

'He might not *want* to but he always does.' She ducked, climbing between the rails.

'Anyway,' he said as she straightened up, 'I hate to tell you this but there is another flaw in your plan. I can't drive.'

'You can't drive?' Natalie looked aghast.

'Well, I cycled everywhere till I was seventeen.' He shrugged. 'And then I got my old BMW motorbike.'

'The Black Bomber.' Eight-year-old Hazel had named it, Natalie remembered. They'd all ridden on it countless times, arms clutched around Matt's waist, thundering down the road to the coast, faces pressed against his leather jacket as they zoomed round curves. Once they even took a trip to the New Forest – Milly on the back of Matt's 750cc monster, Natalie with one of his friends (on a Suzuki 250, not nearly so cool).

'I always had a bike until I went to Ecuador. And there it's such a pain in the arse to rent cars anyway, outrageously expensive, what with insurance, rampant theft, insane roads and suicidal drivers, it's easier to always catch taxis. So I just never got around to taking my test. Also, it's not very eco, is it, to drive one of those stinking gas guzzlers?'

'Your father died in a car accident, didn't he?'

He nodded. 'Skidded on black ice and drove into a tree. My poor mum's always warning me motorbikes are way more dangerous, but they're a hell of a lot more fun. Still, sometimes it's a nuisance to be a non-driver. I'll sort it out one day.'

They were out on the open hillside now, looking down at the cluster of houses below. As he put one foot on the pedal, ready to swing his leg over the bike, she stopped him.

'You know, there's something . . . something I've never told anyone, outside the family. Not even Jeremy . . . especially not Jeremy.'

'What's that?'

'I can't . . .' Natalie gulped, her face turned salmon pink, '. . . swim, I can't swim.'

'And that's a secret – why?' Matt grinned, flicking her lightly on the nose.

'It's not funny. A big wave knocked me under when I was a kid at the beach and I was always scared to death after that. Don't you remember when we went to that swimming pool with the wave machine? I'd always come out when the whistle blew and they started it up. And at the seaside I'd always say the water was too cold. Anyway, our honeymoon's in the Maldives and Jeremy's gone and booked us on a week's scuba-diving course.'

'But why didn't you tell him?'

'I was going to but his last girlfriend was the total outdoorsy type, always abseiling down cliffs, paragliding off them, or spelunking in some maze of caves. I mean, I know I've got to confess but I'll look like a total fool.' Nervously, she chewed on a strand of hair.

Matt moved it gently from her mouth. 'You might not – I have an idea.'

Chapter 20

The same evening Natalie pushed the bedroom door open with her back, her arms full of laundry. She was seething. Seven o'clock and Jeremy still wasn't speaking to her and she was in no mood to placate him. Letting his mother talk to her like that. Abandoning her in the church car park while he and his parents trotted off to discuss mortgages without her, as if she was a right thicko. Hell, her office was wallpapered with thank you letters from first-time buyers who'd looked to her for help when they were overwhelmed by the financial quagmire of house buying. There was nothing she didn't know about interest rates, endowments, repayments, buy-to-let mortgages. And what had Beryl meant with that snide remark about her job?

OK, Dad had been outrageous, she fumed, as she tipped Jeremy's underwear higgledy-piggledy into his drawer, not bothering with her usual obsessive folding into neat little piles. Worse than outrageous, maybe. But that was hardly her fault, was it? Alcoholism was an illness really and Jeremy had always known he'd got a problem. So what had she, Natalie, actually done that merited the Coventry treatment? Gone off alone with an old family friend? Horrors! Turned up later than expected? Big bloody deal! Fallen off a bicycle? Could happen to anyone. (At least that was Matt's explanation when they'd been confronted by Jeremy's thunderous looks back at her parents' house.)

They'd come in the side entrance, Matt propping the bike against the ornamental cherry.

'Jeremy!' Natalie gasped as they walked into the living room. 'I thought your parents were taking you home.'

'I changed my mind. Asked them to drop me off here instead.' His eyes flicked to the briefcase he'd left by the fireplace.

'Oh.' Natalie felt lots of pairs of eyes boring into her.

'But tell me,' Jeremy said in a tight voice, 'where have *you* been?'

'Sorry?' She glanced at her watch, then the grandfather clock by the fireplace. Five to three. Two hours had passed since they'd left the church. Even Hazel and Milly were back from the restaurant and watching a rerun of *Inspector Morse* with Peggy and Erin. 'I was just . . . we came home the long way.'

'Looks like it.' Hazel had a strange expression on her face.

'What do you mean?'

'Better nip to the loo, Nat.' Milly glanced from her to Jeremy and back again.

Natalie hurried down the hallway, face blazing. But it blazed even more when she caught sight of herself in the mirror.

There was a big welt of mud on her cheek, leaves on her hair and the hem had come down from her dress. Worst of all, right in the middle of her nose, was a big streak of bike oil – no wonder Jeremy had stared. She felt like murdering Matt.

'I was just telling Jeremy how you fell off the bike and how your ankle swelled up like a balloon,' Matt informed her when

163

she came back in after doing a quick clean-up job. 'And how long it took to get back . . . with the pain . . . you know.'

'The pain . . . oh yes, my ankle . . .' Natalie rested her hand on the back of the sofa for support and began hopping. 'I think the swelling's going down.'

'I can't see anything,' Jeremy said, suspiciously.

'Trust me, I'm a doctor.' Matt knelt beside her, taking her foot between his warm palms, twisting it this way and that as he pretended to scrutinise it. He was enjoying himself a little too much, Natalie thought. Was this act meant to placate Jeremy or to piss him off? 'Can you put any weight on it now?'

'A bit.' Suddenly she took a grip of herself. 'Well, it had better be OK for the wedding, Matthew Harkness, or you'll have a lawsuit on your hands.'

Now Natalie sat on her wrinkle-free immaculate bedspread in a nest of lemon lace pillows and stared into space. It wasn't like she had said or done anything to be ashamed about, for heaven's sake. Matt had been the perfect gentleman. There was absolutely no reason for Jeremy to get jealous, none at all.

As if stung into action, she sprang up, went to her cupboard and up on tiptoes, reached for her box. Bringing it back to the bed, she ignored the ribbon-wrapped bundle and pulled out a small notebook, turning to the first page.

A List of Future Goals By Natalie MacLeod (aged 13), she read. *1. Marry a wealthy man.*

The door swung open.

It was Jeremy.

'What's that?' he demanded.

'Sorry?'

'That box in your lap.'

'Nothing.' She quickly snapped it shut. Well, at least he was talking now, even though his expression wasn't exactly forgiveness and light. 'Some old papers.'

'Show me.' He went to grab it but she managed to pull it from his grasp.

'No, you mustn't. Thing is . . . thing is . . .' she racked her brains. 'We need to go over insurance papers, car, life, medical, et cetera. To change names. You couldn't get your policy, could you, from the study? I need to keep things together.'

'You're lying, Natalie. I can always tell.' Jeremy was in no mood to be soft-soaped. 'Hand it over.' He took a step towards her. 'Now!'

Avril glanced around. Another impeccable choice by Richard Burdock. Muted lights, candles on tables, convivial atmosphere. Warm yet discreet.

He looked very serious in his dark suit and navy round-necked cashmere sweater underneath. But in a hunky brooding way. God, she'd missed him . . . Over two weeks since she'd seen him (admittedly with Saskia) and two days before that since they'd kissed . . . He'd had another business trip since her return from the States, he'd told her, but still she had to admit these absences only fired her passion.

'So, what was it that was so very urgent you had to see me tonight?' she asked once the soft-soled waiter had padded away with their drinks order.

He studied her carefully before speaking. 'Diane had a phone call.'

'I thought we weren't mentioning Diane.'

He gave a wry smile. 'Things have changed.'

'Oh.' Avril gazed into the candle, and scratched at a sliver of wax that had escaped. 'In what way?'

'Somebody rang her. While you were in New York so I

didn't get a chance to mention it sooner. They apparently felt under some strange obligation to inform her that I was having an affair.'

'No!' Avril dragged her hand from the candle like it was burnt. 'Who was it?'

He shrugged. 'No idea. Anonymous.'

'Man or woman?'

'Woman she thinks. But it was a pretty crackly line.' He paused as the waiter carefully placed two martinis between them. 'Couldn't tell what age.'

'Was she . . . was she very upset?'

'Put it this way, she wasn't thrilled. Diane hates *anything* interrupting her beauty sleep.'

Avril turned the pages of her menu, not reading a word. 'She could have done a 1471.'

'Actually, she did. Unobtainable number, surprise surprise. Strange choice of timing, three in the morning, don't you think? Doubly strange, one might say, because very few people know I'm seeing you. Of course I'm sure we've been spotted dining together but, all in all, I've respected your wishes for discretion. And I've had no reason to confide in anyone.'

'Not even Charlie?' She resisted the urge to add 'or Saskia'.

He quirked his eyebrows. 'Actually, Charlie's one of the few I've told but he's concrete. Trust him with my life. Tell me, did you by any chance talk about us to anyone recently?'

'I mentioned it to Milly,' Avril admitted.

'You did?' He raised his eyebrows again. 'I'm shocked.' She couldn't tell if that was irony in his tone.

'Angry?'

'Not angry. Why should I be angry?'

'But she wouldn't tell a soul, anyway. Apart from my

166

family.' (How often had she told him that her sisters' love of gossip was what kept BT in business?) 'And Brenda knows, naturally . . .'

'Yes, naturally, Brenda . . .' He picked up the olive from his drink and popped it in his mouth. 'Anyway, it's curious but hardly important. Truth is, and this is no one's business either, Diane's seeing someone herself, someone quite a bit younger than both of us. I know, I know. Ouch to my enormous ego, and I can't say it doesn't sting a bit . . . but, well, Diane and I, we know where we stand. We've always been completely honest and we love each other but the marriage hasn't worked for years. We make excellent business partners but lousy husband and wife. We live together, eat together and, up until last year, we worked together, but that's the sum of it.'

'You mean you don't sleep together?'

He shook his head irritably. 'No, Avril.' His voice held a tinge of forced patience. 'We don't sleep together. And neither do we discuss our sex lives. That would be the ultimate in pointlessness. We've trundled by quite happily up till now. The house is big enough . . . We were going to sort things out, we just wanted to wait till Kath finished with college before we started any upheaval.'

'She hasn't guessed?' Avril looked up. The waiter was beside them again, this time with a bottle of wine. Richard tasted it and nodded his approval.

'Probably, she's extremely sharp. We have separate bedrooms after all. But I think she's been grateful to maintain the status quo. Teenagers can be rather self-obsessed.'

How would I know? You're talking to a childless old maid. The words burned unsaid in her mind.

'I suppose what I'm saying, rather clumsily' – he placed his hand gently over hers – 'is that it was bound to happen one day. Diane and I always intended to divorce. But now she's had that phone call, it's made us rethink everything. We had a long talk . . .'

'And . . . ?' Avril could have written the script herself. '*We've realised we can't do that to Kath. We owe it to ourselves to give it another try.*'

'And – I've moved out.'

'OK, then.' Jeremy had cornered Natalie in the room but she was standing firm, holding the box high in the air. 'I'll tell you. It's . . . it's . . .' she struggled to gather her thoughts, '. . . undies for our wedding night. Special undies. You mustn't see them beforehand.'

'Special undies for our wedding night?' Jeremy's eyes lit up.

'Yes, and it's bad luck. You know, like one for sorrow, two for joy, three for a girl, blue for a boy . . .'

'Four for a boy, you mean.' He was thawing rapidly, his dark mood leaving.

'Yes, that's right. No . . . no . . . What I meant to say was . . . something old, something new, something borrowed . . . Jeremy darling.' She put on a little girl voice. 'I'll show you if you really want . . . but things haven't been going too well as it is, have they?'

'I was a bit miffed this afternoon. And rightly so, I'd say, after your father's appalling behaviour – and then you turning up looking like a hooligan from the hills.'

Natalie opened her mouth to say something, but stopped herself in time. Any bite back from her might start him on the box again. She shuddered at the thought. Quickly shoving it under the bed out of sight, she reached out to stroke his shoulder muscles. 'You're so tense, darling. Look, why don't you pop to the bathroom?' She smiled wickedly. 'Get something for me. Something to your advantage.'

'What?' Jeremy said suspiciously, not quite ready to be mollified.

'Some massage oil,' Natalie teasingly whispered into his ear. 'That walnut and bergamot one you bought me. The one we never opened. Go on, quick! And a towel. I'll do your back. Extra special treat for an extra special fiancé.'

That did the trick, already she could hear him rummaging through the bathroom cabinet.

Natalie slipped the box into her bedside cabinet, locked the door and tucked the key under the mattress.

Playing for time Avril dipped a long tall spoon into her chocolate mousse. 'You never told me Diane was having an affair.'

'Why would I?' Richard casually stabbed at her dessert with his fork. 'Off-limits topic, remember?' He leaned back, licking the chocolate, and scrutinised her beneath narrowed lids. 'Or did you, by chance, imagine I was some misogynist prick who whored around unbeknownst to his doting wife?'

'Don't be silly.' She felt ashamed. So many of her exes were like that. And hadn't that been half the thrill, the getting away with something, the dizzying knowledge that you could get caught?

He took her hand in his. 'I told you we were living separate lives. But from now on, we're doing it openly. I've rented a flat in Edwardes Square. Signed the lease this afternoon.'

Avril was silent, her feelings a mass of confusion. How was she supposed to react? Was she appalled or pleased. Relieved? Disappointed? All of the above?

'Could have been worse.' Richard laughed, reading her like a cheap novel. 'I might have arrived on your doorstep with suitcases packed and a hangdog expression, begging to move in with you.'

She laughed. 'Yeah.'

'And what does that mean, "yeah"?' His scrutiny was making her wriggle.

'It meant, nothing. Just "yeah".'

'It was what that "yeah" implied.'

'What did I imply?' Avril suddenly felt uncomfortably hot. Her appetite for dessert had melted away.

'Oh, I don't know. That nuclear disaster might have been more warmly received. Listen, Avril, let's not play games. I think you know I'm in love with you.'

Did she? Playing with her spoon, Avril couldn't think of a single thing to say. Nor could she seem to lift her eyes which were suddenly magnetised by the congealed mess at the bottom of her dish. She was too afraid of what she might see when she looked into his.

Richard leaned over and took her hand.

'I also know how you value your independence. But would it be so really far-fetched . . . that we think of living together –'

'Live together? I'm sorry . . . I . . .' Nausea rose in her throat, her sickly pudding threatening to make an unscheduled return. 'I need some fresh air . . .'

She jumped to her feet, her chair clattering loudly to the ground. Heads turned and eyes popped, following her clumsy rush to the door.

How could things have gone so terribly wrong?

Natalie knelt, legs astride Jeremy, and pummelled away at his back. 'Do you think, babypie, that in our new place, we could get mood lighting?'

'Anything you say, my precious.' His voice was muffled, his face lost into the pillow.

She smiled. The massage was working its usual magic, his

muscles and disposition turning malleable under her nimble fingers. Between groans of pleasure, he'd already muttered his gruff regret for the day's misunderstandings; had actually dared a faint hint that keeping his mother happy was a challenging task. He called it 'nerves', Natalie privately called it 'a bloody nerve', but at least harmony was restored.

'Is this OK?'

'Lower,' he groaned.

'This OK?' she joked, deepening her voice.

'Come here.' He laughed and started to turn over. 'You know, you're looking especially luscious tonight.'

She pushed him back down. 'I'm not quite finished yet . . .' Switching to feather-like strokes, she ran her fingers between his ribs. 'Jeremy,' she began tentatively, 'have you ever wanted to do something wild? Spontaneous? We could surprise everyone. Skip Little Hooking entirely, elope to Gretna Green?'

There was a short silence. 'Don't imagine I haven't thought of it,' he muttered, turning his head to the other side. 'But it's impossible. The invitations have gone out, everyone's accepted. I mean, we're only a week away from the bloody wedding. What would people *say*?' His voice rose slightly, sounding aggrieved. 'You wanted this, remember. You insisted . . .'

'Shh. I know, I know,' she breathed, lowering her body onto his back and nibbling sexily at his neck. 'Don't worry, it's all going to be fine.'

'Mmm, that's nice.' Jeremy was melting under the touch of her descending hands, pleased that for once Natalie had initiated sex. Not that they never did it, just that it had tailed off lately and sometimes he felt she was performing it as a kind of duty.

Rolling on top of her, he started kissing her breasts.

*

Afterwards she lay awake, drawing a mental target on the ordinary humdrum light fixture and circular paper lampshade from Ikea, knowing their days were numbered. Maybe Jeremy wasn't the funniest, brightest or even hunkiest guy in the gene pool, but he was decent, solid, dependable, he obviously loved her to death and most of all they shared the same ambitions. In time she'd win over his harpy mother, though it might take a grandchild to seal the deal. His father would be a piece of apple pie – the old man was a total lech when his witch of a wife wasn't jerking his strings, drooling with happiness if a pretty girl so much as batted her eyes.

All she had to do was pull off this wedding. Jeremy was right, it was too late to change venues. She'd just have to trust Matt when he said he could take care of Dad. Maybe it had been a one-off lapse, maybe he wasn't really on the bottle again. And she'd speak to Mum again, give her strict instructions on protocol. There was no reason for this sense of dread, no reason at all.

When they'd masterminded the D-Day invasion of Normandy, they hadn't had Natalie's attention to detail. Not a single i was ever left undotted, no t discovered sloppily uncrossed. If by chance some evil uninvited godmother should show up, cackling curses, the parking attendants would know exactly where to put her broomstick.

No, everything was going to be perfect. Just perfect.

Chapter 21

It was only ten o'clock but the faint miasma of depression that always swept over Hazel when she came home had sent her early to bed. Downstairs, she could hear Peggy clattering dishes, singing 'Come Fly With Me', one of her all-time favourites. Callum was probably nodding in his armchair, drowsing during the news, sucking on the burnt-out embers of his pipe.

They were little old people, she thought. It was a shock to see how their wrinkles and white hairs had multiplied in her absence, how stooped Dad had become and how Mum had shrunk. Even the house looked smaller and shabbier, the dust and grime accumulating as her mother's eyesight worsened, the presence of atrophy evident everywhere she turned. And even the garden, which in her childhood had seemed to stretch for acres of enchantment, was shockingly normal, larger perhaps than was usual for a house this size, but still no longer the magical kingdom she remembered.

She bashed her pillow to a more comfortable shape, turning over on her side to face the dividing wall between hers and Milly's old bedroom where Matt had taken up temporary residence, except that tonight he'd gone into Codmoreton to visit an old mate from school.

God, she'd worshipped him as a little girl, even if he and the others weren't always nice. Treating her like a pest. Getting her to wander up to women hikers on the Downs when she was just a toddler and ask, 'Are you wearing a bra?' Sending her to face the grumpy old owner of the newsagent's to buy sweets with a selection of shiny stones instead of money.

When she walked into that clinic and saw Matt of all people, grinning down at her with those crinkling impish eyes, it was like kismet. Too much of a coincidence to be anything but fate, but what would come of it?

Being at home again, playing games with her niece and nephews, was bringing back memories of Hazel's own childhood, good and bad. She stared sleepily at the patterned curtains, thinking of those times when Mum would charge into the room where they were watching TV, fists in boxing stance. 'Put up your dukes,' she'd challenge and then attack, arms flailing like a windmill, while they fell about in giggles, helpless to defend themselves. Or she'd unexpectedly whack them and explain, 'That's to teach you life's not fair.'

And the way Dad would hide in his study the minute he came home from work and they'd be ordered to leave him alone. Mum always found extra food at teatime for any of their friends, but Dad would seldom eat with them because his own children's table manners made him ill, or so he always said. But he'd spend hours helping them with their homework, patiently explaining the mysteries of maths and chemistry, bringing history to life with his love of ancient times or declaiming Shakespeare and translating the old Bard so they hadn't a clue what the dickens was going on.

Then there were the days when his hands shook in the morning, his eyes bloodshot, and Hazel would walk into the kitchen and find her mother in floods of never-explained tears.

There were horrible fights too. Milly and Natalie always hustled her into the bedroom, but she wasn't stupid, she could hear them through the walls. And even as a small child, she'd learned to read the signs. There was the happy cheerful Dad, throwing her in the air, carrying her on his shoulders, the one that made Mum grimly quiet but had Hazel laughing with glee. Until it gradually dawned on her how closely he'd be followed by the staggering unsteady Dad, clinging onto the banister, falling into his armchair maudlin and weepy, or the Dad who'd lash out suddenly, foaming with fury, like a monster ready to obliterate the family with a sweep of his massive paw. She could remember peeking through the kitchen door when she was supposed to be in bed, seeing Mum yelling at Dad, Dad forging forward to strike her, knocking dishes from the table onto the floor instead, Milly and Natalie grabbing at his arms. It was like watching something from the telly, strange, surreal and weirdly exciting.

Hazel rolled over, kicking the bed sheets off, a little less sleepy now that her brain had sprung back into its busy musing. Her father was a mass of contradictions: funny and shy, erudite but with simple tastes, a giver of soppy birthday cards 'to my darling daughter' yet terrified of hugging. When he was on a binge, the whole house held its breath, never sure if or when the explosion would come. And in the aftermath Mum would cry and rant, Natalie snub him and Milly try desperately to make everything better, feeling sorry for her dad as only Milly could. Then life would be normal again, Mum laughing and singing as she did her thousand and one chores, while helping Hazel build a fort from cushions or a tent from an old sheet and a washing line. It was like living in the shadow of a volcano. Long periods of beautiful uneventful days punctuated by extreme drama. No wonder Hazel had grown up with a craving for excitement.

By the time Natalie and Milly left home, though, Mum no longer got so angry and Dad usually passed out instead of going on the rampage. Maybe that was why Hazel mostly found his drinking funny instead of being bitter and angry like Natalie and Av. (When had she and Nats ever shared anything, even an opinion – willingly at least?) She'd felt sorry for Dad today at the graveyard, looking bewildered and crumpled, his once blue eyes washed-out with the pallor of a habitual drinker. At lunch he'd seemed confused, toying with his food, saying next to nothing while Mum tried to rally the troops, chatting nineteen to the dozen to cover the scene they'd all witnessed. Actually, that little episode had been quite funny really, apart from Natalie's reaction. The look on Godfrey's face! And what had Dad really done, after all? Hazel would have loved to shove that Mr Poshy-Washy herself. Or bite his wife's other leg. Hooray for Rory and Dad.

Though Hazel did feel for Milly. She'd been clearly mortified by Rory's outburst and had spent the entire rehearsal morning worrying about the children's behaviour – she'd looked frazzled with anxiety by the time she bundled them into the car.

Milly's ultimate aim was to maintain complete calm and avoid any form of unpredictable excitement. Her life was so boring as to make Hazel's teeth ache. Half the time she seemed tired and miserable, shouting at the kids instead of disciplining them, always fighting with Erin. Last week Hazel had gone to Codmoreton to visit her sister but she swore, even though Milly seemed in an unusually good mood, her house was even more disorganised than her parents' and Hazel's lacklustre attempts to help tidy barely made a dent.

She had gallantly changed Ben's nappy, though; an interesting experience. At eight months old, Ben's head was round, shiny and bald, a MacLeod family trait. It was the same with Avril, Milly and Natalie when they were that age, Callum complaining bitterly that everyone else's children had hair except his. Until Hazel – emerging, according to Mum, with a mat of black down from head to toe – sent him into total panic. A baby monkey, Natalie always said.

She was drifting now, finally feeling cooler than she had all day as the night's chill took over. Her eyes closed and she was lost in dreamland.

It was two in the morning when she woke up, her heart pounding until she realised it was only a dream. There had been a man's voice yelling, someone banging at a door and a girl screaming, hysterical.

It took a few minutes for her pulse to return to normal. The details were evaporating even as she tried to seize and analyse them. Had the voices been familiar? The result of watching too many horror flicks? And what, if anything, did it mean?

Avril was relieved when the dawn finally filtered through the crack in her bedroom curtains. What a shitty night. She couldn't bear to remember her headlong flight from the restaurant, yet it insisted on replaying through her throbbing brain like a particularly bad commercial. What on earth must Richard be thinking? Talk about a runaway bride – she couldn't have galloped away faster if she'd been on a bolting racehorse – and poor Richard hadn't even proposed. But what did the bastard mean by leaving his wife? And springing it on her like that?

She got up to brush her teeth, head aching from the brandy she'd consumed on arriving home, hoping to blot out her wretched feelings of shame and guilt. Her nerves had been on edge, watching the telephone, dreading its ring, sick with remorse and fear when she realised he wasn't going to call. How could she face him after this? And did she want to?

The brandy bottle was still on the kitchen counter, the level of remaining liquid startlingly low. Did she really drink all that? Impossible. There must have been less there than she'd remembered. The place looked a bit chaotic but her cleaning lady was due today so that sorted that. What she needed now was a Bloody Mary, get her mind straight.

As she carried the tall glass past the breakfast bar to the comfort of her living room, she had a fleeting thought there'd been a hefty amount of hangovers lately but it was quickly dismissed. She was nothing like her father. She didn't have a drink problem. Didn't stumble around making a fool of herself. She was totally in control.

Too bad there wasn't a single item of food in the fridge. That was what came of eating out all the time. Even if you bought groceries, they inevitably rotted, unused. Besides, breakfast was usually a cup or two of coffee, unless Richard stayed over and insisted on scrambling eggs or bought bagels. He knew she wasn't the domesticated type. If they lived together, would he expect to turn over the Le Creuset cookware to her? Hell would freeze over first.

Let's face it, this place wasn't big enough for two and Avril wasn't about to move. She loved her flat. Loved its Pembroke Gardens location in Notting Hill, the shops and pubs, didn't even mind the tourists constantly asking directions or the bedlam of the Carnival. She'd decorated it some wild colours for someone who'd lived her teens dressed entirely in black. Her dining room was deep red, her lounge a vivid turquoise, her furniture . . . Well, the point was it was all her – Avril's – personality, *her* favourite paintings hanging on the walls, *her* favourite photos and knick-knacks on the mantelpiece and nesting tables. The huge wardrobe and dresser in her bedroom were bursting with her clothes. Richard couldn't possibly expect to move in here. Have him watching TV when she wanted to read. Bumping into each other in the bathroom.

She shuddered, feeling claustrophobic at the very thought.

Like visiting Milly and seeing the demands her family made on her, how she never had a minute to herself. She swirled the ice cubes and scowled at the last of the tomato juice. Milly looked like she'd lost some weight. That was a miracle. The dress fitting had only been a few weeks ago. And she'd been a bit peppier too, when she'd seen her at the church. Maybe Matt's return had been good for her—not that Milly would ever swap her hair shirt for an illicit romance, even if Ivor were a wife beater and her kids had kids of their own. Natalie, in contrast, was more of a harpy than ever. Old maid, eh? Well, better an old maid than a martyr or self-obsessed shrew.

She pulled her bathrobe tighter around her waist. She'd go to the office early today, email Wally, tell him thanks but no thanks. But first she'd take a lovely long soak in her jetted tub. Might as well benefit from this godawful early rising.

And Richard? Well, to quote her heroine Scarlett O'Hara, 'I'll think about that tomorrow.' Or at least not until his call.

Chapter 22

Natalie dipped a cautious toe into the crowded swimming pool, pulling down her sensible black costume. Although the way Matt was looking at her, she'd have preferred one of those ruffled ones her mother chose – with the skirt almost to her knees.

'OK?' He took hold of her hand and helped her down the steps.

'Yes. Whoo, bit chilly.'

'You get used to it.' He shivered, goosebumps visible on his arms. 'It's actually warm once you've been in a bit.'

'Liar.' She gazed around. Two stops on the tube from her office, it was the perfect venue. She could nip out for lunch and no one would be the wiser. 'How did you know about this place? I thought you'd spent the last umpteen years playing Dr Livingstone.'

'Quite so, Mr Stanley.' He flicked water at her still bone-dry chest and shoulders. 'But before the wilderness swallowed me, I did my training in Central London. UCH.'

'So if I drown' – reluctantly she submerged to her neck – 'you know where to take me?'

'In that unhappy event, yes, I know where to take you and luckily the first thing they taught us at med school was the kiss of life.'

'Good, well, right.' She reached for the metal rail on the side and let go of his hand. 'So, what's first?'

'First is . . .' She didn't like the gleam in his eyes. '. . . stick your face under the water.'

'No way!' She jerked back, horrified.

'Yes way. Pretend you're blowing bubbles into a saucer. Just let your face and chest go forward, don't worry, I'm right beside you.'

She felt an unnerving flutter as he grabbed her waist.

'You can drown in a saucer, you know. It's been known to happen.'

'You're quite right, Natalie.' He suppressed a smile. 'But, please, indulge me.' He stepped back, folding his arms across his perfectly toned chest, which, Natalie noted, had just the right amount of dark hair, just enough to be masculine without resembling a bear.

'I can't . . . I don't like . . .'

'Water? Getting wet? Listen,' he said exasperated, 'do you want to go scuba-diving with your beloved Jeremy or don't you?'

Half an hour later, he was walking across the shallow end, supporting her stomach with the flat of his hand, while she kicked her legs and arms.

'*Perfecto*, Nasty. Remember, keep the movement going with your legs.'

'I feel like a bloody frog.'

He laughed. 'Speaking of frogs, I still can't get why you never told Jeremy. Not good to keep secrets, you know.'

'We don't keep many secrets.'

'Only that you can't swim and you're going on a diving honeymoon, hey? Right, now, hang onto the bars again and kick your legs, come on, big splash.' He held onto the side beside her. 'Like this.'

'That wasn't a secret,' she puffed with dogged exertion. 'More of a surprise. He didn't mention the scuba-diving till a few weeks ago.'

'And you couldn't talk him out of it? Suggest more entertaining ways of passing those first precious hours of post-nuptial bliss? You must be losing your touch – or should I say, your whip . . .' He caught her foot as it blasted out to kick him.

'Maybe you'd do better with a float.' He jumped up onto the poolside with noticeable ease and grabbed a brightly coloured piece of foam, while two nubile college-age girls relaxing on beach towels stared longingly at his lean, tanned torso.

Giving them a completely unnecessary smile (Natalie thought), Matt tossed the float into the water and dived in smoothly.

Oh well, Natalie reflected, as she inched her ungainly way down the bar towards him, means to an end.

Dressed in street clothes again, Natalie's hair hastily blow-dried, they stepped into Great Russell Street.

'I'd better be off then.' She hitched her handbag onto her shoulder. 'I told Vera I had a showing after lunch but she'll be wondering what's happened to me.' She found it awkward somehow to meet his eyes. 'Are you sure you don't mind doing this? Because it's so far –'

'Natalie, it's no problem.' He pulled out her collar tip which had got tucked under her thin sweater. 'Like I told you, I'm up here in London all this week anyway. Got a whole bunch of interviews.' He glanced at his watch. 'In fact, I'm going to be late if I don't get going.'

'Interviews? You're thinking of staying?' She couldn't have sounded more alarmed if he'd diagnosed her with Hazel's fabled case of rabies.

'I might stick around – why not?' His wide mouth curved, apparently amused at her reaction. 'It's hard – almost impossible – to maintain a relationship out in the field, you know. And I could stand to suffer a few home comforts.'

'I'd have thought a mud hut in Africa would be right up Hazel's alley.' Natalie couldn't help a waspish tinge to her voice.

'Too bad my old job's in South America then,' Matt said. 'But you might be right. Especially if you throw in a few prowling lions. That girl's afraid of nothing.'

'Except routine. She'd no doubt get bored of prowling lions after a couple of weeks. Want to trade them in for polar bears.'

Well, someone needed to warn him, she reasoned. Hazel was fickle, always had been. Like Avril in a way – neither could make relationships stick. And Matt's admiration for her so-called bravery was galling. He'd only end up suffering when she lost interest in him.

'Dangerous animals, polar bears,' Matt said lightly. 'Still, at least she knows what she wants.'

Was that a dig at her? Natalie wondered. An implication that she, Natalie, didn't know what she wanted?

'See you tomorrow, then.' She gave a kind of awkward wave.

'See ya.'

She walked two steps, then stopped and swung round. 'You think this will work?'

'You mean can I turn you into Flipper in less than five days?' He hadn't moved. And he couldn't be taking these interviews too seriously, she thought, if he insisted on wearing jeans and a rather faded yellow T-shirt – no matter how good he looked in them. 'Probably not, but luckily, my little sardine, you don't need to grow fins to scuba – just think of it as taking a leisurely stroll underwater.'

She was halfway down the tube station stairs, when an appalling idea stopped her in her tracks. What if Milly wasn't the only one shaken by meeting her first love again? What if Matt had quite different reasons for wanting to stay in England? It could explain why he was being so amenable, working hard to ingratiate himself with Milly's family. What if Natalie had it upside down and it were *Hazel* who was heading for heartache?

She stood rooted like a boulder, streams of travellers parting and merging around her, as she tried to dismiss the unwanted notion. Even if Milly were acting weird, surely Matt would never be that sneaky? To sniff around a married woman? Wreck a family? And honestly, she fumed, irrationally upset by the absurdity of her thoughts, love might be blind but surely not enough to ignore how *grossly* her sister had let herself go. The pressure of people forced her into motion again but not until she'd worked up an indignant little speech about the sanctity of marriage. The first sign of hanky-panky and she intended to let them have it.

She would scarcely have been reassured if she'd been able to see Matt fifteen minutes later walk into Victoria Station, stroll over to the departures board and hop on to the first train heading back to Sussex.

Ivor turned over in the king-sized bed, reaching an arm for Milly as his brain slowly registered her absence. His eyes opened and he flopped onto his back and yawned. What a month he'd been having. Working these long hours, worrying about finances, whether some blip in the stock market or the demise of yet another start-up company would scare his investors away before he managed to secure the deal. He felt guilty about Milly, left with the burden of raising their boisterous family. At least she seemed more cheerful with the bustle and activity surrounding Natalie's wedding. Her post-natal depression, if that's what it had been, seemed to have lifted.

But where was Milly? She couldn't be in the toilet all this time. And what was that odd humming sound? Sliding his legs out of bed, he padded in bare feet down the stairs. As he approached the living room, the noise grew easier to identify. But it made less sense than ever.

He opened the door, blinking at the light. Milly was so absorbed, he had to say her name twice over the sound of the vacuum cleaner. Surprised, she spun her head round, looking like a cat burglar caught with a bag marked 'swag'.

'Milly. Milly! What on earth are you doing?'

'Hoovering.' She gave him a smile, guilt mixed with a pretend casualness.

'At three o'clock in the morning?' He had to glance at his watch, not quite able to believe it.

'I couldn't sleep.' She switched the vacuum back on and started swooping under the coffee table. 'Might as well be productive.'

'Right, well, of course.' Totally bewildered, Ivor tried for levity. 'Why not clean the bathrooms while you're at it?'

'I already did. And the understairs cupboard.' She sucked up one of Rory's pieces of Lego. There was a clattering sound followed by a burning smell. The only person it seemed to bother was Ivor. Was he insane to think there was something odd in this situation? He stepped in front of the hoover. Milly looked at him, surprised by his action.

'Darling' – he stretched around and carefully unfastened her fingers from the handle – 'call me crazy, maybe, but I think it's a little early to start cleaning the house. Come back to bed. I won't be able to sleep without you.'

'I can't sleep whatever,' she protested but she still allowed

185

him to lead her up the stairs. 'There's no point,' she added as they crossed the landing. 'I'll just be lying there. Wide awake. Waiting for the alarm.'

'Hmm.' He kissed the back of her neck. 'Maybe I can think of a way to pass the time.'

Hazel ambled into the kitchen where her mother was preparing lunch.

'I didn't know whether to wake you, dear. Should I have?'

'I suppose. I know I've got to stop this lying-in-bed-late lark, but to be honest' – she snatched a pear from the fruit bowl and took a large bite – 'I can't be arsed.'

'Uncle Sidney called. He and Aunt Betty just arrived at the hotel. Said they'll see us at dinner Wednesday night. We're entertaining the out-of-town relatives while you girls enjoy the hen night. Are you all right, you look a bit peely-wally?'

'Well, I've been having these bad dreams lately and . . . I don't know, sometimes I think my whole life is a complete and utter waste . . .'

'You know, I used to have this recurring dream,' Peggy said cheerfully, 'that I was blind and everyone around me was playing rounders, having a whale of a time, and I couldn't see a blasted thing. What do you think that meant?'

'A psychologist would probably say you were being kept in the dark about something. No, it's just I have this weird feeling . . .'

'Oh, I know all about weird feelings.' Peggy patted her hand. 'The first time I saw your father I was a staff nurse on the VD ward. I passed him in the corridor and I thought, uh-oh, the walking wounded, run for your life, Peg.'

'Dad had VD?' Hazel looked shocked.

'No, dear, he was working in the hospital. But he had that

vulnerable air. Like a little puppy looking for love. I tell you, it was devastating.'

Hazel gave up. There was never any point trying to bare your soul to Peggy. Even as children, if they approached her with their mundane problems – a bully in the playground or a best friend turning traitor – she'd either chivvy them into pretending all was well or become so heartbroken on their behalf, they'd end up comforting *her*.

In the living room, Hazel picked up the remote and flicked from channel to channel. Crap, crap and more crap. Reality rubbish, flick, dog-training programmes, flick, Jerry Springer-type shows, flick, flick, flick.

She switched it off and turned back to Situations Vacant in yesterday's newspaper. Waitress. Bike courier. Telesales. Well, no one was going to hire her for anything great, were they? Not with her CV.

Not that she'd never worked. She'd cooked on a yacht in Polynesia, sold time shares in Mexico, even endured two mind-numbing weeks temping in a finance company in New Zealand where she almost got sacked for stealing until they discovered one of the clerks was borrowing the cash to pay for his mistress. But they were hardly jobs to warm a prospective employer's cockles – or even his heart.

It was the same shit that hit her every time she came home. Reality screaming that it was time to grow up. At thirty, she was broke, out of work, in some ways no further along than the day she'd left school at eighteen. It wasn't only Natalie's biological clock that was ticking; the chances of a meaningful career or a real relationship dwindled with every passing year.

This visit she hadn't even bothered calling her three best friends. Julie was something high up in Reuters, driving a Porsche, working impossible hours and earning scads of loot;

Harriet was teaching at a nursery school and raising two kids; and Alice had just given birth to a little boy and was running her own business from a home office. Usually she couldn't wait to phone them and arrange a mini reunion, but honestly, why make the effort? They were as bored with tales of sharks attacking her boat in Papua New Guinea or swinging through the rainforest canopy in Costa Rica as Hazel was with stories of European monetary policy, loft extensions and puréed parsnip.

She chewed on the end of her Bic pen, splintering it to shards. Her bank account was as pitiful as Jeremy's attempts at humour and even her mum's tolerance for unpaid loans was running short. But never mind all that. Natalie's stupid wedding was only five days away. Being polite to Jeremy and his putrid parents would be stressful enough without fretting over what to do with the rest of her life. She'd thought maybe she'd return to South America with Matt, do some volunteer work for a worthy cause, but right now she'd have trouble scraping together the fare to Edinburgh let alone Ecuador.

She didn't know why she'd let them all think she and Matt were involved. Still, it had been priceless seeing Natalie's face, especially when she jumped on her high horse before Hazel could even say a word to the otherwise. True, Hazel wasn't exactly Frigid Fanny where her past history with men was concerned and Matt had slept in her room that weekend when the house was so crowded, but really, just for once, Natalie could have given her the benefit of the doubt without leaping to conclusions.

Not that Matt wasn't fun or still dishy despite his advanced years, but he'd known Hazel since she was a baby. He and Milly had even changed her nappy once, how weird was that! Thinking about sex with him – yuck – she shuddered, it was almost like incest. And going out with someone almost forty – that was almost as bad!

The trouble was, she thought moodily, no one took her seriously. Not her parents, not her sisters, not even Matt. To them she was still the irresponsible, flighty baby of the family; a catalogue of amusing high jinks and crazy whims. Which most of the time she was fine with but just occasionally it sucked.

Irritated, she put her trainers on the coffee table, sending a stack of her dad's Gaelic books tumbling on to the carpet.

Let's face it, coming home stank. You think you've evolved politically, emotionally, intellectually, then the second you're back, you might as well be toddling around, thumb in mouth and trailing your blankie. If Avril hadn't sent her that money and her marching orders when she was too broke to refuse, she'd still be in Ecuador, or more likely Peru by now exploring Inca ruins. Maybe she should buy a lottery ticket. All it would take was five hundred quid and they wouldn't see her for dust.

'You look . . .'

'Like shit, I know. Go on, say it. I haven't been sleeping lately.' Milly stared challengingly at her friend who stood on the doorstep, pushchair at her side.

'No – good. You look good, actually.' Rachel manhandled the pushchair through the door, careful not to wake her baby daughter. 'You've lost a barrowload of weight. And have you done something to your eyes?'

'I plucked my eyebrows. It's Natalie's hen night tonight.'

'And is that why you're dressed to the nines? '

'What, this old skirt? I've had it decades, just not been able to get into it before.'

'Mmm.' Rachel gave her a bemused look. 'Sure you're not off to have a secret love tryst somewhere, dolled up like that?'

'Me, tryst . . .? Now where would I meet anyone? Anyway, you're wrong, I'm not good, I've had a hell of a morning.'

After dropping Rory at school, Milly had been loading her trolley at the supermarket checkout, when someone tapped her shoulder.

She turned to discover Darren's mother standing, unsmiling, behind her.

'Mrs Simpson.'

'Oh, Mrs Hammond, hi there.' She braced herself. 'How are you? How's Darren?'

'He was fine until a few weeks ago when your son decided to take it upon himself to bite him!' The cashier exchanged a shocked look with Milly, then quickly focused her attention on Ben, pulling funny faces at him. 'I'm afraid he's been very highly strung since then. Not his usual self at all. I believe the teacher spoke to you?'

'She did, yes . . .'

'So what have you done about it?'

'Well, I've had words with him, obviously –'

'And?'

'He's sorry, I'm sure he's sorry –'

'He *told* you he was sorry?'

'Thirty-three pounds ninety please.' The cashier raised her eyebrows.

'Thanks.' Milly fumbled in her bag for her credit card. 'No . . . not exactly,' she said half turning back to face Mrs Hammond. To her dismay, she realised her voice had developed a tremor.

The angry mother took it as her cue to go for the jugular.

'I thought as much. What your son needs is a good smack!'

'I don't smack my children,' Milly replied indignantly, all hint of a tremor evaporating. But instead she felt her body flush with heat. Beneath her smock top, sweat began to pool in her armpits.

'I can believe that!' It was a snarl.

'I can't imagine what came over him.' Milly fumbled with the card, rotating it all ways until the cashier finally snatched it off her and placed it purposefully in the machine. 'Honestly, all through nursery he never caused any trouble. He's normally very good.'

'Well, he's clearly not now. Personally, I teach my children not to bite.'

'And so do I,' Milly said through gritted teeth.

'Your number?' The cashier indicated the chip-and-pin machine.

'Well, in your son's case it doesn't seem to have worked, does it?' Mrs Hammond spun on her heels and marched off.

'And then I couldn't think what my blinking pin number was and it took me ages to calm down enough to remember,' Milly said as she helped Rachel fold up her pushchair. 'I spent the whole journey home so engrossed with trying to think of some snappy retort instead of my pathetic "so do I" that a whole queue of traffic formed behind me and a lorry driver gave me the finger. Why am I so bloody inarticulate when it comes to confrontations?'

'Because you're a nice person. Too nice. I would have said, "Funny – I teach my children to bite at least once a term."'

'Or "Takes two to tango."'

'Or "Let's be sure of the facts before we start condemning . . ."'

'Or just "Fuck off, Hammond, you rod arse. Stop leeching off your children's dramas and go get a life."'

They both laughed.

'Cheer up.' Rachel followed her through to the kitchen. 'Old Hammond will get her comeuppance one day. Darren can't always be perfect. They're either monsters at five and angels at fifteen or – Oh my God, what happened here?'

It was the quality of disarray in Milly's kitchen that was

unusual. The oven door yawned open, its blackened surfaces covered with cleaning foam that set Rachel coughing; its stainless-steel racks soaking in the sink. The cupboards, the pantry, even the fridge had contents evacuated so that tins, jars, packets and bottles, all bearing value labels, were jumbled over every work surface while a worn-out sponge and a whole array of cleaning products bore testimony to unmistakable signs of scrubbing.

'I just felt like I had to do something. The whole mess was getting on my nerves.'

Rachel looked at her gobsmacked, then tapped her on the head. 'This is you, Milly, isn't it? Not an impostor dropped down from outer space?'

'It's only a bit of spring-cleaning.' She looked defensive. 'I haven't been so tired lately.'

'It's just I always use you when Mark has a go at me for my slovenliness. All I have to do is say if you think our house is a mess, you should see Milly's. Now who can I use as my standard?'

The sounds of Ben stirring took Milly into the bedroom with Rachel following behind. Rachel leaned over the cot, cooing as he smiled up at her, and suddenly jumped back. 'That's not a dummy, is it?'

'I thought he needed it. I've stopped breastfeeding, you see. Helps take his mind off it.'

'But you fed Rory till he was eighteen months?'

Milly shrugged. 'Just thought I'd quit early. I read this article . . .'

Rachel gave her a strange look as Milly began telling a long, involved spiel about some new research into cot deaths in America and dummies preventing them. She'd known Milly since Erin was tiny. Something didn't quite add up . . .

Chapter 23

'Come on then, repeat after me: "I have the floats, I know the strokes." '

'Hey, Matt, you're a poet and you don't know it.'

'Well, are you going to swim? Or should I push you in?' Matt laughed.

For the third lunchtime in a row, Natalie stepped, shivering, into the water. Matt dived after her, swimming underwater and then emerging beside her, pushing back his dripping hair with his hands. It felt intimate and odd to be so close together, almost naked, while beside them a lone swimmer in cap and goggles forged past in endless laps.

He started, as usual, with one hand under her stomach and one hand holding her up by the chin as she made the swimming movements she'd practised. When his fingers gradually released their touch on her belly, she experienced a sense of loss, wishing them back.

Only for security, she told herself, kicking harder. His hand was keeping her afloat, that was all. Ridiculous to think she might actually like the way it felt. She was doing this for Jeremy. Her beloved fiancé. With all the willpower she was capable of, she intensified her efforts, surging forward to touch the side.

'Not bad,' Matt said admiringly. 'Quite the Little

Mermaid, Nasty, I swear last time I saw someone with a natural action like that he was jumping up to grab a raw fish. And speaking of raw fish, did I ever tell you about our local candiru fish that likes to swim up your pee into your uretha? Way more effective than putting dye in the water. They should borrow a few for this place, guaranteed to stop illicit pee-ers.'

'I wish you'd stop larking around.' Natalie came spluttering to a halt and stood up in the water. 'You're totally putting me off and now I won't be able to think of anything but how much pee there might be in this pool. Why is it you can't say something nice without following it by something completely crass? What are you – twelve years old?'

'I wish,' he said lightly. 'You were so much nicer to me when I was twelve. So what do you girls have planned for tonight's hen party? Whooping it up with the Chippendales?'

'Not quite. Meet in the champagne bar at Kettners, dinner in one of their private rooms, and maybe a club after. Hopefully Milly can get away. Ivor lets her down so often.'

'You don't like him much, do you?'

'I guess no one's perfect.' She put her shoulders against the bar and kicked her legs up and down. Hadn't she read somewhere it would trim the thighs? Though, frankly, hers were pretty trim.

'Apart from the lovely Jeremy.' Matt changed the subject. 'And talking of Jeremy, did you know there's an Amazonian monkey that's as tiny as your fingernail?'

'I doubt it,' Natalie retorted, splashing at him. 'Maybe your big mitts but I happen to have particularly delicate fingers *and* nails. And absolutely no interest in the Amazon in case you hadn't noticed. The whole place sounds awful beyond belief, if you ask me.'

'So where's Jeremy going for his stag night?'

'Scotland. He had suggested Prague, but no way was I risking him missing a flight back.'

'Always running the show, eh, Nasty?' He was laughing at her again.

'I know what I want,' she said pointedly, remembering he'd admired that in Hazel. 'Is there something wrong with that?' She grabbed a float from the side and pushed it in front of her, kicking her legs.

'Nothing at all.' He swam along beside her. 'And does Jeremy always do what you want?'

She kicker harder and glared at him, pretending more annoyance than she really felt.

'What's that supposed to mean?'

'Well, I'm trying to fathom the attraction. Because you must admit, on first sight, he does come across as a bit of a tosser.'

'What?!' Natalie let her legs sink down and panicked as she realised they weren't touching the bottom. Her head went underwater and she came up, spluttering and gasping, as Matt dragged her towards the shallow end.

'He is *not*!' she said when she could breathe again. 'How dare you! You don't even know him.'

'Calm down.' Matt splashed her lightly. 'I said at first sight, didn't I? I'm sure for you to be mad enough to marry him, he must have redeeming qualities.'

'He has. Lots. Tons. He's . . . well, he's . . .'

'Go on.' Matt swam a lazy side crawl, circling her like a shark.

'He's rich, earns lots of money, works hard –'

'Wow! That must really keep your pulse racing.'

Natalie scowled. 'And he's brilliant in bed. A real tiger.' She swam off, grabbing her float.

'Too much information, my petal.' He towed her

backwards towards him. 'But I've never heard you mention love.'

'That goes without saying.' Natalie struggled to keep her head up and hold onto her float at the same time. She kicked with her free leg, hoping to hit Matt but he stayed annoyingly out of reach.

'Does it?' He pulled her round so that his eyes met hers and they weren't laughing.

'I didn't mean . . . Look, I'm marrying him for goodness' sake, obviously that means I love him,' she said defiantly.

'Say it then. Say you love him.'

'Don't be absurd.' They were so close she could see drops of water on his eyelashes. She kept her arms rigid by her sides. 'I don't have to prove my love for Jeremy to you or anyone else.'

'No, you don't. But just humour me. Let me hear you say it.'

'I do.'

'You *do* what, Nasty?'

'I love him, I love him, I love Jeremy Potterton-Smythe. There, does that satisfy you?'

Not waiting for his response, she plunged forward, holding her breath, kicking and flailing. When she grabbed the side, gasping, she realised Matt was applauding.

'Great! Very, very good! Well done!'

'Sorry?'

'You forgot your float. You made it over there all on your own. Way to go, Nasty. My work is done. You're officially a swimmer!'

Stirring her Cup a Soup with a pen, Vera looked at Natalie suspiciously as she walked into the office, grinning from ear to ear.

'What are they feeding you in that new deli? That's the third day you've come back into the office whistling after lunch.'

Natalie smiled mysteriously. 'Whistling maids and crowing hens are neither fit for God nor men.'

'Pardon?' Vera blinked.

'Something my grandmother used to say.'

'Do you even realise how odd you're sounding lately? What's up with you?'

'Nothing. Just that it's a gorgeous Wednesday afternoon and everything's going *swimmingly*. And I'm getting married in three days' time. Can you believe it? I'm getting married Saturday!' She opened the door again and shouted out. A grey little man passing by gave her a nervous look and sped up.

'And I found just the place for you. Ready for it . . .' Vera paused for theatrical effect. 'Stunning new apartment in the heart of Chelsea. Two thousand square feet.'

'Stop, stop!' Natalie put her hand up. 'I don't want to hear any more. I mean, who really cares? I mean, when you're in love, as long as you're together, that's really all that's important.'

Vera gave her a strange look. 'You've changed your tune a bit.' She stood up and walked over, putting a cool soap-smelling hand on Natalie's forehead.

'Now what?'

'Just checking that you're not running a fever. Don't want to waste my new dress this evening if the whistling maid is delirious with food poisoning.'

Natalie giggled. 'You mean for my crowing hen night?'

Vera made a face. 'For once I almost feel sorry for your poor fiancé. I just hope he knows what he's taking on.'

'Which is bigger? Left or right?'

'Left.' Avril squinted, eyes tearing. 'No . . . I mean right.'

197

The heavy frames dug into her nose as the optician took out the right lens and replaced it with another. He clicked a new image on to the screen.

'OK, same again. Which is bigger?'

Who the fuck knew? Or cared. Her eyes were watering so badly from the chemicals the idiot had squirted in them that she had trouble seeing the circles at all, let alone evaluating sizes. Why handicap her before she started? If only he'd try her on an ink-blot test. Avril had always had fun with those. Basically, whatever the shape, you just insisted it looked like a penis.

It was finally happening. Just as everyone said it would, only she'd managed to stave it off till the age of forty-five. At first it was only at night, when she was very tired and the light was poor, that the letters looked a little blurred. She'd be reading a manuscript in bed and have to stop early because her eyes were hurting. Then she started wearing the reading glasses someone had given as a joke present on her fortieth birthday, only at night-time, of course. Before she knew it, it was small print in broad daylight, the *London A–Z* might as well be written in Sanskrit, and lately she'd even found herself squinting at restaurant menus, holding them at arm's length. Yesterday, when a client had handed over her own reading glasses without even a comment, she'd known her number was up.

How humiliating. After years of depending on and gaily abusing her eyesight, it was finally letting her down. All those nights as a kid when she'd avariciously digest her music magazines by the crack of the bedroom door or the dim beam of a torch under the covers. All those scoffed-at warnings that reading in bad light would hurt her eyes when her eyes were so much better than anyone she knew. She couldn't ignore it any more. She was officially old. Decrepit. Falling apart.

Maybe that was why she was so unaccountably depressed as the optician spouted words at her like *presbyopia*, *ciliary muscles* and *hardening of lens*.

'They call it menopause of the eye in some circles.' He laughed gaily as he set about showing her two walls of frames.

Oh great, that made her feel so much better!

Had there ever been a single pair of glasses invented in the entire world that didn't make her appear like a spinsterish schoolteacher or a lunatic boffin? Some people looked good with glasses. She, Avril, didn't. It was as simple as that. Big old sunglasses, yes, she almost felt naked without those, especially in LA, but short of adding a white stick, she could hardly saunter around London wearing them at night.

Contact lenses, the optician was suggesting as she rejected yet another pair of frames, this time Thelma from *Scooby-Doo*. But she hated the thought of sticking her finger in her eyes. Could she go for laser surgery? She'd had one friend who'd dared the operation only to be left seeing double. But those were the early days. They'd improved since then. Hadn't they? And was she brave enough to risk it?

Fortunately the café where she bought her lunch on the way back to the office had its menu marked in large chalk letters on a board. And anyway, she knew what she wanted: smoked salmon and cream cheese on wholewheat bread. The place was packed, a queue almost stretching out the door. When did everyone start looking so young? Even the men in their business suits looked like children playing grown-ups, mid-twenties at most. Their eyes followed a dazzling young blonde, showing off a flat-toned navel with hip-slung jeans, but they didn't even glance at Avril. Why would they? Their own mothers could be younger, and probably were.

She took her sandwich and went back out into the hot

summer street, heading for Jubilee Gardens. Richard hadn't called. Not a peep out of him since Saturday night. She'd almost, once, picked up the phone to apologise but her better instincts kicked in. Why would he want a moody old bag like her anyway? She'd been told often enough she was impossible, a harpy, a ball-breaker. No, might as well face it, Natalie had it right. She liked her spinster existence. She was better off on her own, away from the heartbreak.

In fact, she thought, sitting on a bench and taking a bite of her sandwich, might as well buy the cats right now. Start carrying photos of them in her wallet, telling all and sundry about their latest cute antics. Only she couldn't stand the creatures, plus they made her sneeze. Maybe she could settle for a very small dog, a Yorkshire terrier or a Maltese. Keep it in her handbag and be one of those eccentric old ladies who brought it with her everywhere she went.

What was Richard playing at anyway? Was he furious? Offended? Waiting for her to crack and call, begging? She'd never been good at showing remorse, and anyway, what did he expect? Irritated by the way he was taking over her thoughts, she pulled out her mobile and hastily dialled a number.

'Michael? I got your proposal . . . You've got to be kidding me, this is Cameron Baxter we're talking about here. Studio says what . . . ? Full artistic control, sweetie, remember? I know they like to see the rushes but Cameron doesn't work that way . . . No, that's out of the question. Listen, do you have any idea how many scripts are landing on my desk every day, how many studios are clamouring at my door? Go back to them, tell them when they really get serious, we're ready to negotiate. Ciao. Love you, darling.'

She snapped her phone shut with a satisfying click. She had plenty of work waiting for her at the office. But for once in her life, the thought of going back there was so much less appealing than sitting here, feeling the sun on her closed eyelids, hearing the buskers' banter as they entertained the lunchtime crowd.

And then there was Wally. What had started as an off-the-cuff semi-joking proposition had suddenly turned serious. He wanted her and Wally was used to getting what he wanted. Yesterday, he'd upped his offer, naming a ridiculous salary combined with a benefits package that made the old man at the North Pole look like a positive miser. Her eyes had boggled when she'd read his email, which included a two-week deadline. Of course she'd never do it but it was exciting all the same, and she'd never been more tempted . . .

With a sigh she cut behind a Rollerblader, her high heels click-clacking as she strode briskly towards the Thames. If it weren't for Natalie's bachelorette party tonight – or hen do, as Nats liked to call it – she'd quite happily grab a bunch of her favourite classics from Blockbuster and cocoon herself under a blanket with a takeaway curry and a bottle of red wine. Or make that two bottles and forget the curry.

Hen nights – ugh! The very thought.

Chapter 24

The more Natalie tried to enjoy herself, the more she found she wasn't. Strange that, she thought in a disassociated way. There she was, at her hen party, meant to be one of the most fun nights of her whole life, everyone making a fuss and toasting her future, belle of the ball, and she was loathing every second.

She'd tried a numerous variety of cocktails in the hopes they'd relax her but all those Long Island Iced Teas and Slow Comfortable Screws Up Against a Wall had done nothing for her mood. If anything, they had only made her more morose.

She headed for the powder room and squinted at herself in the lighted mirror against a backdrop of shiny black tiles. Am I tipsy? she thought dazedly. Can't be. I'm never drunk, never ever ever ever. Although saying that, she did look drunk. Her lipstick had evaporated, black smudges sat panda-like under her eyes, her mauve strappy dress seemed to have lost a strap, and God, she had a hole in her tights. Natalie had never been seen in public with a hole in her tights.

'Are you OK?' Vera's reflection suddenly appeared at her shoulder. 'Are you having a really fantastic time?'

'Oh yes, yes, fantastic.' She tried smiling, but it didn't work. Her mouth only moved the merest millimetre.

'Here, have some of this.' Like magic, Vera produced a

small hip flask from her handbag. 'It's triple-proof vodka. Tina brought it back from Moscow. We both smuggled a bottle in past the bouncers. Tina hid hers in her knickers, so you'd better have mine.' She laughed.

Natalie began to giggle as she took a glug from the bottle. The fiery liquid hit the back of her throat and set her coughing. Suddenly she wanted to cry. No, she sniffed, I am not going to. This is the happiest time of my life. Shortly to be Mrs Jeremy Potterton-Smythe. Natalie Aileen Potterton-Smythe.

She'd tried the name on for size quite a few times over the years and mostly it rolled off her tongue – Natalie Potterton-Smythe – but tonight it felt, well, all wrong somehow.

'Say my name.'

Vera looked surprised. 'Natalie MacLeod.'

'No, my name-to-be: My married name.'

'Natalie Pinkerton-Smythe.'

'Potterton. Say it again.'

'Natalie Potterton-Smythe.'

Natalie frowned. 'It's not right.'

'Are you sure you're OK?'

'It's the *Black Swan*. The *Black Swan* all over again.' She closed her eyes and was immediately dizzy. Everything was spinning round and round her head, the name again . . . repeating itself, Natalie Potterton-Smythe, Natalie Potterton, Natalie Smythe, Natalie Scythe, Natalie Harkness. Harkness? Where did that come from?

She felt wet on her neck and put her hands to her face . . . Great rollicking tears were pouring from her eyes – she hadn't even realised.

'Natalie, what's the matter?' Vera had her arm around her shoulders.

'My name sounds horrible. I hate my name.'

'Shall I go fetch one of her sisters?' someone said.

'You'd better,' someone else agreed, and giggled. 'Either that or we're going to have to send for a straitjacket. Tell them she's talking in tongues.'

'Ladies and gentlemen.' Callum stood up, clinking his glass, while in front of him the conversation trickled to a stop. 'I'm saving my big speech for the wedding so I'll keep this short, forty-five minutes or so.' He paused while everyone generously laughed, giving it more gusto than the feeble joke deserved. 'I want to thank you all for being here, in particular Ted and Susan, who've come all the way from Toronto, and those of you who've travelled from Skye, Manchester, Southampton and, yes, such remote places as Golders Green.' Another laugh. 'This is a great occasion, my wee girl's wedding, although some might say at thirty-seven she's no so wee . . .' He swayed slightly and checked himself. 'Still, to me she'll always be that angelic curly-haired toddler, forever scolding us if we didn't wash our hands or wipe our feet.'

Laughing with everyone else, Peggy thought he looked sheet white, sweat pearling on his forehead. It was hot in here. She fanned herself with a menu. Callum never liked the heat. He was holding a glass of orange juice for his toast, but his hand was shaking.

She was puzzled, he couldn't be drunk again, could he? After nearly fifty years of marriage she knew the signs. He'd been so shocked by Natalie's outburst at the grave, for once he'd seemed to sober up right away. Besides, Peggy had turned the house upside down for booze and she could swear he hadn't been out of her sight long enough to buy a bottle.

Nerves, she decided. The poor man was in all probability frightened out of his wits.

*

'Am I going deaf as well as blind?' Avril burst into the powder room. 'Your mate says you're rattling on about a goose or something?'

'Swan.' Natalie had been found a chair and was now sitting on it, head rested against washbasin, looking distinctly green. Vera was rubbing her back and filling up a glass with water. 'The *Black Swan*.'

'Black Swan? What are you talking about?'

'I'll leave you two alone,' Vera said, slipping off.

'Mum. If she'd married Frazer, would she be happier? Would Dad be an alcoholic? Would Milly be so desperate? Would you be married? Hazel settled? Would I be an all right type of person rather than a Nazi?'

'You're not a Nazi. You're fine, honest.' Avril gave her a spontaneous hug which Natalie awkwardly tolerated.

'That's what Hazel called me. Natalie and her Nazi gang.'

'I'm sure she didn't, but . . . so what? Sisters are cruel sometimes. But they don't mean it. Don't forget I'm the shrivelled up old spinster.' She laughed hollowly.

Natalie blinked up at her. 'I never said that.'

'Oh darling, I don't care. I think it's funny actually. And probably true. And, Natalie, if you don't stop crying I'm going to take you home.'

'I'm not crying.' Natalie dabbed at her eyes.

'Yeah, right. You look completely wasted. What have you been drinking?' She inhaled sharply. 'Do I smell dope?'

''S one of Hazel's herbal cigarettes. No nicotine, she said. I only had three drags. Don't tell Dad, shhh . . .' She put one finger to her lip.

Avril refilled her water glass and handed it to her. 'I'll kill her. Drink this. And by the way, who the fuck's Frazer?'

*

Avril had poured as much water down Natalie as possible, which seemed to have helped, along with a little fingers-down-the-throat trick she knew to get rid of excess stomach contents.

'You know, darling,' Avril said, searching for some words of comfort, 'I'm not the marrying kind, never have been, never will. Guess I'm the archetypal old maid after all. But, sweetie, you believe in all that fairy-tale crap. And if anyone should get married, it should be you.'

'It should?' Natalie looked up from her mascara-stained tissue.

'Too right it should. You and Jeremy are the most married people I know. You're like a pair of twins. God, if you can live with each other for six years, you're going to be fine. Do you row?'

'Never.' She sniffed.

'Does he hit you?'

'God, no!'

'Does he drink too much, take drugs, spend all your money on fast cars?'

Natalie shook her head. 'He earns more than me anyway.'

'Well then, he's perfect for you. Now come on, dry your eyes, stick on your slap and paste on your winning smile. Do what you do best, Nats. Face your public, and boogie.'

Milly flapped her elbows and wiggled her hips like a funky chicken while singing at the top of her voice. Dancing, drinking, partying, she'd forgotten how much fun it all was. It was yonks since she'd had a good old bop.

Suddenly over in the far corner, she spied a familiar figure and yelled and waved.

'Hey, Gayle . . . Gayle, over here!'

Gayle caught her eye and bustled across.

206

'Milly? Is that you?'

'Course it's me.' Milly beamed. 'Come on, strut your stuff.'

'But you . . . you must have lost at least . . . You'd better come to my shop first thing tomorrow. Your gown's going to hang like a sack. How on earth did you do it?'

'Ah,' Milly replied, tapping her nose, 'that'd be telling.' She grinned like a Cheshire cat as she bumped her hips against Hazel's, almost sending her youngest sister into the arms of a smooth dark-skinned looker who had been circling them all night. Last time anyone from outside the family had mentioned Milly's weight, it was to ask when the baby was due – three months after she'd given birth to Ben.

How offended she'd been as she'd lumbered home.

How very different now.

'. . . and as I said, I'm sure there'll be more than enough speeches on the big day, so . . .' He paused. 'As one of my favourite patients once said . . .' He stopped again, wiping his sweaty temple.

'Go on,' Peggy urged under her breath.

Callum felt a tingling in his arm, then a pain like no other rip through his body. 'Aaahhhhh' he groaned loudly, clutching at his chest. Someone laughed out loud, thinking it was a joke. At the other side of the table, Matt jumped out of his chair.

With a sudden jolt, Peggy realised what was happening . . . She reached towards her husband, but it was too late. With a clatter his chair fell backwards and his head hit the floor with an almighty thud.

Immediately Matt was at her side, peeling off his jacket and checking for a pulse. 'Call an ambulance!' he instructed urgently. 'Does anyone have some aspirin? Callum, Callum, can you hear me?' To Peggy's horror, Matt began CPR. The invited guests gathered round, watching him work, their faces pale and shocked.

'Please, darling,' Peggy uttered under her breath. 'Please be OK.'

He stared up at her, his eyes like pinpricks, before they began slowly rolling back.

Leaving Natalie to repair her face, Avril returned to the steaming disco where Milly was dancing like a maniac, legs stomping to the beat as she peered through her splayed fingers like an old hippy. Next to her, Hazel was grinding her groin against a handsome Middle Eastern type whose silk shirt was slashed to the navel. Honestly, her sisters!

She tucked herself into a corner of the bar wishing once again she could ditch her high heels for a pair of slippers and a good book by the fire. Or maybe a pair of brandy snifters and some hot sex on the fireplace rug. She checked her phone again, but there were no calls from Richard. Not surprising. After all, the guy had left his wife, asked Avril to share a flat with him and how had she reacted? Like a petrified virgin seeing her first flasher. Leaving him like a fool with a huge bill for dinner and egg – no, make that chocolate mousse – on his face.

She felt her phone vibrate on her lap. She fumbled for it in her purse with a sudden pang of hope.

'Avril . . .' Peggy's voice trembled.

'Mum? Is that you? What's happened? What's the matter?'

But the line was crackly, the reception fading in and out.

'Hang on!' Avril yelled over the noise of the disco. 'I'll call you right back!'

Christ, she thought, racing to the quieter lounge bar upstairs. It had to be bad for her mother to call. And, damn it, now she realised she couldn't call her back – the number was withheld. Would Peggy try again? Or was she waiting at some phone booth, wondering why the telephone didn't ring? With fumbling fingers, Avril dialled the number for information. Now what the fuck was the name of that restaurant?

Natalie felt better. A dab of blusher, touch of foundation, eyeliner and she was ready to face the world. Avril was so right. So sensible. The music had slowed in tempo. Phyllis Nelson's 'Move Closer' was playing.

She remembered the song from a rugby club disco she went to the summer she'd just turned seventeen. She'd done her hair specially and her parents had forked out for a new dress and everyone told her how wonderful she looked. Milly and Matt had been there and afterwards they'd all walked home together, laughing and singing, Matt joking about the hearts Natalie had broken that evening. It was one of the best nights of her life. And then there was another one, barely a year later . . .

No, she wouldn't let it come. If she didn't acknowledge it, didn't think about it, then it might not have happened. It couldn't have happened.

The music grew louder and as much as Natalie tried to shield herself, her mind kept drifting back, back . . .

They were listening to the same song in her Earls Court flat. Matt had shown up unexpectedly to surprise Milly in that brief period when the two sisters lived together. Where had Milly been that day? It was lost in the mists of time, one of those idle bits of information that evaporates as thousands of new bytes flood in. But it had been Regatta week, she remembered that, and so Natalie and Matt had driven to Henley with a gang of others, drunk gallons of Pimm's and got so plastered and wild, her friends had to chauffeur them home, giggling like a pair of loons in the back seat all the way. It was all innocent fun – until they were back in her flat and she was alone with . . . Looking into his dark smouldering eyes as he put down his coffee cup and pulled her up to dance . . . realising, like the bottom falling out of her heart and overturning her world, that she was . . .

And then he kissed her. And it was the most fabulous wonderful kiss in the whole world, and it didn't stop. Emotions flooded up inside her as the memory swept her up.

Natalie Harkness. Natalie Aileen Harkness.

For the first time in almost twenty years she allowed herself to relive that evening. The bliss, agony and shame of realising she was in love – had maybe always been in love – with her sister's boyfriend.

And then out of the mist of people, suddenly Matt was there, in the nightclub. Impossible. He was at the Darlington Hotel with her parents. She blinked. No, he really was there. Tears sprang to her eyes as the truth, the absolute truth, hit her with such an incredible force that her knees almost buckled. What she now knew, for certain, for always, was that she was in love with Matt. Which meant she couldn't be in love with Jeremy . . . which meant that if she went ahead with the wedding in three days' time, she'd be making the biggest mistake of her life.

'Natalie.' Matt took her hands in his and squeezed them gently. 'I had to find you.'

She wrapped her arms around his neck. 'And I had to find you, Matt.' She leaned her body into his, till he was holding her, like he was holding her when she was swimming – supporting her. 'You know that I . . .' she started, but he was pulling her arms down and she was confused. She wanted to kiss him, right in the middle of the floor, blow the world, blow Hazel, blow Milly, blow Jeremy, everyone. Behind his head she noticed Avril weaving her way towards them, her face wearing a peculiar expression, but Natalie didn't care. All she knew was she wanted to kiss him and kiss him and kiss him and . . .

His head slightly tilted to one side as his mouth approached hers, she felt his warm breath as she closed her eyes, lips puckering . . . But almost too late she realised he'd angled off, his mouth heading for her ear.

'It's your father,' he hissed urgently. 'He's collapsed. He's had a heart attack.'

The shock hit her like a tsunami. She felt herself swoon, but Avril was at her side, propping her up. Taking over. Taking charge.

'I've a taxi waiting outside,' Matt said. 'Just by the entrance.'

'OK,' Avril acknowledged, bustling. 'You look after Nat, I'll go fetch Hazel and Milly.'

And then it was Matt with his arm round her waist but none of that mattered any more.

Chapter 25

'He's not going to die, is he, Doctor?' Peggy addressed the cardiologist who was perched on a desk, stethoscope around his neck, clipboard in hand. He was a young-faced man with steely-grey hair and soulful eyes that radiated concern as he looked at the small audience gathered in front of him. He scribbled some quick notes onto a sheet of paper then cleared his throat.

'Well, of course, there are no guarantees, but I'm quite sure he's going to be fine. Just fine. You got him here fast.' He put the clipboard down and wiped the lenses on his round wire-rimmed glasses. He was over six foot three, Peggy was pleased to notice. She'd always had more faith in tall men. 'The blood tests have confirmed the ECG's findings. It was definitely a heart attack. We're giving him an intravenous injection of a drug called thrombolytic which in layman's terms is –'

'A clot buster.' Peggy sniffed. She blew her nose with a trumpet roar on the dinner napkin she'd inadvertently swiped from the hotel.

'That's right.' He gave her a gentle smile.

'Matt here is a doctor too and I'm a nursing sister,' she said, her voice determinedly bright. 'Retired now, of course. I volunteered for years at the local hospital but they finally put me out to pasture.'

'Well then, I'm dealing with experts. And I hear your quick response might have saved his life.' He looked over at Matt. 'Well done.'

Silently, Matt nodded in response.

'But what caused it?' Avril asked.

He smiled at her. 'We can't be certain. Heart attacks are due to a number of factors. Obesity, diabetes, smoking . . .' He counted out three fingers.

'He loves his pipe.' Hazel looked stricken, her hand gripping Matt's arm. On his other side Milly was sitting like a statue, tears running down her face.

'Inactivity . . .'

'I've tried to get him to go for walks with me.' Despite her attempt to keep it together, Peggy's face was lined with worry. 'Sometimes I think he's cemented into that old armchair.'

'Is there a history of heart disease in the family?'

'Not that I know of. But then he is a bastard.'

'Mum!' Natalie scolded.

'In the biblical sense, I mean,' Peggy corrected. 'It was a terrible burden, growing up with that in the Hebrides, his own father living on the same island and refusing to acknowledge him. Mind you, he was a drinker too, just like Callum.'

'Quite.' The cardiologist nodded. 'Well, of course alcohol is another strong factor, as is high blood pressure.' He gave a quick glance at his watch and automatically Natalie also looked at the clock on the wall. Eleven thirty. Less than an hour ago they were all writhing under disco lights, bombed out of their minds, and yet she had never felt so sober. From the corner of her eye she saw Matt reach to cover Milly's clasped fingers in a reassuring grasp, his other arm around Hazel's shoulders. He looked like the rock that was keeping them both from being swept away.

'There are many root causes,' the cardiologist was saying. 'Was he under any stress?'

'Yes.' Natalie stood up, shaking. 'It's my fault, isn't it? All the worry of the wedding. And I told him I hated him, didn't want him there. I did this.'

'Oh, get off your box, why don't you!' Milly suddenly also stood up, eyes flashing at Natalie. 'Just for once can something not be all about *you*?'

There was an uncomfortable hush. Abruptly Natalie sat down.

'What now?' Avril asked anxiously.

'We'll need to keep him here while we conduct some tests,' the cardiologist explained as he made another quick scribble on his notepad. 'Depending on the damage to the arteries, he may need bypass grafting or an angioplasty.'

Seeing a question mark on every face but Matt's and Peggy's, he stood up and began drawing a diagram.

'In the angioplasty, we aim to stretch –'

'He's going to be all right then?' Natalie interrupted.

The doctor paused in his drawing and gave her a reassuring smile.

'As I told your mother, he's going to be fine. Just fine.'

Peggy walked into the small waiting room, her face looking ten years older than the day before despite the cheery smile she'd pasted on. She never failed to surprise them, Natalie thought. The woman could dissolve into a puddle over a Disney cartoon but give her a real crisis and she showed a core of steel. It was now three in the morning. For nearly four hours they'd been snatching bits of sleep when they could between cornering nurses at every opportunity to check on Callum's progress.

'He's awake but very weak,' Peggy informed Milly and

Natalie. 'Avril's gone off to search for a doctor again. I'm going to the cafeteria to fetch us all some hot drinks. Can't just sit around twiddling my thumbs.'

'I'll come with you,' Milly offered.

'No, no, stay with Natalie. Just in case there's any news.' And with that she was gone.

'If I'd had any idea I'd spend the night on a row of plastic chairs I would have dressed more appropriately.' Natalie tugged her thin cardigan closer to her, wishing her dress wasn't so short.

'And I would have brought along a pillow.' Milly attempted to lighten the mood as she paced up and down the waiting room. 'We should have stuck them on Mum's list of things to fetch from home. Hazel's bound not to think of it. Do you remember how we used to use our pillows as horses? We'd hang onto the corners and bounce up and down on the beds, pretending to race each other.' She studied a wall poster of a cross-sectioned heart. 'I suppose I should be grateful that my lot are such good sleepers. Actually, Erin's having an intense love affair with her mattress. Most weekends I've more hope of shoving Rory into a suit and tie and finding him a job as a bank manager than coaxing his sister out from under her downie.'

Natalie watched her fidget about the room, picking up magazines, putting them down. She must have dropped two dress sizes at least. Natalie could actually see her cheekbones, her legs had calves and ankles again, and the bulge which had been obstinately growing since her pregnancy with Ben now looked more like a moderate tummy than a python that had swallowed a goat.

'What's your secret, Milly?' she said, admiringly. 'I can't believe how much weight you've lost. It isn't that Atkins diet, is it, because I've heard eating all that protein –'

Milly blushed, staring intently at a seascape on the wall. 'No. Well, I've been walking a lot. And . . . uh, working out . . .'

'Well, good for you. I'm always at the gym and it doesn't seem to –'

'And eating less. Actually, I've been fasting quite a bit.'

'Fasting?' Natalie said, horrified. 'Oh, Milly, you're not going anorexic now, are you? Because I know I told you at the fitting –'

'I said a bit.' Milly looked hounded and a little annoyed. She sat down again, leafing through an ancient copy of *My Weekly*. 'Bet we drove Mum potty with all that bedtime giggling.' She dropped her pretence of reading and went back to reminiscing. 'Remember our spit races down the bedposts? How gross were we? Mum could never understand why the bedhead had all those strange white marks . . .'

Natalie's eyes glazed over as Milly rattled on. It was obvious she didn't want to talk about her weight loss. But then Milly and weight had always been a touchy subject. It was good to see her animated again, though, not like the wet blanket she'd turned into for quite a while there, moping around and feeling sorry for herself.

'You know, it amazes me' – Natalie irritably tossed her curtain of blonde hair, when Milly finally paused for breath – 'how your memories of our Pollyanna childhood are so different from mine. All this walking the Cuillins, fishing for crabs crap. What about the other side – Dad forcing whisky on our teetotal neighbour, humiliating us the one time he showed up for Sports Day, staggering through Little Hooking completely blotto? How about all the times he threatened to hit Mum –'

'Only when she goaded him.' Milly defended her father.

'And it wasn't always threats,' Natalie snapped back. 'I

mean he *did* hit her. More than once. I saw him. Don't you remember her saying, "Look, he smacked me across the room and not even a bruise"? Because I do. And we used to get it too, sometimes. I mean, what about that time he had you by the hair and I called him a bastard and we both ran and locked ourselves in the bathroom? He wasn't always this funny cuddly old drunk everyone makes him out to be. He practically drove Avril away from home . . .'

'You don't know that for sure.' Milly turned her back.

'Oh, don't be so naive. I might have been only five but I was there. He used to call her terrible names and Avril would scream at him from inside her bedroom, and you used to hide under the covers and Mum would –'

'He could be *dying*, Natalie.' Milly was close to tears. 'How can you be so cruel?'

The door swung open.

'Hot chocolate, anyone?' Peggy entered with four cups in a cardboard holder. She looked at their flushed faces. 'What's going on here?'

Natalie recovered first. 'Oh, Milly and I were just talking about old times. Remember that game, Milly, where one of us would start to fall off the top bunk, pretending it was a cliff? And we'd clutch the sheets until the last possible minute and then shout, "Rescue Service! Rescue Service!"'

'And then the other would shout "gardelous" or "action stations" and jump forward to pull them back up.' Milly sounded sullen, playing along for her mother's sake.

'I always thought one of you was killing the other.' Peggy settled into a chair. 'All those screams and laughter and then howls of tears. And when I'd come in brandishing the wooden spoon, the room would be deathly still, except for faint snores.'

'And after you spanked us, you'd come back crying, apologising for being such a bad mother.' Natalie laughed.

'It never made a blind bit of difference to us anyway,' Milly said, remembering her argument with Mrs Hammond. 'That's why I never smack mine. I think it really did hurt you more than it hurt Nat and me.'

'I hope Hazel remembers everything.' Peggy wrapped her old hands around the polystyrene cup of chocolate. 'I should probably have sent you, Natalie.' She noisily sipped her drink. 'Or Avril. Someone responsible. I do wish that girl would settle down. Oh, but she's always been so fussy. What about that boy she chucked purely because he farted in the cinema? I think his name was Martin.'

'That wasn't Avril, that was me.' Natalie scrunched up her nose. 'And too flippin' right, it stank to high heaven.'

'Do you think that nice doctor's married?' Peggy's attempt at her old self faltered as her eyes began to well and her bottom lip quiver. 'Oh girls, what am I going to do without him?'

They rushed to hug her. 'There isn't going to be any "without him",' Natalie said firmly. 'And that's final.'

The nurse bustled around Callum's bedside, tucking in his sheets, checking the drip. The old man's eyes were closed, his skin sallow beneath an oxygen mask. Even expecting it, Avril was alarmed by how ill he looked.

'He's had an intravenous injection of diamorphine and some anti-sickness medicine,' the nurse whispered. 'He insisted on seeing you but don't stay long. He shouldn't be talking at all really.'

'How are you, Dad?' Avril said as the door softly swung shut and her father's eyelids fluttered. 'You gave us quite a scare.'

'Och, not too bad.' She had to lean forward to hear him. 'Like . . . the . . . vicar's egg – good in parts.'

The lump in her throat almost gagged her. 'Everyone's outside, you know. We're all rooting for you.'

'Hazel?'

'She went with Matt to fetch your things.'

'I asked to speak to you . . . because . . .' His breathing was laboured. '. . . Because . . .'

'Don't try to talk.'

'No, you need to tell her . . . please . . . before . . . it's too late.'

'I will. Soon.' Avril gently took his limp veiny hand in hers, being careful not to disturb the gauze holding the drip in place.

'You must . . . Your mother and I . . . we thought we were doing the right thing. You were just a bairn yourself. We wanted to spare you and the wee one . . .' Each word cost an agony of effort, punctuated by painful breaths.

'None of that matters now. Please, don't think about it.'

'Aye. But . . . I don't want to die without . . .' He took another deep breath. 'If you won't tell her . . . then I will . . .'

'You're not going to die.'

'Promise me . . .' Frustrated, his hand fumbled at his mask. 'Promise me.'

'OK.' Avril sighed heavily. 'I promise. Now get some rest.'

She walked down the corridor and stared out the window. Scanning around quickly to check she was alone, she pulled a small bottle of vodka from her handbag and raised it to her lips. God, how she needed that.

It was no use, Milly thought: catnapping on bucket seats was a physical impossibility – at least for her. She looked down at her sleeping mother and sister, both looking distinctly uncomfortable but still managing to get some shut-eye. For a while, hoping to appease her restless legs, she'd walked the entire length of the Coronary Care Unit from the nurses' station to the small snack bar, but here she was back in the waiting room, feeling as fidgety and hopped up as ever. Ivor would have to take the day off work, cancel all those important meetings. If they were that important. She was beginning to have her doubts. She had a nasty little vision of him hiding out in some cosy little café reading the newspaper and waiting for the last train to escape the dreariness of domesticity and child-raising. It was wicked even to imagine it but, really, how long was she supposed to keep on being penniless and patient?

And this was another terrible thought, but if she'd known how her life would pan out, would she have made the same choices? Seeing Matt these past few weeks had woken so many questions, so much imagining of what might have been. If she hadn't met Ivor and dropped out . . . if she hadn't married young . . . if she'd finished uni, got her degree . . . What great career might she be pursuing . . .? What fantastic adventures might have befallen her . . .? What brilliant things might she have done with her life . . .? Who would Milly MacLeod be now?

Hazel and Matt were in her parents' bedroom, bunging items of clothing into a faded leather weekend case.

'Two pairs of pyjamas for Dad.' Hazel was in overdrive, yanking open drawers. 'Not those holey ones. And slippers, he'll need slippers. And a sponge and . . . Should we take a nightie for Mum? They might find her a bed at the hospital, don't they do that sometimes?'

'Come on, Hazel, we need to get back.' Matt came out of the bathroom, carrying toothbrush, denture fix and a rather shorn and overused shaving brush.

'I know, but I don't want to forget anything.'

By the time they'd crammed everything Hazel wanted into the bag, the zip wouldn't shut. They were walking past the living room, when she stopped. 'What about his pipe? Do you think they'll let him have it?'

'I doubt it. Smoking's hardly something they'd encourage for heart patients.'

Hazel went over to Callum's armchair and stood rigid as if mesmerised by the ashtray. When she failed to move, Matt joined her. She turned, throwing her arms around him.

'I'd like to smash it in a million pieces. Oh, Matt . . .' She buried her face in his shirt, breathing in his familiar comforting scent. 'He's always been so strong.'

He smoothed her hair. 'Hush now, it's going to be all right.'

Eyes filling with emotion, she inhaled the faint odour of Ivory soap, feeling his warm body against hers, the hard muscles of his back. For a second they clung to each other, two shipwreck survivors, both struggling in their internal miseries. Then, like a baby reaching for the breast, Hazel stretched up, pulling down his neck, rising on tiptoe to find his lips, desperate to blot out her unhappiness in the best way she knew how.

Gently, Matt unwrapped her arms. 'Hazel,' he said, his voice husky and apologetic, 'that would be a really bad idea.' He slumped onto the sofa, elbows on knees, head in hands, staring miserably into the unlit fireplace.

But bad ideas were Hazel's speciality. She didn't want to think. Didn't want to be sensible. Had never given a hoot about whether she'd respect herself in the morning and never less so than now. Many a dark night of the soul had been alleviated with sex and why should this be any different?

'Maybe it is.' She planted herself in front of him, chest heaving as she stared him down. 'But who gives a stuff. If it makes us feel better. Look, everything's fucked up . . .' Her

221

voice cracked on the words, tears starting and quickly pushed away. 'I bloody *need* this, Matt, don't turn tight-arse on me now.' She sat beside him, turning his head to face her, green eyes dark with pain. 'Remember that creepy story you and Milly used to scare me with when you were babysitting. Where the spooky ghost used to rattle his chains and moan "No one will know . . ."'

'Vaguely.' Matt almost smiled.

'Well,' she said, her hands reaching out, tugging on his belt buckle, 'no one will know.'

Chapter 26

Avril hung up the waiting-room payphone, feeling slightly guilty for calling her long-suffering assistant at five thirty in the morning. Today *would* be the day she had that ridiculously early breakfast meeting with a writer whose mobile number she'd left on her office pad. Still, Brenda was a notoriously early riser, and besides, that's why she was paid the big bucks. Avril's mouth twisted wryly, knowing her assistant could earn much more if – heaven forbid – she ever left.

'I thought Hazel and Matt would be back by now.' She opened her compact and reapplied her lipstick. 'What do you think they're up to? Shagging for England now they've finally got the house to themselves?'

Preoccupied with her own concerns, she failed to notice the expressions that crossed her sisters' faces.

Natalie closed her eyes as she thought of the fool she'd made of herself earlier that night. Jesus! Throwing herself at Matt. Trying to snog him like some rock-star groupie. What a prize idiot! Thank God he pushed her away. She stood up shakily. 'I've got to get some air.'

Out in the corridor there was a sudden animal noise, a cross between a squeal and a wail. Suddenly a young Asian boy, about Fergus's age, ran past. His face was contorted. 'She's dead . . . Granny's dead! Granny's dead!' he cried, as his mother caught up and grabbed him.

All three sisters stared at each other appalled. Abruptly, Natalie stumbled to the doorway and left.

Avril's head was churning as her mind gnawed at the promise she'd made, dreading what lay ahead of her. She and Milly sat lost in their own private thoughts. Each time she heard footsteps in the corridor Avril flinched, expecting Matt and Hazel to burst in.

How would Hazel react? She was so nonchalant, carefree. Nothing ever seemed to get to her. But then why would it? As the baby of the family, she'd always been pampered and protected. As an adult, she leapt insouciantly from one adventure to another, never stopping to consider the hearts she might be trampling on or the consequences of a misjudged word or deed. The few times she was called to judgement, she felt terrible, of course, but her sincerely felt remorse was soon overshadowed by the next big thing.

And she, Avril, was worse. Not an accidental force of nature like Hazel, who was unthinking as a hurricane, but callous and calculating and heedless of other people's pain. She'd developed this impenetrable skin that had served her well in business but allowed her to wreak havoc in other people's personal lives. Now she couldn't stop the jabbing of a suddenly born-again conscience. All her guilty crimes were reappearing like Scrooge's ghosts – bitter phone calls, excruciating encounters with tearful or angry wives, the humiliating experience of being caught in the wrong bed at the wrong time – choosing this long scary vigil to march in circles through her brain. She'd been hurt early in life, betrayed, shat upon – but how had that given her the right to destroy other people's happiness?

She had to stop thinking about this. She had to stop thinking of Hazel. Of Richard. Of the past. It would drive her crazy.

'Dad looked awful,' she blurted out and sank abruptly back into silence. Flicking through a magazine, unable to take in a word she read, Milly didn't respond.

Half an hour later the door swung open. Avril held her breath and expelled it sharply as she recognised Richard. He appeared quite crumpled, as if he'd thrown on his clothes in a hurry. Black jeans, shirt only half tucked in and wrongly buttoned so that his skin peeked through a gap. His eyes were fixed on Avril, full of concern.

'What are you doing here?' She stood up. 'How did you find me?'

She was aware of Milly beside her staring at the intruder with a sudden return to alertness.

'Brenda called me. Told me what's going on. Oh, baby.' He held his arms out wide and took a step towards her. 'I'm so sorry about your father.'

Avril found herself doing something she'd not done since she was fifteen years old when the bottom had dropped out of her entire world. She fell into his arms, sobbing like a child.

Natalie sat on a stone wall by the car park, fighting back tears, when her phone started ringing.

'Jeremy. Thank God.' She clutched the mobile to her ear. 'Where on earth have you been? I've been trying to call you all night. Didn't you get my texts?'

'Yes, well.' His laugh sounded drunken. 'T'sh my stag do, honeychops. Left my phone in the room. Can't eshpect to keep me on a ball and chain, y'know. Not 'fore the wedding at least.'

'But I called the hotel. I left at least ten messages telling them it was urgent.'

'Everything's urgent with you, old girl.' Jeremy laughed again. ''Sides, I'm calling now. So whass'up? Not lost the cake, have we?'

'No we haven't lost the cake.' Quickly she explained the events of the night.

'Oh, poor devil. Well, you always knew his ticker wasn't up to snuff. Sure all that bloody drinking didn't help either. Is he OK?'

'No he's not OK, he's had a bloody heart attack!'

In the background, Natalie could hear male voices, loud raucous jeering.

'Where the hell are you? It's six in the morning.'

'We've been clubbing it, honeylamb. Playing poker now. Last shot of freedom, you know. Oooh, oh . . . Hold on a sec . . . Brandy's over there. Deal me in, OK? Where are you? I'll call you back.'

'I'm at the fucking hospital, where do you think?' She gripped the phone tight, wishing it were a rock she could whack against his dense skull.

'No need to use language like that. I know it must be upsetting . . . yesh, hang on, Piers. I'll be right along. Jush talking to my future bride here.'

'So are you coming back?'

'What'cha mean, coming back? Henry's got us all going salmon fishing on his eshtate. 'S going to be Laird of Balmucky one day, own half of bloody Scotland. Might wangle us an invite for grouse shooting, get to meet Bonnie Prince Charlie. Can't dishappoint everyone, you know. Not after dragging them all this way. Shhtill, be home t'morrow. If . . . don't looosh my plane ticket with my dashed shirt . . .'

'But my father's seriously ill!'

His voice faded in and out as if he kept forgetting to hold the phone to his mouth.

'C'mon, poopsy, can't be as bad as all that. Got your sisters with you, haven't you?'

'Yes, but –'

'Good-oh. They'll take care of you. Nothing like family, you know. Beshides, there's thirty chaps here who've cost my parents a shedload of . . .'

Natalie pressed the end-call key. She didn't want to hear any more. 'But you're meant to be my family too . . .' she spoke softly to herself, pulling her cardigan closer to her as she curled into a tight ball.

'Oh, there you are.'

Natalie looked up to see Avril standing over her, a tall good-looking man at her side. She recognised his beaky nose from the *Sunday Times* photograph. 'Richard, Nat. Nat, Richard.' Avril made cursory introductions. 'Look, we need to make some decisions.'

'Decisions?' Natalie blinked. 'What decisions?'

'It's Thursday morning, sweetie, and your wedding's on Saturday,' Avril said gently. 'We have to decide what to do. Hopefully Dad will perk up and be home by then or . . .' She paused while she took in her younger sister's appearance. Red-rimmed eyes accentuating her oh-so-pale face, the make-up she'd so carefully reapplied at her hen party now washed off again. 'You might prefer to postpone, in which case someone has to contact all the wedding guests . . .'

Natalie's lips trembled. 'What would you do?'

'Me?' Avril almost laughed as she swapped a look with Richard. 'Darling, you know me, highly allergic to altars. In your shoes I'd be fleeing to the airport with a one-way ticket to Kuala Lumpur. It's your call but . . . if you do go ahead, well, I know Dad'll be sorry not to give you away.'

'Give me away . . . ?' Natalie shook her head at the irony.

To think she'd wanted to exclude her father from the wedding. To think she'd wished her father dead. Of all the prayers to be answered.

Avril touched her arm. 'I don't want to hurry you, but we need to know. Maybe you should get hold of Jeremy.'

Natalie rose to her feet, brushing the dirt off her dress.

'Don't worry,' she said curtly. 'I've made my decision.'

'I told you, you don't have to drive me. I could easily catch a cab.'

'I won't hear of it.' Richard held the passenger door open, waiting for Avril to slide in but at the last minute she baulked.

'No, this is wrong.' She was shaking violently, feet rooted to the car-park cement. 'I shouldn't leave Dad. What if something happens?' The veneer of self-control she'd maintained for Natalie suddenly cracked.

'Nonsense.' He hugged her shoulders, reassuringly. 'You look done in, Avril. You ought to get some rest. It won't do anyone any good if you collapse. Milly will ring if there's any news and then you can relieve her.'

'But Hazel, it's important I talk to Hazel.'

'I'll have you back here in a couple of hours. Or call her on the mobile. Then I'll take you to your sister's flat, we'll get her wedding folder and we can start making calls back at the hospital.'

Her head lolled against the headrest as she tilted back the seat. 'God, I'm knackered. If I could only shut my eyes.'

'Come on. My place. It's nearest.'

'No, mine. I need a change of clothes, check my messages, call the office . . .'

'That can wait too. What you need now is sleep. And food. I know you, Avril. You won't get either if I leave you on your own.'

She was too tired to argue. She watched his profile as he wound his way expertly through the narrow streets towards Edwardes Square, his eyes flickering over to her, alight with concern.

How dear he was, Avril thought as she gave in to his caring commands. And how much she'd missed him.

She ought to be furious with Brenda for interfering but all she could feel was relief. Was this what it was all about? Having someone to back you up, stand beside you when the polar ice caps were melting and a tidal wave was heading in your direction. For so long she'd dared depend only on herself. But now she was exhausted. And then suddenly she just had to tell him.

The words came out awkwardly at first. Stammering. And then as his hand reached over to grip hers, they started to flow. She told him of how she used to worship her father, of the shock when she'd discovered his drinking and violent outbursts, and how quickly he'd fallen off the pedestal she'd put him on. She told him of daily fights, power struggles over homework, pop music, clothes and his refusal to let her date. She'd thought him a hypocrite, preaching at her, trying to run her life, when really he was just a bloody old soak. And then she'd met this boy . . .

She hesitated, not sure if she wanted to go on, but Richard's grasp tightened and she continued. 'And then . . . I found out I was pregnant. I was so frightened.' Her mind flashed back to an image of her parents' disappointed faces, the deathly silence that had greeted her announcement, interrupted only by the ticking of the large grandfather clock. And then the yelling, the recriminations.

'Mum wanted me to have an abortion – for my sake, she said. But Dad wouldn't hear of it and was suggesting adoption instead. Religious reasons, I'm sure, but maybe partly because he was illegitimate himself. Not that we were ever supposed to talk about that.' She looked out the window, staring unseeingly at early-morning commuters lining up at a bus stop. 'Anyway, I wanted to keep the baby. But both my parents kept telling me how dire my life would be. Said I was too young for that responsibility, I'd be missing out on so much, staying home at night, changing nappies and enduring two o'clock feeds while my friends were at parties, having fun. Have to say' – she gave a hollow laugh – 'they were probably right. Not that I cared about that at the time.'

'What about the father? What did he think?' Richard kept his voice neutral, his eyes on the road, as if knowing that the slightest hint of sympathy would unhinge her.

'He didn't want any part of it. Well, can you blame him? He was only seventeen. I thought he was so mature, a rebel, but he was just another confused kid. Into drinking beer and raising Cain not kids. Anyway it wasn't like I had a lot of choices. So it was decided I should have the baby in secret and find it a really nice home. Which we did. One fairly close to us as it happens.'

There was something in the way she'd said it that made Richard glance at her, seeing her clenched knuckles, the bitterness around the mouth. 'Hazel?' he guessed, then jerked his attention back to the road as a taxicab blared its horn and swerved.

'She doesn't know, Richard. I've never been able to tell her. I mean, when's the right time? I used to try and convince myself that when I was older, once I was earning enough money, then I'd be her mother again. But when we were all home, with everyone cooing over *Mum's* new arrival, I couldn't stand it, not even for her. We moved to Little Hooking right away, thinking it would help "the secret", but if anything it made things worse. We were all conspirators in this big lie and I hated it and my parents. They were hot on me finishing my education but instead I split. My first decent job was in the States and I couldn't take Hazel there. Who would have looked after her when I was working?'

A deep sigh escaped out of her like air rushing out of a balloon. 'When I came back I was her big sister, Avril. She adored Mum and Dad. And every year it got harder to say anything. I had my life, she had hers. Why rock the boat? What difference did it make?' She finished just as Richard turned into a square of elegant houses and pulled up to the kerb.

'It made a difference to you,' he said in almost a whisper and pulled her to his shoulder. She found herself melting into his strong arms.

'Maybe I was too selfish,' she started. 'My career . . .'

'Shhh . . . It's OK . . .' And then he was kissing her, full of solid reassurance and tenderness and the words died in her mouth.

Chapter 27

'I can't believe this.' Hazel shifted gear back to second and eased off on the accelerator. For the third time in the last half-hour the traffic almost came to a standstill.

Matt twiddled with the radio trying to tune it into a traffic station.

Hazel shuddered as they went past an array of emergency vehicles and two crashed cars. Well, she certainly didn't want to look. Someone there, either inside that mangled car or in the ambulance that she could hear in the distance, had just had their whole life disrupted. One minute they were driving to work or something, and the next . . . Tragedy, grief, shock.

She felt like she and Matt had been gone for days. There'd been the taxi ride down there, then she'd had a rest and drunk gallons of black coffee wanting to be sure that it was safe for her to drive Callum's car back, grateful that she'd only been drinking at the meal. But when Matt had woken her they hadn't been able to get an answer at the hospital. What was happening with her dad? Jesus, the journey back was taking forever.

'What time is it?' she asked as the traffic finally came to a halt.

'Five minutes after you last asked.' He seemed lost in thought, distracted.

Roadworks, gridlocks and now a complete standstill because of the accident. None of it helped by the new awkwardness in the car. Punishment, she supposed, for her behaviour back at the house. Or was it just her being awkward? Suddenly she couldn't read Matt at all.

Had she ever been turned down before? On top of the anxiety about her father that was tying her stomach in knots and making her drum her fingers on the steering wheel, she felt the searing welt of Matt's rejection. Gone was their easy rapport. Attempts at conversation or Hazel's feeble jokes had landed as leadenly as one of Richard Branson's balloons.

She scrutinised Matt's enigmatic expression as intently as a stage magician hoping to read minds. He seemed engrossed in the sight of bumper-to-bumper cars and concrete. His eyes, what little she could see of them, were faraway and morose – not that they didn't all have good reason to be depressed. Feeling her gaze, he looked at her and as quickly looked away.

It came to her like Moses tripping over the burning bush or a computer hacker finding the secret code.

'You sneaky bastard,' she whooped suddenly. 'You're hiding something. It's a woman, isn't it? You've got a girlfriend.'

Matt's eyes flickered with surprise as he glanced back at her. He crossed his arms and gave her a deadpan stare. 'No,' he denied flatly.

'You have, you have, you have,' Hazel chanted excitedly, her miffed ego forgotten. 'Matt is in lo-ove. Who is it? You might as well spill the beans. I always know when anyone's lying. It's a curse.'

'Well, this time your curse let you down.'

'Is it someone in Scotland? Ecuador? England? Wait, is this the reason you've been taking off every morning?'

He crossed his legs and she sensed she'd scored a hit.

'Come on,' she urged, 'I promise I won't tell anyone.' In mockery of her defeated seduction effort, she jabbed her finger in his ribs and crooned again, '*No one will know . . .*'

Richard backed into the bedroom, a laden tray in his hands as Avril emerged from his bathroom, hair wet, dressed in a too-large pyjama top that clung to her still damp skin.

She plucked the cream collar with her manicured finger.

'Silk,' she observed. 'How sweet. I didn't know men still wore these.'

'Actually, they were a present from my mother. Though they never looked as good on me as they do on you. Here, we have orange juice, croissants and coffee. Hope that serves madam well.' With a flourish he put the tray on the bedside table.

Avril sat on the edge of the bed and winced as she towelled her hair. 'There isn't a brandy or whisky hidden on that tray, is there? My brain feels like it's being crushed by a combine harvester.'

'I guessed as much.' Richard took the towel and gently began rubbing her head. 'That's why you'll notice two aspirin to the right of the single-stem rose.'

'Is sir for real?' Avril swallowed the tablets in a gulp of orange juice. 'Where did you find all this?'

'Avril.' He dropped the towel over her hair, laughing. 'I have a fridge full of food out there. It's not such a novel concept. I could rustle you up bacon and eggs if you want. I might even have some leftover coq au vin.'

'Impressive.' She tore off a piece of croissant realising she was starving. 'And the rose?'

'I always aim to have a dozen or so on hand,' Richard said solemnly, as he ran his fingers down her neck sending shivers through her. 'One for each girl I lure to my bachelor lair.'

'Really?' She swung her legs up and moved the tray to her lap. 'And how's that working out?'

'Kind of lonely actually.' He sat on the edge of the bed and she moved to make room for him. 'I haven't had time to unpack most of my things. Almost everything you see here is part of the rental furnishings, bar a few of my pictures. The flowers cheer things up, make it seem more like home.'

Did his wife buy flowers, she wondered, and keep their house immaculate? Now that she paid attention, the bedroom looked neat but impersonal with nothing on the other bedside table but an art deco lamp. Granted the flat was extremely classy, but kitchen apart, it still had the transient atmosphere of a hotel.

'You should get some sleep,' Richard suggested. 'It's quarter to seven. And maybe call Milly, give her the number here?'

Usually she'd have bristled, perceiving this as bossiness. Instead, meekly, she did as he suggested.

'Everything's stable, apparently,' she said when she put the phone down. 'It's such a cliché – they're really not giving anything away, are they? But better than "a turn for the worse", I suppose.'

'My uncle had an angioplasty last year,' Richard said. 'He watched it all on a monitor. Said it was better than an episode of *The Sopranos*. Do you want me to tuck you in?'

'So decadent' – she relinquished her tray – 'being waited on. I could get used to this, you know . . .'

'Perhaps we should save that for a future discussion.' He leaned forward and gently kissed her lips. She wriggled happily under the sheets as he disappeared into the kitchen. For once his mention of the future hadn't completely freaked her out. Maybe it *could* work. If she could learn not to be so set in her ways. For a second a fantasy popped up of them sharing a big open-plan flat with shiny wooden floors and she and Richard at the piano dressed in white suits and singing duets. Where did that come from? Oh yes, she realised suddenly, the 'Imagine' video. John and Yoko. How ridiculously corny. But yet, appealing all the same.

When he came back in, she grabbed his hand, pulling him to lie on the bed beside her, his front against her back like spoons. She was already drifting away.

'Maybe this'll turn out to be a good thing for Dad. You know, the wake-up call he needed to get his bloody act together,' she said drowsily, as her eyes closed of their own volition. 'Mum'll have her hands full when he comes home. Doctors make horrible patients. Perhaps one day you could meet them both . . .'

'I'd love to.' He wrapped his arm over her shoulders. 'And perhaps you can meet my daughter. She'd like that very much.'

'You've told her about me?'

'I have, yes.'

Another small buzz of pleasure ran through her. 'You're so kind, Richard. I'm sorry, I didn't mean . . . at the restaurant . . . It was just a shock . . . your wife . . .'

'I know. It was my fault, springing it on you like that. Don't say any more.'

'Just half an hour then. Promise you'll wake me.'

And then she was asleep.

'Ivor? It's me.' Milly dropped her aching body on a bench, dedicated to 'John and Freda, who loved the view'. Well, maybe they did once, she thought, pressing her hand to her head, but she'd bet the entire contents of the hospital cafeteria, they wouldn't be impressed with the hideous new estate that was facing her now. Her mouth felt sandpaper-dry as the buildings whirled dizzily before her eyes. She grabbed the bench to steady herself.

'How's everything?' she said, forcing herself to focus. 'Kids all right?'

'Terrific. I put Ben to bed at twenty past nine and he slept all the way through. There was a bit of a fuss around supper time but we both survived. How's your dad?'

'Hanging in there. We should know more this morning but they think he'll come out of this OK.' Now she recognised the background noise that was nagging at her consciousness, a persistent wailing, all too familiar. 'Why's Ben crying?'

'I don't know. I've tried feeding him his formula but he's just being fussy. Don't worry about it.'

An irrational rush of irritation coursed through her jangling nerves.

If he was ever around to help out then perhaps, when emergencies hit, she wouldn't feel that she'd abandoned her brood with a space oddity from a galaxy far, far away. She wouldn't put it past his boffin brain to leave poor helpless Ben out on the front doorstep with the milk bottles.

'The instructions are on the tin,' she said, fighting back waves of nausea. 'Flat scoops, remember?'

'I know. I can read. Really, everything's great.'

Apparently his definition of great included the sound of a whopping loud crash and a barrage of name-calling. 'You bumhole, Rory! Now it's broken!' and 'You're the bumhole, bumhole.' She felt strangely distant from it all, floating somewhere above the bench as she listened to her household fall apart.

Good, she mused with uncharacteristic viciousness. Give him a taste of her daily existence. The boys fighting all over the house, Ben screaming, Erin stomping around like an evil harpy. But all of a sudden her stomach was churning and she was dying for the loo. What on earth was wrong with her? She hadn't weed this much in her entire four pregnancies.

'I've got to run. Don't let Erin leave the house without breakfast.'

'Too late. She's already gone. Wouldn't even down a slice of toast.'

'This early? It's barely seven thirty.' She was jigging on the balls of her feet now, doing Rory's wee-wee dance. She hurriedly started to jog towards the hospital entrance, hoping she'd make it without the humiliation of wetting her knickers.

'Some geography project apparently. Shall I bring Ben up?'

'No, no.' Milly shuddered, as she pushed at the toilet door. 'This is no place for babies. I'll call you later, OK.'

Afterwards, as she washed her hands, she looked up and caught her face in the mirror. Thinner, for sure – and not surprising with these recent bouts of diarrhoea. But her hair looked straggly and the skin of her face and neck had a weird red flush. Anyway, it was worth it, wasn't it? A few niggling side effects against her entire future happiness? When she was closer to her target weight, in a week or two, she'd drop the dose.

But in the meantime she had to muster all her dwindling reserves to get back into that waiting room. Shakily, her fingers fumbled for the plastic cylinder in her handbag. She tipped two pills into her hot moist palm and stared at them for a moment. So tiny, so innocuous-looking. Scooping a handful of water from the running tap, she knocked them back.

Chapter 28

Natalie patted her veil to make sure it was sitting right. Her make-up was subtle yet classy, her hair piled high in ringlets. The gown a festoon of crystal embroidery and cream silk. Gayle Cutting came forward and stooped at her feet to make a few minor adjustments.

She glanced ahead at the church pews, their ends tastefully bedecked with cream roses on a background of plum card. All the relatives were there. Uncle Ted, Auntie Susan, cousins, nephews and friends from afar. Her father held tightly to her arm, no hint of drink, while her mother was smiling warmly in her smart new powder-blue suit. Finally! She caught Avril's eye and tried not to let her expression become too smug.

Reverend Chatham smiled brightly and gave a nod to the organist. She paused at the doorway lapping up the admiring glances all round. Callum gave her hand a couple of comforting pats as they paced forward in perfect time to the music.

But wait! Something was pulling her back, stopping her. She turned and realised the problem immediately. Fergus had tripped on her train and his weight was pulling her down. A large tear ripped down the back, exposing her new satin thong and matching suspenders for everyone behind her to see. A murmur began, she heard someone snigger and then jeering, louder and louder. She looked down the narrow aisle. The top lip of Jeremy's smiling mouth unexpectedly reared up and quivered hideously and then he was laughing, slapping his thigh, the loudest of all . . .

'Nat.' Milly rushed towards her brandishing a horse blanket. 'Nat . . . Nat . . .'

'You can't put that monstrosity next to my dress!' Natalie started back in horror.

But now Milly was holding a bridle, forcing the grass-stained metal bit towards Natalie's teeth.

'Nat! Nat!' Milly shook her sister. 'Wake up.'

'Oh my. Oh my . . .' Natalie rubbed at her eyes as she tried to clear her mind of the nightmare. 'What's going on?'

'Dad wants to see you.'

'Me? What about Hazel? Or Avril?'

'Neither of them are back yet. I've been in with Dad and he asked for you.'

The brightness of her eyes, the hint of agitation, struck Natalie with sudden fear. 'I . . .' She shook her head. 'Last time we spoke I was so horrid. I said such terrible things.'

Milly put her arms around her. 'Don't be so silly. He wants to see you, Nats. Go on, you dopey mare – get in there.'

It took a minute, emerging from a deep slumber, for Avril to realise where she was. Her head on Richard's shoulder, her face pressed into the silver hairs on his chest. Had they really gone to sleep like that? It was one of the mysteries about relationships she'd never understood – the supposed appeal of spending the night together. Was it the agony of your neck propped uncomfortably on someone's rock-hard arm? Or finding him lying under yours, sending it from numb to such excruciating torment that you were ready to hack at your shoulder just to break free?

And yet here she was, glued to Richard like a Siamese twin,

and from the sticking sensation when she prised free her face, she'd been like that for a considerable length of time. Chalk that up to another first. For once she'd actually slept – instead of lying awake, secretly calculating the exact moment she could decently kick her lover out or grab her own clothes and bolt.

He looked sexy when he was asleep, his long mouth so curved and sensuous that she just had to lean in and kiss his lips. He opened his eyes and then closed them again, pulling her into him. Then swiftly they were making love, only with a depth and tenderness to their passion she'd never felt before. Every touch of his fingers seemed to send fire blazing through her skin; if this was heaven, maybe she'd take up religion . . .

'Watch out!' Braced with one hand on the strap above the door, the other on the dashboard, Matt had never felt so close to death or regretted so deeply his inability to drive. 'It's not going to help your dad if you smash us both into the back of a lorry.'

They'd crossed the Surrey–Sussex border and were on the dual carriageway. Hazel was driving like a maniac, swapping from one lane to the other, foot jammed on the accelerator. Nearing their destination after all the delays she was in no mind to pay attention to the reprimanding flash of speed cameras. A sense of foreboding was almost suffocating her. Never had the trip from Little Hooking to town seemed to take so long. That damned accident. It had held them up for hours.

With relief she finally saw the sign for the hospital. She swung into the car park, screeched to a halt in the first available space and tugged on the handbrake.

'Here. Pay and Display's over there.' She chucked Matt the keys. 'Do you mind? I want to see Dad.' Grateful she'd taken the time to change into jeans and trainers at home, she began running, through the Accident and Emergency entrance, up two flights of stairs, throwing open doors, barging past visitors and staff.

'Nee Nee . . . your wedding . . .' Callum smiled weakly, the words a struggle between ragged breaths.

Natalie's eyes filled with tears. She wanted to fall into his arms but he looked too frail.

Her father's fingers tightened on hers, his eyes half closed. Only this time it wasn't his usual alcoholic stupor. Natalie's gut twisted, remembering her last angry words to him.

'I'm sorry . . .' he rasped. 'I've been . . . a fool . . . I wanted . . .'

'No, I'm the one who should apologise. Daddy, I didn't mean . . . Daddy? Daddy?' She watched as his eyes started flickering. Seconds later the green line went flat and the apparatus behind him started beeping.

As often as she'd seen it in all those television dramas, it took a second to realise what was going on. 'Doctor!' she yelled. 'Doctor! Help! Help!'

Two nurses burst through the door.

'Crash!' one said startled.

'Crash!' the other shouted.

'Crash!'

Avril was falling into space, tumbling into a world where everything was warm and dark and infinite, unsure whether she was crying out or laughing in ecstasy, when the bedside phone rang. Returning to earth, she realised her own mobile was tinnily playing 'Toreador'.

Richard rolled off her, reaching for his phone as she grabbed hers.

'Hello? Yes, Mrs MacLeod, she's right here, she just picked up the other phone. Hang on a sec.'

Mobile to her ear, Avril's face was drained of colour. 'He did? When? Natalie, stop crying, I can't hear a thing. Look, Mum's on the other line, let me talk to her.'

Richard handed her the receiver, sliding his arm to her shoulder, but she threw it off.

'Oh, Mum.' Her head hunched into her shoulders as she huddled on the side of the bed, her face crumpling. 'I'm so, so sorry . . .' There was a long pause, when Richard could visibly see Avril falter, pull back her shoulders and shake off the impending tears. 'Milly fainted? She's all right, isn't she? Is Hazel back yet? Look, I'm leaving here right away.'

She hung up, shaking. 'He's dead. My father's dead.'

Kneeling beside her on the bed, Richard thought she'd never looked so beautiful, her dark hair tumbling down her back, her cheeks stained with grief.

'I'll drive you,' he said, reaching out to comfort her.

'No!' Violently she turned and pushed him away. 'Don't you think you've done enough!'

'Avril . . .'

'I knew I shouldn't have left. Why didn't I listen to myself . . .?' She was gathering her clothes with trembling hands, pulling on her underwear, struggling into her skirt. 'My father's dying in some hospital bed and here I am – fucking!' She spat out the word in fury. 'Some daughter I am.'

'Don't do this, Avril.' He tried to sound calm but he realised his heart was beating thunderously. 'Look, I want to help . . .'

'Well, you can't.' Her face was a closed shutter, barring all intruders.

'This isn't your fault, you know.' He stepped on his shirt, discarded earlier on the carpet, and hastily scrambled into it.

'There's nothing to feel guilty about. You needed rest . . .' He grabbed her arm, hoping to slow her angry exit and make her listen to sense but again she wrenched free.

'Rest!' she said bitterly.

'Yes, rest.' Richard realised his hands were also shaking as he let them drop. It was a phenomenon new to him, the red-hot business tycoon who always had control. He wanted a whisky, desperately. 'Look, I understand why you're upset. But don't let this lousy rotten timing spoil what –'

'Why do men always make everything that happens all about *them*?' Steam was almost shooting from Avril's ears, as she shoved her feet in her shoes. She didn't care if she was being fair or not. 'My father's dead, you egotistical prick. And instead of being with him, carrying out his last dying wish, I'm swanning around with you, screwing my brains out. How do you think that makes me feel?'

He rubbed his hand through his tousled hair, staring at her, his shirt unbuttoned, bare feet emerging from the silk bottoms that matched the pyjama top she'd thrown off, knowing that whatever answer he gave would be wrong.

'I guess I have no idea,' he said sombrely, no longer trying to protest or touch her. She was fully dressed now, grabbing her bag from the table, dropping the mobile inside.

'I'll never forgive myself, don't you understand?' Her hair was wild as if every inch of her was throwing off electrical sparks. 'And every time I look at you I'll remember – oh, forget it.' She whirled on her high heels. 'I'll grab a taxi in the street.'

He caught up with her at the door, putting his hand on it to block her momentarily.

'If there's anything . . .' His eyes looked tortured, full of sympathy, dark with pain. 'If you need . . . anything . . . anything whatsoever, call me, OK? I'd be happy to –'

'You're just not getting it, are you?' she said nastily. 'Let's see if I can state this simply – in less than one syllable.' The door slammed behind her with a resounding crash.

Natalie and Peggy were fussing over Milly, Peggy trying to make her drink a glass of water, Natalie wiping her brow with a damp towel when she looked up and spotted the cardiologist walking past, surrounded by a gaggle of students.

An inhuman fury coursed through Natalie as she raced over to him. 'So there are you, Doctor He'll-be-just-fine . . .' Her eyes were blazing, hands at her waist like a fishwife. 'Well, he wasn't fine, was he? He wasn't bloody fucking fine!'

'Cheer up, love.' The cab driver glanced at Avril in the mirror. 'It might never happen.'

Her withering glare made him shudder and turn the radio volume to blasting.

Without a word he pulled into a parking space in front of Natalie's flat.

'Wait here, I won't be a moment.' She rushed up the steps, unaware of the reversed V sign he gave to her departing back.

Now where the fuck would Natalie have left that folder? Under her pillow, probably, so she could make notes in the wee small hours of the exact shade of ribbon for the basket that would hold little paper hand towels in the downstairs loo. Only with that mammoth file, it'd be like shoving your pillow on a microwave oven. How do you know Nat's wedding file's under your bed? Because your nose is touching the ceiling.

She moved quickly from kitchen to living room to bedroom, noticing that Natalie kept things scarily neat. They'd all been horribly messy as children. She remembered her father telling her once as she sat sulking over her boiled mackerel dinner, 'I went into your room today, Avril, and it made me weep. Physically weep. It's a terrible thing, you know, to make a grown man cry.' And what had been Avril's smart response? 'Well, don't go in there then.' She'd have been sent from the table for that one if they hadn't been in the middle of one of their endless feuds about her not leaving until she'd finished everything on her plate. She'd seen that same fish for breakfast and lunch the next day until her mum had taken pity and dropped it in the rubbish bin, accidentally on purpose.

The taxi horn blared outside, adding to her sense of haste. She pulled open the fitted wardrobe door, noticing a huge box. Could it be in there? Tugging on it, the entire thing fell out and split open, scattering the contents across the floor. Photos, odd mementos – a badge from the Edinburgh private girls' primary school Milly and Natalie had attended, which, like Harry Potter's Hogwarts, still believed in the 'house' system. A Bible she'd won at Sunday school for top attendance during her brief religious phase. Her Brownie wings. A photo that looked like Natalie and Matt sitting in a wigwam in the back garden – probably never made the albums because Natalie thought it made her look undignified or something.

Quickly Avril started shoving everything back. A piece of paper caught her eye. Oh God, this was so Natalie.

A List of Future Goals By Natalie MacLeod (aged 13)
1. Marry a wealthy man.
2. Big white wedding like the kind in magazines, with lots of photographers taking pictures.
3. Always look gracious and sofisticated like Grace Kelly or Pam Ewing.
4. Have a nice house with a swimming pool and flowers in vases and a maid to come in every day.
5. Have lots of famous friends, especially Simon le Bon and Princess Di.

6. Have two children, a boy and a girl.
7. Go to Oxford or Cambridge and have everyone amazed at how smart I am.

8, 9 and 10 were blank. Probably hadn't been able to think of anything else. Creative writing had never been Natalie's strong suit. Avril rocked back on her knees, feeling unexpectedly sorry for her sister. Number 1: postponed. Number 2: ditto. Number 7? Well, the university thing hadn't happened and nor, to date, had numbers 4 and 5 although Natalie did a decent job at looking 'sofisticated'. Number 6: well, how exactly was Natalie planning to arrange the sexes? Sperm selection? Wouldn't put it past her.

She was just about to close the lid and put the box back when she realised something had fallen further into the wardrobe. Reaching out her hand, she tugged out a shoebox and a ribbon-wrapped bundle of letters. Glancing at the return address, she gave a gasp.

'Natalie,' she said. 'Oh, Natalie . . . How could you?'

Chapter 29

'Oh, hi, Milly . . . Yeah, we're about to head off to choose the coffin.' Hazel tucked the phone under her chin, making faces at herself in the hall mirror. 'Nat's concerned if Mum gets her way, Dad'll meet his Maker in cedar-coloured cardboard. She told her that she and Avril were paying for it, but you know Mum, hates anyone wasting money.'

'I'd chip in but . . .'

'Yeah, brasso like me. Don't worry, you know Av's loaded. All those canny investments she's been buying into for years. And Natalie's insisting on putting some of her honeymoon spending money in there.'

'Poor Nat,' Milly said. 'She's still feeling guilty about that fight with Dad.'

'I know. But if it makes her feel better and it gives Dad a good send-off . . .' At the hospital Hazel had looked stunned, white-faced, staring away from them up at the ceiling or at the blank wall whenever tears threatened. She wasn't the type to flaunt grief publicly, even with her own family. Milly could sense her cheeriness now was just for show. 'So what's your vote?' Hazel continued. 'Got any special requests?'

'Hearse pulled by six plume-decorated black stallions?' Milly tried to match Hazel's upbeat tone although she herself had been crying almost every minute since the death. Part of her just couldn't believe it, but the part that did was devastated, wanting only to bury herself under the bedcovers and seek oblivion in sleep. Needless to say, with it taking all the effort she could summon to do the minimum of tasks required, the house had quickly reverted to a disaster zone.

'Can you imagine? Nat would have a cow if some over-dressed nag let out a steaming pile of dollop. Mum'd be pleased though. Remember how she'd rush out with the shovel whenever one of the Pheasant Farm horses disgraced themselves?'

'How's she holding up?' Milly asked in a hushed voice.

'Surprisingly chipper.' Hazel lowered hers to match. 'Although she has her moments when she thinks no one's around. And Nat's taking it really well, considering she's had to cancel her wedding.'

'She must be gutted.'

'Yeah, although arranging the funeral's kinda taking her mind off things.' Oh how Hazel wondered at Natalie's ability to compartmentalise. Give her a job to do and she seemed able to block everything else from her mind. Dad's death. Her wrecked marriage plans. Either event devastating in itself but after her initial meltdown at the hospital, Natalie had sprung back into remarkable sangfroid. Or perhaps, Hazel surmised, she had the type of myopic brain that filtered only the task in hand: writing the obituary notice, filing the death certificate, setting up their appointment with the undertakers.

Avril was a dynamo too, though there'd been even more frenzy than usual in the manic way she launched into marathon telephone sessions. Ninety-five guests and Avril had personally contacted more than half of them, informed them the wedding was off, gave them the funeral details instead and whisked back to the office, but not before allotting lists of names and responsibilities to her siblings and even Matt.

249

Everyone breathed a little easier when she was gone. Certainly she was a huge help and you could see the ruthless efficiency that had led to her big success but she vibrated like a high-tension electricity power line in the seconds before it snaps. Definitely not comfortable to be around.

'Is it terrible I'm not there helping?' Milly sounded tearful. 'Only I've got the most blinding headache.'

'Nah. There's going to be four of us on the case as it is and you've got the kids to look after anyway. Oh, I must tell you what happened yesterday, it's hilarious. Nat and Mum were at the Births, Marriages and Deaths place when Mum had to fill in her details on this form, and you'll never guess what?'

'She forgot her address? I suppose she has been having a bit of trouble with –'

'No,' Hazel cut in. 'She's been lying about her age. All the time she's been saying she's seventy-six, when she's really seventy-eight! Can you believe it?'

'But why?'

'God knows. We've been teasing her about it all morning. Listen, I'd better go. Mum's waiting in the car in her best Sunday hat, humming "It's a Long Way to Tipperary".'

'Tell her to change it to "Danny Boy", it's a lot more appropriate,' Milly managed to joke.

'I will. See ya.'

'And now' – steepling his fingers, Mr Hodgkins, the funeral director surveyed them sombrely like Count Dracula leading a group counselling session – 'we come to perhaps the most important decision. The choice of caskets.' He pushed a colour-photo laminate page at them, lowering his tone to a reverential hush that heralded big money. 'Many of our sorrowing bereaved feel that this is their last chance to show –'

'Well, I was wondering,' Peggy interrupted. 'Could we freeze-dry him?'

'Mum!' Natalie choked on her glass on water, an image popping into her head of a jar of Nescafé freeze-dried coffee granules with her father's head sticking out. 'Be serious.'

'You don't mean . . . uh, cremation?' Mr Hodgkins blinked, and tugged at the cuffs of his black suit. 'Because we already discussed –'

'Not cremation,' Peggy said impatiently, 'promession. Look.' She pulled out a folded newspaper clipping. 'I saved this from the *Daily Mail*. "Crewe Council is proposing to freeze-dry bodies to minus 321 degrees Fahrenheit,"' she read aloud, '"And then put them on the vibrating pad which reduces them to powder within a minute. Nothing but compost remains."' She passed the clipping over the glossy desk. 'Callum loved his vegetable garden – he'd have approved of that.'

'And if that doesn't stop you eating up your carrots . . .' Hazel whispered in Matt's ear. '*Bleagh!* I bet even Milly would go back to eating meat.'

Natalie glared at them both, infuriated by the sight of her youngest sister giggling with Matt – in this of all places! While they were finalising the details of her father's eternal rest. Though strictly speaking Matt wasn't giggling, still she was annoyed at him for encouraging – or at least not reprimanding – Hazel. She couldn't help but wonder, had he told Hazel about her foolish behaviour at the nightclub? Were they both secretly laughing about it? She thought of Avril's remark about them shagging for England and suddenly, standing behind the lugubrious undertaker, Matt looked sexier than ever, but in a malicious demonic way. A regular irresponsible James Bond, using his lithe body and broad impish grin to indulge his sick little fetish for – why not call it what it was? – Pussy Galore.

251

Much as her mother already seemed completely dependent on him, as lost under his spell as the rest of her bewitched family, Natalie couldn't wait for him to leave, to run back to South America or anywhere as long as he was well and truly gone. Only every time he so much as suggested he might pop up to Manchester or check in on some mates in Bath, Mum acted like Herod had threatened to slay her firstborn. And being a grieving widow, Natalie couldn't even scream at her and tell her to butt out and let him go.

Even now, her cheeks burned at the memory of her hen-party faux pas. And since she was currently staying at Mum's – under the not-unreasonable pretext of being needed but mainly because she was so disappointed with Jeremy she couldn't look him in the face – the tension was almost unbearable. Possibly worse, she could almost swear Matt was intentionally keeping out of her way. What must he think of her?

'Ah yes, promession.' Nodding wisely, Mr Hodgkins gave the clipping back. 'Not legal in this country yet, I'm afraid.' He raised the corners of his lips slightly. 'Perhaps if you actually looked at some of the caskets . . .' The funeral director led them into the adjoining parlour where urns of chrysanthemums were tastefully interspersed to lighten the effect of the rows of coffins. He opened a lid to reveal an oyster silk lining. 'Now this is one of our most popular models . . .'

Natalie's mind drifted back to the afternoon before, when she'd caught her mother lurking in the potting shed, her shoulders shuddering as she clutched Callum's old tweed jacket with the darned elbow patches. 'Foolish of me, I know.' She managed a watery smile as Natalie had walked in. 'After all, he could be a dreadful man in some ways. But it's all been such a shock.'

Awkwardly Natalie squeezed her arm. 'It's all right, Mum.

He *was* your husband. You *are* allowed to cry.' They'd all broken down at sometime or another; still, it was funny how none of them liked to do it in front of witnesses, as if it made them vulnerable and exposed. Only Milly seemed incapable of holding back floods of tears.

She pulled out a large upturned flowerpot, checked it for woodlice and gingerly sat down, watching Peggy fondle the well-worn collar.

'All those years, he never once took me dancing or out to dinner. And he said some terrible things when he was drunk, things I could never forget. But you know, he had a kind heart and he loved all of you so very much.'

'I know, Mum.' It was a familiar litany.

'He used to get so upset when I made him mince for dinner. But it was all I could afford, trying to make ends meet on the miserly housekeeping he gave me.'

They'd all hated their mother's mince, Natalie forbore from saying, mainly because it was inevitably burnt. But she'd had such inventive ways of getting them to eat her culinary disasters, halting their wailing complaints by pretending, 'I made it specially for you, Natalie. I know it's your favourite.' And then you'd hear her say exactly the same thing to Milly and Avril and Hazel until finally it was Callum's turn.

'Woman!' he'd bellow, while his daughters giggled behind their hands. 'For crying out loud, haven't I told you a thousand times, I hate mince.' And then plaintively to the girls, 'Does she do this just to upset me? Does she go out of her way to cook me things she knows I cannae abide?'

'Ah, well.' Peggy slipped on Callum's jacket and put out a hand to pull Natalie up. 'You know what they say, laugh and the world laughs with you . . . How's Jeremy, by the way? The two of you haven't had a falling-out, have you?'

'To be honest, we're barely speaking.' Natalie sighed

heavily. 'I can't . . . well, I just can't forgive him for not being there when I needed him. All he was concerned about was letting his friends down. He didn't even consider coming back to support me.'

'Did you ask him to?'

'Not in so many words.'

'Well then. You know some people are very funny about illness. We had this nurse once, why she was ever a nurse –'

'Don't make excuses for him.' Natalie closed the potting-shed door behind them, pulling on the string that had been a temporary latch for the last ten years. 'He let me down – badly.'

'You know, dear, he might not have realised how serious it was. None of us knew, did we? Not even that nice doctor.'

'But even once he'd . . . passed away . . .' Natalie gulped. Deceased, dead, departed, passed over, it seemed impossible to say any of them without stumbling. 'All Jeremy cared about was how much it would cost to cancel the wedding and how to tell his friends.'

'Practicalities are important too.'

'Truth is, when the chips were down he just wasn't there for me. Unlike . . .'

Unlike Matt, she wanted to say. Those desperate moments after Dad died, Matt's arrival had been as welcome as the first medic on a battlefield. Except his first aid had been hugs and words of comfort and his bandages practicalities that really mattered: calling Ivor, getting Avril a taxi home (she'd flown in looking like a banshee, demanding to see the body, distraught about what she saw as her defection), quietly talking to the hospital administrator about their next step when everyone else was too distressed. And then cooking dinner that night for the shell-shocked crew and coaxing them all to eat. Even upset as she was about Hazel and Matt, Natalie had to reluctantly concede that the whole ordeal would have been twice as hard without him.

What a contrast to Jeremy, who'd finally appeared at the house the next evening looking fractious and irritable about having to drive to Sussex with his hangover, barely staying long enough to sit down and positively bristling with embarrassment and unease at the emotional maelstrom of a household in mourning.

'Unlike?' Peggy's glance was suspicious.

Natalie watched her feet scrunch on the gravel path, avoiding her mother's enquiring eyes. 'Like he should have been.'

'Oh, Natalie, look, Jeremy's taken a long time to grow on me, but you two are . . .'

'Go on, say it, like twins. Peas in a pod. Well, maybe I don't want to marry someone who's the same as me. Maybe I want someone the *opposite* of me. In fact, Mum, I feel like calling off the whole bloody wedding altogether!'

'Oh dear.' Peggy stopped, astonished, and slid her arm around her daughter, pulling her close. 'Darling, are you serious? I was going to say "so sure of yourself".' She reached out for Natalie's hand and patted it comfortingly, searching her eyes. 'I've never thought the two of you are like twins! But please, promise me you won't rush into any decisions right now. Remember, we've all been under a lot of stress.'

She paused to pull the faded blooms of a climbing rose. 'Death makes people act in all kinds of odd ways,' she mused. 'You know, when my father was dying your uncle Ted went to visit and the nurse told him, "Oh, your mother's in there with him now." And when he walked in, there was a lady Ted had never seen before at the bedside, holding his hand. So Ted turned and left, never even bothered to find out who she was.'

Natalie stared at her, baffled. 'Do you think Grandpa Dartford was having an affair?'

'That or he was a bigamist!' She said the word with relish, clearly loving the idea of a family scandal. 'We'll never know. Your grandparents weren't well suited, really. My father was a brilliant self-made man and my mother, God rest her soul, was a very silly woman. She told me when the estate was settled, some of their savings seemed to have vanished as well as his car. And there were a heck of a lot of people we didn't recognise at his funeral.' She linked arms with Natalie as they approached the house, Natalie still trying to assimilate these fresh skeletons that seemed to have crawled out of the family closet into the sunny garden. By the back door, Natalie pulled them both to a stop.

'You know Frazer . . .'

'Frazer?' Her mother's brow wrinkled as if trying to place the name.

'The *Black Swan* guy. The one you almost married. Did you have any regrets?'

'Well, it was the most beautiful boat. Of course, I –'

'No, not the boat. The man. Do you think you should have waited?'

'For Frazer?' Peggy burst into surprised laughter. 'Of course not. Oh, the man was utterly charming – he always made me think of that song, "The Sailor with the Navy Blue Eyes" – but he was a complete scallywag. Had a different girl for every day of the week. And besides, I was in love with your father.'

What could you do with the woman? Natalie thought now, watching her mother trying to see her face in the mirror-like shine of a brilliant walnut casket. She was enough to drive anyone crazy. Or to drink.

'Did your husband prefer teak or mahogany?' Mr Hodgkins was still trying the hard-sell approach.

'Well . . .' Peggy pulled another makeshift handkerchief, an old sock this time, out of her sleeve and rubbed absent-mindedly on the gleaming surface. 'He was very fond of a teak chest we got as a wedding present. And his uncle in India once sent us a marvellous mahogany wardrobe. But honestly, Mr Hodgkins, Callum was a simple man. As often as not he'd just as soon save his money and buy that rubbishy melamine. I can't see him spending . . .' She leaned over to read the price tag. '. . . eight thousand pounds on a box that's just going to rot.' She straightened up and gave Mr Hodgkins a dizzying smile. 'He'd think me absolutely gaga.'

There was a funny snuffling sound from Matt. He turned his back and looked intently up at a corner of the ceiling, as if examining it for spiders' webs, but Natalie could see his shoulders shaking.

Automatically she sent the man in front of them a look of sincere apology, conveying – as she had so often in the past – her complete lack of control over her mother's behaviour. She'd sent that same look to the owner of a King's Road antique shop where she'd once made the great mistake of taking Peggy. Oh, the humiliation of trying to look like a worldly patron of fine things while your mother ran delightedly from Wedgwood vase to Victorian pine dresser, asking for a price on every item and shrieking with dis-believing horror at each reply. Who the hell had Natalie been trying to impress? she wondered now.

This mission was doomed. However willing Avril and Natalie were to splash out, they were heading for the simplest pine box the funeral home offered.

And even Mr Hodgkins seemed to realise it.

'Too bad we can't send him off in his MFI wardrobe,' Peggy said, nudging Hazel cheerfully. 'It's falling to pieces as it is.'

And then all of a sudden Natalie was seeing the funny side, digging her nails into her palms to stop herself giggling. For as long as she could remember, she'd cringed with embarrassment over her mother's eccentric behaviour, not wanting to be seen with her, terrified about what outrageous thing she'd do or say next. As awful as was the fear her friends might catch sight of her dad staggering around the house, red-faced and banging into walls, almost as bad was Peggy boasting about Natalie's brilliance in front of Natalie's unimpressed classmates or telling them some convoluted anecdote that involved various venereal diseases, or announcing loudly, 'I'm sorry, I'm not allowed to talk to you. Natalie's forbidden me to say a word,' and then pretending her lips were glued shut.

But she was after all her mother. She was spunky and clever with a hilarious sense of humour, and when they were little, the friends who did visit always wanted to hang out in the kitchen with her instead of going up to Milly's or Natalie's room to play records. And really, why should Natalie care what people thought of her so much? The bottom line was that she loved her mother. Had loved her father too, not that she always showed it. Death had a way of making you more appreciative of the living even as you were mourning the dead. She caught Matt staring at her and from his understanding smile realised their thoughts were running on similar lines.

Quickly, she jerked her head away, humiliation surging again from her toes to her hairline, and turned her attention back to the job at hand.

Chapter 30

The hearse pulled up outside the house and Mr Hodgkins made his way slowly down the front path, head lowered and hands clasped discreetly behind his back.

Inside, Peggy was fussing over Matt, picking lint off his jacket. 'What a smart suit.' She fingered the lapel. 'Surely you didn't have it with you?'

'Borrowed it from a mate,' he said. 'Steve Bolton who runs the Codmoreton post office. Said he only wore it twice, once to his wedding and the second time for his divorce. But now I feel like an incredibly boring stuffed shirt next to Hazel. Don't you think she looks stunning? She reminds me of a hummingbird in that outfit. Or maybe a scarlet macaw.'

'Sure you don't mean a scarlet woman?' Hazel returned, jokingly. Her slender body was brilliant in a crimson two-piece unearthed only last week in a vintage clothing shop. She was as thrilled by its low-slung hipster flares, very sixties retro, as she was by the scandalised look from Natalie when she put it on that morning. But who said funerals had to be all about black?

The doorbell rang. Looking pale and anxious, Milly rushed to answer it. 'Limo's here.' She'd spent the night so Peggy and her daughters could all ride together. Ivor and the kids would meet them at the church.

Natalie came down the stairs, coiffed and Jackie Kennedy-like in a cropped tailored jacket and matching navy skirt that just shielded her knees. Still, she thought, neither of them could pull it off like Avril whose enviable height gave her a model quality and whose simple Chloé washed silk tuxedo dress made her appear more elegant than ever.

'Come on.' Peggy took Matt's arm and tugged him towards the door.

Matt shook his head, looking much less shaggy now that his tawny mane had been cut for the occasion and the sun-streaked ends swept away from the barber's floor. 'I don't think so. The limousine's meant for immediate family. One of the neighbours will give me a lift.'

'Fiddlesticks.' Peggy dragged him past the uniformed driver, her brown eyes alight. 'You're like an adopted son to me . . . and you were to Callum too.'

No one noticed Avril flinch.

'It's like four weddings and a funeral,' Milly whispered as the driver took off at about five miles per hour behind the hearse that carried her father's body. It was probably the stress of the last few days, she thought, but she still had this migraine that wouldn't quit.

'But without the weddings,' Hazel joked. 'Oops. Sorry, Nats.'

'Four daughters and a funeral,' Matt said.

'And a surrogate son.' Peggy patted Matt's knee.

'Flattered, I'm sure.' He grinned at her.

'How long are we going to dawdle on at this speed?' Hazel hissed. 'Not all the way to church, surely?'

'Till the end of the street,' Peggy said. 'That's what they did with Mrs Chimmenoski three doors down. Callum got very irate with them, I'm afraid. He got stuck behind the last car when he was late for a dentist's appointment and had no idea he was tangled up with a funeral procession. Kept blaring his horn and trying to overtake. I almost died myself when I heard about it.'

Hazel smiled and stared out at the long overgrown hedges as they inched slowly past. A small group gathered at a bus stop goggled at them with unabashed curiosity, trying to peer inside the hearse as they stopped to let a pedestrian cross in front of them.

Peggy nudged Matt. 'Cost a fortune, this troop of thieves,' she said in a loud stage whisper, with a meaningful nod towards the back of the driver's head. 'If Callum were here he'd hit the blimmin' roof.'

They all stared out the windows, then one by one, shoulders started shaking, lips started being bitten. First one started to go, then the others, like dominoes. Avril was the last, but even she eventually collapsed.

'Stop it, everyone.' Tears streamed down Natalie's face as she tried to regain control. 'It's . . . well, it's blasphemous.'

'Sacrilegious, you mean,' Hazel corrected between snorts. 'Blasphemous would be taking the Lord's name in vain. Get it right, Nats. You're the one who starred at Sunday school.'

That caused another round of rib-aching giggles. Avril tried to stuff one of the hankies Peggy had foisted on to them all into her mouth, Matt ground his knuckles into his forehead, Hazel dropped her head in her hands, staring at the floor mats while Natalie focused on the driver's large ears sticking out from under his cap, refusing to look at the others in a hopeless effort to calm down before they set her off again. Even Milly, who'd been feeling nauseous ever since they stepped into the vehicle, had to bite her lip, her miseries temporarily forgotten.

'Well, blasphemy or not, thank Christ for tinted windows.'

Natalie held her stomach. 'Can you imagine anyone going past now, and seeing us all giggling away like –'

'Hysterical hyenas,' Avril and Milly screeched in unison.

'I wish you'd tell your mother to stop her cackling.' Jeremy scowled through the hatch at Peggy holding court in the living room. 'She sounds like a hen that's just laid an egg.'

'Oh, she's just pleased to meet up with all the relatives again.' Natalie pulled some precooked sausage rolls from the microwave and placed them on the table in front of Milly. 'Most of them haven't visited in years.'

A pang of regret stabbed her as she stared at the horrible shop-bought puff pastry she was doling out instead of the wedding caterer's gourmet appetisers and delicious salmon.

'But this is her husband's wake. She should at least tone it down. Thank God my parents aren't here to see.'

'And what *was* their excuse?' Milly glared fiercely at Jeremy. 'Some "long-standing" bridge invitation? I'm sure that was *far* too important to cancel.'

'Actually a charity fund-raiser,' Jeremy sneered back, clearly irritated by her attack. 'My mother's on the board, you can hardly expect her to miss it.'

Milly caught Natalie's pleaful don't-make-waves expression and stifled the furious outburst simmering in her throat. 'Do you think there's enough food, Nat? I don't want to underfeed them.'

'I think there's enough for us all to last the winter.' Natalie removed cling film from a large plate of chicken tikka bites. 'You've really gone to town.' In gratitude, she refrained from saying pineapple-laden cocktail sticks were positively seventies. There had been a rocky bit earlier on as the coffin was lowered into the grave where Milly had almost fainted for the second time that week. She'd suddenly grabbed Ivor and her sisters rushed protectively to help but, although deathly white, she'd insisted she was fine.

'He deserves a good sending-off.' Milly looked tearful again. 'That's the least we can do for him.' In a high bright tone, she changed the subject. 'It went well though, didn't it? All those people from Edinburgh and beyond. And didn't Matt give a great eulogy? So sweet when he said Dad was the man who inspired him to become a doctor.'

'He really loved Dad.' Natalie caught sight of Jeremy's expression and felt impelled to add: 'Well, he did. So did lots of people. You never really got to know him.'

And no regrets there, Jeremy's face seemed to be saying, but he choked it back by stuffing a sausage roll in his mouth, his cheeks swollen as he chewed. God, everything he did today seemed to be annoying her. All during the service, Natalie had found his presence by her side almost unbearable, standing there in his stuffy suit, looking like a big slab of beef, his red face pompous and condescending. Her eyes kept straying to Matt, finding it impossible not to compare his broad shoulders, strong lean body and cheerful kindness with the attributes of her groom-to-be, and having her fiancé coming up wanting. Bad enough that every time Matt smiled at someone she suffered a surge of irrational jealousy, wishing those smoky-grey eyes were staring down at her instead, but standing next to Jeremy, accepting condolences, she felt as if they were under a spotlight, with a huge foam finger marked 'Plonker' pointing directly at his head.

His Adam's apple bulged as he swallowed the last chunk. 'And that bagpiper,' he said sourly, 'bursting in like that, full tartan regalia, and piping that dire music. Only your mother could think that was appropriate.'

'It was the "Skye Boat Song".' Natalie fussed over the tray so he wouldn't see how his words stung. 'And Mum didn't hire him,' she added, arranging pizza fingers in perfect lines. 'I did. He was booked for our wedding.' She'd felt so proud too as he'd marched solemnly up the aisle, clad in feathered bonnet, sweeping shoulder plaid and with a tiny knife fighting for sock room with his well-muscled calves. Tons of people had come up after and said how touched they'd been. Why was Jeremy choosing today of all days to be . . . well, to be such a *tosser*?

'You know it'd be nice if you actually went out there,' Avril said, shooting them all dirty looks as she swept into the room, empty plates in each hand which she swapped for two full ones, 'instead of leaving it all to me and Hazel. After all, half these people probably wouldn't be here if it weren't for you, Natalie.' She pushed against the door with her bottom and flounced out again.

'What's up with her?' Milly gawped.

'I think she and lover boy had another falling out. He's conspicuously absent, haven't you noticed?' Natalie picked up the sausage rolls and steeled herself to enter the fray, almost colliding with Hazel as she burst in.

'Bloody hell! You should have heard Mum just now, an absolutely fucking hoot! Pardon French, JJ.' She sneaked a carrot baton and dipped it into a pot of chilli sauce. 'Another of her penis stories. About a patient who had genital warts. Apparently, after he died he got in touch with his wife in a seance and sent Mum a message.'

'What type of message?' asked Milly.

'Tell the little nurse my problem has cleared up. And then she said the man's name was Mr Cockburn, only of course she mispronounced it as Cock instead of Co! I didn't get the rest, I was laughing so much and Auntie Cyn almost choked on her melon ball. Honestly, one glass of Harvey's Bristol Cream and she's anybody's.' Hazel grabbed a corkscrew from the worktop. 'Right, refills all round. If I can get Uncle Ted pissed he might do that trick where he balances a spoon on his nose and waggles his ears.' She slipped out again, snatching yet another bottle of wine as she left.

'You see what I mean,' Jeremy hissed at Natalie. 'Does your family have no decorum?'

Through the crowd, she caught sight of Matt, his back to her, his newly cut hair curling gently above his collar. She felt the blood throb faster in her pulse.

Oh, go screw yourself, Jockstrap, she thought.

Avril was smoking outside the back door, when there was a crash, followed by another coming from her father's tool shed. She was in a foul mood, plain tired of being polite to uncles and aunts she'd not seen in donkey's years, and chatting to second cousins twice removed that she didn't recognise. She'd done her stint while Natalie and Milly had hidden in the kitchen, now it was over to them.

She stubbed out her cigarette and slowly she made her way down the windy garden path, intrigued as to who she might find. Through the glass pane she could just make out a silhouette. They must have heard her. A cigarette suddenly flicked through the air, hit the ground and was quickly stamped upon by a killer heel.

Music had started up. 'Lost My Heart in San Francisco'. Her mother must be digging through her old record collection. Avril's mouth twisted wryly as she neared the door. All these years, if Mum took out her few beloved albums – Elvis, Perry Como, Andy Williams – to play on their ancient gramophone, then the next thing, Dad would search out his old Gaelic seventy-eights, light-hearted ones such as 'Stop Your Tickling Jock' and the more hauntingly beautiful by his namesake Callum Kennedy with titles such as 'Morag

O'Dunvegan' or 'The Skyeline of Skye'. The girls would love those sessions, kicking their heels up around the living room, making up their own version of the Highland Fling or the Gay Gordons.

Avril pulled the string latch and poked her head around, surprised at who she found in there. The air was blue. No guesses why. A shelf was hanging down at one side, clay pots smashed and scattered on the ground and the unexpected occupant was crouched down, picking up the evidence of an accidental collision.

'Bad habit that,' Avril remarked laconically.

'What?' Erin blushed guiltily as a peal of laughter came from inside the house.

'Biting your nails, whadya think I meant?' She lifted Erin's hand and pointed to her fingers.

'Oh . . .'

'You know when I was a kid, I did the same, except then I had to paint on this revolting stuff. Tasted like fucking earwax.'

'Gross.' Erin giggled. Her mother would never use language like that in front of her. It was refreshing. Made her feel quite grown up. 'You *had* to put it on?'

'Oh yes, your grandmother would make me. She was pretty strict back then. Not the lovable old lady she mellowed into. Kinda nippy out here, isn't it?' She noticed Erin shivering.

'I'm OK. So what else did she make you do?'

Avril kicked a few clay shards into a corner, helping Erin to put back the shelf. 'Just embarrass me at every opportunity. When she turned up to parents' evenings, man, that was terrible. She'd tell the teachers that all I thought about was boys. That I was too busy giggling with my friends on street corners to lend a hand and that I spent so much time up the tree on the back green, spying on Michael Mahovsky, that his parents threw a bucket of water over me.'

'And was it true?'

'Yes.' Avril gave a wry smile, remembering her conversation with Matt. 'I seem to have got soaked a lot.'

'At least your mum came to parents' evening.'

'What do you mean?'

Erin's face clouded. 'Don't matter.'

'Your mum goes, though, doesn't she?' Avril pried gently. Milly had always taken an avid interest in her children's school activities. Always attending every fund-raising venture they organised. Yes, because she used to moan about having to drag all the kids with her, because Ivor wasn't home.

'Not for the last one. Nor the music nights.'

'Music nights?'

'When all the kids in school do their thing. Steel band, jazz band, pianists, choir, whatever.'

'So what do you do?'

'Violin. I'm thinking of giving it up though. Dad's never there to watch, Mum doesn't care any more. She was a lot nicer when she was fatter.'

'Of course she cares. She dotes on you.' Involuntarily, Avril flashed to the dress fitting. Milly's unhealthy flesh erupting from that hideously small dress. She must have dropped two sizes since then. You would think Erin would be ecstatic not bummed out. Kids! They were an alien race.

Erin fidgeted uncomfortably but Avril could sense she didn't want to go back to the house.

'So how is school?'

Erin shrugged. 'Useless. I'm going to fail everything.'

Ah, maybe it wasn't just her grandfather's death that was making her look so woeful and drawn. Probably stressing over exams. Well, at least she was taking them. Avril had never had the chance. Not a single O level, what with everything that had gone on.

'Rubbish. Milly's always boasting how smart you are. What subjects are you doing?'

'Maths, English, PE, Spanish, the usual. But I'm pants at them all.'

'Tell me about it!' Avril laughed. 'I couldn't even pass a fucking eye test. But hey, Hazel's fluent in Spanish, she could help you. And your mum, well, God, you should be getting top marks at English, kiddo. Your mother was brilliant at it when she was young.'

'She was?' Erin looked surprised. 'She never told me.'

'God, yes, she got distinction or something in her A level and she wrote an incredible story for a newspaper competition, all about having an artificial leg, and it was so convincing that when she went to pick up her prize, they'd arranged a special ramp for her.'

Erin gave a disbelieving snort.

'Scout's honour.' Avril nodded encouragingly. 'You should ask her to help you.'

Erin shook her head. 'She's too . . . I don't know. Freaked out, I guess. I try and speak to her and she just walks away. It's like she doesn't know I exist.'

'Listen, sweetie,' Avril said gently, 'you have to understand it's really hard for her right now.'

'Mmm.' Erin didn't sound convinced.

'Still, biting nails is nowhere near as bad as smoking, eh!' Avril teased with a swift change of subject. She pulled a packet from her pocket and turned it over to the back. 'Doesn't say "Smoking kills" on here for nothing. Lung cancer, cancer of the tongue, cancer of the mouth, lip . . . I read once that they opened up this guy and he was dripping black inside from all the tar.'

'Yuck. Well, we were shown a photo at school of two lungs and they were all purple and blue like they were bruised, with dots all over them. It was completely disgusting.'

'And you get wrinkles round your mouth.' Avril snapped open her lighter. 'And boys don't want to kiss you because you smell so foul.'

'How sad is that?' Erin managed a reluctant laugh. 'So what's that thing between your fingers?'

'Why do you think I'm a childless old spinster?' She took a long, slow drag. Well, if the boot fitted, might as well stick it on and tighten the buckle.

'How are things going?' Matt found Peggy temporarily alone for the first time all day and gave her a one-armed squeeze. 'They're not tiring you out, are they?'

She looked frail, he thought, despite the reappearance of that same old coral lipstick and a dusting of face powder. The past week had been a strain on them all, but Peggy had to have felt it most. Again he thought how much he admired her. Whatever her troubles, she always managed to stay cheerful.

'Who, me? Oh, right as rain.' She stared around the room at the little groups of friends and family talking and drinking. 'Did you know Callum's old nurse just came up to me, said how much his patients missed him at the practice? So sweet of her. I could never make him believe that anyone cared.' She waved her empty sherry glass at the mobbed room. 'I keep thinking how Callum would have hated this. All these people. He only agreed to our hosting the wedding reception at home because it was Natalie who asked. Poor thing, she worked like a Trojan putting that wedding together and now here we all are. Ah well, what can't be cured must be endured.'

Not for the first time that day, she pulled him over to admire a gigantic flower arrangement displayed proudly in a huge ribbon-wrapped vase. 'I still can't believe darling Dorothy sent these.' She clasped the card to her chest. 'Aren't they magnificent! Oh, I do miss her, Matt, she was the most wonderful friend.'

'She was so sorry not to make it.' He smiled at Avril as she refilled Peggy's glass. 'And devastated to hear about Callum. But it's a twenty-six-hour journey. And she has this dreadful sciatica.'

'She's not to worry. And we all have to struggle these days. I have to wear elastic stockings myself. Look, Jeremy!' She stretched out to grab her future son-in-law who was slinking by, accidentally splashing sherry on to his cuff. 'Aren't these splendid? Matt's mother sent flowers all the way from Adelaide.'

Jeremy brushed irritably at his shirtsleeve, making a big deal over his stained cuff. 'I somehow doubt they came from Adelaide,' he scoffed. 'I bet if you look at the card it says Codmoreton Florists. Interflora makes it bloody simple these days. Damn.' He jerked back, spilling his drink on himself, as Matt, moving forward, stepped hard and deliberately on his toe.

Hazel, walking by with the last of the ham sandwiches, caught the exchange and just managed to stop herself snapping, 'Yeah, so easy neither you nor your parents bothered.' She saw Matt staring at Jeremy as if studying a fascinating Petri dish of some deadly flesh-eating disease. So at least she wasn't the only person who found the jerk unbearably rude. Granted, Mum had been carrying on all day as if Auntie Dorothy's floral gift were ruby-studded and gold-plated but so what if it cheered her up?

Peggy blinked, then turned her head and began manically waving at someone across the room. 'I must go and rescue Dr Habib. He's looking terribly lost.'

Jeremy yanked at his tie, loosening it from his collar and poured himself a gin and tonic from the drinks table.

'Hate events like these, don't you? Total bloody ordeal,' he said, in the longest exchange he'd had with Matt yet. 'How long does one have to stay at these blasted things anyway?'

'Oh, I think you could leave any time,' Matt said easily. 'No one would miss you.' Over Jeremy's shoulder he could see Natalie by the buffet laughing and chatting with one of the hipper cousins. She flicked her hair, caught him looking and gave a quick smile before returning, more animated, to her conversation. *A tiger in bed?* he thought. *You've got to be kidding, Nasty. This joker's more like a rhino.*

Jeremy was still scowling with undisguised animosity as he tried to decide if he'd been insulted. Finding no clue in Matt's face, he snorted and stared around him with contempt.

A few yards away, Aunt Susan, Uncle Ted's wife, collared Hazel, laying her short bejewelled fingers on Hazel's sleeve. 'I was just saying to your mother, how terrible for dear Natalie, having such a tragedy happen three days before she was due to wed. I understand the poor girl should be on her honeymoon by now. Do we know if they've set a new date?'

'Let's hope not.' Hazel glanced over at Matt and Jeremy across the room. 'Her fiancé's a dickhead. You can't miss him, he's the one who walks like he's carrying a billiard ball up his backside.'

She strolled off with the sausage rolls, leaving Aunt Susan blinking in shock.

Chapter 31

As the first to leave gathered bags and hats, Avril headed unsteadily upstairs, holding on to the banister to support her suddenly weary legs. It was irrational, she knew, but the longer she made small talk, the more angry she became until the mob below all blurred into a sea of faces, chomping down on Milly's cocktail snacks, drinking their free booze and spouting meaningless sentiments. 'So sorry.' 'Such a tragedy.' 'Sorry for your loss.' 'He was a good man.' How trite the words sounded. Well, they should be bloody sorry. Half of them couldn't give a stuff about her dad anyway. For years, he and Mum had been virtual strangers to their own relations and now he'd snuffed it, the worms all crawl out of the woodwork.

'Bugger the lot of them,' she said to herself, and then, grinning loopily, she repeated it, pacing each step carefully in time with the word. 'Bugger. Bugger. Bugger.' Her mouth curled with satisfaction, thinking blurrily of her mother's story of how a three-year-old Avril had scandalised a waiting room full of Callum's patients by tackling the stairs to their upstairs flat in this very same way, each cautious step punctuated with her first ever swear word. Only a toddler but already a rebel.

As she passed by the large bedroom on the landing, she

could hear the sound of squabbling. She paused, hand on the doorknob, taking a deep breath to steady her head.

'If you don't let me have a turn, I'll tell Mum where you were last night,' Fergus was growling.

'If you do, you're dead.'

'Hey, hey,' Avril said, walking in and assuming her best authoritative manner. 'What's going on?'

'Erin's calling me names. I'm going to tell Mum.'

Erin put her arms out in front of her and started trembling them. 'I'm shaking, I'm shaking,' she said sarcastically.

'Stop it now, all of you!' Avril gave them her sternest look, the one she usually reserved for negligent writers who'd overshot their deadlines. 'Where are your parents?'

'Dad's putting Ben down. And Mum's resting in Nanny's bedroom.' The writers were usually abashed. Erin sounded less so.

'Right, stay where you are. I'll go get her.' Avril marched down the landing. She found Milly lying with her eyes closed under the duvet in Peggy's big double bed.

'Milly?' she whispered, shaking her shoulder. 'Honey, are you awake?'

'Yes . . . Yes . . .' Milly began to get up. 'What? Is something wrong with Ben?'

'He's fine. Ivor's taking care of him.' About time he loaned a hand with his own kids.

'I'd better get up.'

'No, stay where you are.' Poor thing, Avril sympathised as she sat at the side of the bed. She looked terrible, practically green. It seemed Callum's death had hit the usually well-balanced Milly hardest of all. 'Thought I might take the kids out. They're going a bit stir-crazy.'

'*You?*' Milly opened her droopy eyes a fraction. '*You're* taking them?'

'If they're allowed to go.'

'Of course they're allowed. Yes. Yes. Do you want some money?' She tried to sit up again.

'Don't be daft, sweetie.' Avril bent down to kiss Milly's cheek, trying to remember how much she'd had to drink, if she should be worried about the breathalyser. Not much, she decided. A little wine, that was all. 'Get some rest now. Don't let the bedbugs bite.'

'Hey, dudes,' she called out as she headed back into Hazel's old bedroom. 'What say we escape this joint and go find us some ice cream?'

'Yes, yes!' Two voices in excited unison and the third morose: 'Yeah, all right, whatever.'

'Right then.' She chucked her set of keys at Fergus. 'Last one in the car's a hairy gorilla.'

'Come here.' Natalie beckoned Hazel from a crack in the door to Callum's study. Quickly she pulled her inside. 'Did you see? Over to the right, by the piano, talking to the vicar.'

'Oh my God!' Hazel marvelled, recognising Peggy's hated next-door neighbours. 'Joyful and Mr Beastly. Do you think they gatecrashed, the nosy parkers? Shall we get Matt to chuck them out?' She closed the door and leaned her back against it, grateful for a few moments of reprieve. It seemed like they'd been socialising for hours and the hangers-on were still hanging on. Would they never go?

'Mum probably invited them. You know her. More the merrier. Never could hold a decent grudge. Not like Avril, who bears them like banners.'

'Yeah. If there were a sulking event in the Olympics . . .' Hazel giggled then stopped as she caught sight of a half-finished crossword lying on her father's desk.

Natalie came to peer over her shoulder.

'I just can't believe it,' she said. 'I just can't believe my father's dead.'

'Our father,' Hazel corrected automatically. She always said that, Natalie. *My* dad. *My* mother. Like they belonged exclusively to her. Or as if she were the centre of the universe. But Hazel's heart wasn't into bickering now. They'd just buried their father. His was the first dead body she'd ever seen lying on a gurney in the hospital mortuary, his skin unreal and plastic-looking. This was the first truly momentous thing ever to have happened to her. She was half an orphan. An adult. Ridiculous thing to say but somehow she'd never really felt that grown up before.

Her sisters always said that, as the baby, Hazel had had it easy. They'd already fought the battles for her. By the time Hazel was of a dating age, Callum was a lot more lenient about how late she stayed out and what parties she could go to. Nor had his occasional lapses devastated her the way they had the others. Whether it was their tumultuous household that had caused her quirky sense of humour or her quirky sense of humour that allowed her to laugh at it, either way she didn't give a hoot. If you don't like me, fuck off, had become her creed. And that went for the way she lived her life. To hell with the conventional path. There would be no regrets when Hazel went to meet her Maker, none of her father's self-sacrificial wallowing in unfulfilled dreams.

'Where are you off to this time?' he'd ask, as she packed her rucksack.

'Greece, Dad.'

'Ah, Greece.' His eyes would mist over. 'All my life I've dreamed of going to Greece. Athens. The Parthenon. The Colossus of Rhodes. Now that must be a sight.'

Walking past the door, her mum would let out a derisive snort.

'Did you know, Hazel, lass,' he would continue regardless, 'that when Zeus turned himself into a swan . . .' And off he'd be with another rambling story about legends and myths.

'Well, then you should go.' To Hazel it was that simple. 'Book a flight. Take Mum.'

'Dream on!' Hazel could still hear Peggy clattering pots and pans in the kitchen, expending her frustration on innocent cookware.

'The cheapskate's never once taken me on holiday, except to Skye which was no holiday at all slaving on his mother's crumbling house. Unless you count that B&B weekend in Blackpool. And him, walking downstairs in the morning room, dressed in shirt tails and underpants. The poor woman serving breakfast – her eyes almost popped out of her head.'

'What's the old groaner saying?' Callum would turn his head. It seemed they had this same conversation every time Hazel pulled out her Karrimor. Practically word for word.

'Never mind. You should go, Dad. You can afford it.'

'Och, away with you, Hazel. Do you think money grows on trees?' He'd shake his head as if wafting away an impossible vision.

And then next time.

'Away to Italy, are you? Och, I've always wanted to see the Colosseum . . .'

Natalie threw the newspaper down. 'Any minute now you think he'll walk back through the door.'

'Joking about the wifies gossiping in the newsagent's that morning,' Hazel added.

'Or moaning about the state of the roads.'

'Or the government.'

'Or every other country's government. Remember how he'd never miss a single episode of *Coronation Street*? And if you dared to talk through it, he'd hush you out of the room, never mind if he hadn't seen you for months.'

'I can still smell him, that stinky old pipe . . .' Hazel's eyes looked suspiciously moist as she turned her head away from her sister's gaze.

Natalie felt a stab of sympathy. Her better instincts prodded her to go over and give Hazel a comforting hug but as usual she held back. She'd never been a touchy-feely person. It was one thing she had in common with her father who tended to shudder from affectionate displays, his expression wavering between tortured or embarrassed half to death. Now she regretted it. He hadn't kissed or cuddled her since she was a little girl. But then why would he when she had been so horrible to him? Hardly ever coming home. Pretending she didn't know him at her own engagement party. Taking Jeremy's side against her own father. She was an awful, awful person.

Hazel slumped in Callum's armchair and kicked off her shoes. 'And now Matt will be leaving soon,' she said gloomily. 'He told me he's off as soon as he can get a flight to Ecuador. And I'll have to find a job. Everything's going to be horrible.'

'You're not going back with him?' She knew it. They'd had a bust-up. Or Hazel had got bored. Dumped him. How could she treat people this way?

'Doesn't look like it, does it?' Hazel yawned, shrugging off her jacket, exposing her shoulders and arms in a very skimpy bra top.

'But what about . . . he told me he was going for interviews. Jobs in London.' Natalie felt her stomach drop.

'Matt? Working in London? No way. Mum keeps trying to talk him into Sussex but she doesn't realise he'd be totally miserable. You should see him out there, Nats. He loves it. Happy as Larry without a hint of civilisation, not another white person or even a flush toilet for miles around.

277

Remember how he used to say he wanted to be an explorer and a vet? Save wild animals from poachers and treat the ones which were wounded. Well, except that he's taking care of people instead, he's pretty close to living the dream.'

This time Natalie's heart fell along with her face. When Hazel said it, she could see it. Matt hacking his way through the undergrowth, machete in hand, surrounded by small people with blowpipes, huge hairy tarantulas scuttling out of their path. She shuddered, knowing that Matt's idea of paradise was her idea of hell. They were as incompatible as ice and fire. Each had its place but it wasn't together. But why had he lied about the interviews then? Her belly tingled as if her very skin was reliving the touch of his strong capable fingers.

'Besides,' Hazel continued blithely, 'I'm almost positive he's got a girlfriend somewhere. Mum'll be shattered though.'

'But I thought Matt came back with you because the two of you were *so in love*.' Natalie's voice took on a stinging note, as she thought of the hornet's nest Hazel's arrival had stirred up.

'Oh that.' Hazel studied a loose crimson thread. 'Actually, I never said any such thing. You were the one who jumped to conclusions.'

'Conclusions? What do you mean, conclusions? You purposely let me think –'

'Don't you think we should go back?' Hazel leapt from the chair in one smooth move. 'Drinks are probably running dry and Jeremy will wonder where you've disappeared to.'

'Well, Jeremy can go toss himself, can't he?'

Hazel turned to her, mouth agape. If Natalie had said she was going to cycle naked to Chichester, she couldn't have been more shocked.

Avril pulled into the main road, indicating left. She was sure there was a row of shops up here somewhere. Was she supposed to have gone right at the post office? Or was it the turning after? She looked across at Erin sitting next to her staring out of the window and for the millionth time today thought of Hazel. She'd still not managed to speak to her. Still not fulfilled the promise to her father on his deathbed. There never seemed to be the right time, either she was surrounded by the others, or feelings were running too high, but she knew she had to do it and soon.

From out of nowhere a young muntjac deer jumped into the road. Avril slammed on the brakes but the road was wet and the car skidded.

'Oh fuck!' Avril tried spinning the wheel to the right but the car didn't respond. She jerked the gearstick into second and pressed on the brakes again. But instead of stopping, the car began spinning round and round. She felt her head banging hard against the side window. Half concussed, stars blurring her vision, suddenly she realised they were facing the other way and the car had drawn to a halt.

Silence.

'Is everyone OK? Rory, Fergus?' Fumbling with her seat belt, she tried to turn her head but a sharp pain stabbed at her neck which suddenly seemed frozen.

'I've white chocolate Magnum all over my new trousers,' Erin moaned.

'What about you, Fergus?'

'I finished my Magnum.'

'No, I meant are you OK? Do you hurt anywhere?'

'I think I bit my tongue.'

'Rory?'

Silence.

'Rory? Rory!' Her whole body hurt with the effort to wrench around.

'You said the F-word,' Rory's little voice piped up.

'Did I? Sorry.' She looked in the mirror to see a flashing blue light. 'Shit!'

'Now you said the S-word,' said Fergus.

Christ almighty, Avril felt like Bill Grundy, the presenter fired from *Nationwide* after he encouraged the Sex Pistols to swear on live television.

In the mirror she could see the lights coming closer. She put her head in her hands and groaned. Now she was for it. If they breathalysed her she'd be more than likely over the limit. That'd be her licence taken away for sure. Her car sold off, back to taxis and trains. The noise stopped and when she opened her eyes, she realised the police car or ambulance or whoever it had been had passed by.

She'd got away with it.

A sense of relief floated over her a second before another horrific thought struck which made her heart sink to the depths all over again.

Milly

must

never

find

out.

Sitting on the floor of her mother's living room, cross-legged in front of the hunting print sofa, Hazel was laughing so hard her ribs hurt. With most of the attendees already gone, the wake – in the best Scottish tradition – had turned into a party. It had started when Uncle Ted – so respectful and quiet until they left the cemetery – had sat down at Peggy's old piano and started banging out 'I'm Forever Blowing Bubbles' and Uncle Mike – who had more bad jokes than the Royal Mint had gold bars – had jumped in with the comb and paper. Not to be outdone by her own brothers, Peggy had joined her voice to theirs and now she was leading everyone in 'Roll Out the Barrel', while the few mourners who weren't singing along clapped like ranch hands at a hoedown and even Reverend Chatham was showing an unlikely talent for playing the spoons.

Smack in the middle of the revelry, Matt spun Natalie round in a circle, tears of mirth falling down her cheeks.

'How about "Donald, Where's Yer Troosers"?' Peggy's brown eyes were dancing as she wiped damp tendrils of hair from her forehead. 'Callum loved that one.'

'We'll get all the war songs next,' Matt whispered, his breath tickling Natalie's ear.

Hampered by her three-inch heels, Natalie clutched his right bicep as she hopped on one foot, struggling to undo the strap of her left shoe. She'd just sent it sailing into the air when, by her other shoulder, she heard Jeremy's voice and jumped guiltily out of her skin.

'You have to shut her up,' he demanded. 'Get them to stop this.'

'Why?'

'Why?' He sounded incredulous. 'Why? Because it's shameful, that's why. Your mother's making a damn fool of herself. Never mind yourself.'

'So what?' Natalie eyes held a strange glint. 'It doesn't seem to be bothering the clergy. Christ, Jeremy, she's seventy-six, or rather seventy-eight,' she quickly corrected, 'years old! Does she still have to explain herself?'

'Pardon?' Jeremy was taken aback.

But Natalie had arrived on her soapbox and there was no way she was leaving. Her voice grew louder and people began to turn.

'If Reverend Chatham doesn't object, why the hell should you? Can't she have a good time without you coming up here with that mug that would turn milk sour, wanting everyone to be a right old miseryguts like your –'

'In the kitchen.' Jeremy's face was poker-straight as he crudely grabbed her elbow. 'Now!'

Twenty minutes later and Hazel was sitting on the loo in the downstairs bathroom, her ears still ringing from Natalie and Jeremy's screaming argument. What had come over her sister? Whatever it was, good for her. She hadn't even seemed to be that upset when JJ stormed off after she refused to leave with him.

'Get lost!' Hazel and everyone else still at the wake had heard her shriek. 'You stuck-up pompous prick! I wouldn't go with you if the house were on fire.' Then there'd been the slam of the front door and the roaring throttle of the departing MG.

Grinning at the memory, Hazel was brought back to the present by a sharp rapping.

'Won't be a mo!' she yelled. Jesus, it wasn't like there were no other toilets in the house and she'd only just gone into this one. Couldn't they use another?

A second knock.

'I said . . .' She paused, realising the knocking was coming from the window, not the door.

She zipped up her trousers and peered through the mottled glass. There was someone out there. Unscrewing the lock, she opened the window a fraction.

'Boo!' Avril's face appeared from the left.

'Bloody hell, Av, you almost gave me a heart attack!' She stopped when she realised what she'd just said. 'I mean a shock. What are you doing here? Are you pissed or what?'

'Just let me in.'

Hazel opened the window and Avril began squeezing her way through.

'Sorry to be so dramatic, sweetie,' she said when she finally stepped on to the floor and brushed herself down. 'I didn't want everyone making a fuss, that's all. Particularly Milly.'

'So how did you know it was me in here?'

'Your crimson outfit might have been a slight clue. You could see it halfway down the street.'

'Oh well, Dad always liked me in vibrant colours.' As Avril lifted up her fringe to study herself in the mirror Hazel noticed a large cut on her forehead. 'Jesus, what happened?'

'I had a bit of an accident.' Quickly she filled Hazel in. 'Kids are fine. No scratches and sworn to secrecy. I bought them all a second ice cream. Ouch.'

Hazel was dabbing at her head with a bit of toilet paper. 'You really should get Matt to look at this. It might need stitches.'

'It's not first aid I need, darling, it's a good dollop of foundation.'

'You can't put make-up over that, it'll get infected.'

'I've been around a long time, Hazel, you can put make-up over anything. Now get to work.'

Ten minutes later, Avril inspected herself in the mirror.

'Good as new.' In the reflection she caught Hazel's eyes and for a second her hand touching the bump stilled. She took a deep breath and turned round, crossing her arms in a strange hunched-up way. 'Look' – she hugged her ribs a little tighter – 'now I've got you here on your own. There's . . . Well, there's been something I've been meaning to tell you . . .'

'Spit it out then.' Hazel gave a puzzled laugh.

'I'm not sure how to say this.' Avril sat down on the bath, gripping the edge with white knuckles. Hazel wondered if the accident hadn't been a bigger shock than she was admitting. 'Once . . .'

'. . . upon a time.' Hazel grinned encouragingly.

'No. Once,' Avril began again and faltered. 'This is serious. When I was fifteen I got involved with a guy –'

'Oh great,' said Hazel, putting down the toilet cover and settling onto the fluffy pink shag. 'I love stories. Tell me all.'

Avril smiled in an odd way. 'He was two years older than me, had just signed on as a merchant seaman. Spiky hair, tartan scarf – a raging Bay City Rollers fan. Anyway, I thought he was the coolest boy I'd ever met, turning up to meet me from school in his battered old Ford Cortina.'

'I don't know,' Hazel countered, laughing. 'Cool and Bay City Rollers – those aren't two words you usually find in the same sentence.' She was enjoying this. She'd heard plenty of stories of Avril's wild youth from Milly and Nats but her eldest sister usually preferred to avoid Memory Lane like it was Plague Alley.

'Anyway, we . . . I . . . fell in love.' She suddenly looked very vulnerable, so that Hazel caught a glimpse of the pain those words cost her.

'God, you in love, Avril? Was it snowing in hell or . . .' Her voice faded. Her usual jokey manner didn't seem appropriate.

'To cut a long sordid story short,' Avril carried on quickly, 'I got pregnant.'

Hazel nodded, suddenly anticipating what she was about to admit. Maybe the day and the car accident had shaken her. Brought up the old guilt.

'Don't tell me – you had an abortion. And you never told, did you? Oh, Av, it must have been –'

'No' – Avril brushed away her sympathy like an annoying fly – 'you've got it all wrong.'

'Then what are you saying?' Hazel frowned. This whole conversation was too odd. Why was Avril looking at her like that?

'I'm saying I didn't have an abortion.' She stared into

284

Hazel's eyes and, as Hazel stared back, she had a strange sickly feeling that turned her bones to icicles. It was like there was something she'd always known, had never wanted to delve into . . .

'You're kidding,' she said, trying to laugh, to keep the truth at bay. 'You're making all this up, aren't you? Maybe it's concussion – you should have Matt look at that bump.' She pushed away the taunting images crowding her brain. Their all too similar hair colour, skin tone. The fifteen-year-age difference. The many never-explained mysteries of Avril's past.

Avril gulped. 'You've got to understand, it was really hard. I had the baby but –'

'I don't need to hear this.' Hazel jumped to her feet, refusing to believe what her mind was now yelling at her. Avril could have had a stillbirth. Or, please God, the kid was put up for adoption. 'It's ancient history anyway. I'm sorry, but I think we should –' She bolted for the door but Avril was ahead of her, blocking her way.

'It was you, Hazel. You're my daughter.'

They were inches away. Avril raised her hand to touch her, her mouth open as if searching for the words to make it better but Hazel was already pushing past.

'You bitch! You lying fucking bitch!'

Chapter 32

Five days since the funeral and Natalie was back at her desk. Vera had told her time and again to stay away, that she could easily cover, but Natalie insisted on turning up bang on the dot each morning.

Having to concentrate on making phone calls, showing clients around, and even Vera's constant babbling, kept her mind from dwelling on the mess that paraded as her life.

'You shouldn't leave him alone too long, you know,' Vera said for the sixth time that morning.

'I told you, I don't want to talk about Jeremy.'

'It's just that you never know how a bit of loneliness can affect a man. Ignore the Loos equation at your peril.' She picked up a *Hello!* magazine from the pile under her desk and began tapping at a glossy photo of David Beckham. 'Left to fend for himself in Madrid . . . Rebecca Loos, waiting like a viper in the wings . . .'

'Allegedly.' Natalie found another *Hello!* and flicked through the pages, looking at a photo of Posh with cropped blonde hair and huge sunglasses. 'But now he and Posh are the toast of LA and the Spice Girls are suddenly in the news again. Eat your heart out, Rebecca.' She flipped through the stack of magazines. 'Some of these are years old, don't you ever throw them out?'

'Maybe they are. But if I was you, I'd move back in and set a new wedding date. And all that commuting from Sussex. You must be knackered in the evening.'

'It helps me sleep at night.'

Vera's expression softened. 'Missing your dad?'

'Yes.' She didn't mention her desperate concern for Hazel and the shock of her disappearance because then the whole thing would have had to emerge.

They'd all heard the shouting, her furious departure and then Avril, hysterical, ranting at their mother before running out.

Natalie still couldn't believe it. She and Milly found themselves reeling and stunned as, after the last of the guests had hastily left, their mother sat them down and told them everything.

Hazel – Avril's daughter? Never in their wildest dreams had they suspected. Their whole childhood had been built on a pretence. And if she herself felt this way, then how must poor Hazel feel?

Natalie realised Vera was looking at her curiously.

'The house seems so empty without him,' she added. 'And think what it must be like for Mum. She needs me now. I don't want to abandon her while she's still getting over the shock of it all.'

'I thought your horrid sister Hazel was there, with her horrid boyfriend?'

Natalie flushed. 'I never called them horrid.' She was grateful when the conversation was interrupted by the tinkle of a bell as the street door opened. A handsome aristocratic man in a dark casual suit over a white silk shirt strode briskly over to Vera's desk. 'I wonder if you could help me?' he said. Gawping with admiration, Vera madly fluttered her eyelashes at him and hastily shoved her nail polish in a drawer.

'Richard?' She'd only heard it once but Natalie would know that rich deep voice anywhere.

Richard turned round. 'Natalie? What are you doing here?'

'I work here. This is my office!' she exclaimed as she stood up.

'No kidding. What an extremely small world. I dropped by to pick up some details. Chelsea, two-bed flat, period building. Just come on the market.'

'Yep, that's right. Draycott Avenue. Vera, can you fetch us the brochure? It's on Henshaw's desk.'

Vera glared at her and stomped off. Richard fiddled with his cuffs looking vaguely uncomfortable.

'Sorry about your dad. You will give your mother my condolences?' He stared around at the pictures on the wall and then back at Natalie. 'And please let me know if there's anything, anything at all, that I can do.'

Avril's name hovered unspoken between them. Natalie made a quick decision. 'Fancy a coffee?'

'Sure.' He glanced at the coffee machine.

'No, I mean outside.' She flicked her head at Vera's departing back. 'Away from prying ears. There's a quiet little café down the road.'

'Lead the way.'

'Coming to work, or are you going to stay in bed all morning?' someone shouted through the door.

For a second Hazel couldn't figure out, a) where she was, b) what country she was in, c) who was talking, and d) work? What did that mean?

She turned and squinted her eyes at the window. There were thick rusty metal bars outside. Could it be a prison? Turkey perhaps? Afghanistan? Some *Midnight Express*-type nightmare. Then thud – it all came back to her.

She was thirty years old, penniless, jobless and had recently found out that everything she'd ever thought about her family was a façade.

And again the flashbacks came as they had done every morning these past few days and she felt sick to the pit of her stomach.

'Can't lay there all day, you know, girl.' Jonno, the landlord of the Flying Ferret, popped his head round the door again.

'God, you sound just like my mother . . .' She stopped as she realised what she'd just said.

He smiled sympathetically. He knew the story. She'd turned up five nights ago ordering vodka after vodka, yabbering on about her ol' man's death. Jonno remembered her from her previous visit, the laughing devil-may-care girl who'd bantered with him and Drew and joked around while she shouted her friends some beers. It was one of his talents, his memory for people. He was surprised to see her alone, and by the desperate manner in which she had knocked back her drinks.

Come closing time she was completely stonkered. He asked her how she was getting home and suggested if she was crook maybe one of her sisters could come fetch her and suddenly she lifted her head from where it was resting against a pillar, opened her eyes and growled in this extremely loud almost exorcist-like voice: 'They're not my sisters. They're not my fucking sisters!'

Next thing he was sat next to her with his arm around her shoulders and it all spilled out.

That night she slept on his sofa and the following morning they came to an arrangement. Drew had left the previous afternoon for Cornwall – some big event at Fistral beach, volleyball, live music, and surfing, which was his passion. So if she wanted a room she could have it as long as she didn't mind covering Drew's shifts, kept the dunny clean and took her turn at cooking.

'What time is it?' she croaked as she propped herself up on her left elbow.

'Near half eleven.'

'Oh God,' she groaned. 'I've slept in again, haven't I? I told you to wake me.'

'I'm waking you now, darl.' He stepped in. 'Here, drink this. Careful, it's hot.'

Hazel squinted at him as he walked over to the bed and handed her an oversized mug of tea with 'World's Biggest Farter' written all over it. Not much to look at with his bald head, bullneck and short stocky body, but he'd been an absolute star since she'd loaded herself onto him. His constant barrage of wacky humour was just what she needed under the circumstances, and the fact that he was gay took the threat of unwanted romantic advances out of the equation. She suspected he missed Drew far more than he admitted and having her around, even as a fall guy for his constant barrage of jokes, probably distracted him from his loneliness as well.

'Cheers,' she said, taking a large slurp of tea.

'Nothing better than a good hot cuppa, eh!'

'No.' She smiled at the ridiculous cliché. Trite rubbish maybe but comforting nonetheless.

Bolting from the wake in her dad's Toyota, Hazel had driven blindly, tears blurring her vision, no idea where she was heading, only that she had to put as many miles as she could between herself and Little Hooking. She'd taken roads at random and somehow found herself on Coulsdon Common driving past the Flying Ferret. As her befuddled brain recognised the sign, she realised she needed a drink. Desperately.

'Right, well. I'll leave you to put your strides on and I'll see you downstairs. There's a fair amount of bottling up to do.'

She hopped out of bed and rummaged in the wardrobe for something to wear. As she pulled on yet another of Drew's oversized sweatshirts and trackie bottoms, the same hard facts went over and over in her brain.

Fact 1: Her sisters weren't her sisters.

Fact 2: Callum wasn't her father.

Fact 3: Peggy wasn't her mother.

Fact 4: Avril was . . .

What was that poem about how your mum and dad fuck you up? Well, this time they sure had.

'Avril was with me when she got the news.' Richard stirred his cappuccino. 'I would have come to the funeral but, ah, let's just say I don't think I would have been entirely welcome.'

'You don't need to explain. I've known Avril a lot longer than you have.'

'So how is everything?'

'Horrible. And on top if it all, there's been a bit of a family crisis . . .'

'Oh.' A flicker of a shadow crossed his face, just enough for sharp-eyed Natalie to pick up.

'You know, don't you? About Hazel?'

He sighed. 'Avril told me the morning your father passed away. I take it the revelation didn't go down well?'

Natalie gulped. 'Oh, Richard, it was horrendous. Hazel ran off before Avril had a chance to explain properly. I've never seen either of them look so upset. We've rung all her friends. Milly even called some missing persons line and the police but they're not terribly concerned.'

Her mind flashed to the endless night after the wake which she and Milly had spent going over and over the whole thing, until they were dizzy from rehashing it. They'd each been every bit as shocked as the other.

'And yet I can see it all now.' Milly had paced the living room, practically wearing a groove in the carpet from their father's threadbare old armchair to the bay window. 'That eight-week stay Mum had at Granny Dartford's before Hazel was born. I always wondered, why did she have to go? I mean, you'd think if her mum really was ill, they could have found someone else, someone not seven months pregnant to look after her. I was so mad at her for leaving us, especially with Nana being as strict as she was.

'The so-called *boarding school* that Avril attended.' Natalie shook her head sadly. 'There was me all those years, feeling resentful and jealous because she was given the opportunity to have a super-fun time sharing dormitories and having pillow fights and midnight feasts, just like in an Enid Blyton novel . . . While in reality, she was pregnant and living with Granny Dartford, stuck in some horrible town where she didn't know anyone.'

'So how's Avril bearing up?' Richard brought Natalie back to the present.

'She's gone into her usual retreat-into-her-shell mode. Won't take our calls. Phone's off at night, busy busy during the day. God, have you ever known anyone to hide behind work as much as she does?'

Richard smiled. 'Quite truthfully, no.'

'Anyway, I've left a message, pleading with her to come over next Sunday, told her Mum needs all our help to sort out Dad's belongings. Milly and I are going to be there so hopefully it'll give us all a chance to talk.' She stirred her coffee. 'Would you like me to send her your love?'

'I doubt she'd want it.' A cloud descended on his face.

'Oh, Richard.' Natalie put her hand over his and squeezed it gently. It was obvious by his concern how much he cared for Avril. She felt guilty for her earlier hasty judgement. 'All I can advise is give her time. This Hazel business has completed freaked her out.'

Richard drained his coffee and shook his head 'There's no pressure from me. She can take all the time she wants.'

Well, Natalie wondered, what did that mean? Was that a good thing or an 'I've washed my hands of her'? But she didn't know Richard well enough to ask.

'I can't for the life of me imagine where Hazel has vanished to.'

Peggy peeled a hard-boiled egg, throwing the shell in the bag put aside for rubbish. 'Those girls are so high-strung and bloody-minded sometimes, I swear they take after Callum's mother.'

Matt and Peggy were sitting on an old picnic blanket at one of their favourite haunts, perched on top of a rolling hill, with farmland spread below like a chequered flag.

It had been Matt's idea to come up here for an extended lunch break, get Peggy out of the empty house for a few hours where, with Hazel gone, Natalie at work all day and no Callum, it felt as if Peggy were the ghost, forlornly rattling her chains.

'Oh, you know Hazel,' he reassured her. 'She probably got a wild notion in that crackpot brain of hers and decided she just had to visit Findhorn or see Stonehenge at the break of dawn. Probably camping in a Gypsy caravan with a bunch of travellers or some such crazy story. She's nothing if not spontaneous.'

In fact, Matt felt more than a little pissed off with the entire bloody-minded lot of them, high-strung or not. Granted, Hazel had her provocations but had she the slightest idea of the turmoil her disappearance had caused? He'd been on the phone for hours, calling every friend her sisters and Peggy could remember, but with absolutely no success.

Then Avril, dropping her bombshell and fleeing the scene of the crime, but not without first screaming her rage at Peggy, and capping it all by giving the rest of them the cold shoulder, as if everyone in the world were to blame except for her. Matt was furious at her immaturity over the whole situation.

And finally Natalie. Of all the times he'd dreamed of her coming up to him, eyes shining, raising her face to be kissed, she had to pick the most impossible moment – the night of her hen party, the night her father died. And now she was staying with Peggy, having some kind of spiteful tantrum with that tool she was engaged to, and wouldn't so much as look Matt in the eyes.

If he didn't care so much for her, he'd say something, tell her exactly what he thought of her behaviour. But what was the point in stirring things up again? All that family had quite enough to deal with.

It was with much relief that he'd upped sticks to Codmoreton to temporarily stay with his old best mate Steve in a blessedly oestrogen-free zone of beers, pizza and *Die Hard* films. He'd arrive to paint and do odd repairs to The Briars after Natalie had left for work, cycling back to Codmoreton before she caught the evening train home. He hated to abandon Peggy with the Hazel mystery left unresolved. Quite honestly the house could use a bit of TLC and he wasn't the kind to sit around all day twiddling his thumbs.

'Yes, well, she'd better not have flown to America because once I've had my bunion operated on, if all goes well, I've decided she and I are off to the Yukon to find a nugget of gold and make our fortunes. To be honest' – Peggy patted Matt's leg – 'I don't worry about that girl at all. She might be small but she's a fighter. Like Avril! And sharp as a tack. I don't doubt she'll survive whatever calamity life throws at her. How else do you think I could bear her travelling on her own all this time? Anyone that tries to tackle Hazel will find more than he bargains for, I can tell you that.'

'You can say that again.' Matt tore off a chunk of crusty bread and loaded it with cheese. 'She's little but she's mighty. When she gets angry I've seen seven-foot thugs quivering in their boots.'

'And then there's Milly, a latent genius,' Peggy mused, reaching for the Thermos, 'but languishing, I fear, in the security of a happy marriage. I know you haven't had a chance to get to know Ivor but I like him very much. Such a relief to have one of them settled.'

'Hmm.' Matt took a swig of beer, staying non-committal. In fact, of all of them, it was Milly about whom he was most concerned. At the funeral she'd looked overwrought, her face ashen, with dark circles around her eyes, and he'd noticed her furtively shake a small pill on to her trembling palm and knock it back. What was it? he wondered. Some kind of antidepressant? Tranquilliser?

But it had been the wrong moment to question her and since then she hadn't been making her usual visits or answered the door the one time he tried to drop round, and maybe it was better to let it rest a few days, let the Hazel thing settle, instead of butting head first into that particular china shop.

'You should go to Australia,' he suggested now. 'Visit Mum. She'd be thrilled to bits to see you.'

'Oh, wouldn't that be fantastic?' Peggy beamed, diverted as he'd hoped. 'I could go for their summer. It'll be so strange here by myself once it's winter and I don't even have the garden to distract me. Living with Callum, well . . .' Her eyes glistened. 'Sometimes, especially when the kids were young, it was like being marooned on a recently erupted volcanic island.

But now I miss the dratted man. Isn't that always the way? Oh well, we do ourselves no good to harp on about the past. Onwards and upwards, that's what I say.'

'. . . so I said to her, well, if you want your children downing alcopops at their age, then that's your business. Though with mothers like that, it's no wonder thirteen-year-olds like that poor Lily Williams end up passed out on the golf course.'

It was mother-and-baby morning and Geraldine Prior's busybody mouth was spreading its usual poison, but Milly had barely heard a word. Her eyes wandered round the small church hall. Orange juice and digestives were laid out on the counter alongside a saucer for donations; babies lazed back in rockers or were placed on the floor surrounded by brightly coloured toys. And round the other side, toddlers climbed up small slides or rampaged at the wheel of sit-in cars.

As Geraldine wittered on, Milly stifled a yawn. She'd have happily given it a miss this morning. She felt on edge, longing to crawl out of her skin. Twice today she'd found herself opening the fridge door for no reason, staring at the contents and closing it again. And all the while her fingers itched to delve into her purse, find that bottle with the little white pills.

The buzz of energy they'd given her at first no longer lasted more than a minute or two. Between doses, she was lethargic, bloody exhausted really, summoning every inch of energy just to change Ben's nappy or put the clothes from the washer to the line. She felt like she was floating, watching herself from a distance, as if the poor slob going through the motions of normality had nothing to do with her.

Geraldine was looking at Milly expectantly.

'Sorry?'

'I was just saying it's a shame Erin missed that test Wednesday. Tanya said it was really important.'

'Test?' Tanya and Erin were in the same classes for most subjects.

'Geography.' She scooped Finn, her eighteen-month-old, on to her lap and fed him an organic rice cake. 'How is she by the way?'

'Oh, fine. Yes, quite fine.'

'Just, well, Tanya says she's not been at school these past few days. I assumed she was sick.'

'No . . .' Milly said slowly as she tried to clear the fog in her head. 'I mean, when I say fine, well, she's feeling a bit . . . fluey . . . and she has . . . diarrhoea . . . and . . . You see, we've all been down with it. We're thinking of painting a red cross on our front door,' she quipped.

'Oh.' Geraldine's sharp nose twitched in alarm. 'Sorry to hear that. But Ben's OK?' She indicated to Ben lying on his stomach making eyes at himself in a small plastic mirror woven into the cloth.

'He caught it first. I wouldn't have brought him if he wasn't one hundred per cent OK.'

'No, of course. Oh, oh. Singing's started. Are you coming?'

'I think I'll head off actually, check on Erin.'

'But you've only just got here.' Geraldine's beady eyes peered in surprise through her granny-like glasses.

'It's Ben's naptime too. The illness put him right out of kilter. See you next week.'

'OK. Give my love to Erin.'

Milly manoeuvred Ben's tiny arms into his jacket as Geraldine placed herself cross-legged on the floor with the other mothers at the far end of the hall who were belting out 'Wheels on the Bus' at the tops of their voices while manipulating their babies' arms in circular motions.

'I'll give her a darn sight more than that,' she mumbled under her breath.

By the time Milly put the key in the lock she was fuming. She parked the buggy in the hallway and marched straight upstairs to Erin's bedroom. Skipping school for the past few days? Where the hell could she have been? And missing a test. How many times had Milly tried to instil in her that she shouldn't waste these valuable school years?

As for her room . . . She glanced around. Admittedly it was cramped but even so what a tip. *And* she hadn't cleaned out her hamster. How many weeks had that been? The stench from the cage was worse than a horse stable. And when had Erin last let it out – or was it destined just to spend its nights going round and round on that awful metal wheel?

'Here.' She plucked a couple of chocolate nibbles from a half-opened packet and pushed one through the thin bars. Cruel, really, how they were condemned to these small cages. 'You poor thing. Poor, poor thing.'

At the sound of the bars being rattled, the hamster sleepily lifted its head, took the chocolate from her and stored it in his cheeks before snuggling back under its cotton-wool bed.

Milly began rummaging through Erin's desk not really knowing what she was looking for. Textbooks, mock exam papers, broken protractors, loose ink cartridges and then a light blue sheet of lined A4. She turned it over and peered closer. Signatures . . . fourteen rows of them, all the same, or almost the same. But what worried Milly most of all was . . .

It wasn't Erin's signature.

It was Milly's.

Chapter 33

'Alan Alda. Two o'clock. And the woman with him – Kate Winslet.'

'She's nothing like Kate Winslet, her head's too small and she's at least twice her size.'

'Kate Winslet when she was pregnant?'

'And what about that guy in the corner?' Hazel pointed to an elderly drunk. It was their afternoon amusement – match the celebrity to the punter.

'Dean Martin.' Jonno rested his elbows on the bar. 'No. The guy from *High Noon*. Gary Cooper.'

'You've seen *High Noon*?'

'They do have films back in Aussie, we're not that backward.'

'Just I didn't imagine westerns would be up your street.'

'Oh?' His monkey face crinkled into a smile.

'But then maybe they would be. Fancy a night in with a video?'

'I'll consult my engagement diary.'

'And I'll consult mine.'

They both laughed.

'Go on then, who's that couple?' Jonno indicated the handsome man and the fiery redhead who'd just stepped in. 'Keith Urban and Nicole Kidman?'

'No way. He's taller than her for a start and she's much more Jane Goldman.'

'Who's Jane Goldman?'

'You know nothing.' She punched him playfully on the arm. 'She's Jonathan Ross's wife. Writes books about paranormal stuff. Hair's exactly the same colour. Ignorant Aussie.'

'Whinging pom.' They smiled in comic unison as the guy reached the bar.

'So what would you like?' he asked his girlfriend as he put his arm around her waist. 'Wine?'

She smiled curiously. 'Better not. Make it a St Clements.'

He turned to Hazel. 'St Clements and a pint of Stella, please.'

Hazel put the glass under the tap and waited while the amber liquid slowly poured in. She'd got pretty good pulling pints, changing barrels, working the till, mixing cocktails. She'd done bar work before, but in somewhat more laid-back, hippy venues – Phuket, Goa. But wherever it was, she'd always liked that she could hide behind a counter and people-watch. Not having to make conversation if you didn't feel in the mood.

The couple paid and took their drinks over to the snug area. Hazel could see the electricity between the two of them. He couldn't take his eyes off her, touching her elbow, pulling out the seat for her, holding her hand. And she obviously basked in his attention.

It made Hazel feel wistful. She'd never been in love. Something always stopped her getting close enough to a guy to give things a real chance. And on the rare occasion she had convinced herself she'd fallen head over heels and lingered long enough to delve into their innermost core, searching for the hidden diamond this fascinating creature must surely have buried in the deepest vaults of his heart, it usually turned out to be a worthless rock. So off she'd be to the next captivating thing, leaving the poor bugger reeling, wondering what hit him.

It was a character trait that had got her into trouble more than once. Out there somewhere were a string of past victims more than willing to brand her as a heartless tease when really it was more a failure to keep up with her imagination. At the first twinge of boredom – which for Hazel usually came right about the time they started getting mushy and clingy – she was off.

Just like Avril.

No! Not like Avril, she thought furiously. She was nothing like *that woman*. Avril had shown more consideration to a dog than she had to her own daughter. Daughter. The very word made Hazel want to throw up.

Half an hour later found Hazel scrubbing frantically away at the bar as her whole sorry story regurgitated around and around her head. She couldn't face anyone, didn't want to face anyone – not yet. Maybe not ever. There were so many questions she wanted to ask, but she was just too angry right now. How could her whole family keep such a massive secret like that? she thought bitterly as she took the worst of her venom out on the bar. What a fool they'd made of her.

'Bluey keeps staring at you,' Jonno whispered in Hazel's ear.

'Bluey?'

'The redhead – that's what we call them in Oz. Of course it could be the manic way you're polishing those work surfaces. Jeez, I can just about see my face in them.'

'Ugh, well, don't look too hard, it might crack. Actually, I thought it was you she was staring at. Perhaps she fancies you.

Doesn't know that you're g—' She almost said gay, but just managed to add 'game for a laugh'.

'Game for a laugh?'

'Pommy expression. From an old TV show. Oh, oh, she's coming over.'

'I'll leave you two alone. Maybe she's "game for a laugh".'

'Pint of mild and another St Clements?' The girl put her empty glasses back on the counter.

'Sure.' Hazel flipped the lid off the orange bottle.

'Do I know you from somewhere?' The girl half frowned.

'I don't think so.'

'Not Amanda by any chance?'

'No.' Though that name might have suited her. She'd often thought about changing her name. Hazel being way too boring and tree-like. Maybe something exotic like Miranda or sultry like Drambola. That's one of the reasons she liked travelling. The constant moving on, the total reinvention of yourself if and when it took your fancy. She could be the bookish bespectacled woman seriously studying the archi-tecture in Mandalay, the fun-loving dippy blonde bombshell or even the mysterious brunette needing to be on her own. But last week, wow. The rug had really been pulled from under her feet. Her whole family had reinvented themselves. Her sisters were now her aunts, her nephews and niece her cousins, and Callum and Peggy her grandparents.

'Ice and lemon?' She studied the woman. Up close she was really rather stunning.

'Just ice. Sure I don't know you? You're not from around here?'

'No.' Hazel picked up two ice chunks and dropped them in. 'You?'

'I live in Brighton.'

'Cool.' Hazel smiled. 'Love the shops.'

'They're great, yeah.' The girl smiled back and gathered up the drinks. 'Well, see ya.'

'See ya.'

Hazel's mobile bleeped twice, signalling another incoming message. Damn, not again. She pulled it from her back pocket. It might be easier if she'd just switched it off, but something was stopping her. Curiosity perhaps . . .

She skimmed back over the texts that had been coming in over the last few days:

1. Nat – *WHERE R U?* Delete.
2. Avril – *Call me*. Delete.
3. Milly – *PLEAD ROING MMMMMM* (Actually that one tickled her.) Save.
4. Avril . . . Delete.
5. Avril . . . Delete.
6. Avril . . . Delete.

'Richard stopped by my office this morning.' It was six thirty and Natalie was sitting at the kitchen table chopping onions while Matt painted the wall behind her a bright sunshine yellow that Peggy had picked out and Callum would surely have detested. For once Natalie had caught the early train home only to discover that Peggy was in Codmoreton, checking out an evening class that Janet from the library had suggested. Funny how people reacted so differently to her recent widowhood. Either, Peggy had confided in Natalie, they crossed the road to avoid her or they jumped in with endless suggestions to help her get over her bereavement. Why they couldn't just leave her alone to grieve in peace! After all, it had been less than a fortnight since her husband had died. Still, the sound of Belly Dancing For Seniors had proved too much temptation to resist.

'Richard? Avril's boyfriend?' Matt was almost finished, kneeling on the floor in his ripped jeans as he carefully painted around the plug socket. 'The married guy you called the spawn of Satan?'

'Very funny.' Natalie's face coloured. 'We went for a coffee.'

'Oh, and?'

'He was really nice. Concerned about Avril *and* Hazel. Avril had told him her big secret before us even. Incredible, huh?'

'They're obviously closer than she lets on.' Matt put his paintbrush in the empty pot of emulsion and went to the sink to run water in it. He had paint in his hair and on his T-shirt and smelt slightly of sweat. It had been with a touch of awkwardness that she'd invited him to eat with them tonight. His nightly absences had been a source of almost equal relief and letdown.

'Too bad she won't call him. But she's like Mr Darcy, "My good opinion once lost is lost for ever." ' Natalie had seen *Pride and Prejudice*, the one with Keira Knightley in it, five times and had quite a crush on Matthew MacFadyen. In fact just the other night she'd had a dream about it, only instead of the dark brooding actor emerging towards her out of the mist, those piercing grey eyes had belonged to . . .

'*Damn Avril!*' She slammed the three-inch blade into the pile of onions wishing she could as easily cut the thread of her overactive imagination. 'And damn Hazel, acting like a selfish brat as always, no thought for Mum or anyone else. Why do my bloody family have to be so dramatic?!' She stabbed the board, creating an inch-deep groove.

'I have no idea.' Matt put a restraining yellow-spattered hand over hers and gently prised the large chopping knife out of her hand. Pulling the board and onions towards him, he tipped them into the frying pan. 'Not to change the subject,' he added lightly, 'but how's Jeremy? You are still getting married, aren't you?'

'Yes. Yes, of course.' Natalie squirmed under his scrutiny. She washed her hands under the cold tap and said to her reflection in the tap, 'Only we can hardly set a new date when we don't know if Hazel's dead or alive, can we?'

'Oh, I'm sure she's alive. She survived Colombia, I think she can cope with southern England.' When she looked up, Matt was staring at her with an intensity that made her breath catch in her throat. 'You're blushing . . .' he pointed out, pulling a strand of hair from her red cheek and tucking it behind her ear.

'I'm just hot.' Natalie sprang away and filled the pan with water. 'Right, spuds next. Can you pass me the bag?'

'You don't have to, you know.' He leaned against the counter, juggling an earth-laden potato from hand to hand, still staring.

'I just fancied some mash.' She ducked her head, letting her hair drop in a curtain again.

'No, I mean marry Jeremy.' He placed the potato in her hand, staring at her intently as she looked up. 'You don't have to marry Jeremy.'

'What do you mean, don't *have* to?' Natalie immediately bristled. Who was he to tell her what she could or couldn't do. 'Of course I know *I don't have to do anything*. I'm marrying Jeremy because I want to.'

'Well, that's good then,' he said with too much enthusiasm as he looked into the bag of potatoes.

'I mean, if I didn't want to, if I wasn't marrying him, I'd tell him, wouldn't I?'

Matt hardly seemed to notice this, as he picked up four more spuds and started a quite impressive juggling routine, two in each hand and then all four in a circle. Whistling a tune she didn't recognise, he kept his eyes on the flying objects, moving around the floor to keep them all within reach.

His lack of response infuriated Natalie.

'And I'd tell everyone else,' she ranted on. 'I wouldn't just be postponing the wedding, I'd have called it off for good. What? What are you smirking about?'

'The lady doth protest too much, methinks.' It was one of her father's favourite quotations. Crazy how hearing Matt use it now made her feel ganged up on.

'I'm not. It's just . . . it's none of anybody's bloody business what happens between me and Jeremy.' She grabbed at the nearest airborne object and all four went crashing to the floor.

'Not even Jeremy?' Picking up the fallen spuds, he dropped them into the sink beside her. 'Doesn't he have a right to know?'

'There's nothing to know!' Natalie's voice upped a tone.

'And I'm a blue . . .' With the words '. . .-arsed baboon' hovering on his lips, he caught her dangerous look and with a glance at Peggy's flower vase found a more innocuous substitute. '. . . blue iris. This is me you're talking to, Natalie.' Matt leaned against the worktop and scrutinised her from head to toe. Natalie's traitor heart suddenly accelerated and her face burned. 'Maybe I'm dense but you certainly don't give me the impression of a besotted bride-to-be. Where is Jeremy anyway? You've seen him what, once, twice since your dad died? But of course that's normal when you're so in love you can't keep your hands off each other. I'm sure you're both just too *frightfully* busy.' Sarcasm made his voice sound low and gravelly.

'Well, I have been busy, in case you haven't noticed, taking care of Mum.'

He put his hands on her waist and turned her so that she couldn't avoid the burning pupils of his slate eyes, searing into her own, reading things she didn't want him to see. 'Be honest, with yourself, if not with me. You know if it's a wedding you're after' – he quirked his eyebrows, his voice husky and faintly mocking – 'why not consider a doctor? Poorly paid, limited prospects, but a great kisser. And you have to know I've always been mad –'

'Mad?' Her heart was beating so fast she thought it might erupt out of her chest. Was he serious? Or was this his twisted attempt at humour? For a second she wavered and then the thought of Jeremy's parents' scandalised faces tipped her over the edge. 'You're insane! My life isn't a joke, you know.' She jerked away, saved by a sudden surge of anger. How dare he suggest that all she cared about was the wedding! Like she was some pathetic bimbo desperate for a gold ring on her finger. 'Look, let's get this straight. You are nothing to me. I am nothing to you. You haven't seen me for twenty years, you don't know the slightest thing about me. And I don't care for *your* opinion! I'm marrying Jeremy because I love him. So save your pathetic attempts at psychoanalysis, it's clearly not your forte, *Doctor*.'

Matt jerked his hands away as if she were scalding.

'Sorry.' His face was stiff, his gaze suddenly flint. 'My mistake. You're right, it's none of my business. I should stay out of it.'

He slouched moodily towards the back door but Natalie was on a roll now, a red mist clouding her eyes as all the stress of the last few weeks and the injustices of the past rose up to taunt her.

'You're dead right it's none of your business. And I'll tell you another thing you should stay out of. My family. This house. The country. Hazel said you're going back to the Ecuador so why don't you hurry up and go! Get out! Get the hell out!'

Unthinkingly, she snatched up the nearest item to hand, a still unpeeled potato from the bag on the counter and flung it at his head. He ducked and it missed by a mile but the failure only provoked her more. She grabbed another and another, throwing them in a wildly erratic barrage.

'I hope the mosquitoes eat you alive! I'm sick of your interfering and I bloody hate you!'

'Don't worry.' Arms raised to protect his head, Matt's initial response of surprised laughter at the attack was pushed aside by a sudden corresponding anger. 'I'm going. There's just one last thing.'

Swiftly he marched into the onslaught, grabbed the saucepan from the stove and poured the contents, cold water, potatoes and all, over her head. Natalie gasped with shock, hair and clothes dripping as he glared down at her.

'I've had it with you, Natalie MacLeod. I always knew you were a spoilt princess but I never figured you for such a complete cow. You might have all your family and Jeremy terrorised but you don't impress me. I've had it up to here watching you run roughshod over everyone's feelings.'

He threw a tea towel at her and stormed into the hall. Still stunned, towelling her hair with the striped fabric, Natalie stepped to the kitchen door to see him pick up his daypack.

'I'm out of here. Have a nice rest of your life. I would say I hope Jeremy makes you happy but frankly I don't give a shit. You deserve each other. Tell Peggy I'll phone her before I leave.'

Natalie had never seen his eyes so cold. In all her childish squabbles with Matt, he'd always been the one to come to his senses first, tease and plague her until she reluctantly laughed and forgave him. But somehow, instinctively, she knew this was different. She had the sudden sickening feeling that this time there'd be no apologies, no making up. She opened her mouth, not knowing exactly what she wanted to say.

The words that eventually tumbled out weren't exactly the peace flag she had in mind. 'Go on then, get lost. If you were a real man you'd feel completely emancipated, cycling off on your little bike, you . . . you . . . non-driver.'

Matt slung his daypack over his shoulder, looking far from crushed. 'Well, at least I'm not emasculated which is more than I can say for any man who chooses to hang around you. And unlike that ball-less wonder you love to bully, I actually like having a vote.'

While she was still working this out, the front door slammed. Belatedly, shocked into motion again, Natalie rushed to tug it open.

'Matt!' she yelled, looking both ways down the street.

No sign of him. And suddenly everything was horribly wrong.

Chapter 34

'Yes, Mrs Pettigrew.' Natalie was on the phone the next day. 'I absolutely understand.' She made a face at Vera who gave her a sympathetic look. 'Yes, I know. Entirely immoral and so disappointing but . . .' She held the phone two feet from her ear as the angry squawking rose to descant. 'I promise you, we can find you another house just as –' A slam and the phone went dead.

'Stupid bitch. Not my fault if the surveyor found subsidence, is it?' She looked up as the door opened. To her surprise, Jeremy was in the lobby, gazing around at the walls plastered with photos of luxury mansions, as if he wasn't quite sure he was in the right place.

'What are you doing here?' Natalie gasped. Jeremy worked in the depths of the City and claimed he never had time for lunch. Seeing him now in her office was a bit like seeing a crocodile lurking in Kensington ponds; she almost wanted to rub her eyes. He looked sharp though, in his Harvie & Hudson shirt and pinstriped suit. Out of habit, she mentally checked her own appearance: smart but sexy Joseph jacket with matching skirt, hair twisted on top of her head with a jewelled clasp and she'd just reapplied her make-up minutes before. Not that it mattered. 'Why didn't you ring?'

'Because I thought you might be out, *again*.' He ran his

finger uncomfortably round his collar, looking about as relaxed and friendly as an on-duty guardsman.

Natalie exchanged a swift look with Vera, whose eyes were on stalks.

'It's so nice to meet you at last,' Vera gushed. 'I've heard so much about you.'

'How do you do?' Jeremy shook her outstretched hand briefly before turning back to Natalie. 'Is there somewhere we can talk?'

'Yes, sure. Um . . . OK then. Vera' – she reached for her bag – 'I'll have my mobile on. Call me if there's anything urgent. Oh, and if Mr Gleeson rings, tell him I'm onto it.'

'Your usual?' The young waitress smiled down at Natalie, recognising her from the previous day's visit with Richard. Natalie wondered if she found it strange – her, having coffee with two different men on consecutive days. She probably thought she was having an affair.

'Yes, and a . . . what are you having?' Natalie turned to Jeremy.

'Espresso. I thought what we needed to say, we needed to say face to face,' Jeremy said darkly as the waitress slipped Natalie a wink before walking off with their order.

'Sounds ominous.'

'It is . . . well, it isn't. It's . . .'

'You look like you've been sent on a mission.' She almost laughed, but stopped when she saw his face freeze. 'You *have* been sent on a mission? Don't tell me . . .' The penny was dropping with a clang. 'Your parents?'

'No. I mean. I'm sorry . . . I . . . What I'm trying to say . . . I mean, what I . . .'

Irritation battled with a strange sort of sympathy for his discomfort.

Natalie shook her head. 'Stop. Stop. This is not between your parents and my family. This is just us now, Jeremy – you and me.' In her peripheral vision, she was aware of the girl behind the counter now, watching them as she put cups on saucers, no doubt sensing yet another emotional drama. 'If you met me now, knowing me, knowing how we are together, knowing – let's face it, what my family are like – would you want to marry me?'

He lowered his eyes. 'No.'

'And Jeremy, darling,' she said quietly, with a hint of a smile, 'I don't want to marry you.' Some part of her mind was congratulating herself on how well she was handling this scene. She was Celia Johnson in *Brief Encounter*; Ingrid Bergman saying farewell to Bogie in *Casablanca*. Jeremy, she could see, was impressed and not quite sure how to take it.

A movement to her left made her look up. Their coffees had arrived.

'Anything else?' The waitress placed the drinks in front of them.

'No, thanks,' they both said in unison and she walked away with a strange smile on her face. The giant bowl-sized cup in front of Natalie had a crack and a big chip on the rim that surely meant it should be tossed immediately in the bin but this wasn't the time to make a fuss.

'But . . .' Jeremy looked confused.

'It's silly, isn't it?' She put her hand over his and gently traced her finger over the engagement ring she'd so wanted at the time he'd proposed. 'But I think I was always wrong for you and perhaps you for me. We brought out the worst in each other. All our insecurities, our faults.'

Jeremy attempted a weak smile. '*I* have faults?'

'A few perhaps.' She smiled. 'I just think that maybe apart we'll have a chance to be the people we truly want to be, not two neurotics caring about what everyone else thinks, too frightened to step out of the corporate line.'

She abandoned the coffee, pushing the cup away. 'Now that we're over, maybe we can be friends.'

'We're over?' Jeremy stuttered. He looked baffled at the unexpected turn of events. 'But I wasn't meaning . . .'

'Oh yes.' Natalie slowly nodded, once again sensing an invisible director's silent applause. 'We're definitely over. We don't have to announce it right away, though, if you don't want. Give it a few months and everyone will have forgotten we ever had a wedding planned in the first place. It'll be easier then. We might even get away with not returning the presents.'

He forced a smile. 'You mean we each get to keep a toaster?'

She couldn't tell if he was relieved or crushed. He looked like he was flitting somewhere between the two. But of one thing she was sure, his rotten parents would be dancing for joy.

'Oh, Jeremy.' She leaned forward to hug him. She knew, heart of hearts, they wouldn't stay friends but, at the same time, she knew she'd miss him. Six years, after all. Six years of living together, sleeping together, planning a future together. And yes, she'd miss what he represented, the two point five kids, the central London house, no money worries. But – it was shocking to realise – the sense of freedom was immense.

They stood up, leaving their coffees untouched. For a second they held each other in a long embrace. Jeremy was the first to step away.

'Well,' he said, his mouth twisting cynically, 'congratulations. Now you can run after your gardener with a clear conscience.'

'What?' Natalie looked up at him, shocked to see the bitterness in his eyes. So much for it all being so easy.

'Oh, don't play the innocent. We both know you can't stand being on your own. And I've seen the way you look at him. I'm not a bloody idiot, you know.' He snatched his brief-case and marched out, not waiting for her startled response.

She sat for a while after he'd gone and then dropped some change onto the counter and made her way to the door. Just as she reached for the handle, something caught her eye. It was a little old lady standing in the corner clutching the largest bunch of flowers Natalie had ever seen.

'He just gave them to me,' Natalie heard the old lady chuckle to her friend. 'For no reason. What a nice young gentleman.'

'Did he catch you?' Vera was all agog when Natalie swept triumphantly back into the office.

'Who?'

'Matthew Harkness. Blimey, you didn't tell me he was a total hottie. He's your sister's horrid boyfriend?'

'He was here? Matt was here?' Natalie felt her head swirl.

'With this massive bouquet, looking for you. I sent him over to the café – I thought that's where you'd be? Now what were they?' She put a finger to her temple, thinking. 'Not carnations, not tulips . . . Hmm. I'm really rubbish with flowers. Oh yes, I remember! Irises, they were, blue irises.'

Natalie stared straight ahead, feeling her smile wobble. Only sheer willpower kept it pasted to her face. The envelope had been opened, the cameras were on her, and against all odds, the Oscar had gone to someone else.

Chapter 35

'Squeeze it.'

'No.'

'Go on, squeeze it.' Jonno took a step nearer to Hazel. 'Feel its texture, smell its ripeness. It has to have just the right amount of softness, yet not be squidgy.'

'Well, it is a bit squidgy.'

'Right, so we put it down.' He took the avocado from Hazel's hand and placed it back among the others. 'And go check out another stall.'

They were in the market rooting out ingredients for tonight's meal. Only rooting out didn't even begin to cover the endeavour. Hazel had never been on a grocery trip like it. Jonno spent what seemed like hours at each stall, minutely inspecting each and every salad item. Smelling, touching, probing, like a sultan selecting from the latest shipload of potential concubines. Cabbages too green, peppers too ripe, cucumbers too hard or large, or whatever. She supposed she was lucky he didn't suddenly whirl around and check out her teeth. If not to tell her age then at least to see if her pearly whites were worthy of biting into such precious objects.

'A tomato is a tomato is a tomato.' She jigged with impatience, watching him pore over the fruit – or was it a vegetable?

'But that's where you're wrong, sheila. There's all sorts of tomato, different shapes, different flavours. Over ten thousand varieties in actual fact. Great White Beefsteak, Golden Peach, White Queen, then there's vine-ripened, hothouse. Shall I go on . . . ?'

'Well, they're all going to get bunged in a salad, so who cares?'

'I care. OK, test question, what's this?' He produced a bunch of green leafy stuff from his basket which to Hazel actually looked more like a weed.

She hazarded a guess. 'Parsley?'

'Coriander! Here, take a sniff.' He grinned as Hazel backed off, making a face.

'Ugh, I hate that stuff. Worse than tofu. When I was in Ecuador, they put it in everything. Even scrambled eggs. Tastes like soap.'

'You kidding? It's my favourite herb. Now come on, back in the car. I've got to go to the butcher's to pick up an order of meat. Want to come along?'

Hazel shrugged. 'Might as well, I've nothing better to do. At least not until I get some dosh together.'

She hefted three bulging carrier bags, dropping them beside Jonno's armload of purchases on the back seat, and pulled down the passenger-side sunshield to check her reflection in the attached mirror. Yep, she looked different all right. Hair cropped close to her head and spiky and Jonno had helped her colour it a shockingly unnatural blonde. Even without her current outfit of borrowed cut-off cargo pants held up by a belt and one of Jonno's sleeveless Ts, no one could say she looked like Avril now.

'Have you always been this fussy about food?' she asked, glancing back at the bulging shopping bags.

'Since I was a nipper.'

'You know, I spent a season grape-picking in France once. They were obsessed with food too, just like you. Family of ten lived in this chateau and they didn't even own a tin-opener. Went berserk if you put the Camembert in the fridge, and anyone daring to add fizzy water to their Pouilly Fuissé would be hanged on the spot. Whereas Mum –' She stopped suddenly, remembering Peggy wasn't her mum and studied her nails intently.

Jonno looked at her sympathetically as he pushed the car into first. 'Families, eh? What a trip.' He scrunched the gearbox of his old Fiat. 'Take mine, for instance, and I mean take them, please. I have two brothers. The eldest is a right mongrel, as useful as a tail on a tortoise. The other's a psycho – can't walk into a bar without starting World War III. As for Drew's family, phew, where do I begin? His sister has four children by five different fathers.'

'How come?' Hazel perked up, diverted by the illogical maths.

'Two of them are fighting paternity. She's refusing a DNA test. I tell you, it beats *Neighbours* hands down. And my father has the reddest neck in the state of Queensland – thinks Abos should be shot on sight and gays should be smothered at birth.'

'God,' Hazel exclaimed, 'that must have been *so* hard for you.'

'Yeah, especially when I took up hairdressing. Why do you think I left Brizzie?' His eyes caught on a building. 'Now this manoeuvre is known back in dear Oz as chuckin a U-ey.' He yanked the wheel around. 'Come on, darl, I'll shout you lunch.'

'There must have been a reason, though.' Jonno cradled his pint half an hour later.

'Like what?' Hazel gulped her drink. 'Shame on the family? It's not like Dad was any virtuous angel. And from the sound of it nor were the rest of the relations.'

'Nor were mine, darl. My father once called my mother a whore and I punched him in the smacker. I kicked him out, told him if he ever set foot in the house again, I'd wallop him all the way to Ayers Rock and leave him for the dingoes' dinner.'

She smiled. 'Were you particularly close to your mother?'

'Yeah . . . Yeah, I was. Am.'

'Was she quite . . .' Hazel stopped. She was going to say domineering but ended up compromising, '. . . a strong character?'

Jonno gave her a fishy look.

'You could say that. Don't you try and get a measure on me, my girl, or you'll be trying all night. All right, your oldies screwed up, but it doesn't mean there was no love there. And they might have had their reasons. I think you should give them a fair go – at least talk to them.'

'I can't.' She set her chin stubbornly

'All families are dysfunctional, kiddo. I don't know, maybe you just have to change the perspective.'

'What do you mean?'

'Tilt the mirror, sheila, so it's not always pointing at you.' He gestured to the 'It's All About Me' slogan emblazoned across her chest. 'We all buy into the perfect life. Everyone's happy, we should be happy, but the reality is look behind those closed doors and that neighbour's being beaten up, that teenager's being pressured for sex, that rich old lady is dying of loneliness because her kids can't be bothered visiting. All I'm saying, darl, is don't just think why did it happen to me, but why did it happen to my mother, how did my grandmother feel, you know . . . And once you've come up with the questions.' He stood up and held out his hand to pull her to her feet. 'Then maybe it's time to go search out the answers.'

'No, Bruce.' She stuck her arm through his. 'Nice speech, but maybe it isn't.'

Chapter 36

Peggy fussed around her three daughters offering the contents of a large flowery china plate – almond slices and coconut macaroons. 'And I've cake in the kitchen. Dundee. Shop-bought.'

'Just sit down, Mum,' Avril ordered. 'We don't want you waiting on us.'

'But I feel guilty everyone running around after me. Doesn't seem right.'

'It's about time we took care of you,' Natalie insisted, as Milly opened the window to let in some fresh air. 'Mum, are you sure you want to go through Dad's things now? It could wait a few weeks.'

'No, it can't,' Avril contradicted. 'I can just see Dad's clothes hanging around forever, full of moths and the whole house getting infested. I'll do the upstairs, if you like.'

'I just meant . . .' Natalie felt a momentary flash of annoyance at Avril's bossiness. After being incommunicado for over a week and practically having to be dragged down here, *now* she wanted to take over? 'It seems awfully soon. I don't think the moths are going to fly in for at least a fortnight, do you?'

'The church jumble sale's next Saturday.' Peggy sat down in Callum's armchair and bit into a macaroon. 'And I expect it'll take my mind off poor Hazel. What did the police say again?'

Despite her initial brave stance, Hazel's extended absence had started to truly worry her.

The sisters exchanged glances. Avril turned her back and stared out of the window. Milly busied herself with Rory's shoelaces.

'They said they have every man on the street out there.' Natalie crossed her fingers. 'First sign of her they're going to call straight away.' Truth was Hazel was over twenty-one and had left of her own free will. The police couldn't have been more disinterested if they'd reported a stolen bicycle.

Peggy smiled. 'I've always had faith in our boys in blue. I remember Dorothy's brother Roland was going to join the Metropolitan force but he was too small by half an inch. He walked the streets for hours to make his feet swell so he'd be taller. Didn't work, though. So you think Hazel will be back soon?'

'Yeah, don't worry. She's bound to be home for Milly's birthday. After all, it's a big one this year. We'll have to arrange something special.' Natalie kept her voice more reassuring than she felt. You never knew with Hazel. She could already be on a plane flying over some distant ocean. Long gone. Just like Matt.

Two hours later Milly was busy in the kitchen while Rory played at her feet and Ben gurgled happily away in his rocker. She'd finished the dishes, cleaned the surfaces and put away the meagre leftovers from Morrisons' finest deli offerings. No more Tesco for Milly, not since the Mrs Hammond encounter. As it was, she couldn't stroll through Codmoreton without feeling the need to peer round every corner to make sure the coast was clear.

'Fuck it!' Rory exclaimed as his Lego machine broke into two.

'What did you say?' Milly dropped to her knees like she'd been shot from ten paces by a Colt 45.

'I said, fuck it,' he repeated, his face utterly serious.

'Rory!' She turned him to face her and looked him square in the eyes. 'You mustn't say that word. Ever. I repeat, *ever*.' She shuddered as visions leapt into her head of being called in to the school as Rory parroted it to all the children in his class. 'Do you understand?'

'Auntie Avril said it,' he defended himself, sounding aggrieved.

'Avril?'

'Yes.' He nodded, then smiled as he spotted the yellow astronaut he'd spent the last ten minutes searching for. 'When she crashed the car.'

'She did what?'

'Crashed her car.' He clicked the astronaut into position on top of his spaceship. 'And it rolled round and round. Whee . . .'

'Whee?' She could almost feel the smoke gathering in her nostrils. 'Whee!'

He nodded. 'And she said the S-word as well.'

'Right, that's it!' Milly ripped off her Marigolds, throwing them at the sink. 'Don't move from this room. And put your hands over your ears.'

Avril was in their parents' bedroom pulling clothes out of her father's wardrobe. There was a pile on the floor as tall as Rory.

She sighed as she held up a couple of ties before bunging them in a black bin bag labelled 'Oxfam'. Everything was musty and old and she was developing an allergy. Her eyes were swelling up, her throat was scratchy. From the dust probably. It was all so sad and pathetic somehow. Her dad's life possessions – a bundle of moth-eaten wool suits, some cotton shirts and a few exam certificates proving he'd once passed through medical school. All there was to show of his existence. What was the point of it all? Or was there no point? You just left a pile of genes behind – if you had children, that is – and your flesh turned to worm fodder. Was that it?

Really, she thought, checking inside the pockets of a pair of trousers, she just wanted to finish the job in the shortest time possible, head back to her cosy flat, down a pile of Nurofen and shut the door on everybody. Her mother, her sisters – especially her sisters. She wouldn't have come today if Natalie, the eternal nag, hadn't called her again and again, refusing to give up until Avril finally picked up the phone. But being home only reminded her even more sharply of how badly she'd screwed up.

With her parents.

With Richard.

And, most of all, with Hazel.

Watching her mother torment herself over the fate of the young woman she'd raised as her own daughter, Avril felt crucified with guilt. Where could she be? Was she ever going to return? And if she did would she ever forgive Avril for her selfishness? Because really that's what it had been. Selfishness – and, yes – cowardice. That had come into it too.

Big old scary Avril was no more than a shrinking violet.

Against all that, the fate of her on-again, off-again romance with Richard really shouldn't matter. Although somehow it did. Not that she would ever call him. That would go against everything she believed; her ferocious pride was all that kept her just barely clinging on. Stopped her from sitting in a nice hot bath with a friendly razor. Or driving off Beachy Head. And not that she would take his call, even if he tried, which he hadn't. If she paid any attention to the few brain cells she still had functioning, this really was the absolute worst time to get emotionally attached.

However nice the guy might be.

And however much she missed him.

Since Hazel's disappearance Avril had been holed up in her flat, drinking away her heartaches with the time-tested remedy of alcoholic oblivion, barely making an appearance in the office, leaving poor Brenda to fend off the calls from neglected clients. Her mouth tasted like a lockerful of sweaty socks, her eyes were bloodshot and squinted from the painful daylight that only accelerated the pounding of manic little dwarfs pickaxing their way through her skull.

At least for once Natalie had the good grace not to tell her how terrible she looked, but both her sisters had appeared shocked when Avril walked in, her usually glossy hair greasy, unwashed and slovenly pulled back into an untidy ponytail.

And they didn't even know the latest news. Baxter had left her. Run off to Hollywood and signed with Creative Artists. For all his avowals of eternal loyalty, the golden goose had flown the coop.

Suddenly the door burst open and Milly stormed in, face puce with rage. 'What happened the other day?' she snarled. 'The day of the funeral.'

'Let's see.' Avril bunged two patched-up cardigans in the throwing-out box, followed by a pair of dog-chewed old slippers. 'Matt made a great speech, we had a wake where Mum had the time of her life, Hazel ran off after I hit her with the truth of her existence and . . . oh yeah, sometime in there we buried Dad.'

'During the wake. You know only too well what I'm talking about.'

'Well, if you know what you're talking about, sweetie, then maybe you'd kindly enlighten me.' Avril was in no mood for games and she didn't much care for Milly's tone of voice either.

'You crashed the car, didn't you?'

Avril felt dual blades of guilt and remorse stab her below the breastbone but the sentiments were quickly overshadowed by her already foul mood and her inability to take even one more thing. Was this why they'd dragged her down from London – so they could accuse her? Having Milly shout at her was really the last straw in what was already winning awards for the lousiest summer on record. Obviously Milly had heard some version of what had happened, but instead of coming to discuss it, was choosing to twist a briefly terrifying but thankfully fairly non-eventful incident into a monumental cause for massive hysteria.

'Actually,' she said, coldly, though she did in fact feel terrible about it, 'no, I didn't.'

'Rory said you did.'

'You're talking about the trip to the ice-cream parlour? Yes, all right, hands up, bang bang, I skidded the car slightly and we ended up facing the other way. I tapped my head but apart from that no one was even faintly scratched. It wasn't even a fender-bender, let alone a crash.'

'And you didn't even have the decency to let me know? What if the kids had whiplash injuries? What if they had internal injuries that didn't show? What if –'

'Internal injuries that didn't show?' Avril scoffed. 'Good God, Milly, stop being so melodramatic,' she added dismissively, as she held up a dressing gown. 'What do you think, charity, chuck or pass to Ivor?' Even as she'd said it, she wondered if she'd gone too far. The worry and torment of losing her daughter, her lover and her business within weeks of losing her father was turning her spiteful.

Milly glowered, pure loathing in her eyes.

'Look.' Avril softened, feeling bad after all. 'No one was hurt. They were wearing seat belts. It was no big deal.'

'How can you say that?' Milly was infuriated at her sister's attitude and ignorance. These were Milly's babies they were talking about, her whole reason for being. And there was Avril who could have killed them with her stupidity, and she was just shrugging it off, like . . . like it was a nothing. Like Milly herself was a nothing. 'Rory said the car rolled over.'

'Well, he's a kid, isn't he? Bound to exaggerate. It kinda spun round slightly, so it was facing the other way.'

Milly's heart was thumping violently, her head ready to explode. 'I knew there was something up when you all got back. Fergus was ashen, Rory was quiet and I'm sure I heard Erin vomiting in the bathroom. It all fits together now.'

All fits together? Who did she think she was, an amateur sleuth? A modern-day Miss Marple? Avril fumed silently as she carried on emptying the wardrobe, surprised at how good it felt to direct her anger at someone other than herself.

She could have mentioned that if Milly had bothered to pay attention she might have spotted Erin sneaking out the back door with a couple of lime Bacardi Breezers crammed under her cardigan. But then it wasn't up to Avril to snitch on her niece. She'd only inflame the situation and by the look of Milly that wasn't a very good idea. She was the mother lion protecting her cubs.

'Did the police come? Were there other cars involved?' Milly's questions were like machine guns in Avril's ear. Da da da da da . . . Da da da da da . . .

'I told you. There was no other car. It was a muntjac. I swerved to avoid a deer. And no, darling, it wasn't hurt and I didn't hang around to call the cops.'

'So if there was no other car . . .' Milly narrowed her eyes. 'You were drunk, weren't you?'

'Of course I wasn't!' Avril said, contemptuously.

'Well, it'd make a change.'

'What exactly are you implying, Milly?'

'That you're a drinker. An alcoholic. A soak. Just like Dad!'

Avril's voice turned razor-sharp. 'How dare you!'

'Come on, we all know the truth. Admit it. How much do you drink? Every night? Every second night? Every day? All day? I can smell it on your breath right now.'

'Who do you think you are, Judge sodding Judy?' Avril scrambled back to the wardrobe, pulling things out in a frenzy. 'I'm surprised you even noticed Erin was ill. Most of the time you hardly acknowledge she's there.'

Milly couldn't believe her ears. 'I acknowledge she's there, all right. I acknowledge that she's sullen and sulky. That she won't help around the house. I acknowledge that she's bunking off school, that her marks are going down, that she's had endless detentions. What the hell has that to do with you?'

'And have you seen the teachers about it? At *parents' evening*.'

'None of your business. Don't you think I've enough on my plate with the boys . . .'

'Well maybe that's why.' Avril folded her arms. 'Perhaps she's feeling neglected.'

'Neglected!' Milly felt her blood boiling up.

Avril hadn't meant it to come out in quite that way. 'I just said, maybe she *feels* neglected. What with the boys taking up your time.'

'I can't believe it. *You* – *you're* giving *me* a lecture on parenting!' Milly's voice escalated, her whole body shaking. 'You stupid spiteful cow!'

Natalie and Peggy were in the shed rifling through Callum's tools. 'They're no use to me. I don't even know what half of them are for.' Peggy picked up a wooden pump-type thing and stared at it bemused.

'I think it's a spray for insecticide,' Natalie guessed. 'Maybe you can use it for your garden.'

'I can?' Peggy seemed pleased. 'And this?'

Natalie took the object from her mother's hands and cautiously turned it over. 'Looks like something from a torture chamber. You know, you might be able to sell some of this stuff at a boot fair, or even on eBay.'

'No, I wouldn't want to sell it. Maybe Matt'll want these when he gets back.' Peggy missed Matt badly. She'd grown used to his help and companionship. It seemed odd him taking off like that and even his friend Steve seemed clueless as to where, but she could give a good guess why – he'd probably discovered Hazel's whereabouts but didn't want to get her hopes up. Any day now she expected the doorbell to ring and the two of them to be standing there, grinning like the PG chimps. 'I owe him still, you know, for all the work he did even though he insisted I should pay him in kind with my tatty scones. And I'm sure Callum would love him to have them. After all, Ivor hasn't time with all his meetings and now you and Jeremy have gone your separate ways . . . Oh, Lordy, Lordy!' Peggy suddenly exclaimed. 'What's all that shouting?'

Natalie listened. The sound of screaming and yelling filtered from an upstairs window. 'Stay here,' she commanded. 'I'll go check.'

Natalie opened the kitchen door to see Milly and Avril going for it hammer and tongs, Avril storming down the stairs, with a black bin bag in her hand, Milly on the landing yelling at her. 'You're a lousy aunt!' Milly's face was so red she looked about to burst a blood vessel. 'Not once have you taken any of my children for a weekend or had them to stay overnight or read them a bedtime story or . . . or anything. You're late with their birthdays, nine times out of ten forget their Christmas presents –'

'And do I feel like giving out Christmas presents' – Avril whirled round with her hand on the banister and snapped back – 'when they're too lazy to bother writing thank-you letters? I mean, for Christ's sake, can't you even teach them some manners? What kind of a mother are you?'

'Stop it! Don't. Avril, Milly!' Paralysed to her spot at the foot of the stairs, Natalie's eyes swung wildly from one to the other, horrified by the unleashed fury she was witnessing. 'Stop this now!'

'Well, I might not be the world's best mother,' Milly sneered, descending after Avril, 'but I'm a darn sight better than *you* ever were!'

There was a frozen silence as the words hung in the air. Natalie shook her head willing it all to be taken back.

'Yep, you got me there,' Avril finally said in a trembly voice as she ran a finger down an imaginary blackboard. 'Point for you.' She grabbed her jacket, thrown over the railing, and put it on.

'Milly, you shouldn't have said that,' Natalie cut in. 'That was really too much . . .'

'Oh, you can butt out.' Milly's eyes were like gobstoppers, as she ran down the last few steps, spittle forming at the corner of her mouth. 'You've always been a spoilt little madam. You know why Dad had a go at Mr Potterton-Smythe? Well, do you?' She didn't wait for an answer. 'Because he was going on about you being a common little tyke who wasn't good enough for his darling son. And Dad and I overheard. But there you were with your snobbish blinkered attitude. Attacking him. Making him feel bad . . .' A film of liquid covered her eyes. She sat down suddenly and put her head in her hands.

'She wasn't to know,' Avril defended Natalie. 'Dad was pissed.'

'Yes, well, that's another thing,' Milly said bitterly, raising her eyes, this time addressing Avril. 'If you'd been a halfway decent daughter, instead of turning your back on him, you might have got him some professional help. Spent some of that money you flash about paying for therapy.'

'He wouldn't have gone,' said Natalie flatly. She was standing between Avril and Milly, holding the banister as if she needed its support. 'Mum tried for years to get him to AA.'

'Well, he might have listened to Avril. She never even brought them out to LA. I mean, talk about tight-fisted,' Milly ranted on. 'There she goes travelling business class everywhere, staying at top-class hotels, when I'm saving up for a mop.'

'And why are you saving up for a mop?' Avril said bitterly as she shrugged on her jacket and started doing up buttons. 'Because you're married to a pig of a man, that's why.'

'You leave Ivor out of this!' Milly spat.

'That's not hard,' Avril scoffed, slinging her handbag over her shoulder. 'He leaves himself out of it often enough.'

'It just burns you that I'm happily married, doesn't it?' Milly sprang to her feet in a way she could not have managed a month ago and glared at Avril, standing in front of her, blocking her exit. The cheek of her criticising Ivor! 'You might have an oh-so-successful business but you're going to end up a lonely old woman . . . and you're jealous as hell.'

'Jealous?' Avril said incredulously. 'Christ, I wouldn't have Ivor if he came free in a fucking goody bag! If that's a relationship then I'm the Queen of the Nile.'

'At least he's *my* husband,' Milly tore in. 'Not somebody else's. It's not me that's screwing married men. Have you ever thought maybe Richard Burdock's daughter feels neglected?'

'Milly, no!' Natalie moved as if to step between them, afraid it might turn physical, the way she and Milly had bitten and scratched and pulled each other's hair as kids. 'That's not fair.'

'Oh, you can shut up too, you hypocrite!' Milly whipped round like a wildebeest attacked by two lions. 'You're the one with the picture.'

'What picture?' Avril looked confused.

'Don't, Milly.' Natalie shook her head. 'Don't, please . . .'

But Milly ignored her. 'She brought an article about your Richard to the pub. Showed it around. She said you were "a homewrecker with the morals of a rutting rabbit". Go on, Nat.' Her voice was strangely high-pitched. 'Admit it. Admit it to your big sister.'

Avril waited for a reply, her eyes swivelling to the accused.

A second went by, then another, while Avril looked icily at Natalie standing rigid. Her face said it all.

'Well?' Avril finally spoke.

'It wasn't like that,' Natalie spluttered. 'It . . . It . . .'

'How can you condemn me, Natalie,' Avril said coldly, 'when you screwed Milly's boyfriend behind her back?'

'Sorry?' Natalie said, genuinely confused, the attack so out of left field that Avril's words didn't register at first. Then colour flooded her face.

For a horrified moment, Natalie and Milly stared at each other.

'Go on then,' Avril defied. 'Why don't you enlighten Milly about what happened between you and Matt?'

Natalie opened and closed her mouth like a goldfish who's found itself one minute swimming happily round the bowl then the next lying on the kitchen floor tail flapping.

'It wasn't . . . It didn't . . .'

'I saw the letters, Natalie,' Avril carried on spitefully. 'Now tell me who's the one with the morals of a rutting rabbit.'

Backing away from her inquisitors, Natalie turned and escaped to the kitchen, slamming the door.

'Hazel was right. You are a bitch!' Milly yelled at Avril. 'And I never want to see you again!'

'Don't worry, you won't.' Avril kicked at the black bag of clothes, sending them spilling on the hall carpet, and then wrenched open the front door. 'You can finish the rest!'

Milly was still shaking so badly it took her five minutes to fumble the key into her front door. She pushed Rory ahead of her into the kitchen, dragging Ben behind her in the push-chair. The house was lit up like a Christmas tree, curtains half open, showing the chaos inside. A proper pigsty – did no one care apart from her?

Immediately, as if he'd been lurking behind the door instead of holed away playing video games, Fergus popped out of nowhere and started his complaints.

'Where were you?' His whining voice grated on Milly's eardrums. When had her eldest son turned into this demanding little gnome? She could almost see his nose grow, the warts and whiskers sprout until he was ready to be planted in one of Peggy's flower beds with a rake or shovel in his hand. 'You promised you'd be back by two. I missed my football match.'

Football match? What day was this? Her head whirled dizzily, spinning with confusion. It was Saturday, wasn't it? No, wait, yesterday, they'd . . . She felt her stomach jump in panic. What had they done yesterday?

Ignoring Fergus, she whirled on her heels and followed the sound of the television to the living room where Erin was sprawled in the armchair, mobile glued to her ear. Quickly she switched off the call as Milly walked in, putting her feet on the floor and standing to face her mother. Her lower lip was trembling, her hands twisting nervously, but Milly was too distraught to notice.

'Mum. I need to tell you . . .'

Milly felt a wave of nausea threaten to overtake her. She struggled with the urge to vomit on the threadbare carpet.

'And I've things to say to you, young lady, but later. Here.' She shoved Ben into Erin's arms. 'Take care of your brother, it's about time someone else helped around here. I'm not feeling too good, I need to lie down.'

Already the room was spinning. Only by a supreme effort of will did she manage to make it up the stairs and collapse on the bed.

Avril flung open the door to her flat and slammed it with a well-aimed kick, grabbing her post from the mat and flicking through it in a flaming rage. You see, that's what happened when you got close to people, you ended up either hurting them or getting hurt yourself.

As she ripped up the junk mail and stuffed it in the bin, her anger was undercut by regret. Why had she said those things to Milly? She knew the Ivor comment would really get to her. They were all under so much stress. Of course, Milly had said some dreadful things too. Whatever, Avril was sick of it all.

She fished her mobile from her bag and began furiously tapping in a number. No reply. She stared into space a few seconds longer then she dialled again. After a few seconds it answered.

'Wally? Avril MacLeod.'

'Avril?' He sounded pleased to speak to her. 'You've come to a decision?'

'Yes.'

'And? Come on, honey, don't keep me in suspense.'

Chapter 37

'Milly! Milly!' Ivor's voice roused her from the first deep sleep she'd had in weeks. She rolled over and saw him standing in front of her, his face contorted with worry and anger. 'What's going on with you? You've been in bed for almost fifteen hours. Aren't you feeling well again? And what do you know about these?'

She squinted blurrily at the objects he was waving, then at her watch – eight thirty . . . in the morning. But what day was it? A school day? And what was Ivor flapping in her face?

'What are they?'

'Bills,' he said. 'Bills, bills, bills. Final reminders, most of them. Do you realise we're about to have the gas cut off? And the telephone company have put a collection agency on to us.' He waved the bunch in his left hand. 'These came in today's post.' He flourished his right hand. 'And these I found shoved in a drawer. Crammed under the tea towels. Look at this. Visa . . . huge late fees. Mastercard's about to cancel our account. Half of them threatening legal action. When did it get so out of control?'

'I . . . I don't know. I suppose . . . I forgot . . .'

'This is the worst possible day for this to happen. I've a really important meeting this morning. I told the kids I'd drop them at school. Ben's in his cot playing with his toys, but he won't be happy for much longer. You need to get up.'

When she staggered into the kitchen half an hour later she could see from the war zone in front of her that Ivor wasn't lying. The place was a shambles. Dishes shoved in the sink, clothes all over the place. The best cure for this mess would be a match – burn it all down. The old Milly would have been appalled but this new one was far too tired to care. It all seemed unreal to her, unimportant and remote, as if she was watching someone else move through her life.

She sat down on the nearest chair, head in her hands. Everything was so confusing right now. Her head swam as memories and thoughts whizzed around her skull. Snippets of conversations. Sounds of shouting. Her eyes were heavy.

'Mum. I've really got to speak to you.' Erin's voice brought Milly back to the chaos with a bump. Why wasn't she at school?

'Not now, Erin. I have to . . . get ready.'

'For what?' she demanded sullenly. 'This is important.'

'I don't know . . . Maybe I just need a lie-down. I'm . . .' Her voice trailed off.

'But this is urgent,' Erin wailed. Her face looked pinched and pale. 'Mum, I desperately need some money. I'm –'

'Money!' Milly's heart began thudding faster, the tension shooting up her backbone, until suddenly she was incandescent with fury. 'Is that what this is about? You selfish little madam. Go out and get a job. Apply to Woolworths. I'm fed up with everyone bleeding me dry, do you hear?'

'You know I can't work till I'm sixteen and it's not like that . . .' Erin looked shaken. 'It's for –'

'Me! Me! Me! That's all I get from this family. Well, I'm sick of it.' Now that Milly had cracked the floodgates of

335

resentment with Avril, it seemed she couldn't stop. It was as if she'd tapped an endless source of anger that had been simmering for years, waiting for its moment to erupt. Always she'd put people before her, always she'd been the doormat for them to walk on, a verbal punchbag for their emotional worries. The lumpy old shoulder for the world to lean their heads against and have their tears mopped and noses wiped. Well, not any more. 'Sick of it, do you hear?' she repeated. Avril's words suddenly echoed round her head. 'And what do you mean telling my sister you're neglected?'

'I never . . .' Erin blushed in alarm. Why was her mum speaking so fast? Why were her eyes bulging? It was like she was watching a video on fast forward. Her head seemed to be trembling from side to side.

'Telling her I'm not giving you enough time. Mummy's neglecting me . . . Mummy's leaving me out . . .' Her mother spoke with a strange, high-pitched voice.

'You know nothing about me!' Erin shrieked, matching her tone. 'Nothing. And you know what else, I don't want you to either! I hate you!'

'Apologise this minute!' Milly's face was inches from Erin's as she screamed at the top of her lungs. 'This minute, do you hear, or I'm telling your father.'

'So what?' Erin swung her Nike bag over her shoulder.

'Pardon?'

'So *fucking* what!' Erin stood defiantly in front of her mother. Daring. Provoking. 'You're a rotten mother anyway. You don't even know why Rory bit that kid, do you? Everyone else in the world knows but you. You're the shittiest, most useless –'

SLAP.

Erin only saw it coming the second before it struck her. There was no time to turn away.

Cheek stinging, dumb with shock, Erin wheeled around and jerked blindly at the kitchen door.

'Oh no, Erin!' Milly cried out. 'I'm sorry. I'm sorry, I shouldn't have . . .'

But it was too late. The glass pane rattled in its frame and Erin, as she herself would have expressed it, was 'outta there'.

One thing Avril could do well was organise herself in record speed. She swallowed the lump in her throat as she swooped under the bed for her suitcase. She couldn't believe she was doing this. So many years of being independent, answering to no one. But, then again, so many years of heartache and angst, knowing that she and she alone was responsible for paying the rent, the office expenses, the accountant, Brenda's salary, plus babysitting the careers and lifestyles of all those clients that relied on her. If she was ill, if she couldn't make it to the office – well, she'd always had to. More than a few days' absence and the whole juggernaut would come rolling to a stop.

That's what someone like Milly could never understand. She'd always been married, always had someone to share the burden. How could she ever imagine all those nights Avril had lain alone in bed sweating, wondering if her business was about to come tumbling down? Wondering how once again she could conjure up that much-needed contract or if the whole house of cards would collapse? All Milly saw was the flashy outfits, the fancy cars, the first-class hotels, not realising that long before she could afford them, Avril had known that, in her business, image was everything. If you didn't look successful, no one would deal with you. You couldn't demand a million dollars driving a VW Beetle and dressed by Miss Selfridge. Simple as that.

It would be so different now. Salary. Profit-sharing. People to cover for her. And yet . . . Would her clients – all those

English TV writers that loved to pop in for lunch or end-of-day drinks – think she'd defected? But if they did, so what? She knew how far their loyalty extended – and it wasn't nearly as far as their egos. Clients were like puppies. The minute you stopped stroking and coddling them, they were off searching for someone new to play with.

Wally had sounded shocked when she'd announced Baxter's defection but Avril was quick to proclaim that give her a week or two and she could get him back.

She'd let things slide, that was all. Wasted too much time feeling sorry for herself. She was done with all that now.

She cast an eye around the bedroom, checking she hadn't forgotten anything. She'd miss this place, but as she kept reminding herself, it was only going to be rented, not sold. The estate agents would manage it and maybe when she was a little old lady, retired from business, she'd return to England and live here again with a couple of those miniature dogs. She stuck the last of her underwear in the suitcase and heaved on the straps. With a final tug, she managed to clip the buckles together and lugged the case off the bed. Heavy or what! Thank God for wheels.

Wally had insisted she should come right away. Sign contracts. His lawyers were already drawing them up. Spend a short while getting to know the rest of 'his people'. Her future colleagues.

Oh well, until things were settled, Brenda would have to hold the fort. That was one thing she'd been adamant about: that her faithful assistant should be offered a job in LA with her. Though poor bemused Brenda – on being informed of developments just this morning – hadn't sounded quite as keen as Avril on leaving the land of Fortnum & Mason and Typhoo Tea.

Now what? Her flight wasn't until six o'clock tonight. She

needed to be at the airport, what, three hours early due to extra security, that still gave her quite a bit of time before the taxi was due to arrive. It felt odd not to be in the office, working till the very last minute, but for once in her life she didn't feel strong enough for Brenda's reproachful stares.

Fresh from his breakfast meeting, Richard had just opened his laptop for the day and poured himself a cup of steaming hot coffee when his extension began to ring.

'Richard?'

'Hi, babes. How are you?'

'Fabulous.' He could hear the smile in her voice, almost see her face radiant under those vivid red Pre-Raphaelite curls.

'So, what's put you in such a good mood on this drizzly Monday?'

'You know when I asked you – in Brighton – that question . . .'

'You mean . . .' He could hardly say it. 'If you ever got pregnant . . .'

There was a long pause. 'Well, I am.'

Rachel rang the doorbell three times and, getting no reply, turned the handle and stuck her head in.

'Anyone home? Milly?' The grandfather clock in the hallway chimed eleven thirty. There was no answer but she could hear Ben wailing from upstairs. Then Milly staggered from the kitchen, her face blotchy and eyes swollen, as if she'd been crying for hours. She held the door frame for support, looking blindly towards Rachel.

'Oh, Milly.' Welling with concern, Rachel rushed forward. 'What's happened?' She wheeled her daughter into the kitchen, closing the door.

Sitting her friend at the table, she ran upstairs to find Ben

339

in his cot, red-faced and screaming with outrage. She picked him up, soothed him and brought him down. Two minutes later his soaking nappy was changed, his face wiped clean and he was perched in his high chair with a jar of baby food while Rachel boiled the kettle.

'Here, drink this.' She pushed a hot cup of tea in front of Milly and stared at her anxiously. 'Listen, don't take offence, but I've got to ask you something. Are you on drugs? I wouldn't say anything only one of my ex's got into trouble once with speed and your pupils look just like his did then. And you've been so strange lately. Not returning my calls. Up and down like a yo-yo.'

'Speed?' Milly gave a bizarre laugh which to Rachel's alarm showed no sign of stopping. 'I'm a fat forty-year-old house-wife,' she spluttered, hysterically, almost rolling off her chair as her eyes desperately darted around the room, looking anywhere but at her friend. 'Where would I get speed? The pusher at Rory's playground? Church volunteers at toddler group? Anyway, you know me, Rach, I don't even take aspirin.'

'Well, something's going on,' Rachel insisted stubbornly. 'This place is a disaster. You're being bloody weird. What is it? Are you feeling depressed again?'

'It's a phase.' Milly hiccuped and waved her hand airily. 'Nothing but a phase.' She lurched to her feet and tipped the rest of her tea in the sink.

Rachel stood up too, her eyes scouring the kitchen and lasering onto a small plastic bottle. She beelined over there and picked it up.

'Yeah, right, just a phase.' Worry made her voice sound scornful as she scrutinised the label. 'Oh my God, Milly – these are diet pills, aren't they? I've read about this very brand.' She stared at her friend with huge eyes. 'Are you out of your mind! Don't you know these things are so dangerous they've banned them in America? Tons of people have had heart failure, seizures – even died! I read the other day someone tried to strangle his own mother while on them. Look, Tristan told me about Darren Hammond calling you fat and upsetting Rory but that's just playground nonsense. How long have you been taking them? You're . . . you're not addicted, are you?'

'No. I . . . I've hardly . . .' Milly rubbed her face, staring at her friend blankly. Rachel's words, slow to sink in, were penetrating like acid rain. She felt her stomach twist with panic, temporarily lifting the foggy veil that had enshrouded her. 'Listen, Rach, if you really want to help, look after Ben for me. I . . . I've got a doctor's appointment and I don't want to take him along. You know those places are breeding grounds for germs. His food's in the fridge. Don't worry, I won't take long.'

Grabbing her handbag from the counter, she sang almost gaily, 'I'll be back in a tick.' And walked out the door.

Richard drained his now cold coffee and put his feet up on the desk while he waited for a pause in Felicity's excited monologue. 'Babes, that's fantastic!' he jumped in when she finally took a breath. 'Stay put. I'll be right over with a bottle – no, a magnum of champagne.'

'I mustn't drink,' his cousin replied laughing. 'But you can meet me for lunch if you want and buy me a smoothie. I have a real craving for mango and pineapple. You know, I still can't believe it,' she gabbled on. 'They said I had no chance without this new sperm treatment. It was fifty trillion to one or something. But it worked. It bloody worked!'

'Felicity, you've completely made up for what has otherwise been a pretty lousy month. You must congratulate Tommy. Say well done from me.'

'So you will be the godfather?'

'Of course, darling. You wait, I'll be the best godfather your baby could ever have. Spoil the little tyke rotten with pony rides and fishing trips and maybe a Labrador puppy. I'll even take him or her to church if you insist – unless . . . you're not still a Buddhist, are you? I can't wait to tell Kath.'

'Oh, Richard.' She laughed. 'Steady on. We must keep it among ourselves. Just till the three months are up, you know how it is. Oh, and there's another thing I've been meaning to call about, but what with everything here . . . You know that picture you have on your desk of your on–off, off–on, girl-friend . . . the pretty one, auburn hair, dark skin. The one you've been keeping hidden. Amanda is it?'

'Avril.'

'Ah, I knew it began with A. Well, funny thing is, I'm sure I saw her the other day. Tommy and I visited this country pub, outskirts of Surrey, and I'm positive it was her behind the bar. You know how nosy I am, I've admired that picture a dozen times and she is very striking.'

'Sorry, not possible. She runs her own company. It couldn't have been Avril.'

'No, no. She's working there as a barmaid and – sorry, to say this, Richard – by the looks of things she could be hitched up with the landlord. They weren't exactly holding hands but they seemed dead close. I'm telling you she was the spitting image, only her hair's different now. Somehow makes her look younger than the photo. Maybe she's in some witness protection programme!'

'You've been watching too much . . .' Suddenly Richard's brain clicked into gear. 'Hazel. It must have been Hazel. Was she young? Early thirties?'

'At the most. You old dog. Who's Hazel?'

'Long story. Look, if you don't mind can I take a rain check

342

on that celebration lunch?' A small detour might be in order. 'I need the address of that pub.'

'Thing is, mate, it might not be cordon bleu,' Jonno told Hazel as he stirred the bubbling pots in the pub kitchen, 'but the Flying Ferret combines my two true loves – food and lager – and it's bonzer grub, if I say it myself. Told my old man I wanted to go to cooking school when I was eight years old, poor bastard almost burst a blood vessel. I was a jackaroo for a while though and the cook on the station taught me a thing or two.'

'Jackaroo?'

'Aussie cowboy. You should see me on a horse.'

'Milly used to ride. Spent her whole childhood at the stables, mucking out, cleaning tack, giving lessons in return for rides. She was always begging Mum for a pony of her own.'

'She never got one?' Jonno added more pepper to each steaming pot.

'Nah. I remember once, she and Natalie thought they might be able to talk Dad into it when he was drunk, so they pulled out the tape recorder – to capture the evidence – and Mum walked by just as Dad was agreeing, saw what was going on and gave this derisive snort. So they recorded him slurring, "*Och, sure you can have a horse, dear, as long as your mother doesn't go –*" and then he breathed in hard through his nose twice – "*sniff, sniff.*" Milly and Natalie thought it was hilarious. They kept playing it over and over again, had that tape for years.' She was babbling, Hazel suddenly realised. Telling a story that could make no possible sense except to the people who had been there. Really, she was as bad as Mum. Granny. Peggy. Whoever.

'Here.' Jonno put out a hand to cover hers. 'What harm has that lettuce ever done you?' Gingerly he removed the knife

343

from her fingers. 'Stop hacking into it like you're Freddy and today's Friday the thirteenth. They get distressed, you know.'

'Distressed?' Hazel laughed and wiped her arm on her forehead. 'And what should I do about that? Offer it a hanky and a cup of weak sugary tea?'

'Tear them, darl.' He kissed her nose. 'Tear them with your hands.' He dipped a spoon in a simmering brew he'd been nurturing and smacked his lips. 'Now open your mouth and close your eyes.'

'And you shall have a big surprise?' She grinned. Obediently she squeezed her eyes shut and opened her mouth like a baby bird. When she was little Milly and Natalie were always playing these kinds of games with her. Games of Guess What This Is. She well remembered sticking her tongue in some powdery stuff Natalie had put in her hand and discovering as her mouth caught fire it was very hot mustard. From a slit under her lashes, she saw Jonno scrutinise her.

'Nope.' He took a step back. 'I don't trust you, you're peeking. Wait there a minute.'

When she turned to see where he'd gone, she found him heading towards her with a long dishcloth. He began wrapping it around her eyes.

'Oi.' She pulled away.

'Oi what?'

'Oi, you could be a mass murderer for all I know. Next you'll have me chained to your bed.'

'Not with the lunch crowd due in fifteen minutes. And if I was a mass murderer, I would have strangled you last night. Stop that sodding snoring of yours. I could hear it down the corridor.'

'I don't snore. Anyway, how do I know you won't stick an ice cube down my back?'

'What do you think I am? Six years old?' He finished tying

344

the cloth. 'Now open wide.' She felt a spoon being pushed in between her teeth.

'Mmm.' She rolled the mixture around her tongue. 'It's ab . . . so . . . lutely delish. More.'

'Pretty please?'

'Pretty pretty please.'

He grinned as he saw her mouth open again. 'You think it's good?'

'It tastes yummy. But the way you've been all hunched over and secretive, I bet it looks like cat's puke. What is it?'

'My new veggie special. Goulash Hazel. Pretty rapt with it myself.'

Hazel squealed in outrage as she felt the familiar shock of cold ice sliding inside her T-shirt. Tearing the dishcloth off, she hit him with it and made straight for the stove.

'Just a little bowl,' she said, grabbing the ladle and filling her dish. 'What's the recipe?'

'Top secret.' Jonno grinned. 'But I will tell you two ingredients. Coriander. And tofu.'

'No! You bastard.' Once again he had her in fits of laughter. Watching him fool around the kitchen, pulling items out of the industrial-sized refrigerator, juggling pots and pans, she realised that for all his tattoos, biker bulk and pug-like face, there was something really very appealing about him. Perhaps it was the self-assured way he bounced around his little kingdom, completely in his element, busy as hell, but having a good time with it. Maybe that was why Drew, the miniature stud-muffin with perfectly chiselled cheekbones would fall for this otherwise ugly mug. Or perhaps Mr Tiny but Perfect Drew swooned over Masterful and In Charge Jonno.

She gave herself a little shake. Who cared why the pair were together? She had a great thing going here. Better than sex. She'd found a good friend. Someone who could rabbit on more than her. Someone who liked to laugh. And he wouldn't ruin it – as with so many other male 'best friends'. There'd be no sudden declaration of undying love followed swiftly by refusing to see her again – or worse, taking up with one of her female friends. In her experience the whole platonic thing with a heterosexual guy was a complete myth.

Maintaining friends and travelling was difficult anyway. However important at the time, other people always slid in to fill the void of your absence. Or you discovered that whatever had made you so compatible was long gone. The friendships that lasted years and spanned continents were rare and precious indeed.

Look at her sisters. Milly's mates were the mums' groups, fussing around their broods like a great lot of cackling chickens – most of her single crowd had run off by the time she popped the second one. Avril's were the smart set, usually related to work, a revolving door of people she chatted to, emailed, texted daily until they crossed her in a business deal and were dropped like scalding King Edwards. And Natalie just seemed to have couples, dinner-party guests, whose names were 'The Mullions', 'The Fotheringtons' or 'The Dashford-Snells'. Never Liz and Dave or Pete and Sharon, and from what Natalie told her, they thrived on malicious gossip about each other – that's why it was important not to miss a gathering.

Whereas Mum . . . or rather Peggy . . . well, she could walk into a supermarket or stand at a bus stop and thirty seconds later she and the person next to her would be exchanging life histories. While Callum never got to first-name terms with his colleagues of years – they were still respectfully calling him Dr MacLeod on his retirement day – every person Peggy met was a new best friend. She'd always berated her daughters for being shy. 'It doesn't cost anything to say hello,' she'd say. 'It doesn't hurt you to be friendly.'

'Wakey-wakey.' Jonno's voice in her ear made her jump. 'Those doors won't unlock themselves, you know.'

One forty-five. Avril glanced at her watch. Just time for a coffee before the taxi arrived. As she flicked on the kettle, her mobile began to ring with a number she didn't recognise.

'Hello?'

Silence.

She was about to put the phone down when she heard a strange gulping noise. It sounded like a woman, a young woman. In fact, an exceedingly young woman?

'Avril, I . . . I . . .'

Erin? 'Hey, Erin? What's up?'

Sound of deep breath, then gulp. Another deep breath, then a pause. 'I . . . I'm pregnant.'

'Pregnant?' Avril closed her eyes a second. This couldn't be happening. Not now. Not today. Not ever. 'Erin, does your mum know?'

'No.'

'Oh.' She glanced at her packing cases. 'Are you at home?'

'I'm in King's Cross. Outside a clinic.'

'Is anyone with you?'

'No.'

The fear of God rushed through Avril's very soul. Alone in King's Cross. A pretty young teenager. Pretty young vulnerable teenager. There could be anyone out there, waiting to grab her. Pimps. Slave traders. Paedophiles.

'Whereabouts?'

'You'll let Mum know?'

'Sure, I'll let her know.'

'No, I mean . . . I don't want you to.'

'But I must. Now tell me where you are.'

'If you're going to speak to my mum, then I'm not saying.' Erin's voice sounded flat. 'We can just forget it. Bye –'

'Listen, no. Don't hang up, Erin. Please don't hang up. Let's start again. What can I do? What do you want me to do? I'll do anything, sweetie. Anything, just say.'

'I need three hundred and ninety pounds.'

'Oh.'

'I'm going for an abortion. They say . . . they say they'd like me to bring a family member with me if I could, but they'd still do it without,' she added almost defiantly. 'I've already given them sixty pounds, which is all I had in my savings account. I'll pay you back. I'll give you my Christmas money or I'll –'

'Christ, Erin, paying me back is the last thing I care about. Can I meet you somewhere?'

She was quiet a moment. 'Only if you promise you won't say anything to my parents.'

'You know this'll get me into a heap of shit, don't you?'

'Mum's doing my head in right now. Going on at me all the time. It's like . . . it's like she's gone mental or something . . . One minute she's OK, the next she's like a witch . . . It's freaky. I just can't speak to her . . .'

'Oh fuck . . . er, I mean, flip. OK, here's the deal, I promise I won't say anything if you promise to at least consider telling your parents afterwards.'

'OK, I promise . . . to consider, that is.'

'Right.' Avril grabbed a pen. 'Now shoot.'

Chapter 38

'So what do you reckon on that one?' Jonno nudged Hazel. Hazel glanced at the tall, well-dressed man as he weaved his way through the tables.

'War correspondent? Roving reporter for the *Mail on Sunday*?'

'Nah, he's more like some high-powered barrister. I can just see him in one of those funny little wigs and a big black gown, leaning on the rail, charming the knickers off the jury.'

'Journalist,' she hissed.

'Barrister,' Jonno hissed back as the man's eyes scanned the huge assortment of beers.

'What can I do you for?' Hazel twinkled her green eyes at him.

'Pint of mild, please.' He pointed at a pump.

'Sure.' Hazel put the glass under and pulled the handle. There was something about the guy, she recognised him from somewhere, but where? She gave him a brief once-over as his gaze roved around the bar. 'Two pounds fifty, please.' Hazel placed the drink in front of him and waited for him to retrieve a wallet from his inside pocket. 'Anything else?'

'Nope. That's all.' He handed over three coins. 'Hazel, is it?'

Hazel started. 'Yes. Yes, it is. Do I know you?'

'I came in last week. There was a gang of us.'

'Oh yes.' She vaguely remembered a large rowdy mob crowding out the place to standing-room only. Rugger-buggers, all raucous laughter and smutty jokes. Loud and lary. From some big insurance office nearby. Funny, but she wouldn't have pitched him there. Oh well, neither she nor Jonno were correct.

'Thought I'd return for the great beer. Cheers.' He lifted his glass and took it to a nearby table.

'Was I right?' Jonno came across and put his arm around her shoulder.

She shook her head. 'Was in last week. Works in insurance, very boring. So you don't even get half a point.'

'Probably fancies you.'

'Or maybe you.' Hazel poked him in the ribs. 'Don't worry, I won't tell Drew.'

'Oh?' He quirked his eyebrows. 'Big of you, mate.'

But her eyes kept returning to the table. Why was she so sure she ought to know him? She'd definitely seen him before – and not just behind a bar.

Richard headed off the minute he'd downed his drink. It was odd meeting Avril's daughter. Like her in so many ways. Similar characteristics, similar smile. Damn the woman. He was still trying to fathom her out. For a brief moment there, the day he'd visited the hospital, she'd really seemed to open up, let him in as she never had before. When they'd made love it was as if they'd gone to a different level, reached a depth and intimacy he could only have dreamed of attaining. And then – kapow! Shot down in flames and blown out of the water before he had a chance to raise the white flag or lift a hand in self-defence.

Of course the timing was miserable. Her father's death. The

shock of that phone call. He wasn't an insensitive clod, he could understand the grief she was obviously feeling and then the torment of having her daughter disappear. But he was done with chasing. Where was the line anyway between ardent suitor and harassing pest? But it didn't mean he couldn't do her this one last favour before he galloped off into the sunset.

As he strode back to his car, he flicked open his mobile and scrolled down his list of contacts, through the As.

'Avril, come on,' he breathed as he heard the voicemail click in once more, 'where the hell are you?'

Natalie heaved a big black rubbish bag through her bedroom door and put it down next to a box containing books and CDs. Almost everything she owned in the world lay in bags and clearly marked boxes, leaving the flat looking starker than ever, with great gaps on the mantelpiece and bookshelves – as if they'd been plundered by obsessively tidy burglars. Without Natalie's few photographs, now crammed in the box named 'Decor', the white walls, white doors and white carpet reminded her of the inside of a freezer – an apt metaphor, she thought now, for six years spent in limbo.

To think that once she'd been adamant that all guests remove shoes for fear of soiling those pristine fibres, and how she'd hovered compulsively over red-wine drinkers, terrified of the potential stains. Had she been out of her mind – or just locked into Jeremy's? Well, now his entire cricket team could stomp in with muddy boots and she couldn't give a stuff. Let them wreck the place. Jump all over his ugly soulless furniture, leave uneaten pizza slices behind the beige cushions and spill beer over his glass-and-chrome coffee table. Maybe it would finally look as if someone actually lived here.

She walked back into the bedroom, remembering the wild and crazy day when they'd actually been inspired to paint their sleeping wall a daring shade of cream. The hours they'd spent over charts trying to decide between names like Ash, Barley, Almond, Linen and, yes, Jasmine White. She couldn't even remember what they'd chosen in the end. Only that the project had taken hours longer than expected and Jeremy hadn't liked the final result, said it was too pink. And he'd acted like it were all her fault, the shitbag. Luckily, he was at work. The last thing she wanted was him standing over her, arguing about who had bought the Coldplay CD, though a hand to the car with all this stuff would have been nice.

She pulled the last box – 'Personal' written in large felt-tip pen – from its place by the almost empty wardrobe. The wedding folder took up most of the space, and on top of its mammoth bulk sat the innocent-looking shoebox that had caused so much trouble. Natalie's knees buckled and she sat down beside it, remembering Avril's outburst. Almost against her will, she tugged off the lid and withdrew the packet of letters. She untied the ribbon and opened one at random. *'Dear Natalie,'* she read. *'Please, please, don't throw this one away.'* Her heart pounded as she quickly scanned to the last line. *'Remember, I'll always love you, Matt.'*

When her mobile rang, she almost jumped out of her skin, thinking for one guilty second it was the doorbell and Jeremy returned. Slightly breathless with surprise, she answered it. It was a male voice.

'Natalie? It's Richard.'

'Oh, hi there.' Well, of course they'd swapped cards but she hadn't actually expected him to ring.

'Sorry to disturb but I'm looking for Avril.'

At least one of them had decided not to be stubborn. 'Have you tried her mobile?'

'It's off.'

'Oh.' Unusual.

'It's just that I've found Hazel. I'm outside this pub . . . It's in Surrey, near Coulsdon. Called the Flying –'

'Ferret.' Natalie couldn't stop herself interrupting. 'The Flying Ferret.'

'My cousin Felicity rang me. Said she'd seen a photo I keep of Avril and, well, to cut a long story short, I came to check it really was her. She's working behind the bar.'

'Did she know who you were? Did you speak to her?'

'No and no. I didn't want to scare her off.'

'Quite right.' Natalie was thoughtful. Hopefully Hazel hadn't recognised him from that magazine article she'd bandied around. 'Look, I think the best thing is we both try Avril, and if you get through to her first, tell her I'm heading out there now.'

For the third time that day Avril opened her mobile, scrolled down to Milly's number, hesitated, then snapped it shut.

After Erin's phone call, her day had turned into one manic rush. Postponing her flight, emailing the sleeping Wally her change in plans, telling her radio cab to take her to King's Cross instead of Heathrow. And thank God, for when she caught sight of Erin at their arranged meeting place – Burger King – she was shocked at the sight of her. Her long blonde hair, normally meticulously straightened and brushed to a shine, was a straggly mess. Her beautiful blue eyes were puffy from crying and her porcelain skin was whiter than a swan's. Instantly Avril knew she'd done the right thing. The only thing.

'Erin Simpson?' the receptionist called out.

Erin looked at Avril and rose to her feet. 'Come on then.' Avril tucked her arm through her niece's. 'Let's face the music together.'

The nurse sitting at her desk swivelled her chair as they entered the small room. 'Hello again, Erin.' She smiled.

'Hi,' Erin said in a small voice.

'Your mother, I take it.' The nurse turned her attention to Avril. 'I see the resemblance . . .'

'No, I'm her aunt.' They briefly shook hands. 'Her mother's sister.'

'OK.' The nurse jotted down some details on a sheet of paper before her. 'Well, I'm glad someone's come with you this time, Erin.' She turned to Avril again. 'So, anyway, Erin's filled you in, yes?'

'If you mean do I know she's pregnant and considering an abortion – yes.' Avril looked around the small olive-painted room. It was clean enough but sparse and depressing. A calendar on the windowsill, a couple of posters talking about STIs and a clock on the wall informing them it was two minutes past three.

'She's already seen a doctor who's declared her fit for the operation. And she had a counselling session earlier this week. Her mind seems very firmly fixed on going ahead with the termination tomorrow. Don't worry, dear,' she added to Erin in reassuring tones, 'there'll be other girls your age going through exactly the same thing, so you won't be alone.'

'Does she have to stay overnight?'

'No, but before she leaves, we'd like to speak to her about contraception.' The nurse dug around in a drawer for some leaflets. 'Now regarding the operation, have you any questions, Erin?'

'Is it going to be painful?' Erin said in a tiny voice.

The nurse smiled. 'Like a strong period pain. Cramps. Bleeding may last up to fourteen days.'

'Will it be general or local anaesthetic?' Avril asked.

The nurse flipped through her paperwork. 'Erin indicated she wanted to be asleep. She'll only be out for about ten minutes. And she'll be able to leave the clinic about three hours later – after another check-up, of course. Now if you can sign this . . .' She handed Avril over a form.

'Right. Just one thing . . .' Avril's pen was poised in the air. 'Something I can't quite get my head around. You're actually allowing a girl of her age to do this without her parents' knowledge? You do realise she's only fifteen?'

'All perfectly legal, yes,' the nurse replied stiffly. 'Under the 1967 Act, as long as we have the signatures of two doctors and we can ascertain the child is mentally stable.'

'Surely that's not fair on the mother?' Avril didn't like this at all. She had a feeling it was all too rushed.

'Look, there are many kinds of parents with many differing outlooks. Our primary concern is for the mum-to-be. In this clinic we strongly encourage our younger patients to inform their families and in an ideal world, they would but . . .' She pursed her lips. 'Ultimately, if we weren't a confidential service, we wouldn't have them coming to us in the first place and the result would be many more teenage births and dangerous backstreet abortions. And that wouldn't be a good thing, now would it?'

'I guess not.' Patronising old boot. Avril swapped a glance with Erin. Reminded her of the tone the midwives had used on her when she was having Hazel. Some things hadn't changed a bit.

By the time Natalie pulled into the car park of the Flying Ferret it was after three and the lunchtime crowd were long gone.

How odd it felt, remembering when they were last there, talking to Matt, planning her wedding, chatting with Hazel about the place settings which seemed oh-so-important at the time.

She made her way across the faded carpet, keeping her fingers crossed, praying Richard's arrival hadn't spooked Hazel. The number of times she'd have happily strangled her . . . But now, petty feuds were a mere blip compared to this. Natalie had never wanted to see her more.

Her eyes wandered across to the bar and then behind it. At first she didn't recognise Hazel. Her hair was shorn like a hedgehog, brassy as Courtney Love, and the too-large camouflage trousers and tight muscle T-shirt on her skinny body made her look more fragile and petite than ever. Her eyes were firmly fixed on the barman and Natalie was surprised to notice she was laughing – like she hadn't a care in the world.

Natalie cleared her throat as she approached. 'Hazel?'

Hazel spun round at her sister's voice and the smile melted from her face.

'Nat.'

Natalie's eyes filled with tears and silently she leaned across the bar, hands outstretched. The next thing Hazel was sobbing in her arms. Who went first, who knows, all Natalie remembered afterwards was that for once in her life she hadn't held back.

'Think you sheilas had better move to somewhere more private,' Jonno said in an oddly gruff voice, wiping his sleeve against his eye. 'Don't want to put the punters off their pints.'

'Mr Simpson. Oh good, you *do* exist.' The voice in Ivor's ear was cool and crisp with disapproval. 'I'm sorry to disturb you at work only I'm afraid there's no answer from the other numbers in my file. Poor Rory has been waiting here since three thirty. Someone needs to pick him up from school.'

'Richard Burdock? So that's who it was, I knew I'd seen that face before.' Hazel poured hot water into two mismatched mugs.

'Apparently his cousin, Felicity, recognised you from a photo. Came in a few days before. She thought you were Avril.' Natalie glanced around the kitchen. She'd never been in the living area of a pub before. It was nice, tiled counters and backsplash obviously updated. Copper pots hanging from the ceiling. Slate floor that looked really old. And everything put away, not a single dirty dish in the sink or on a draining rack. The owner obviously kept things neat but it still felt homely and comforting.

'I'll bet it was that redhead. Jane Goldman. She called me Amanda.'

'Oh, Hazel.' Natalie took the Snoopy mug Hazel offered her and cradled it in her hand. 'We've all been *so* worried about you.'

'I suppose you were in on it as well?'

'In on it?' Natalie put down Snoopy. 'No.' She shook her head violently. 'God. How could you think that? Milly and I only just found out ourselves.'

'You swear? You swear you both had no idea?'

'Not a clue.'

Hazel felt an overwhelming sense of relief. Somehow knowing that she wasn't the only one kept in the dark made everything kind of easier to deal with. Milly and Nat had been deceived too. Somehow it mattered.

'Look, you know how hopeless I am with secrets.' Natalie reached for Hazel's hand and squeezed. 'Don't you think if I'd been told, it would have come out?'

Hazel considered this. 'True,' she acknowledged.

'You have to come back, Hazel. We need you at home.'

Hazel stared into her mug as if reading tea leaves. 'I can't. I'll never come back.'

'But why not?' Natalie tried to quell her disappointment.

'You don't understand what it's like. I feel so . . . betrayed.' Her voice wavered. 'It's taken everything and turned it on its head. It's totally destroyed me.'

'Well, don't let it.' Natalie stood up. 'I mean it, Haze. You know the old saying, it's not what cards are dealt to you that makes you strong, it's how you play them.'

'Oh, it's all right for you, Nat, the deck's always been stacked in your favour.'

'Stacked in my favour? Are you kidding? I'm as fucked up as anyone. Let's see, just last week I was all set to marry a man I didn't particularly like – let alone love –'

'*Was* set?' Hazel said aghast. 'You mean you're not marrying JJ, I mean Jeremy?'

'We broke it off.'

'Him or you?'

'Let's just say the Poshy-Washies started it and I finished it.'

Hazel quickly suppressed an ear-to-ear grin. 'Oh, Jesus. I'm sorry, Nat. You must feel awful.'

'In actual truth, Hazel darling, I'm relieved. I feel like this ruddy great mountain has slipped off my back. I mean, can you imagine, I'd have been forever trying to keep up with the Joneses, pretending to be something I'm not, denying my background, my personality. God, even my own father. Now I just want to be, well, myself I guess. I know it might sound like pansy-arsed psychobabble but at the ripe old age of thirty-seven, I want to find out who I am.'

'Doesn't sound pansy-arsed to me. You're actually sounding real for the first time, Nat.' Hazel spontaneously gave her a hug. 'I couldn't stand that perfect Stepford Wives routine. I always suspected you were a robot.'

'Gee, thanks.' Natalie raised her brows in irony.

The familiar wicked glint of Hazel's eyes returned. 'So

you're no longer, Natalie "Whatever will people think?" MacLeod?'

'No. And I'm hoping after all this, you've matured past Hazel "Let's see who I can humiliate next" MacLeod.' The echo of Natalie's old waspishness made them both laugh.

As Hazel escorted her out, Natalie decided to give it one last try. 'Mum's desperate to see you,' she said, as they walked past the back staircase into the bar area of the pub. 'You need at least to speak to her. And Avril. Talk it over. Find out *their* reasons.'

'Jonno said something like that.' Hazel flipped open the counter flap, shoving her hands in her pockets as she led Natalie to the door.

'Jonno?'

'The landlord.' Hazel flicked her head at Jonno's sturdy back.

'Wise words from him then.' Natalie glanced over at the barman who was now busy bottling up. 'Look, everything's gone to pot at home. We all had the most furious row yesterday afternoon and now no one's speaking to anyone else. I'm trying to hide it from Mum because she's suffering enough as it is, and Matt's not around any more, thanks to me, and bottom line is, I can't cope with this on my own. Oh God, please, Hazel, you have to come back. You can't leave me to sort this out by myself. I need you with me. I need your advice.'

'*My* advice? *You* want *my* advice?' They were in the car park now, Hazel glancing at the gunmetal sky, thinking that it looked like it was about to rain. Big Nasty Nat wanted advice from *her*, the baby of the family, Miss Irresponsible Personified?

'Come on, what do you say?' Natalie coaxed, dangling her car keys.

From her handbag, her mobile started to ring. It took a search through several compartments to finally produce it.

Hazel watched her expression change as she talked.

'Hey, Ivor . . . Sorry . . .? What . . .? When?'

She covered the phone briefly and mouthed, 'Milly's disappeared.'

Chapter 39

Avril and Erin were perched on Avril's small couch as *Pulp Fiction* played on cable.

Neither were taking any of it in, probably just as well since it was exactly the sort of film Milly would never allow her kids to watch. Still, Erin had the remote control and Avril didn't feel like making an issue of it. She kept glancing across at Erin, who looked nervous and edgy – all that brash teenage bravado replaced by little girl lost.

After filling in the necessary forms and writing out a cheque to the clinic, they'd decided to head back to Avril's flat. They were advised by the nurse to both get a good night's sleep before next morning's 'procedure'.

Fat chance. Avril's fingers were itching to pour herself a drink but she couldn't do that. Not at four o'clock in the afternoon. Not in front of Erin. But God, if she ever needed one, it was now.

She stared at her niece, contemplating her choices. Somehow she had to persuade Erin to call home, if only to stop Milly sending out a search party. And say what? Even if Erin could invent some convincing excuse for visiting her aunt, Avril was still stuck in one of those rock and a hard place dilemmas that had no possible happy resolution. If she told Milly the truth, she'd be betraying Erin. If she didn't and Erin had this abortion without her mother's knowledge, Milly would never, ever forgive Avril for keeping it secret. And who could blame her? One way or another either her sister or her niece would probably never speak to her again.

Avril focused briefly on the TV screen. Violence, blood and foul language. Usually she enjoyed action films, considered Milly idiotic for her squeamishness, but sitting here with a teenager, she feared for the world they were living in, when watching torture and death were acceptable forms of entertainment. No place you'd want to bring a sweet innocent baby into, that was for sure.

She scanned her brain for some words of comfort, but everything she tried out in her head sounded clichéd, patronising and trite. There, there . . . It'll all come out in the wash . . . All be forgotten in the morning . . . Although it wouldn't, would it? Whatever way it turned out, it wouldn't be OK. And how could Avril, someone who'd made such a stinking mess of her own life, advise a girl like Erin, who even at her tender age seemed almost intimidatingly smart and on to all the grown-ups' bullshit. Christ, Milly nailed it, Avril couldn't even manage to bring up her own child . . .

That was it.

Sod.

Well, it was going to rear its ugly head sooner or later. She took a deep breath.

'I got pregnant too, you know, when I was around your age.'

'You what?' Erin turned to her in cynical disbelief and obviously saw something that made her change her mind. 'How come?'

'How do you think, how come? Same way we all do, sweetie. Hormones running crazy, brain temporarily disengaged. I was fairly naive about contraception and anyway I was scared to visit any doctors in case they knew Dad.'

'Did . . . did you tell the boy?'

'Unfortunately, yes.' Avril paused. 'He wasn't too thrilled. Did you?'

'No.'

'Who is he?'

'Just some lame-o in my class. They say you can't get pregnant on the first attempt.'

'Yeah, and I was told if the guy pulls out straight away . . .'

'I was curious . . . Don't really see what all the fuss is about.'

'You will one day.' Avril pulled her feet up onto the sofa. 'It's different when you're in love.'

As she said the words, Avril had a most uncomfortable vision of Richard bringing her breakfast in on a tray. She felt her heart wring with grief.

'We only did it the once.' Erin looked morose. 'I'd dumped him before I even found out.'

'Life sure sucks sometimes, doesn't it?'

'Yeah . . .' Erin turned back to the TV. John Travolta was just jabbing a syringe into Uma Thurman's heart. It was a minute before she spoke again. 'So what happened with you?'

'What happened to me? Well, there's a story and a half. I'll go fix us some food, and then I'll tell you everything.'

Natalie snapped her mobile shut and found Hazel's chin almost resting on her shoulder in a fruitless attempt to listen in.

'Come on.' She grabbed her elbow. 'You're coming with me, this is urgent. Milly's family need us.'

'What's happened?' Hazel wailed, agog with curiosity, as Natalie rushed them both across the car park.

'Everything!' Natalie beeped the keyless unlock on her remote and slid into the driver's seat, Hazel close behind.

'Milly's gone AWOL.' She buckled up and revved the engine. 'She wasn't there to pick up Rory from school, she left Ben with a friend and didn't come back, and Erin didn't go to school today and isn't answering her mobile. Ivor's tearing his hair out. He's busy calling round everyone they know but so far no one's come up with anything.'

'Has he tried Mum's?' Belatedly Hazel realised she'd been snatched without a minute's chance to tell Jonno she was leaving. What on earth would he think? Abandoned with all the after-work tipplers expected in just over an hour? She grabbed Natalie's mobile and started to dial the pub number. Somehow even when she tried to be a responsible citizen, fate wouldn't allow it.

'Yes, but no joy.' Natalie shifted abruptly into third gear and then changed her mind and shifted back. 'He tried Avril too but only got her voicemail. Anyway, he wants to stay at the house in case Erin comes back or phones in so I told him we'd check Mum's again and anywhere else we can think of. He's beside himself. Can you imagine Milly leaving her kids? And that's not all.'

'What? What?' Ear to the phone, listening to it ring unanswered, Hazel clutched onto the seat belt as Natalie swerved round a corner. It wasn't often she received a taste of her own driving and it certainly wasn't like Natalie to career along so recklessly.

'Her friend told Ivor that Milly's been taking pills.'

'Pills?' Full attention on Natalie now, Hazel clicked off her phone. Jonno was probably rushed off his feet, cursing her, but this was far more important. 'What type? Valium? Ecstasy? Extra-strength aspirin?'

'Slimming tablets. From America. Glorified speed with some very dangerous side effects.

'And Milly got hold of them? How?'

'God knows. Here, grab the *A–Z*, will you? Which way at the next junction?'

'I tried to confide in your granny so many times, but couldn't find the words.' Once Avril had begun, the words came tumbling like a rockslide. She began by telling Erin how she'd first met the boy who would become her daughter's father. How in love she'd thought they were. The shock of discovery, the agony of trying to keep it secret, hiding her morning sickness, pushing it to the back of her mind until it was almost too late for an abortion. The excruciating sense of betrayal when her boyfriend rejected her and swiftly signed onto a ship heading for Cape Town. She told Erin details she'd shut from her mind for the longest time. Things she hadn't quite had the courage to say to Richard, things she hadn't had time to say to Hazel. But watching Erin, this child thirty years her junior, seeing her nods of understanding and empathy, it just seemed to all gush out.

'Your grandma was rushed off her feet as it was. Nat was sick with asthma and kept having to take time off school, your great-grandmother, Nana we used to call her, was living with us because she'd just had eye surgery, and your grandad – he had quite a drinking problem. He could barely hold it together during the week and weekends were pure hell. Anyway, none of them thought I was capable of raising a baby – they were all pushing for adoption. Nana had a big say in things then because she'd just loaned your grandad money to buy into a new practice and it was her money supporting them. And believe me, it might have been the 1970s but as far as she was concerned, women's lib, free love, the right to choose and all that jazz, had never taken place. She thought fornicators should be put in the stocks and stoned.'

'It must have been terrible.'

'Yeah, but as you and I know, shit happens. Or, as your mother would say, "sugar happens".'

That brought a small smile to Erin's face.

'Anyway,' Avril continued, 'apparently it was a case of whatever Nana said, went. I wasn't strong enough to fight them all.'

'But weren't you very sad . . .' said Erin in a tiny voice, 'About them taking your baby from you?'

Avril gave an awkward laugh, tucking her hair behind her ears, but a shaft of pain flitted across her eyes. 'Furious. I was mad at all of them. I ended up moving out. Running away really. Oh, I did visit occasionally. A couple of times, I even made a big drama about them giving her back to me, but they said they were only thinking of the baby's good, and mine too, of course. They said that they wanted me home, that I was just being stubborn. But I was sick of all the lies. I couldn't stand to be around them then. So even if it meant leaving Hazel –'

'Hazel?' All this time and Erin had only just twigged who they were talking about. 'Auntie Hazel, you mean?'

She nodded. 'Mum and Dad pretended she was theirs.'

'God! Wow!' It took another few moments to sink in. 'Does she know?'

Avril grimaced. '*Now* she does. That's why she ran off.'

'I wondered why she called you a bitch.' Erin tucked her hands in her sleeves and hugged her knees, momentarily diverted from her own problems by the delicious soap opera of the MacLeod family saga.

'You heard?'

'We all did, even Rory.'

'Oh God.' Avril threw her head back on the sofa and cast her eyes to the ceiling. 'You know, you kids want a crash course in swear words, just hang with me a while.'

'I wish I could. I wish I could stay here and live with you forever.'

Avril smiled. 'That's very flattering, honey, but . . . you know, to be honest, I don't think I'm the child-raising type. I wouldn't be a very good role model. I drink too much, I smoke too much and I'm the worst possible example when it comes to men.'

'But I'm not a child. I don't need raising. That's why it'd be so cool.'

Avril didn't change expression but she shuddered inwardly. 'Listen, darling,' she said gently, 'if you want my real honest-to-goodness opinion, I think you need to tell your mum. Sooner the better.'

'I can't. She'll have a fit. I know she will.'

'She won't, I'm certain of it.'

'How can you be so certain?'

'Because she's my sister. I've known her thirty-nine years. In fact, to be precise, thirty-nine years, eleven months, two days. I know how much she loves you, Erin. She'd do anything for you.'

'I wish I had a sister. Instead of loathsome little brothers. What's it like?'

'What's it like? How can I explain?' Avril put her feet on the coffee table and tapped a long stream of ash into the ashtray. 'You know, sweetie' – she blew a smoke ring at the ceiling – 'it's kind of like parents. How they embarrass the hell out of you because you identify with them, only more so because, with sisters, it's as if you share the same skin. You watch them walk through a room or mingle at a party and every gesture, every inflection is so familiar because it's how you walk and talk; you see when they're feeling shy or awkward or humiliated because you react in exactly the same way, often at the same type of things; you know how they're thinking and

367

feeling. It's like catching yourself on video or hearing a recording of your voice. And while often it's great, and it certainly makes you closer, sometimes it can be way too much and you're there squirming with shame, for them *and* for you.'

She stubbed out her cigarette and took a stray flake of tobacco from her tongue, grinning at Erin.

'And they know your weak points – boy, do they too. All that shared history – they'll say exactly the right things to slice you to the bone. But then again, there's that shared sense of humour, the stuff that will have you all in hysterics while everyone else stares blankly, and knowing that however much you fight and rant and rave, you'll always be there for each other. You know, you can name-call your sister all you will, but if someone else has a go at them, then by God, you'll defend them to the death.'

Wistfully, she reflected that however much the MacLeod girls had fought among each other, they'd always been ready to stand shoulder to shoulder when one of them was being pushed off the swings at the park or threatened by the neighbourhood bullies. 'Friends may come and go,' she finished, 'but you're always stuck with your sisters and they're stuck with you.'

She wondered, as she ended on this happy note, if it were true. If she and Natalie and Milly ever would make up. She knew plenty of sisters who loathed each other, some who'd fallen out over some trivial thing and hadn't spoken for years. God, she hoped that wouldn't happen to them. There had to be some way of making it right.

'Your mum'll support you through whatever decision you want to make, I'd bet my entire wardrobe of Vera Wang on it. Right.' She stood up, needing to do something. 'How about a nice cup of cocoa?'

Chapter 40

'Fantastic.' Peggy took off her coat and threw her handbag on the couch. 'I've wanted to see that *Kiss Me Kate* for so long. It's so good of you come with me, Matt.'

'No worries. I never knew amateur productions could be so, uh, entertaining.'

'Oh, they're no patch on Howard Keel and Kathryn Grayson, of course, but still I thought Mrs Bradbury from the Woolwich did a very good job of playing Kate.'

Matt grinned. 'Very spirited rendition and rather daring casting I'd say, giving the lead role to someone quite so amply endowed.'

'I used to do some amateur theatre, you know. I couldn't dance or sing, but I was the only young woman they had so I always got the lead. And did I ever tell you that I once had an audition for a film when I was fourteen?' She switched on the kettle and began searching in her cupboard for clean cups.

'You did?'

'Yes, I heard that a famous producer was shooting in the neighbourhood so I called him up and begged him for a role, insisted I was the next best thing to Elizabeth Taylor. Anyway, I got him laughing and he agreed to see me but my father wouldn't let me go. Thought being an actress was one step away from prostitution. You know, I've never been to the Dog and Donkey before. Did I tell you that?'

'Twenty times.' Matt laughed. One gin and tonic and she was away with the fairies. It was a spur-of-the-moment decision, taking her out, but he couldn't leave the country without saying goodbye, especially after she'd been so welcoming to him.

'I mean, how could I go when I'd barred Callum from the place.' She opened the fridge and peered inside. 'I'd look like the worst hypocrite imaginable. You are going to have supper with us, aren't you?'

'Actually . . .' Matt looked at his watch. 'I really do have to run. I've my flight to catch.'

'Well, just something quick, beans on toast. Natalie should be back any time. She'd hate to miss you.'

'Don't know about that,' he said darkly.

'You know she's moving out of her flat today?'

'Moving?' Matt raised his eyebrows.

'Had a small spat with Jeremy, from all accounts. And, well, you know Natalie. Has to take it to gigantic proportions.'

'Did she say what it was about?' Unconsciously he leaned forward, momentarily not breathing, his whole body waiting for her response.

'No, but no need to worry, dear.' She pulled out a couple of cans and began opening them. 'They'll make it up, they always do. Her emotions are all up in the air right now. Give her a week and she'll be running back to him, cap in hand. You mark my words.'

Pouring beans into a pan, she missed the slightest sag of his shoulders and the expression on his face as he glumly sat down.

Avril went back into the lounge carrying two mugs of cocoa.

But the sight in front of her melted her heart. Erin was asleep on the couch, her blonde tresses sweeping the floor.

With a blinding flash, Avril suddenly saw what her mother's eyes must have seen all those years before. Her niece – however stroppy and rebellious, however worldly-wise she might think herself – was just a child, a pregnant child. But even so, way more mature than Avril had been at that age, her former naivety about anything except music and clothes shocking to her now.

How on earth would she, Avril, have coped raising a kid? Even helped by her parents, how quickly would she have started to resent the shackles stopping her from flirting with every boy she met, wearing out every dance floor in town? How much fun would she have found it, giggling with girlfriends on street corners with a baby attached to her boob? Or worrying about colic and night-time feeds while her friends' biggest concerns were the Top Twenty chart and chasing boys.

All those things Avril wouldn't have been able to achieve if she'd kept Hazel. All the places she'd never have seen.

Of course her mother had been acting in Avril's best interests. Peggy had never given a fig for money or reputation and deep down Avril had always known it. She'd offered her daughter a huge gift, presenting her with what could have been possibly the best of both worlds, and it was only Avril's ridiculous pride that had refused to accept it gracefully. All those years of blaming Peggy for what had probably been the most unselfish act a mother can do for her daughter – sacrificing her own freedom in order that Avril could have hers.

Her parents hadn't insisted on adoption by a stranger, they hadn't forced her to abort, kicked her out in the street, disowned her. No, they'd taken the baby into their own home where Avril could see her every day, watch her grow up, be a very real part of her life.

But oh no, Avril couldn't settle for that. She had to goof it up. Nurse her grudges, nurture her resentments. And slam the door on her parents and her daughter.

She sighed as she picked up her phone to check her messages.

'It's obviously a family trait – running off,' Natalie said, as the hedges of Little Hooking brushed past the window on the narrow lane that led to The Briars. 'Mum used to, all the time, when we first moved here. Just for the day, though. She'd go and visit her aunt Maude in Worthing and Dad would be pacing the carpet, wringing his hands and fretting, "I'm so worried about her, so very very worried. Do you think she's ever coming back?" And then when she did, he'd complain that neither Milly nor I had made him so much as an egg to eat all day. You know Dad, too helpless to open the fridge.'

'Yeah.' Hazel breathed on the window and drew circles in the steam. In one way it was best he had gone first. He had been really pathetic whenever Peggy was away and comically hopeless even when she was there. When they were younger, he'd wander into the kitchen, covering his eyes in horror, and shuddering, 'I can't go in the bathroom, there's some disgusting women's thing in there, I couldn't look,' and they'd rush as one to remove the monstrosity – what could it be? A box of tampons? Something worse? – only to discover an innocuous teen bra lying on the floor. And the way he'd bang on the bathroom door when one of them had snuck in there with a book, shouting, 'What are you doing in there? Have you fallen down the bowl? Shall I call a plumber?' Really, he was hysterically funny half the time.

'He loved to complain that none of us knew how to boil water,' she said to Natalie. 'But that was his generation and besides all that, deep down and without the booze, he was a really loving man. His friends from Skye talked for hours about how special and kind and brilliant he was.'

'I know that,' Natalie said gently. 'You don't always have to defend him, you know.'

'I wasn't defending him,' Hazel replied edgily. 'I was just stating facts.' Now she was closer to home, she was getting nervous again. Should she still call Peggy 'Mum?' Nothing would ever be the same again, no matter what Natalie said. Restlessly, she put her feet on the dashboard and took them down again at Natalie's frown.

'Poor Mum, when you think of it,' Natalie rattled on into the silence. 'Always scraping for money, Dad not wanting her to get a job for all those years and, anyway, how could she with us kids to look after? Actually, I've always thought, out of all of us, you're the one most like her.'

'Scraping for money, you mean?' Hazel teased.

'No.' Natalie smiled. 'The way you're both complete bookworms, hate housework, loathe ironing, can't cook for toffee.'

'Me?' Dusting off her footprints, Hazel looked up in surprise.

'Yes, but at the same time you're always laughing, joking, not giving a hoot what anyone thinks of you. Not all uptight and huffy like Avril and me or timid and self-conscious like Milly.'

'Yes, but Mum's way nicer.'

'True,' Natalie agreed, smiling. 'Mum is way nicer.'

'What does that button do?' Hazel reached across and pointed at the dash.

'Raise the roof, I think. I never use it.'

'You have a convertible and you never use the sunroof! Are you mad?'

'Mildly eccentric, I like to think.' Natalie chuckled. 'But then again . . .' She was interrupted by her mobile buzzing and shuddering. 'Answer that quick!'

Hazel flipped it open. 'Hello . . . Yes . . . It's Avril,' she hissed. 'Hi, Av.' There was just the slightest quaver over the name. Only the fist clenched in her lap gave away her tension. 'Yes . . . Yes, I'm with Natalie. She tracked me down, ha ha . . . Yes, I know. I'm sorry, I didn't mean to make everyone worry . . . Oh, that's OK. Did Ivor get hold of you? . . . Oh, so you haven't heard? Well, apparently Milly's run off now.' Relaying this, Hazel felt a sudden inappropriate urge to giggle. Their whole life turning into a Keystone Kops caper. 'And Erin too and it wasn't even her turn . . . She is? Thank God for that.' She turned to Natalie. 'Erin's at Avril's.' She spoke into the phone again. 'You'd better call Ivor. He's frantic.' She put her hand in front of her eyes as Natalie swerved again, narrowly missing an ice-cream float. 'Don't worry about Milly, Natalie "Call me Starsky" and I are on the scent. If we hear anything we'll ring you and vice versa. And by the way, you'd better phone Richard. Yes, lover boy, Richard. He's turned out to be a regular Sherlock Homes. Oh, and Av . . .' Her voice rang strong and assertive as she paused dramatically. 'Keep your bloody mobile on.'

'Oh dear, what a shame,' Peggy said, answering the door, 'you just missed, Matt. Hazel!' Peggy suddenly caught sight of who was hiding behind Natalie. 'Oh my giddy aunt!'

'No, she's the giddy aunt.' Hazel pointed at Natalie. 'Hi, Mum.'

'You bad, bad girl,' Peggy scolded as she flung her arms around her. 'You scared the living daylights out of me.'

'Oh.' Hazel shrugged. 'You know me, bad penny . . .'

'Matt was here?' Natalie's heart hit the deck, thudding like a hammer at the mention of his name. Her mouth was suddenly dry as automatically her eyes scanned the hallway as if some trace of him might be lingering, like ectoplasm.

'Just this minute pulled away. He had a taxi pick him up for the airport.'

There was a knock on the door.

'Oh, that might be him back. He forgot the hanky I gave him, belonged to Callum, especially monogrammed.' She opened the door but Natalie was disappointed to see Ivor, Ben in arms, a worried frown engulfing his face.

'Any news?' said Hazel anxiously.

'Nothing. I don't know what to think. It's my fault. I was rather sharp with her this morning. I found these bills. I feel terrible. Poor Milly. So nobody's heard anything?'

'No.' Natalie shook her head. 'We've been trying and trying on her phone. Left tons of messages.'

'Although you know Milly and mobiles,' Hazel joked. 'She'd never know how to pick them up. Did Avril call you?'

'Yes, she said she's got Erin visiting.'

'Erin visiting Avril?' Peggy looked confused. 'Good Lord!'

'Main thing is, she's safe and Milly's not. These pills are lethal. God knows how long she's been taking them.'

'I'll go and make some tea.' Peggy disappeared to the kitchen.

'Have you asked all the people she knows around here?' suggested Natalie.

He nodded. 'Fergus has been helping all he can. He was great actually, picked Rory up from school for me, while I was stuck on that blasted train. I've left him at home taking care of Rory, but I really couldn't leave him with Ben.'

'No, of course not.' Natalie smiled reassuringly at her brother-in-law. She'd never seen him so het up. He really did look worried sick.

Half an hour later they were still musing.

'I've driven the boys to the park, the school, Morrisons, the bottle bank. I was going to wander around the town a bit, check out the cashpoints. Thanks.' He accepted the top-up of tea Peggy was pouring into his cup. 'Maybe see if she's drawn any money out but I'll have to go back to put Rory to bed soon. They've got –' Ivor stopped as his mobile began to ring. 'Yes . . . Yes . . . Where . . . ? I'll be right over, Judy. Thanks.' He clicked off his phone.

'What is it?' Hazel asked.

'One of her friends just spotted her car. Abandoned at Codmoreton railway station. Doors wide open.'

'Oh my God!' Natalie exhaled. Everyone was momentarily speechless with worry. 'Look, we'll go. Give us the keys and you sort out the kids,' Natalie finally broke in, taking command.

'And I'll be Base Control and take care of Ben.' Peggy took her grandson from Ivor and sat him on her lap. 'Good luck!'

'So we're going to ask at the railway station, right?' Hazel stared in amazement at her sister as she tooted her horn impatiently at the Mazda in front. This was a new Natalie she was seeing. Or maybe, when the crisis was bigger than a broken fingernail or someone forgetting to return the wedding acceptance card, her sister was made of stronger stuff than she'd ever realised.

'Yup.' She overtook the Mazda, almost knocking over an elderly lady in the process. 'See if they remember selling her a ticket. Oh God, you don't think she's having some kind of breakdown or anything, do you?'

'Milly? No,' Hazel gave the lady an apologetic wave. 'Of course not.' She crossed her fingers. 'Course not.'

'Sorry, love, not a clue.' The man behind the ticket booth, rubbed his chin. 'It's been one of those days. People coming and going, haven't had a minute to catch my breath. And anyway we've those automatic machines now, don't we?' He indicated behind them. 'Your sister might have used one of those. She could be anywhere.'

'Fat load of use he was,' Hazel muttered under her breath as she and Natalie despondently walked back over the railway bridge.

'Yes, but he's right. She could be anywhere.'

'How about mates? Anyone who'd take her in? Ivor said he'd checked the Codmoreton ones but are there any others? Maybe ones that he doesn't know about?'

Natalie searched her memory. 'I think she still writes to one of her old school pals in Edinburgh.'

'Oh God, don't,' Hazel groaned. 'We can't drive all the way up there.'

'Besides, I doubt she'd have the fare. You know how she hates credit cards and she's like the Queen, never carries cash.'

'Never has any, you mean. Yet another reason why she wouldn't use the machine.'

'Well, it doesn't help us, does it? But now what do we do? It's like a needle in a bleeding haystack.'

Hazel spotted a lighted sign in the shopping strip across the road. 'I'm starving. Look, it's past seven. Let's get some food and regroup.'

*

In the steamy grease-laden interior of the chippy, the two sisters perched on high stools planning their next move.

'OK, what have we got?' Hazel stuck a chicken nugget into Natalie's small carton of ketchup before Natalie primly passed her over her own. 'That she had a row with Erin. That she's been taking diet pills that can make you psychotic and terminally depressed. And that her car was found at Codmoreton railway station.' Milly's friend had kindly closed the doors but a quick glance inside had revealed nothing before they locked it up. 'And by the way, you're not getting back in mine until you've finished those.' Natalie handed her a wet wipe. 'I can't stand sticky handprints all over my nice clean leather.'

'Some things never change,' Hazel said with a sigh.

Milly stumbled through the streets heading for the lights, the noise, smiling like a loon. She'd just hopped over a barrier, just like that. Like a young thing. A young, thin thing. The station staff at either end never saw, or if they did, they'd ignored it. 'Couldn't do that while I was a porky-pie,' she muttered to herself. 'No way, *Jose*.'

The noise was growing stronger, cheering, singing, chanting. The lights were blinding now. And words, words of a song were running through her head.

Bruce Springsteen, that's who it was.

She began to dance, sweeping her hands from floor to the moonlit sky above her. Waggling her hips.

Dancing in the dark.

She was back in the eighties.

Dancing in the dark.

She was the girl Bruce pulled on to the stage.

Dancing in the dark.

Suddenly the noise was on top of her and she found herself

being swept along with a pile of people heading somewhere.

She wasn't alone, there were hundreds of people around her. All dancing in the dark, singing in the streets. It must have been like the end of the war. Mum would talk about it, VE Day, when she was about fifteen and she'd sneaked off to Trafalgar Square without telling her parents and she'd kissed loads of boys.

About fifteen, same age as Erin . . .

Erin . . . The pain suddenly cut through her making her want to retch.

Erin was cross with her.

Ivor was cross with her. Ivor was never cross with her but now he was cross with her.

Fergus was cross with her, Ben, Avril, everybody.

Blank it out. Block it out. Block everything out.

Sing, Milly, sing!

And there she was, her voice mingling with other voices, chants and the force of the crowd turned her round and suddenly she was leading them. This mass of singing people, like a drum major being followed by a marching band and she was in front, stamping her feet, march, march, march. Left right, left right. Had a good job and I left right, left right.

She was swinging her arms, in time to the music. Her face pointing at the stars. Laughing, laughing at the moon.

'This is odd,' Hazel observed, idly flicking through Natalie's car manual.

'What is?' Natalie slowed as she reached a blind bend in the road. Everything about today had been odd as far as she was concerned.

'Us two in the car together, spending all this time alone. Travels with my aunt. Are we ever alone together, *Auntie Natalie*?' She flicked her eyes at Natalie to see how she'd react.

'Oh, don't! Don't!' Natalie took her left hand from the steering wheel to touch Hazel's right. 'I don't care whose womb you came from. You'll always be my horrible sister, Haze. Besides,' she added, 'Auntie Natalie from you makes me sound so old.'

Hazel burst into laughter and Natalie did too although she hadn't really meant it as a joke. Bad enough having a teenage niece let alone one Hazel's age.

'You were old when you were with JJ. I'm glad you dumped him, Nats. He wasn't good enough for you.'

'Yeah, right.' Natalie looked at her sideways, waiting for her to barb it up with her usual backhanded compliments. But Hazel's face remained impassive.

'No, really. You need someone who's fun to be with. Someone who'll make you laugh. Who won't care if your clothes are a mess and that you haven't showered or brushed your hair for a week.'

'That'll be the day. I don't care who this someone is, I'll scratch his eyes out before I let him take away my hairbrush. And I'd have to be stuck in prison or somewhere before I gave up my shower. You'd just love that – Natalie, the Birdwoman of Cell Block H.' She chewed her lower lip thoughtfully. 'You know, Haze, I was always a tiny bit jealous of you.'

'Jealous of me?' Hazel swivelled to face her, looking flabbergasted.

'For one thing, you knocked me off my baby-of-the-family perch. Everyone used to rave about how cute I was until you came along. And Milly doted on you, defended you even when you were being obnoxious. Avril – well, she might not have brought you up, exactly, but she thinks the world of you. You always made her laugh, even if she was in a stinking mood with the rest of us. And Milly and I used to go on and on, asking Mum and Dad who they liked best, who would they rescue first if the house was on fire, that sort of stuff. Well, once Milly did set the chimney on fire and you should have seen how quick Mum rushed you outside.'

'Probably because I was too small to walk. That doesn't mean a thing, Nats.' She noticed Natalie's eyes were suspiciously bright.

'Oh, they adored you, you know they did. Mum's life revolved around you. And then you were so fearless. You climbed a ladder on to our roof when you were just a toddler – Mum nearly lynched Dad for leaving it there. And you never care what anyone thinks, you wear all these mad clothes . . .' She looked across at Drew's tight vivid orange 'Windsurfers Do It Standing Up' T-shirt. 'What I mean is, you've always taken risks. You don't go with the crowd, you lead the crowd, while I've followed the rules, tried to fit in. You know, getting a good secure job, keeping myself well presented, making sure my nails are painted.'

'They always look nice.' Hazel automatically looked at hers, short and ragged.

'Big achievement, eh? Natalie MacLeod. Renowned for her immaculate cuticles. Jeremy liked them. Anyway, enough. I don't need you to get any more conceited or there won't be room in the car for your ginormous head.'

'Cow.' Hazel grinned.

'Bitch.' Natalie grinned back as she pulled up behind a double-decker bus collecting a line of passengers.

'Takes one to know one.'

'So, that barman . . .' Natalie said casually, switching on the windscreen wipers as the rain began to cascade from the skies. They'd been touring the streets and villages around Codmoreton for the last couple of hours, but there was no sighting of Milly anywhere. 'It was pretty generous of him, taking you in like that, wasn't it?'

'I guess,' Hazel said dreamily.

'Ulterior motive?'

'Nah. He's just a nice guy. Gay.'

'Didn't look gay.'

'Oh, and what's gay supposed to look like, clever clogs? Freddie Mercury moustache and tight satin shorts showing off a bulging packet?'

'I was thinking preppy haircut, improbably square jaw and impeccable dress sense,' Natalie returned. 'So he told you he was gay?'

'OK, so he doesn't like to talk about it but his partner, Drew, did. You know, the small camp one. When I first met them both at the pub that time he said Jonno was a dag. Dag's Aussie for gay.'

'Dag? Dag doesn't mean gay!'

'Of course it does,' Hazel snorted.

'Hazel,' Natalie said as she turned into a small cul-de-sac and stopped the car, 'you might think you're a big-shot world traveller but I know a thing or two about Aussies. Bob, my boss, who I've worked with every day for seven years, is from Melbourne. You're confusing it with fag. A dag is slang for a nerd, you know like a geek. Oh, Hazel, you didn't put your foot in it, did you?'

But Hazel was too busy thinking in appalled silence to answer. Her mind replaying every conversation, frantically trying to picture every moment they'd spent together. What if Drew wasn't his boyfriend? Jonno had never actually admitted anything. And, OK, much as she hated to buy into clichés, he did own a battered old leather jacket, loved to cook and took up hairdressing at one point, but she couldn't begin to imagine him with a Freddie Mercury moustache.

'Try her mobile again.'

'Is there any point?' Natalie tapped away anyway. 'I've filled up her message box with messages and it's not –' Her eyes widened. 'She's answered!' she suddenly exclaimed. 'Milly, where the hell are you?'

Chapter 41

'What's she saying? What's she saying?' Hazel placed her head against Natalie's.

'Shh! I can't hear.' Natalie shoved her off and covered her left ear with her hand. 'When you walk . . .' she said slowly.

' "When you walk"?' Hazel repeated. 'What the fuck does that mean?'

'Something about a storm?' Natalie continued.

'Give it here.' Hazel snatched it from Natalie's grasp.

It was a man. Gravelly voice. And he was singing in a very much out-of-tune Liverpudlian accent.

'Liverpool. That's the song,' Natalie said. 'Ask him who he is?'

'Who are you? Where's my sister? What have you done with her?'

'Liverpool, Liverpoooooooool.' Click, and the line went dead.

Natalie tried frantically to call him back. 'It's no use,' she said dismally after a minute or two. 'It's going straight to voicemail again.'

'Do you think she's been kidnapped? By a Liverpool supporter?'

'Or run off to see a match? You never know what people will do on drugs. It sounded like there were other people there.'

'Is there a match on? Couldn't be, could there? It's Monday. Do they play football Mondays?'

'How would I know?' Natalie despaired. 'Jeremy never watched anything but cricket and rugby. Said football was for yobs.'

'Yeah, well, that's Jeremy for you – Mr Snobalmighty. Hold on, I'll be back in a tic.' Haring across the main road, Hazel ran into a shop and then back, screeching up to Natalie's open window, doubling up and panting for breath. 'They're playing Brighton. Withdean. Kick-off was seven forty-five. Two hours ago.'

'You're a star!'

'Brighton it is then.' Hazel slid back into the car, clicking in her seat belt and slamming the door. 'And don't spare the horses, Nats, old girl.'

It was ludicrous how nervous Avril felt when she finally dialled Richard's number. Four times in the last few hours she'd picked up the phone and put it back again, scolding herself for being so scared. But she was. Scared stiff, she realised.

Maybe she didn't need to say anything. But she did. Of course she did. Richard had only ever been nice to her and now . . . finding her daughter? That wasn't something you could brush off, pretend hadn't happened. It didn't matter that she'd acted like a prima donna throughout their entire relationship. It didn't matter if he hung up, refused to speak to her, or gave her a piece of his mind about her insufferable behaviour. She'd just have to swallow it, that was all.

And he didn't even know the half of it. That phone call she'd made to his wife while she was in New York. What on earth had she been thinking? She'd been pissed, that's all. He'd been getting too close and she'd started to have anxiety attacks, wanting him near but at the same time wanting to push him away. Telling his wife about the affair was supposed to put an end to it. Send the errant husband running home. Instead, it had exactly the opposite effect. Oh God. She punched in the numbers before she could think of it further.

'Richard?'

'Hi, Avril.' His voice, neutral though it was, prompted a suspicious prickling at the corner of her eyes.

She grabbed a cigarette to soothe her nerves and took a deep breath to calm her thudding heart. 'I was just . . . I wanted to say . . . About Hazel . . . I'm so grateful . . .' Listen to herself, stammering, not able to finish a sentence.

'It was nothing. Don't think about it.' A long silence and then he sounded a fraction warmer: 'How have you been?'

'Great. Well, not great really. You know . . .' She shrugged though he couldn't see her, keeping her voice low, not wanting to wake Erin still asleep on the sofa.

'Are you at home? Do you want to talk about it?' This time she could tell he was melting. His deep voice could always get to her, smooth as liquid chocolate, sexy as a smouldering sax solo.

Did she want to talk? Yes! She wanted to pick up that crippling pride and dump it in the nearest dustcart. Wanted to run over there right now, or have him run over here, so she could throw herself in his lap, kiss his lips off, exchange every secret she'd been keeping bottled up for years, listen to his entire inner-life story, make love like animals and stay in bed for an entire week.

Erin stirred on the sofa, rolling over and coughing, her eyes flickering open for a brief second and closing again. Was she awake? The last thing she needed was to overhear Avril and be sick with worry about Milly. And Hazel or Ivor could call back any minute.

'I can't. Not right now.' She felt her belly clench with

dread, hoping against all reasonable expectation he wouldn't think she was snubbing him again. 'It's complicated. There's stuff going on . . . I can't explain . . .'

'Perhaps some other time then,' he said coolly, and put the phone down.

Avril stared at the receiver for too long before she dropped it back in its cradle. The cigarette in her long fingers had broken in half, still unlit. She threw it on the coffee table and went over to her niece, shaking her gently on the shoulder.

'Come on, sleepyhead,' she whispered softly. 'You'll be more comfortable in bed.'

'It makes sense in a way, I guess,' Hazel said as they walked past Gayle Cutting's shop, all closed and shuttered for the night. 'Running off to some place familiar. Like me ending up at the Flying Ferret, even though I didn't really mean to.'

'But on the other hand that singing drunk could have been anywhere. He might not have been going to the actual game.'

'I know.' Hazel shrugged. As she spoke, a small mob of Brighton supporters milled out of a pub and staggered towards them, arm in arm, waving blue-and-white scarves, toasting their victory. Natalie moved to the wall to give them plenty of room but Hazel didn't budge an inch, causing them to divide around her and spill over on to the road.

'I think Ivor should call the police,' Hazel said when the two women were side by side again. 'Tell them about the lead.'

'Yeah, we could sing our clue to them down the phone,' Natalie scoffed. 'How did it go again, "When you walk through a storm"? Maybe they'll record it and send it through the radio to all the other forces. You were missing almost two weeks and they couldn't have cared less.'

'To think I put you all through this kind of stress,' Hazel

said sombrely. 'You know, I just needed to escape. Get my head together.'

'Well, apparently Milly felt the same way,' Natalie said, not completely letting her off the hook.

The football stadium was a total washout. 'Not that anyone could find anyone in that crowd,' said Hazel as they scoured the seafront where they now stood feeling more hopeless than ever.

'What about trying the train station here? Ask around, find out if anyone's seen her,' said Natalie.

'What, you mean after all our success at the last one? Well, you get to describe her this time. Or . . .' Hazel's eyes lit up as she focused into the distance. 'By God, I'm a clever chook.'

'A clever what?'

'Come on, quick!'

Avril pressed the send button and sat back. She glanced at her watch, mission completed, eleven thirty. Five minutes from the time Hazel had called her, saying they were in a late-night Internet café in Brighton. Well, at least Hazel was talking to her again. Pity she was too worried about Milly to find much relief.

She double-checked the email had gone, then closed down her laptop and stood up, heading for her drinks cabinet and the nearest bottle of red wine. The corkscrew had pierced the foil and was halfway through the cork when she stopped. Milly was right. Her drinking had been getting out of control. In reality, that was why she'd been so angry at her sister's accusations. The truth had sharp teeth.

She began opening bottles and pouring the contents down the sink. Rather a waste and she was sure she'd regret it when she next had guests over, but for the moment it seemed wise to put all temptation firmly out of reach.

It took a second for her to register the noise from the next room. She heard it again. A soft moan. She walked through. Erin was lying on the bed, legs curled up underneath her.

'It hurts,' she said. 'It really hurts.'

A violent red stain oozed out onto the white Egyptian cotton sheets.

'Nah, hundreds of people disembark here of a night.' The station guard drew his hat back and stared at the paper in his hand. The scanned photograph of Milly that had been taken just this Christmas failed to show the weight loss, the new gauntness to her features. 'I could never pick out just one. We have those that want to come. Those that don't.'

'What do you mean? Those that don't?' Hazel thought he sounded purposely sinister, like the ancient villagers in the pub in *American Werewolf in London* or some other creaky old horror film. '*There be strange 'appenings on the moors at night, missie. And them as dies'll be the lucky 'uns.*'

'What do I mean? Ah, we get people staying on trains. Late at night. Have a few bevvies too many, shut their eyes a sec, intending to get out at Redhill, next minute they're here, stranded.'

'So what do they do?' Natalie looked appalled, as if missing her station and arriving at the end of the line was a nightmare indeed. Hazel, experienced traveller, and itching to continue the chase, yawned and fidgeted.

'What do they do?' he repeated. 'Well, sometimes they wait on the platform for the next train home. Sometimes it's too late and they try to get a hotel room, but mostly they just go have a kip. Just till the 4 a.m. back to Gatwick.'

'OK, cheers.' Hazel decided it was time to pull Natalie away.

'Thank you very much for your time,' said Natalie, disappointed.

They were walking back down the steps when Natalie abruptly stopped. 'Hang on a minute.' She turned and sprinted back to the top, leaving Hazel eating her dust.

'Kip?' She grilled the stationmaster again. 'Where do they have a kip? Is there a waiting room or something?'

'Oh, not here. I send them to the cemetery down the road.'

'The cemetery! Yuck.' Natalie clutched her handbag as if feeling the presence of ghostly fingers.

'Safe as anywhere else round these parts.' He looked somewhat offended. 'Although I do tell people to watch their belongings, purses and wallets, like. Anyways, like I say, I often send people there if they're caught short. Saves them hanging around the station. Be a few there tonight, I bet, Liverpool supporters, getting drunk, missed the last train.'

It took a while to walk around the fence of the cemetery to find an entrance. It was pitch black too, the darkness of trees and empty space seeping through the iron railings or perhaps it was just their eyes having to adjust. At Natalie's insistence, Hazel kept the beam of her newly purchased torch pointed on the ground to illuminate their way and avoid dog mess.

'Hang on a minute, just got to do my shoelace.' Hazel stooped down while Natalie waited ahead. When she turned round, Hazel had stuck the light under her chin and bugged her eyes. 'Woo, wooo,' she said in a high-pitched voice.

'God, don't!' Natalie squealed and seized the torch from her. 'Milly used to do that to me. Scared me rigid. And then she used to jump out of the cupboard at me with boot polish all over her face. She was an evil child.'

'Oh well, to hell with her, then.' Hazel pretended to spin round. 'She's not worth saving, let's head home.'

'Don't even joke . . .' Natalie glowered.

They walked on in the still dark night, the only sounds coming from the squeak of Hazel's borrowed trainers and the occasional click where Natalie's metal-tipped kitten heels met gravel. Finally they approached the huge ornate gates of the entrance.

'Sure this is the right one?'

'That's what the guard said.'

'You know, talking about things Milly used to do . . . I did a bad thing to you not that long ago.' Hazel opened the creaky gate. 'Remember your engagement party?'

'How could I forget?'

'Well, I told Dad where it was.'

'Oh my God!' Natalie stopped in her tracks. 'It was *you*. How could you *do that* to me! It was one of the *worst* evenings of my entire life.'

'I know.' Hazel winced. 'I'm sorry. I don't think I liked you very much then. And you never invited me.'

'I only didn't invite you because I didn't want you making wisecracks about me to my friends.' They walked side by side down the concrete path.

'But if they were your true friends, would they care?' Hazel shrugged. 'OK, I admit I was a rat to you a lot of the time. Only it was such fun watching you cringe. Anyway, I really didn't imagine he'd actually go all the way up there and I'd been on the wacky baccy if that's any excuse.'

'No it isn't, and that's another thing –' She stopped as they both suddenly realised they weren't alone. Huddles of bodies were there, leaning against tombs, propped up on benches, lying on grassy knolls, mooching against memorial stones. Hazel stopped in amazement. It was like the thriller video, only spookier.

And real.

'What next?' Hazel asked, conscious of the dozens of sleepy eyes on her.

'Shout,' said Natalie before yelling, 'Milly! Milly!'

'Milly, Milly,' numerous voices echoed, most of them inebriated by the sound of it.

'Milly!' Hazel tried.

'Milly, Milly,' they echoed again. Like a pack of wolves baying at the moon.

'Hey, I'm Milly,' said a girl's voice from the left.

'No, I'm Milly,' giggled another girl from the right.

'I'm Milly,' boomed a deep Welsh voice.

And then the fun and games began, followed by howls of laughter.

'Oh God,' Hazel groaned. 'All we need. A pile of old dossers doing a sodding Spartacus routine on us.'

'What shall we do?' All of a sudden Natalie's eyes brightened. 'I know.' She climbed onto a white marble orb and stood up, raising her voice to the maximum. 'Rescue Service! Rescue Service!'

A little voice piped out, 'Gardelous! I'm here, Nats. I'm over here.'

The sound seemed to be coming from a small bench. Natalie and Hazel raced over. On a half-broken bench was a large, shabby, battered-looking coat from under which a ghostly pale face peeked out.

'It's her,' came a familiar voice. It bounced around her head. She drew the coat tighter to her.

'Is that you, Milly?' Hazel's voice now. But Hazel was missing, wasn't she?

Milly squinted as a beam of light was pointed in her eyes.

'She looks ill, she's almost blue.'

'Come on. Help me lift her.'

Milly could feel arms tugging at her. Disembodied conversations echoed through the blackness. She tried to lie down. Sleep forever.

'I don't want to go,' she protested thinly.

The arms tugged again.

'But you can't stay here.' It was Hazel again but she sounded far far away. 'Why do you want to stay here?' she was asking.

'I don't want my life,' she whispered.

'No one wants their life, Milly.'

'Don't say that,' Natalie groaned. 'It'll depress her even more. You have to come home. Milly? Milly? Doesn't look like she can hear us.'

Milly felt nauseous as she drifted in and out of sleep.

'Milly, what have you taken?' Was that Natalie? 'You have to tell me.'

'We know what she's bloody taken, you clot,' Hazel was saying. 'Help me get her up.'

Now Milly was having this great dream, about flying and then swooping down and diving into water. In the distance she could hear . . . what? Cheeping, squawking . . . She was listening, but not listening. Knowing, but not knowing.

'Erin needs you,' said Natalie, shaking her firmly.

'Erin?' She could feel herself slowly coming round.

'She's in London.' Now Hazel's hands were pulling her up as well.

'London?' Milly tried to make sense of it.

There were lots of urgent whisperings, Avril's name was mentioned. Hush noises and then a mobile phone was pushed against her ear and there was Avril. Her voice strong, cutting through the fog in Milly's head.

'Milly,' she commanded. 'Get over here now. We're at the hospital. Your daughter needs you. She wants her mother.'

Chapter 42

Natalie walked into the dining room with a dark blue velvet box and a tin of Silvo in her hand.

'What do you think? Best silver instead of Mum's old tat?'

'Where did you find that?' Milly interrupted her task of putting down the place mats to take a closer look. The last few weeks had done her the world of good, Natalie was pleased to notice. She looked so much better, the colour returning to her cheeks, the feverish look gone from her eyes.

'Top of the bookshelves in the study.' Natalie blew off a covering of dust. 'One of Mum and Dad's wedding presents, probably. We might as well give them an airing, don't you think? It's not every day Mum turns seventy-nine after all.'

'Especially since she wasn't supposed to for another two years. You do realise she'll be eighty next year? I can't get used to her being so old.'

'Are you kidding, she's younger than all of us. I wish I had half her energy.'

'I can recommend a pill, if you like,' Milly joked.

'Don't!' Natalie commanded. 'Has Hazel told you how dangerous those pills were? She had a friend almost die when she was in the States because she got so hooked on them – liver and kidney failure, damage to heart and blood vessels. How could you do that to yourself?'

'Desperation, I guess. And stupidity. I thought I was too fat for anyone to love me. But Ivor tells me he actually prefers a woman with curves.' Milly put down the last place mat and topped it with a plate from a stack she pulled out of the china cabinet. 'He's been amazing, Natalie, since this all happened. It really shook him up. He keeps telling me how much he loves me, how terrified he was of losing me.' She made a face. 'And talk about bonding with the kids. He's out fishing with them at the moment, even Erin. They're loving all the extra attention.'

'So no more Ivor the invisible.' Natalie rubbed hard at a tarnished fork. 'How's Erin?'

'She's recovered well since the D&C she had to have after the miscarriage – physically that is.' Milly shivered. 'It's probably for the best . . . what happened, but she's got a way to go until she feels emotionally stronger. As least she's got the school holidays now to give her a break. But I still can't believe she had to go through that and I was no help at all. You know, I think there's a part of me that will never forgive myself.'

'Oh puh-leeese. You're the best mum I know. Mother Teresa couldn't be more dedicated. If you ask me, all of our family could use a good healthy dose of self-esteem. Look at us, we're a mess. Drowning our sorrows in drink, using drugs to solve our problems, running away from the slightest crisis.'

'I'm not sure Hazel's situation counts as a "slight crisis",' Milly said. 'But she seems to be dealing with it OK. She and Avril had a good old heart-to-heart, got a lot of things aired apparently. What do you think? Paper napkins or real ones?'

'Real ones, of course.' Natalie huffed on a spoon and tilted it to see her reflection. Inwardly Milly grinned. It was so typical of Nat to find some totally unnecessary task to occupy her for hours while Milly ran around doing all the real work.

'Doesn't this remind you of the day the Poshy-Washies

came for the pre-wedding lunch. Amazing how long ago that seems. Yet it was only a couple of months. Do you ever hear from Jeremy?'

'Nope and I don't want to.'

Milly laughed. 'You know, Natalie, I think you're the strongest of the lot of us.'

'Rubbish.'

'It's true. Dad used to say to me all the time, "If there's one of you girls I never have to worry about, it'll be Natalie." He admired your spunk.'

'You mean he knew I could be a bitch on wheels.'

'Don't be silly, he loved you. And anyway' – Milly gave an impish smile – 'in the bitchiness stakes, you've always been a rank amateur compared to Avril – or Hazel at times.'

'Maybe, but no one can beat me for nagging.' Natalie began work on another fork while Milly went to fetch water glasses.

When she came back, Natalie said, 'Dad really told you I was spunky? You know I always felt so insignificant, next to the rest of you. I wasn't a go-getter like Avril, a risk-taker like Hazel or even Mother Earth personified like you. I was always Nasty Nats, the inadequate.'

'You were never really nasty,' Milly soothed. 'We started calling you that because when you were six, you decided your name was going to be Princess Anastasia, remember? So we called you Nasty for short. Anyway, you could be really sweet. I remember Hazel once had this first date with some guy she really fancied and you got a train all the way from Victoria to Little Hooking just to lend her your leather trousers.'

'I did?' Natalie placed the fork carefully on the left of the plate.

'Yep.'

Natalie shrugged. 'It was probably because she planned on traipsing off in torn jeans, disgracing the family name.'

'Ha ha,' Milly scoffed. 'Problem with you, dear sis, is you can't admit you're a marshmallow at heart.'

'Grrrr.' Natalie pretended to growl, baring her teeth. 'You're such a saint, you think everyone else is too. Anyway, first dates are important.'

'Mmm,' Milly said reflectively, then laughed suddenly. 'I remember the first time Matt came to The Briars to pick me up when we'd just begun going out. I was all shy about it so I gave everyone strict instructions not to answer the door or show their faces. As we were leaving I happened to look up at Hazel's bedroom and I just caught the curtain twitching. The little minx didn't realise she was completely busted.'

Natalie flushed as her mind switched back to the argument they'd had with Avril the day they were clearing out Dad's clothes. 'Oh Milly.' She swallowed hard. 'It wasn't Hazel up at the window, it was me!'

'It was?' Milly quirked her eyebrows humorously. 'You perfidious wretch.'

It was the sort of thing the Milly of their youth might have said, the young girl who'd studied Chaucer and Shakespeare, the young girl Natalie had betrayed.

Natalie took a deep breath, squirming with shame.

'I need to speak to you about – you know – the argument. When we were clearing the clothes.'

'Oh heck, Nats, I'm sorry. I know I was so out of order. It was the pills talking and, well, most of it's a blank.'

'No, I mean about Matt. Thing is . . . it was true what Avril said . . . the letters, I mean. Matt and I . . . I've felt so bad for so long. I never meant it to happen. I didn't answer them. Any of them. I promise.'

She hung her head, fixing her blurry gaze on the cutlery she'd been distracting herself with.

For what seemed a long time there was no response. When

she peeked up, Milly's face was a study of conflicting emotions. Her elder sister sank down on a chair, still clutching an empty water glass, and actually seemed to laugh, albeit ruefully.

'Oh, Nats, what idiots we are. If only I'd known. You've no idea of the agony you could have spared me . . .'

'But you were so upset when Matt broke up with you. You cried for weeks. I don't understand.'

'Because I'd acted atrociously. I was too much of a coward just to come out and say it was over so I literally forced him to do it – break up, I mean. I'd met Ivor, you see, and I was totally loopy about him. Oh God, the first time I saw him, he looked like he'd stepped out of a Russian novel, so dark and tortured, and intense. I thought I'd melt into the floor when those black eyes looked into mine. Next to him Matt was such a boy.'

How amazing it was, Natalie marvelled, the way everyone looked at the world through such different lenses. The idea that any red-blooded female could prefer Ivor, that lanky, slightly geeky beanpole, over Matt. Yet Milly clearly considered him a cross between Heathcliff and whoever the big lunk was that ended up blind in *Jane Eyre*. Probably if Ivor *had* been blind, Milly would have found him doubly irresistible. Natalie closed her eyes as she took it all in.

'I was sure Matt dumped you. I've given him such a hard time over it.' She felt sick with shame, remembering the cruel things she'd said to him, the way she'd never give him a chance to explain.

'Well, he did, in a way, but only because I couldn't bring myself to end it and one of us had to. I was so cruel, Nats. I could barely talk to him or look him in the face. I felt as if I was suffocating if he even tried to kiss me – let alone anything else. Then, when he'd ask if something was wrong, I'd lose my nerve and say no. Anyway, he wasn't stupid. It wasn't as if we'd ever been madly in love, but we were the only people each of us knew when we started uni, it was sort of natural to start going out. But it wasn't ever *serious*. And then, when he told me there was someone else, I was sure he was only saying that so I wouldn't feel so dreadful about driving him away.'

'I thought you loved him.' Natalie shook her head. All those years of pining, feeling like a treacherous worm believing she'd ruined her sister's happiness. She could just see Milly staying in a relationship that bored her to tears because she suffered from terminal niceness. 'You know I never answered a single one of his letters even though I couldn't bear to throw them away. I was sure I'd ruined everything for you. I remember you crying and crying that weekend you came home and told everyone it was over.'

'Because I felt so guilty. Ditching my best friend. And I knew how much Mum worshipped him, the whole family did. It made me feel so rotten. He didn't deserve me treating him that way.'

Nothing compared to the way I've treated him, Natalie thought, miserably.

'And quitting university. What was all that about then?'

Milly groaned and dropped her head on the table.

'Me being a total drongo. Ivor decided he knew way more about computers than anyone at uni could teach him and that he was completely wasting his time. He'd been earning tons of money since he was fifteen, working freelance for all kinds of companies. He had all these big conglomerates offering him jobs, wanting him to work for them right away. So he left and I left too because I was besotted and I only wanted to be with him, even though he argued that I should finish my degree.'

'But are you happy, Milly? Honestly?'

'Honestly?' Milly looked up with sparkling lashes. 'Yes. I

love him, Nats. Oh, he drives me insane at times. He can be wholly impractical and – please, please don't ever tell anyone this, especially not Avril – truth be told, we're almost bankrupt. He's obsessed with this new CTI project he's working on, thinks it's going to make us millions, but in the meantime, I can hardly afford a pint of milk, we haven't got a bean to pay the mortgage, he refuses to take a corporate job, and after the last crash, all the investors are steering clear of start-up companies like they're selling eight-tracks and Beta when the world has switched to DVD. That's why he's been invisible these last few months, trying to tie up all the loose ends on this deal he's hoping to put together. But if anyone can make it work, he can. I just have to have faith, that's all. And I have again, I truly have.'

With her shining eyes, Natalie thought she looked like a particularly devoted follower of an evangelical preacher. If Ivor told her Halley's Comet was a spaceship coming to take her off to Planet X, she'd probably be the first lining up for her intergalactic passport. She just hoped Milly's faith was justified. Was anyone ever good enough to marry your sister? she wondered.

'You know' – Milly spooned the French mustard from a jar into a small silver container – 'I wondered about you and Matt, lots of times. You always seemed so angry at him, like you hated his guts, and I didn't know why. I thought I was to blame for that too, you used to be such good friends. But then sometimes I'd catch the way he looked at you, like his eyes were always drawn in your direction. But I know you and your high principles so well, Natalie. You were always so down on anyone who did anything even slightly unethical. The whole thing seemed impossible so I thought I had to be imagining it.'

'Well, I guess I'm not the bearer of the high moral standard after all.' Natalie resumed placing knives and forks on the next items she vowed to discard as soon as her mum's back was turned, the mismatched scratched old place mats depicting Highland cattle and faded Victorian London street scenes.

'You know I wouldn't care if anything did happen,' Milly said gently. 'In fact, I'd rather like it.'

'Well, too late for all that. Anyway, teaches me to think twice before I judge people.'

'What do you reckon?' Milly asked as her eyes swept the table. 'Candles? I know it's only lunch . . .'

'Definitely. There's those brass candlesticks in the study, you could fetch those.'

All right, so what if she'd done 90 per cent of it, Milly thought, as they stepped back to admire the finished product. She had to admit Natalie's sterling silver provided an unusually elegant note to dinner at the MacLeods'. Which, come to think of it . . .

'Help!' She screamed, rushing for the kitchen. 'We're burning the roast.'

Milly and Natalie were scraping the pan when their mother walked in the back door.

'Smells wonderful.' She sniffed the air. 'Oh, you are dears, doing all this for me.'

'Mum, that smell is charred beef.' Natalie's fingers still throbbed from grabbing the scalding pan.

'Oh, scrape the black bits off, sprinkle pepper and a few herbs over it and call it French. That's what I always do. Now, Milly, Ivor and I have just been talking about your fortieth next week. We've had the most wonderful idea . . .'

'Ivor?' Milly looked astonished. 'But I thought he was fishing. Hi, Fergus, hi, Rory, oomph!' She gave a sound like the air punched from a beanbag as they ran into her.

402

'It's here! It's here!' Rory tugged her hand. 'Come outside and see the surprise.'

'Already?' Peggy looked flustered and bustled towards the garden door. 'I distinctly told Mr Carter not before five o'clock.'

Finding herself dragged in the same direction, Milly shot a questioning look at Natalie who shrugged her shoulders.

'Not a clue.' She took off her apron. 'Only one way to find out, right?'

Chapter 43

They discovered Ivor, Erin, Peggy and a big ruddy-faced farmer in deep discussion by the cab of a large van – a removal van Milly thought at first.

'Hey.' Ivor broke away when he saw his wife and hustled towards her, arms outstretched. 'Now I know what you're going to say' – he pulled her into a swooping kiss – 'but if you give us a chance to explain . . .'

Mr Carter was already walking towards the back of the van, pulling open the big double doors.

'We got you a horse!' Rory blurted as a bay gelding, big-boned and sturdy, hopped out on to the driveway. 'For your birthday!' It discovered a patch of dandelions on the side of the gravel and began to eat them with relish.

'A horse!' Milly didn't know whether to cry, laugh or pummel Ivor into a bloody pulp. She felt like doing all three. The man was hopeless. Impractical? – he was certifiably impossible. A touch of depression and Ivor bought her a horse? They were on a financial jetliner nose-diving towards the Sea of Bankruptcy and instead of searching under the seats for the floatable cushions he was gaily consulting with the stewardess about duty-free!

'He's ginormous,' Natalie said, walking at a safe distance around the animal.

'Only fifteen-two hands,' Milly answered, automatically assessing the animal with an experienced eye.

'Bombproof, so Mr Carter's daughter said. You could have a car backfire beside him and he wouldn't even flinch. She needed to find him a good home.' Peggy stroked the white strip running down his long nose. 'Jenny in the baker's told me. She used to hunt him but she doesn't ride any more, isn't that right, Mr Carter?'

The horse raised its head and snorted – sneezed almost – a spray of moisture flew towards Natalie's horrified face.

'We can't keep him of course,' Milly said, putting on her best no-nonsense voice. 'Mr Carter, I'm sorry, you'll have to take him back.'

Mr Carter looked in some surprise at Peggy.

'No, no. It's OK, Mr Carter.' Peggy offered the soft muzzle a handful of grass. 'Listen, dear, Ivor and I have had the most wonderful talk. We've decided you should all move in here with me. I'm like an old skeleton rattling around these empty rooms. There's oodles of space for all of you and I'll be able to see my grandchildren every day and give you a hand with everything. It's going to be such fun, darling. Ivor can let your place so the mortgage is paid and he can use the attic here as his new office to save the rental money he's paying at the moment.'

They were as mad as each other. Milly visualised the mounds of junk at the top of the house and Ivor sitting on her father's wicker lobster creel, laptop perched on Hazel's old crib. Her mother and her husband – making plans for her future without even consulting her. Some wives would go loopy. But as she thought about it, she had to admit the idea had appeal. She'd always loved this house and the children doted on their granny.

'We can talk about it. But now the horse . . .' she began sternly. One of them had to show sense.

'Oh, he won't cost us a thing.' Peggy waved that off. 'Mr Dodd's nephew has an old paddock he never uses. It's knee-high in grass. He said he'd be happy to have a horse to eat it down, save him mowing and plenty of manure the other end. Wonderful for my roses.'

'But there's hay costs. Vets. Shoes . . .'

'Phooey,' her mother responded. 'Your father never spent a penny while he was alive, always saving to enjoy his retirement and where is he now? As soon as the estate is settled, I plan on giving all you girls a big chunk of money. I'm an old lady, what am I going to do with it? Keep it for the taxman? Blow that for a lark. All right, Mr Carter, you can just put Firefly in the garden for now and close the gate when you leave.'

Scratching his head, looking at the flower beds, envisioning the fate of the vegetable plot, Mr Carter did what he was told. They followed him into the garden.

The horse decided the lawn was much better than dandelions and started grazing around the wrought-iron table, not even flinching when he knocked over a chair.

Bemused, Milly stared at her present. Fergus was trying to give Rory a knee-lift onto his back, Ivor was holding up Ben to touch his mane, Natalie gingerly patting his neck at what she thought was a safe distance from dirtying her clothes. Erin held Firefly's rope, already looking as besotted as Milly had been when she was a girl. What a sight. She had to admit Ivor was a genius after all.

'Don't look now, sweetie, but there's a horse in the garden.' Avril appeared, as always a wave of Opium trailing behind her, arms laden with bags of fruit. Giving up alcohol had given her a wicked craving for sugar which she was trying to stave off by popping grapes and slices of satsuma into her mouth at ten-second intervals. 'He's walking all over Dad's potato patch.'

'I know,' Milly answered. 'It's mine.'

The words gave her a ridiculous feeling of glee. Of course they shouldn't keep it. Any sensible person in the world could see that. It seemed like a nice gelding, calm with a kind eye and an imperturbable manner. But money aside, when would she ever have time to ride it? And what if it hurt one of the kids? Stepped on Rory's foot? Bucked Fergus off? Trampled Ben in his pushchair?

But still her heart was having flashbacks to a younger Milly, galloping across the South Downs. Fearless. Flying. Why had she ever given up riding? It had always been her one great passion. And they did say teenagers who were into horses were less likely to indulge in drugs or sex. This could prove a good distraction for Erin. That's if Ivor ever relented and actually let her leave the house on her own. At the moment she was indefinitely grounded.

Lost in daydreams of Erin eschewing spotty teenage louts for the pleasure of clear rounds and blue ribbons, Milly suddenly became aware of Avril pushing something in her face. It looked suspiciously like a chequebook.

'. . . and I feel so terrible about it . . .'

Milly had lost the first part of the speech. What was she talking about – oh yes, the row.

'You were right,' Avril continued humbly. 'I've been a rotten sister and a terrible auntie. Natalie told me about your money problems. Don't be mad, I know she promised, but I got it out of her. Let me . . .' She opened the flap and started writing the date with a fancy roller pen. 'It's the least I can do. And you don't have to worry about paying it back. Now, how much?'

Milly put out her hand and stopped her. 'It's OK,' she said. 'We're sorted. Mum and Ivor worked it out.'

'Mum and Ivor?' You'd have thought she'd said Pinky and

Perky from Avril's astonishment. Her face fell. 'Oh, Milly, are we still friends?'

'No, we're sisters, better than friends.' Milly stepped into the Opium cloud to hug her. 'Although there is something I wanted to ask you, what you said, you know in that argument . . .'

'Yes,' Avril said warily.

Milly's eyes flicked from side to side, searching for hidden children. 'Who the fuck's Judge sodding Judy?'

'Mum, I was thinking.' Avril cornered Peggy as she came out of the downstairs toilet. 'As soon as I'm settled in California, how about coming out for a visit? I'll take you to Disneyland, SeaWorld –'

'Oh, I'd love to dear but I'm far too busy. I'm going to Australia for a month. First of December. To see Dorothy.'

'But what about the house?'

'Milly and Ivor are moving in with the kids. They're going to keep me company and it'll help them sort their finances.'

'Well, later then? Next spring perhaps?'

'Booked a coach trip to Rome. Saga. I've always wanted to see the Colosseum. Ever since I watched that sexy rexy Charlton Heston race around it in his chariot. Your father wasn't the only one with an itch to travel. Oh, Avril, dear, are you sure you still want to leave? What about your clients?'

'Funnily enough, a surprising number of them like the idea.' Avril laughed hollowly. 'Turned out Baxter's not content with being Top Gun, he wants to direct *Top Gun* – the fifteenth sequel, of course. Part of his conditions for staying with me is that I base my office in LA.'

'Ignoramus! After all you've done for him. I remember when you got him his first TV commercial, that thing with the singing frogs.'

'It's business, Mum.'

'And what about that lovely chap you were seeing? Natalie says he's absolutely charming.'

'He doesn't want to see me,' Avril said, as the doorbell rang. 'And how often have I told you – I don't *do* lovely chaps.'

But her mother was already rushing to the door, the skirts of her flowery dress flapping around her legs.

'Hazel!' She almost broke ribs with the force of her bear hug.

'Hi, Mum.' Hazel pulled away when she finally needed some air. She looked over Peggy's shoulder at Avril. 'And hi . . . Mum! Something smells . . . burnt.'

'Can't smell anything.' Peggy sniffed before smiling at the figure behind her. 'Ah now, and who's this gorgeous hunk of manhood?'

'Well, are you going to let us come in?' Hazel questioned as they all crowded in the doorway. 'I want you to meet my fiancé. He's Australian,' she whispered in Peggy's ear.

'Fiancé!' Avril gasped. She looked behind Hazel at the man hovering there, a pleasant smile on his rather squashed features.

'Australian?' Peggy's eyes lit up.

'Jonno' – Hazel pushed him forward – 'meet Mum number one.' She indicated to Peggy. 'And Mum number two.' She waved at Avril.

Oh well, it was too much to expect that Hazel would let a situation like this pass without getting some mileage out of it, Avril thought, as the stranger in the leather jacket stepped forward and stretched out his hand. If she were making jokes, it had to be a good sign.

'Mind if I just call you Peggy and Avril?' Jonno suggested.

'No probs, me old cobber.' Peggy grasped his big mitt in both of hers. 'I'm practising the lingo. Goodness, don't you sound like Rolf Harris? Blime me kangaroo down, sport.' She pretended to rattle an iron sheet. 'You must be a brave soul to take on a daughter of mine. I've got to warn you, all four are terribly headstrong. But you look like a man of mettle.' She squeezed his biceps appreciatively. 'Are you really going to marry my little Hazel?'

'Too right.' Jonno grinned. 'I'm going to shackle her to the kitchen sink and force feed her tofu.'

'But remember, Mums.' Hazel tapped her nose. 'Mum's the word.'

'Look at me,' Peggy's eyes shone as she lorded over the table. 'I've four wonderful daughters, four delicious grand-children' – she grabbed the arm of Rory, sitting beside her, and blew a raspberry to make him giggle – 'a marvellous son-in-law,' she said with a wave of a fork at Ivor, 'and another daughter about to be wed. Who could be luckier?'

'Mum!' Avril and Hazel chorused disapprovingly as every-one snapped to attention.

'Wed?' Milly gasped. 'Who's getting wed?'

'Oh.' Peggy's hand flew to her mouth, eyes wide and innocent. 'Wasn't I supposed to say anything?'

All heads turned to Avril, Milly and Natalie's jaws dropping in amazement. Erin stared at her incredulous. Ivor began beaming like an idiot, pushing back his chair as if ready to spring over the table to give Avril a congratulatory kiss. Only Rory and Fergus were unaffected, too busy in a secret battle, kicking each other under the tablecloth.

'You made up with Richard!' Natalie enthused. 'Well, about time! Why didn't you bring him?'

Avril sighed and nodded towards Hazel. Hazel grinned at the astonished faces and raised her glass.

'S'right,' Jonno laughed uproariously. 'It's me and Haze that are getting hitched.'

Natalie shook her head in disbelief. 'You're having us on again, right Hazel?'

'Would I joke about something like that?' Hazel turned to Jonno and planted a big smacker on his lips.

'You're actually . . . marriage . . . really?' Milly was lost for words. 'You're serious?'

'Deadly serious.' Hazel seemed delighted at the reaction her news was having on her family. 'I know a good thing when I see it. I'm not letting him get away. This one can cook!'

'And he's Australian,' Peggy said proudly.

'Hazel, that's fantastic!' Miracle of miracles, Natalie had tears in her eyes as she rushed to hug her.

'Good on you, both!' Ivor jumped up and shook Jonno's hand vigorously. 'Welcome to the family! I've got to warn you though, they're all barking mad!'

'So I've heard.' Jonno grinned back.

'Oh, I'm so happy for you.' Milly rushed to squeeze Hazel from the other side. 'It's blinking brilliant!'

'Way to go, Auntie Hazel,' Erin croaked out.

Suddenly everyone was exclaiming and firing questions, all talking at the same time.

'Are you marrying over here or over there?'

'Where do you think you might settle?'

'When's the big day?'

'Did you get down on one knee?'

Catching the excitement Rory and Fergus abandoned their chairs and fell to the floor, wrestling with enthusiasm, ignored by all the women crowding around Hazel and Jonno.

'Isn't it truly tremendous?' Peggy grabbed Jonno's hand. 'You know you've picked a real smasher in Hazel.' She looked around. 'Not that they're not all smashers.'

'It's wonderful.' Avril's eyes were also suspiciously bright as she too embraced first Hazel then Jonno.

411

'I'll fetch the champagne.' Ivor put his arm around Erin and pulled her against him, ruffling her hair. 'I've a bottle in the boot, waiting for a special occasion. We never thought we'd see Hazel settling down!'

'And now that I'm going to be part of an official couple we can join your dinner-party circuit, Nat.' Hazel glowed in triumph.

'Don't hold your breath.' Natalie wrinkled her nose as two champagne flutes and a mish mash of whisky, wine, sherry and what looked like ancient medicine glasses were hurriedly produced and Ivor came back and started unpeeling gold foil. 'I doubt I'll be hosting a dinner party for a very long time. Most of those couples were Jeremy's fuddy-duddy friends. No, now I'm on my own, I'm going to be hitting the bars with all the other hip young singles.'

There was a loud pop, the cork flying across the room narrowly missing Fergus much to Rory's delight.

'Right,' Avril said, when their glasses were filled. 'Well, here's to Hazel and Jonno.'

'Hazel and Jonno!' they chorused.

'And Haze, if you need a wedding dress,' Natalie added, 'I think I might have one spare.'

'So – no Richard?' Hazel was sitting out on the patio drinking coffee, Natalie and Avril one side of her, Milly and Ivor the other. Jonno had been cornered by Peggy who was showing him all Hazel's naked baby photos.

'Nope. All quiet on that front.'

'Too bad.'

'Ah well, I guess, we can't all be raging romantics, sweetie.' Avril snapped her lighter against her cigarette. 'It would never have worked out anyway. I've been on my own too long.'

'You're probably right,' Natalie agreed. She swirled her cup thoughtfully. 'Besides, he isn't such a great catch now, is he?'

She looked up to see four pairs of puzzled eyes.

'What?' Her eyebrows arched over the rim of the cup as she delicately sipped, small finger extended. 'Don't any of you read the papers? His wife took him to the cleaners in the divorce settlement, left him practically penniless.'

Her foot pressed meaningfully on Hazel's.

'Oh yes,' Hazel exclaimed, a bit too forcefully like she'd popped out of a jack-in-the-box. 'I *did* see that! Old Richard, uh . . .' She snapped her fingers, searching for his name.

'Burdock,' prompted Natalie.

'Yeah, Richard Burdock. She even got full custody of the daughter.'

'Kathy?' Avril looked puzzled. 'But she's eighteen.'

'Maybe it was the dog then. Did they have a dog?'

'I'm not sure,' Avril reflected, realising how much she'd missed on all those personal little details. 'I think he mentioned a parrot once.'

'That was it,' Hazel said decisively. 'African grey.' She winked at Natalie.

'Same thing happened to a friend of mine.' Ivor's arm lay loose over Milly's shoulders. 'Got kicked out of his house, court awarded everything to his wife, ended up homeless for a while. Milly and I had to let him sleep on our sofa to keep him off the streets till he got himself together again. Mind you, after three days of the kids fighting over the PlayStation and jumping on him at dawn, he was beginning to like the idea of a cardboard box under Waterloo Bridge.'

'I can't believe it.' Avril was in shock. 'Poor Richard. Oh well.' She sighed. 'Maybe Saskia will take him in.'

'Saskia? Who's Saskia?' Hazel said.

'Some girl who's got the hots for him. Stunning redhead, skin like –'

'A peach? Looked like Jonathan Ross's wife? That's not Saskia. It's Felicity, his cousin. Pregnant married cousin.'

Avril's jaw almost hit the patio and she felt her stomach lurch. 'I have to dash.' She jumped to her feet. 'Say goodbye to Mum for me. Kisses all round.'

They watched her bolt towards her Sprite.

'African grey.' Natalie shook her head at Hazel. 'You're too much.'

'I know, I know. But you were brill, Nats. How did you know she'd fall for it?'

'If she did, it was only because she wanted to.'

Richard opened the door and stepped back in mock horror.

'Avril! What brings Mohammed to the mountain?'

'This.' She kissed him hard on the lips and dragged him to the sofa. 'I just wanted to say you can move in with me if you like. Temporary, permanent, you name it. I can't believe that money-grubbing bitch would take the parrot too.' She stared at his beautiful astonished face. 'Or we could get married . . . if you wanted to, that is. Oh shit, listen to me, I sound like a sodding space cadet. Bottom line, buster, do you still want me or not?'

'I thought you were moving to the States. The canary's been singing again.'

Brenda. Avril snorted. Her assistant either was compulsively indiscreet or the most ardent matchmaker.

'I must get that beak securely bound. She's worse than a leaking tap. But did she mention I still haven't signed the contracts? I can tell Wally and Baxter. Or we could both go, if you like. I'll pay.'

'Avril' – he grabbed her hands to shut her up – 'what's happened?'

'I heard about the divorce settlement. About you losing all your money.'

'My money?' Richard stared thoughtfully into the middle distance. 'Oh, yes. That. Shocking, wasn't it?'

He nuzzled into her neck, then pulled her towards him. When she finally came up for air, Avril's lips looked swollen from kissing, her pupils dark and smouldering.

'Are you very upset about it?' She flipped him on his back and stared at him challengingly. 'All your hard work?'

'Not as much as you'd think.' He rolled her over so that he was on top, pinning her arms to the side of the sofa. 'Tell me, would you still love me if I were wealthy? You do love me, don't you? I mean, that's what this is all about, isn't it?'

'Yes.' She struggled to break one wrist free. 'And yes.' Tugging vainly at the other, she resorted to biting his forearm. 'And yes.' She sat up triumphantly, her long loose hair a tangled mess.

'D'you know' – Richard wryly examined the teethmarks on his arm – 'that's actually an enormous relief.'

'Incredible.' As the sun set over the hedges, Hazel and Natalie sat together watching Milly, Ivor and the kids lead Firefly down the road. Peggy was marching along with them, sword-fighting with Rory as they went. It was one of those perfect Sussex summer evenings where the evening air was balmy and velvet and thick with the scent of ripe grass and the faint hint of distant sea breezes. 'Everything was such a disaster just a few weeks ago and suddenly it seems like it's all come right again.'

'Yes.' Natalie felt sad and happy at the same time. Happy because her sisters were OK, sad because . . . well, because . . .

'So what's up with you?' Hazel eyed her closely.

'Me? Oh, I'm fine,' Natalie said, stiff upper lip. 'After everything with Jeremy I think I'm really going to enjoy spending time on my own. You know, I never have, not really.'

Hazel guffawed rudely.

'Pull the other one, it's got bells on it. I know you love him, Nats. Why don't you go and get him? Heck, if stiff-neck Avril can race across London then you –'

'Get who?'

'Matt, of course. Milly told me everything.'

'But she promised.' Natalie was outraged.

'Only because she cares for you. Besides, there shouldn't be secrets between sisters. So what about it?'

'In case you haven't noticed,' Natalie said with dignity, 'Matt's in Ecuador. And I've just put a month's deposit on my new flat.'

'So?'

'It's the other end of the world. And I don't think he wants to come back.'

'So?'

'You think I should email him?' Natalie said hopefully.

Hazel laughed so much she almost choked on the beer she was swigging from the bottle, half of it running up her throat and down her nose.

'Yes, Nats,' she managed when she could breathe again. 'That's exactly what I think.' Her voice was larded with irony. 'Email the Amazon. Where he is, they don't even have a phone line, you soppy cow.'

Chapter 44

Milly sat back on her heels and folded the flaps on the last cardboard box with a feeling of relief. Finished, practically. The moving men were coming tomorrow morning. The furniture would stay, all except a few favourite items – The Briars was cluttered enough as it was. It might have taken weeks to get it together but the house in Codmoreton was rented to the most delightful family and off to Little Hooking they would all go.

There was just one thing she needed to do first.

At this time of day, Saturday morning, she knew exactly where she'd find her. The park playground was full of familiar faces, toddlers and parents, older children fighting over the swings. But Milly walked past them all with only one target in mind.

'Mrs Hammond.' She stood in front of her former nemesis, her spine straight, determination in every line of her body.

'Mrs Simpson.' Sitting on a bench, Mrs Hammond avoided Milly's blazing eyes, pretending to be searching for something in her capacious bag. Conversation paused as other mothers looked over, scenting a confrontation. Geraldine Prior edged a little closer, away from the knot of women she was talking with, keen not to miss a word.

'I found out why Rory bit Darren.' Milly took a step

forward and put her hands on her hips. 'I thought you might like to know.'

Mrs Hammond looked up at that, brows arched.

'Ah, so he's finally admitted –'

'He bit him,' Milly cut in sharply, 'because apparently Darren was taunting him, pushing him and calling me fat. Well, fat I may be, but you know something, Mrs Hammond, maybe I haven't got the biting lesson quite in there, but I teach my kids not to discriminate against people for race, religion or size, and I suggest you do the same!'

She turned on her heel and stalked proudly away, winking at Geraldine's astonished face as she passed. Good. With old gossip-features as witness, word would spread around the mother circuit like chickenpox at nursery school. If only her sisters had been there too – they could all have high-fived!

As the boat came speeding down the muddy river, Matt had to rub his eyes twice to make sure he was really seeing what he thought he saw.

Perched on the front seat was a female figure in a pristine safari skirt and matching jacket of the type only seen on toothpick models in the pages of *Vogue*. On her head was an old-style pith helmet, worthy of Allan Quartermain on his way to King Solomon's mines, with the addition of a built-in mosquito veil. Even if he hadn't recognised the trim figure, the distinctive way she was clutching the handle of a large white leather handbag was a dead giveaway.

A horde of mostly naked children ran yelling down the muddy trail to greet the new arrivals. Matt followed, almost as fast, trying to hold back his laughter.

Natalie strolled towards him, having some difficulty negotiating the mud in her white sandals. Only one-inch heels admittedly, but heels nonetheless.

'Natalie MacLeod.' Matt reached her and stood, thumbs in the pockets of his shorts, grinning like an idiot.

'Well, it's not Pocahontas. I thought you might need a hand.'

She stared around, taking in the bamboo huts with palm-frond thatch, the dirty faces surrounding her smeared with snot and flies. Then she looked at Matt, feeling her insides twist, her heart sing as she revelled in the familiar contours of his beloved face.

Matt's grin widened as he forbore to mention that she was a few thousand miles off in her choice of historical characters. He picked up her rucksack, recognising it as Hazel's old one. At least she hadn't turned up with a full set of matching leopard-print luggage.

'Nice outfit,' he commented drily, eyeing the safari suit and sandals with disbelief.

'Oh, this?' She glanced down, smoothing the creases out of the skirt. 'Hazel helped me pick it out. At that fancy travel store in Covent Garden. She said these jungle lodges weren't really as rough as I imagined.' She glanced dubiously towards the visible dwellings. 'That there'd be air conditioning . . .'

'Oh, we have air all right,' he agreed. 'Whenever the wind blows.'

'And hot and cold running water . . .' Natalie sounded accusing.

'The river,' he said equably. 'It's tepid mostly. But you'll have to watch out for piranha.'

He held out his hand to her and she moved cautiously towards him, trying to see the funny side to this ridiculous situation she suddenly found herself in. Continent aside, it was nothing like the *Out of Africa* encounter she'd envisioned. Where were the tall cool drinks served on a shady veranda by smiling servants with silver trays? Come to that, where was the veranda?

'So JJ didn't mind you coming out?'

'He's not JJ.'

'I know, I'm sorry, I –'

'No, I mean he's JG. Jeremy the Jerk is now Jeremy the Gone. And now that we've got that sorted – shut up and kiss me.'

Matt obliged, purposely planting on her the most slobbery kiss imaginable. Drawing back, Natalie wiped her mouth.

'Thanks a lot. That was certainly worth the trip from hell. Now I know what I've been missing all these years.' Pretending to leave, she swivelled on a heel, which sunk into the mud with an embarrassing squelch. 'So, if you don't mind, I think my boat's going . . .'

Laughing loudly now, Matt pulled her back and wrapped her in his arms. This time it was a real kiss, full of a tenderness and a passion that took her breath away.

'That's better,' she said with a sigh as they finally separated. Her heart soared in her chest. She bent down to prise her heels out of the mud, slipping out of her unsuitable sandals. 'God, I couldn't wait to get those things off.' She wriggled her toes. 'A joke's a joke but not when it gives you blisters. Hazel's idea. She insisted I brought the handbag too. You've no idea of the looks I've been getting. Hand me my rucksack, will you?' Taking it from him, she pulled on a pair of far more suitable leather hiking boots, admittedly clean and new.

'Wait,' Matt said, as she stood up. 'One more thing.' He touched his finger on the muddy footwear and drew a streak down Natalie's nose. 'I've always preferred you with a bit of mud on your face.'

They walked companionably as if this was the most familiar place in the world to be together, arms around each other, up to his small hut. She ducked through the low doorway of the one-room building, a swift glance taking in the mud floor, the small hand-hewn table with only one chair, the single bed in the corner and a bright green lizard running up the wall.

'So this is it,' she said in a non-committal tone as Matt watched her slightly anxiously. 'Desirable detached dwelling. Needs a little TLC,' she said in her estate agent's selling voice. 'Let's see.' She looked around. 'Maybe a few rubber plants. And Ikea sells those really nice fake palm ceiling fans. We could squeeze in a tropical loveseat from Habitat, add some bedding from Heal's Safari collection.' She perched delicately on the edge of the wooden seat and wiped the sweat from her brow. 'I'm parched. Got any Perrier water? Lots of ice please.'

This time it was Natalie's turn to laugh at the expression on Matt's face. From his place a few steps into the room, which was as far as anyone could go in these tiny quarters without tripping over furniture, he was tilting back his broad-brimmed hat and scratching his head in bemusement. He looked completely foxed but also incredibly foxy.

'Joking,' she said, putting his mind at ease. 'I'm joking.'

'You know, you're funny.' He threw his hat on the table, grinning and came in close.

'Funnier than Hazel?'

He kissed her. 'Twice as funny.'

He crossed over to the bed, moving aside the mosquito net and patted the space beside him. 'Sit here next to me. It'll be a lot more comfortable.'

Undulating sexily, Natalie crossed the room in two steps and did as she was told.

'Mmm,' she said, throwing herself under the net. 'I've always thought these looked so romantic.'

'And useful,' Matt agreed, snuggling up beside her.

Natalie jerked her head. 'What do you mean – useful? You

421

don't mean there's . . .' She flinched as a high-pitched buzzing swooped inches from her head. 'What's that funny whining noise?'

'You'll find out, sweetheart.' Matt distracted her with kisses. 'You'll soon find out.'

In the middle of the night, Natalie rolled over. Matt was awake, head on crossed arms, staring at the inky starlit sky through the glassless window.

'Oh, by the way,' she said snuggling into his shoulder, 'I forgot to tell you. You're invited to a wedding . . .'

Acknowledgements

A world of thanks is owed to our wonderful agent Caroline Hardman for her hard work, terrific advice and encouragement and to the rest of The Marsh Agency for everything. And of course huge thanks also to our talented editor Emma Rose and all the team at Arrow Books for liking *Sisters* and so skilfully (but gently) whipping us into shape.

We're also grateful to have two understanding husbands in Ian and Gary who endured burnt dinners, messy houses, empty fridges, huge phone bills and being woken up at 3 a.m. (Pam never could get the time zone right) – all of which only got worse once we started writing. Thanks also to Pam's children, Sam, Lucy and Alec, who have learned to cook for their own survival. Thanks to our parents-in-law, Esther, Rene and Vic for believing in us always, and to friends too numerous to mention but particularly the inspirational Carol Smith, who was there from the beginning, and Koni, Christine, Elaine, Auntie Annie, Bob and Sophie, all the Boulder crowd plus Vanessa, Beccy, Phil, Carmella, Marisa, Jon, Nigel, Deena, Ced, Anna, Lynn, Dawn, Sheila, Chris, Mike and many others who have supported us along the way. Thanks also to the magazine editors who bought our short stories over the years and made us feel that we were writers after all.

And a special thanks to all sisters everywhere, especially Jo and Sheena, who have shared so many adventures with us. We (Pam and Lorraine) also owe so much to each other, for keeping the other one going and for making it – mostly – fun. Writing a book with a sister was at times frustrating, even harrowing, with banged-down phones and blistering emails, but it was also a great excuse to call each other daily, laugh and gossip for hours and realise we'd run out of time to actually write anything. It was also a huge relief to know that when one of us was blocked, skiving off or stuck for inspiration the other one was, with any luck, beavering away.

And though she didn't get to read this, we can't forget Maya who was so excited and pleased to hear we were being published. She was an incredible friend, a staunch ally, a beacon of courage and a constant source of encouragement, now greatly missed.

ALSO AVAILABLE IN ARROW

Recipe for Disaster

Miriam Morrison

A funny and warm-hearted tale of kitchen disasters, domestic calamities and love against all odds.

Jake Goldman and Harry Hunter have been deadly rivals all through culinary school. Now at the top of their game, fate throws them back together again when they open their first restaurants in the small town of Easedale, just a few hundred metres from each other. Sharp knives and heavy pans at the ready, they start cooking up a storm to entice the locals their way.

Kate Walker has just lost her boyfriend and is about to lose her reputation at the local paper. Her only hope of salvaging her career is a down-and-dirty, tell-all feature about the seedy underbelly of the restaurant business. When one of Jake's waitresses deserts him to join the dark (i.e. Harry's) side, Kate applies for the job, hoping the undercover investigation will get her all she needs to sort out her dead-end job – and maybe even her no-hope love life! Little does she know, when she follows the alluring smells into Jake's kitchen, that she is in for a major surprise . . .

arrow books

ALSO AVAILABLE IN ARROW

The Accidental Wife

Rowan Coleman

How do you know if your life has taken a wrong turn?

Alison James thinks she might be living the wrong life. She loves her husband Marc and their three children but somehow, in the process of building a perfect life for her family, she seems to have lost herself. And sometimes she worries that she's being punished for how it all started – for the day she ran away with her best friend's boyfriend.

Catherine Ashley knows she's living the wrong life. She adores her two daughters, but she'd always thought that at thirty-one she'd be more than a near-divorcee with a dead-end job. In those dark middle-of-the-night moments that come all too often these days, her mind still flicks back to the love of her life: Marc James. And she still wonders whether Alison stole her life as well as her boyfriend.

Alison and Catherine have been living separate lives, a hundred miles apart, for fifteen years – since Alison and Marc ran away. But now Alison's moving back to Farmington, the town in which they both grew up. And they're about to find out just how different both their lives could still be . . .

arrow books